PENGUIN BOOKS

Judy Nunn's career has been long, illustrious and multifaceted. After combining her internationally successful acting career with scriptwriting for television and radio, Judy decided in the '90s to turn her hand to prose.

Her first three novels, *The Glitter Game*, *Centre Stage* and *Araluen*, set respectively in the worlds of television, theatre and film, became instant bestsellers, and the rest is history, quite literally, in fact. She has since developed a love of writing Australian historically based fiction and her fame as a novelist has spread rapidly throughout Europe, where she has been published in English, German, French, Dutch, Czech and Spanish.

Her subsequent bestsellers, *Kal*, *Beneath the Southern Cross*, *Territory*, *Pacific*, *Heritage*, *Floodtide*, *Maralinga*, *Tiger Men*, *Elianne*, *Spirits of the Ghan*, *Sanctuary* and *Khaki Town*, have confirmed Judy's position as one of Australia's leading fiction writers. She has now sold over one million books in Australia alone.

In 2015 Judy was made a Member of the Order of Australia for her 'significant service to the performing arts as a scriptwriter and actor of stage and screen, and to literature as an author'.

Visit Judy at judynunn.com.au or on
 facebook.com/JudyNunnAuthor

T0363041

Books by Judy Nunn

The Glitter Game
Centre Stage
Araluen
Kal
Beneath the Southern Cross
Territory
Pacific
Heritage
Floodtide
Maralinga
Tiger Men
Elianne
Spirits of the Ghan
Sanctuary
Khaki Town

Children's fiction
Eye in the Storm
Eye in the City

Short stories (available in ebook)
The House on Hill Street
The Wardrobe
Just South of Rome
The Otto Bin Empire: Clive's Story
Oskar the Pole
Adam's Mum and Dad

JUDY NUNN

Khaki Town

PENGUIN BOOKS

PENGUIN BOOKS

UK | USA | Canada | Ireland | Australia
India | New Zealand | South Africa | China

Penguin Books is part of the Penguin Random House group of companies
whose addresses can be found at global.penguinrandomhouse.com.

First published by William Heinemann, 2019
This edition published by Penguin Books, 2020

Cover photography by iStock and Getty Images
Cover design by Adam Laszczuk © Penguin Random House Australia Pty Ltd
Internal design by Midland Typesetters, Australia
Typeset in 12pt Sabon by Midland Typesetters, Australia

Printed and bound in Australia by Griffin Press, an accredited
ISO AS/NZS 14001 Environmental Management Systems printer

A catalogue record for this
book is available from the
National Library of Australia

ISBN 978 0 14379 518 6

penguin.com.au

To the memory of my brother Robert Nunn

I miss you, Rob

This book was inspired by the story 'Ross River Fever' by Michael Roberts

A Note to Readers

Khaki Town is about racism and there are some passages that readers may find offensive and even shocking. I have made no attempt to soften this. Even in sections of the narrative where I am referring to government and military views, I have chosen to write in the language of the times because to modernise the vernacular would not be true to the era, both historically and dramatically.

PROLOGUE

1964

There was a tap at the north-east door.

Seated behind his desk by the windows, he looked up expectantly, knowing who would be announced.

The door opened, not fully, just ajar, and the secretary popped his head in. 'Senator Kennedy is here, Mr President.'

He rose from his chair and stood erect, back ramrod straight, a big man, around six feet, three inches in height, an imposing figure. And he knew it.

'Yes, yes, of course,' he said in his Texan drawl.

The secretary opened the door wide, Kennedy stepped into the room, and the secretary retired wordlessly, the door closing behind him with a gentle click of the latch.

'Robert . . .' He circled the desk, hand extended, and greeted the younger man with a welcoming smile. 'Good to see you, so glad you could come.'

'Mr President.' Kennedy returned his own boyish smile, albeit a little tightly. Close to six feet tall himself, he was dwarfed by the president, both in height and build.

The men shook hands.

'Do sit, please.' Lyndon Baines Johnson gestured affably to one of the two carvers on the visitors' side of the desk facing the bay windows that looked south over the leafy grounds of the White House.

Bobby sat. He loved this view. How often had he sat in one of these carvers, no-one else in the Oval Office except him and his brother, sharing a Scotch, talking about anything but politics, escaping the pressure that stifled them daily. He felt a stab of melancholy. God he missed Jack.

'I thought we might share a drink,' Johnson said, lowering his burly frame into the other carver and gesturing to the bottle of spirits and the two tumblers on the desk before them. 'We'll raise a toast to the memory of your brother, what do you say.'

Bobby was startled. Had Johnson somehow divined his thoughts? Was this a show of *sympathy*? If so, how strange, he told himself with more than a touch of cynicism. Lyndon's hardly known for his sensitivity.

Johnson went on, blithely ignoring the younger man's air of antagonism, which didn't in the least bother him. 'I know we haven't always seen eye to eye, Robert . . .' he said, picking up the unopened bottle of spirits and breaking the seal.

Something of an understatement, Bobby thought.

'But this is a moment I rather wanted to share with you.' Johnson poured them both large shots of a dark-brown liquor, more the colour of brandy than Scotch, from a bottle the label of which Bobby didn't recognise. 'It's a moment I'd like also to share with John,' he added, handing one of the glasses to Bobby, 'or rather to the memory of John, knowing how close the matter was to his heart.'

Both men remained poised, glasses in hand, while Bobby awaited the explanation that was obviously coming.

'I have right there,' Johnson announced, stabbing a dramatic finger at the file that sat in the centre of his

desk, 'the final version of the *Civil Rights Act*.' He paused
for further dramatic effect. 'I am about to sign those
papers, and the *Civil Rights Act* of 1964 will become law
tomorrow. I thought it only fitting you should be with me
and that we should share a toast to your brother on such
an occasion.'

Bobby was puzzled by this uncharacteristic act of
generosity – Lyndon rarely gave credit to others. The
announcement had been delivered with the man's customary
arrogance certainly, but Bobby was touched nonetheless.
How could he fail to be? The gesture was magnanimous.

'That's very thoughtful of you, Mr President,' he said,
'very thoughtful indeed. It was a piece of legislation Jack
cared for deeply.'

'As did you,' Johnson replied, 'as did all three of us,
I swear.' He raised his glass. 'To the *Civil Rights Act* and
to John,' he said.

'To the *Civil Rights Act* and to John.'

They clinked glasses and drank.

Bobby gasped at the sting of the liquor. 'Good God,
what the hell is that?' he queried, gazing down into the
contents of his glass, where even the fumes held a certain
threat.

'Yeah, pretty lethal, isn't it?' Johnson agreed. 'Grows
on you though. Aussies mostly drink it with ginger ale
and ice, or Coca-Cola these days, so I'm told, but I prefer
it neat.' He downed another hearty swig. 'Got a kick like
a mule.'

'Aussies?' Bobby was understandably baffled.

'Yep, that's right, Australians.' Johnson picked up the
bottle and poured himself a second slug. 'This here's Bundaberg Rum, all the way from Queensland, Australia,' he
said, flashing the label at Bobby. 'It was given me as a
gift when I was serving there during the war in the Pacific
and I've been carting it around for over twenty years, just

waiting for the right occasion to open it. Well, I figure that right occasion is right now and right here. Can I top you up?' He offered the bottle.

'No thanks,' Bobby said hastily, rather wishing he had some Coke and ice. 'I'll sit on this for a while.' His interest was piqued. What the hell is Lyndon up to, he wondered. Is he going to tell me all about his active service in the Pacific? Does he really think I believe that story?

Bobby took another tentative sip of his rum, not sure what to say by way of reply. He and Jack had often talked over the years, and always derisively, about Johnson's military award. The Silver Star for gallantry in action had been presented to him by none other than General Douglas MacArthur himself.

'The whole thing was a beat-up,' Jack had confided to his younger brother. 'I heard Lyndon volunteered as an observer on an air-strike mission to New Guinea – B-26 bombers. His aircraft wasn't hit as reported, it turned back because of generator trouble; at least that's what I heard. The plane never reached its objective, it never came under fire. A couple of the guys even said the official flight records showed that when their aircrafts were near the target and under fire, Johnson's plane was recorded as having landed back at the airbase.'

To many in the know, it appeared common knowledge that, despite being in the military, Lyndon Johnson had never seen active service. But his official war record did not show that.

Bobby answered with care. 'Jack also served in the Pacific during the war,' he said tentatively, wondering where all this was leading.

'Yes, yes, of course he did,' Johnson agreed with a hearty nod and a salutary wave of his hand, 'and most nobly. My active service was limited to the one mission only, but the truth is, on this particular occasion I was ordered to

Australia for a purpose far broader than combat duty. A purpose that remains secret to this very day,' he added, tapping a forefinger to the side of his nose in classic conspiratorial manner and even lowering his voice, although there was not a soul within earshot. 'And there's a certain synchronicity between that purpose and the toast we just made to the *Civil Rights Act*. Which is why I decided to open my bottle of Bundaberg and share my story with you, Robert.'

Bobby was now very much intrigued. It appeared Lyndon was not about to boast of his citation and his dubious war record, but something altogether different.

As Johnson raised his glass, Bobby followed suit and both men took a further sip of their rum, acknowledging this rare moment of camaraderie.

'I was called into this office when I was several years younger than you are right now,' Johnson went on to explain. 'The year was 1942 and I was to receive orders directly from President Roosevelt. General Eisenhower was also present, just the three of us. That was actually the first day I'd met Ike. He was here in the Oval Office when I arrived and FDR introduced us personally, quite an honour. As you would well know,' he added, 'Eisenhower was coordinating the Pacific War strategy from our end while MacArthur was commanding the forces in the field.'

Johnson gave a smile that was intended to be a mix of humility and self-deprecation, neither of which worked. 'As a young congressman, you can well imagine I was somewhat overawed at finding myself alone in the company of FDR and Ike.'

He hadn't been overawed at all. He'd recognised the magnitude of the moment for exactly what it was – a God-given opportunity for the advancement of his career. The young Lyndon Baines Johnson's ambition had been boundless.

And I was proved right, wasn't I, he now reflected with pride. Just to think, three US presidents together, here in this very room! Well, two of us didn't know at the time we were destined for presidency, he told himself a little smugly, but in hindsight the memory of us three together sure as hell is impressive.

Lyndon could recall every moment of that meeting with vivid clarity.

'I have a job for you, Congressman,' Franklin D. Roosevelt had said, wheeling his chair out from behind the desk and gesturing for the other two to sit, which they did.

'A rather serious incident has occurred in the South Pacific – in Australia of all places – an incident that requires discreet investigation. This investigation must be conducted by a highly trusted political aide, Lyndon, and I intend that political aide to be you.'

The words had been sweet music to young Lyndon Johnson's ears; he could still hear to this day the president's every syllable and every nuance. FDR had been his hero, the man he'd hoped and prayed to one day emulate. Which was exactly why he'd decided, should that day come, he too would be known by his initials.

And so I am, he now thought with an overwhelming sense of satisfaction. And so I am. Why, my whole goddamned family is LBJ, every darn one of us. His wife's childhood nickname had always been 'Lady Bird' – how fortuitous was that? They'd named their two daughters Lynda Bird and Luci Baines, and they'd even had a dog they'd called Little Beagle Johnson. And the name of his property? Why, the LBJ Ranch, of course. Cufflinks and clothes and household items like ashtrays and mugs all proudly bore his initials. 'LBJ' was a loud and clear statement to the world.

'This incident involves trouble with our black troops in a large, northern Australian port called Townsville,'

FDR had continued, 'and if it were to become public knowledge the consequences could be disastrous. Despite the fact that as a society we are not yet integrated, our army must be perceived as a united front, black and white soldiers serving our great country side by side. Which is why this most unpleasant incident must be thoroughly investigated. When it has been and the full truth is known, correct action will be taken, of course, but all findings are to be kept strictly confidential. And we need to bear in mind,' he'd added with a touch of derision, 'there's the damned Australian Government we have to contend with. Although given their stance on racial issues, I'm sure they'll be only too happy to have the whole wretched business swept under the carpet.'

Lyndon had looked a little blank, so Roosevelt had given a nod to Eisenhower for a succinct explanation, which Ike had been happy to deliver in his customary blunt manner.

'They have down there what they call "the White Australia policy",' he said. 'When we first raised the prospect of sending Negro troops they said they didn't want them.'

'Hell,' this was news to Lyndon, 'what did we say to that?'

'We said if no black troops,' Roosevelt barked, 'then no US troops! Period!'

'Needless to say, they changed their tune,' Ike went on, 'but the situation remains tense. They need all the help they can get. The bulk of their army is either serving in North Africa or captured by the Japs in Singapore.'

'I see. How many black troops do we have there?' Lyndon asked.

'Currently in excess of three thousand Negro soldiers,' the general replied, 'and more on their way; there'll be over seven thousand by August. They're employed as work units – building airstrips and infrastructure needed for defence-and-attack bases in the Pacific conflict zone. MacArthur is fully aware he needs a plan to get them off the Australian mainland as soon as possible.'

'So, Congressman,' FDR said, 'I want you down there to investigate. As a courtesy, upon arrival in Australia you'll notify MacArthur, who's currently at GHQ in Melbourne, after which you'll proceed to Townsville, where you'll get to the bottom of this mess and report directly back to me. You'll report to me and no-one else, you understand?' He shared a look with Eisenhower, who nodded, the two men having obviously reached an agreement.

'Yes, Mr President.'

'And keep a goddamned lid on it, Lyndon, lest it explode in our faces.'

Johnson scoffed back the remains of his rum and poured himself a third healthy measure. He'd enjoyed reliving that long-ago scene, which he firmly believed had been the first major stepping stone in his rise to the top.

'C'mon, Robert, keep up,' he urged, 'you haven't even finished your first slug of the stuff.'

'Sure.' Bobby obediently drained his glass, the alcohol no longer having an abrasive effect, but rather producing a warm glow. 'It does kind of grow on you, doesn't it?'

'Sure does. And you want to know why I decided to open this bottle today of all days? You want to know why the synchronicity between my trip to Australia in forty-two and the toast we just made to the *Civil Rights Act*?' He didn't wait for an answer. The younger man's interest was evident and his questions had been rhetorical anyway. 'Well, I'll tell you.'

LBJ settled comfortably back in his chair. 'Roosevelt sent me out to Australia to investigate a race riot, the findings of which were to be kept top secret. As I told you, that secret remains to this very day, and I'll tell you something else – the few Aussies in the know are only too happy for things to stay that way. Ever heard of the White Australia policy?'

'Can't say I have,' Bobby answered, a little bewildered by the apparent non-sequitur.

'It's not officially referred to in international circles as the White Australia policy,' Johnson admitted, 'but I can promise you, that's what the locals call it, and that's just what it is. A discriminatory policy intended to deny entry to the country of all races non-Caucasian. It was the first legislation passed when the country formed a Federal Parliament and it was called the *Immigration Restriction Act of 1901*.' He shook his head in whimsical fashion. 'By golly, those Aussies really are something, a breed apart you might say.'

Bobby looked a query.

'We've long been criticised for our segregationist policies, Robert, as you well know, so in some ways we haven't been all that different from the Australians. We put black people in boxes; we don't give them the same advantages as white folk; we view them as inferior —'

'That may have been true once,' Bobby interrupted, 'but it's about to become a thing of the past.' He indicated the all-important file that sat on the presidential desk.

'Exactly,' Johnson agreed with enthusiasm. 'We are on the eve of monumental change in this country, which makes our current conversation particularly pertinent in my opinion, and I'll tell you why. In these enlightened times the White Australia policy is still alive and well.' He raised his glass as if in triumph. 'Like I said, those Aussies are a breed apart.' A swig and he went on. 'You want to know why I was sent down there in forty-two?'

Another rhetorical question, so Bobby merely nodded, although he was keen to hear the story Johnson appeared so eager to share. What exactly was this well-guarded war secret?

'Ever been there yourself, Robert?'

'Nope.'

Johnson swirled the dark liquor in his glass, studying it intently, remembering the first time he'd had a slug of 'Bundy' as the rum was fondly known in Australia. At least that's what Val had told him. He'd only been in Townsville for those several days of his investigation, but he remembered too when Val had given him the very bottle that now sat on the desk before him.

'Well, it's something else I can tell you,' he said, 'particularly a place in Northern Queensland. A place they call Townsville.'

PART ONE
THE CIVILIANS

CHAPTER ONE

1942

Val Callahan gazed about the main bar of her pub, marvelling at the surrounding sea of khaki. It was half past four in the afternoon and she'd only just opened up – beer rationing already a force to be reckoned with, there was no point in opening earlier. Good thing she had Baz on side with his black-market contacts; she'd need to be calling on him soon.

She joined young Betty and Jill behind the bar in order to help out with the influx of drinkers streaming through the open doors that led to the busy corner of Stokes and Sturt streets.

Khaki wherever you look, she thought as she started pulling beers. Here in The Brown's Bar, the mob queued up outside, passers-by in the street, barely a civilian to be seen, just military everywhere. Army, navy, air force, you name it, and all in khaki. Various shades and styles sure, but khaki nonetheless.

It seems to have happened overnight, Val thought. How extraordinary. We've become a khaki town.

No-one could argue that the military invasion had happened quickly. The citizens of Townsville had been taken by surprise, as had those in many other North Queensland townships. Unlike the civilians of the Northern

Territory, the local population had not been evacuated
south in order to create a restricted military area. Those
in North Queensland had been left to carry on as usual,
as if somehow the war in the Pacific was something that
needn't concern them.

None of us gave things much thought really, did we, Val
mused, counting out a bloke's change. Well, we bloody
well should have! She was actually surprised that she of all
people had been caught so unawares. A tough old broad
like me who's been around the traps, I should have known
better, she told herself. But crikey, there was only a handful
of Aussie troops stationed here, and watching them drill
was a joke. Hell, they wore shorts and sandshoes and no
shirts, and when one lot had finished they'd hand their
rifles over to the next lot so they could have a go. No
wonder we didn't take things seriously.

She grabbed a bottle of bourbon from the shelf and
started pouring another bloke's order, a Yankee officer
with the rank of major, giving him a saucy smile as she
did. Even at the age of fifty-three, Val always flirted. It was
good for business and she knew she could get away with it.
Old broad she might be, but she looked after herself; kept
her hair blonde, never a strand of grey to be seen, still had
good tits, she could pull a trick if she wanted to. Not that
she did – that part of her life belonged in the past. She was
a respectable pub owner and had been for many a year.
But old habits die hard, don't they. At least that's the way
Val saw things.

'There you go, mate,' she said, handing the major his
two bourbons on the rocks – he was buying a round for
his buddy – and giving him another special smile.

Of course, it was the fall of Singapore that did it, she
thought. Then four days later they bomb bloody Darwin!
Some wake-up call! No wonder we all had the fear of God
put in us. The Japs were on our bloody doorstep. And

they're getting closer by the minute what's more. Thank God for the Yanks.

Leaving Betty and Jill to man the bar, she weaved her way through the khaki throng, collecting empty glasses here and there, playing hostess and generally spreading bonhomie.

Just look at them, she thought, her eyes once again roaming those in the bar and through the windows those in the street. Some Aussies, sure, but mostly Yanks; they've taken over the whole place, and Christ alive it's not even mid-March!

The sleepy settlement on the north-east coast of Australia had certainly undergone a dramatic metamorphosis. Of all the coastal townships in this northern region of Queensland, Townsville was considered the most picturesque – locals and tourists seemed to be in agreement upon this. The other coastal towns of course boasted the same tropical splendour: lush palms, banyans and pandanus trees, the heady scent of frangipani, vivid aqua-blue ocean and white sandy beaches. But none could claim a Castle Hill and a Magnetic Island.

Townsville was not only a picture-postcard-perfect image of the tropics, Townsville had a drama all its own. Towering above the settlement and dominating the landscape from every perspective was the 950-foot-high red-rock edifice of Castle Hill, a very spiritual place known to the local Indigenous community as Cootharinga. And lying barely five miles off the coast was Magnetic Island, aptly named, for in the changing light of day it did appear to beckon, luring people with the promise of paradise. All in all, Townsville was an ideal holiday setting, offering an easy lifestyle for the locals and a magical hideaway for visitors.

Not anymore, not these days. The tourists no longer visited, and the locals now lived in a garrison town. The peace had been well and truly shattered, the people of

Townsville rudely awakened to the fact that they were right in the firing line. And they were frightened.

The seemingly instant arrival of thousands of troops, together with the endless shipments of heavy equipment and the barrage of military vehicles that clogged the streets, was immensely disruptive to everyday life. Over time, the military would requisition properties: hotels would be commandeered as officers' quarters; pupils evacuated and schools taken over for conversion to hospitals; many cinemas, halls and even some private residences of those prepared to move south would be used for military purposes. Allied army camps were currently springing up in the Botanical Gardens and parks and in Armstrong's Paddock; tent cities appearing out of nowhere. And of course there were the Yanks. The US airmen and support staff were to be stationed at airfields to be built strategically across the north for American bombers on their runs to New Guinea.

These airfields, and other military infrastructures, were to be constructed by work units consisting of black American troops commanded by white officers, which provided a further element of fascination for the people of Townsville. Few had ever before encountered an American Negro, and certainly none had witnessed the numbers that now flocked through town.

'They're different from us, aren't they,' Aunty Edie had succinctly remarked to Val a week or so ago when they'd stood together at the railway station watching the black troops pour out of the carriages. They'd heard there was another troop train of Yanks arriving and they'd gone to the station to get a good look. 'Nothin' at all like my mob,' Aunty Edie had said, studying them closely. 'Whole lot bigger for starters. Good lookin' bastards,' she'd added with begrudging admiration, 'but I wouldn't want our blokes to get in a fight with 'em.'

Aunty Edie was Djabugay, from around the Cairns region further to the north, but having spent well over a decade of her forty-something years on nearby Palm Island, she referred to herself as a Bwgcolman woman. Pronounced 'Bwookamun', it was the name adopted by all Palm Islander Aboriginals, meaning 'many tribes – one people'.

Val had laughed at the comment – Aunty Edie was famous for cutting through the bullshit. 'Well, I've met a few of them, and I can tell you the fellas who've come to my place are gents, Edie,' she'd said. 'Our Aussie boys could pick up a few manners from those Yankee black-fellas, that's for sure.'

Val had no intention of encouraging only whites to frequent her pub, and in particular the ever-popular main bar known simply as The Brown's. Admittedly, American segregationist practices instilled as they were, white and black soldiers had, for the most part, adopted their own favoured R and R haunts, but as far as Val was concerned, anyone who behaved themselves was welcome at The Brown's.

Indeed, it seemed the Australian Government's fears about the acceptance of Negro troops were proving relatively unfounded, at least so far. The local populace did not seem as offended by the presence of vast numbers of black men as had been originally predicted. Australian officialdom agreed, however, that it was fortunate the American Commander-in-Chief of the Pacific Theatre, General MacArthur, had been sympathetic to the situation at hand. MacArthur had categorically stated that all coloured troops would be withdrawn 'at the end of the Australian emergency', and that as he 'respected' Australia's racial views, Negroes would be assigned to bases 'far from urban centres'.

Townsville was, of course, just such a base, as was the inland mining township of Mount Isa, nearly 500 miles to the west. Both were ideal locations for the building of airstrips and military bases, and both were certainly 'far from urban centres'; in Mount Isa's case, probably as far as it was humanly possible to get, most would agree. Both towns were therefore flooded with the arrival of black Americans, who in these early days of arrival – their jobs being to build the actual bases – preceded and outnumbered their white counterparts.

Val circled the bar, dumping the empty glasses for the girls to wash. 'G'day, fellas,' she called to a group of four black GIs who'd just arrived; young privates, in their very early twenties. She recognised one of them, a big handsome bloke; Ben was his name. Ben had visited the bar several times and on each occasion with a new set of mates.

'Hi there, Val,' Ben called back.

While one of his buddies headed for the bar to buy the beers and lay the bet, Ben led the others directly to the snake pen, just as Val had expected he would. Ben had been unable to win the bet himself, but was obviously determined to witness one of his buddies who could.

The snake pen was how the pub had gained its reputation, and even its very name, which had stuck as a personal and fond title for the pub itself. Newcomers constantly asked, and had for years, 'Who are the Browns?', ignoring the apostrophe in the title and presuming the Browns must be the owners of the pub. But they were quickly set straight. 'The browns aren't a who,' they were told, 'the brown is a what. This is the *brown's* bar.'

The brown, as it turned out, was a snake – an eastern brown snake to be precise, highly venomous and extremely aggressive. In reality, the snake pen was a large glass enclosure that sat upon a two-foot-high granite plinth in the very centre of The Brown's Bar. It might have appeared nothing more than a decorative addition, rather like a fish tank, and certainly seemed so to the locals, who paid little attention to the reddish-brown reptile inside, which was either dozing or contentedly slithering about. The snake pen, however, served a purpose far greater than decoration. If any bold newcomer wanted to test himself, a house bet could be laid at the bar as to whether he could keep his hand resting on the glass while the snake struck. Val was happy to agree to whatever sum was offered, paying three to one in the punter's favour. With the bets coming in at around five bob a time, or at the most a quid, the enterprise wasn't a big money earner for her, but it wasn't intended to be – the snake pen provided excellent entertainment for the drinkers, and attracted people to the bar.

There were rules to be observed. From among those watching, a referee was elected whose job it was to stand on the opposite side of the glass enclosure and remain solely focused upon the contender, ensuring that at no time did he close his eyes or glance away. Another was elected to stand beside the contender, striking the granite plinth with a stick and tapping the glass, sending vibrations that would agitate the snake, urging it to attack. Then, as the reptile showed the first signs of aggression, the contender was to press his hand flat upon the glass at chest height to attract the snake's attention. Furthermore, closely observed by the referee, the eyes of the contender must remain upon the eyes of the snake.

The snake's intention was eminently readable throughout. Once successfully aggravated, the eastern brown would raise the front part of its body horizontally from the ground, swaying from side to side, flattening its neck, black tongue flickering. Then preparatory to attack, it would rear up vertically, showing its paler cream underbelly, coiling its neck into an S shape and opening its mouth wide.

In the wild, the snake would be so high off the ground at the moment of its strike that most bites would result on a person's upper thigh. Here in The Brown's Bar, however, the enclosure being already elevated, the snake's attack was invariably closer to chest or even head height, and in the seconds before it struck, the contender was required to remain looking into the yellowish-orange-circled black eyes of his attacker. Needless to say, the experience was unnerving and no-one ever passed the test, which was why there were rarely any surreptitious bets on the side, and certainly not from the locals. If there had been, the money would always have been riding on the snake.

The first frenzied bout of bar service now over, Val paused to take in the activity around the snake pen. She'd accepted the young man's five quid – a good healthy bet, but then the Yanks were well-heeled – and now she watched as Ben's mate took up the challenge, eyes trained on the snake, placing his hand on the glass as the creature started to display hostility.

The outcome will be the same, she thought, it always is; today won't be any exception. She watched the snake rear up, admiring the arch of its body, the broad, deep head, the frighteningly bulbous cheeks and the wide-open mouth. Spectacular, she thought, a magnificent creature.

Val loved her snakes. In fact, over the years she'd spent travelling the outback, she'd become quite a talented amateur herpetologist. She had several cages at the rear of the pub, each housing a decent-sized eastern brown, which she kept regularly supplied with the live mice and frogs provided by young Tom, Betty's enterprising thirteen-year-old brother. She never worked the creatures too hard, rotating them on a weekly basis, and it never ceased to amaze her that no-one ever noticed the snakes were different, at least no comment was ever made. People just don't look, do they, she thought, probably because they just don't care. Yet the snakes were different – quite noticeably so, particularly in colour. Eastern browns actually being of the black snake genus, their colour was distinctly variable. One of her snakes was darker, one was lighter, and one even had a greenish hue, but all were nonetheless 'eastern browns', all lethal and all aggressive. And to Val, all extraordinarily beautiful.

Then, with lightning speed, the snake struck. And instinctively – it seemed with a lightning speed that equalled that of the snake – the man's hand was whipped away. Ben's buddy had failed the test. A round of applause went up, either for the snake or for Ben's buddy, or simply for the entertainment itself.

Yep, same outcome as always, Val thought. Of course it would be, wouldn't it – human nature, that simple – we're all the same really. Black, white or bloody brindle, we're all the same. She glanced about at a number of the white American soldiers. Some people just don't seem to get that though, do they?

Ever observant, Val had been aware of tensions riding high, particularly when Ben and his mates had walked in. There'd been tension before the arrival of the black Americans certainly, but it had emanated from a bunch of Aussies in the corner. You could sense their animosity towards the white Yankees, who outnumbered them. But that's only normal, she thought. They're jealous. The Yanks in their spruced-up uniforms with money to burn have got a hell of a lot more to offer the girls. Crikey, she'd seen it before often enough, hadn't she? There's always a problem when men are competing for women and the stakes aren't even, she thought. She glanced at the group of several white Yankee soldiers who were propped at the far end of the bar. But this? This was something altogether different.

Her steel-grey eyes, which could be disconcerting at times, remained focused on the group, watching for the first sign of trouble. Their outrage at the presence of the black GIs was palpable, and had been from the moment Ben and his mates had shown up. They certainly hadn't been among those applauding the snake's triumph and the entertainment in general.

Ben thumped his mate on the back. 'Better luck next time, Sam,' he said, and Sam gave a nod and a smile in a tremulous attempt at bravado, his brow beaded with sweat, the ordeal having been far more taxing than he'd anticipated.

The others joined in a toast and the four downed their beers, after which Ben collected their glasses and crossed to the bar to buy the next round.

'Hello, soldier, what'll it be, same again?'

It was young Betty who served him, and with the brightest of smiles. Twenty-year-old Betty, fair-haired, blue-eyed, was exceptionally pretty.

'Yep, thanks, ma'am.' Ben grinned flirtatiously in return, wondering if there'd be any chance of asking her out. 'What time do you knock off?'

'Don't push your luck, boy,' a voice snarled. It was an American voice and the accent was clearly that of a southerner. 'Don't you get above your station.'

One of the group from the end of the bar sauntered towards Ben. 'You're allowed in this place, I gather that,' the soldier, a sergeant, said, 'but don't you turn your charm on a white gal, you hear me? You want to play black stud then you get served by that other gal.' He pointed to Jill, who was working a little further down the bar.

Jill was also young, and also very pretty. But Jill, whose father had been English, or so it was supposed, had blackfella blood in her. Jill was Aunty Edie's daughter.

'Hey, you there, Missy,' the American called, 'you want to come here and serve this boy?'

Val was about to intervene, but it proved unnecessary.

'No, Jilly, don't bother,' Betty called, very loudly for all the bar to hear, 'I'll serve this good-looking bloke.' Then to Ben, 'What's your name, soldier?'

Jill gave the broadest of smiles and a thumbs-up to Betty, while Val let out a hoot of laughter. She was so proud of her girls, whom she thought of more as daughters than hotel staff.

'You want to watch yourself, mate,' Val called to the southern Yankee, 'or you might just find nobody here wants to serve you.'

The southerner slunk off to join his buddies at the far end of the bar, but not before casting a look of utter loathing at Ben, quickly followed by one of equal loathing to Val.

Val assumed, and quite rightly, that she'd lose this particular group's patronage, but she didn't care in the least. Good riddance, she thought as she watched them knock back their drinks and head for the door. I don't need your shit. People are people, mate, black or white. She felt suddenly proud, not only of her girls, but also of her bar – The Brown's, a shade somewhere in between – and besides, her browns were true levellers, weren't they? Everyone was the same when it came to snakes.

Val had always been surprised that people found her snake pen such a novelty. In her past life, she'd bumped into many a similar form of betting – man against snake, always a highly venomous and aggressive snake, a mulga or an eastern brown – snake pens were no novelty in the bars of the outback towns she'd worked. Hell, she'd even bumped into the odd bloke who didn't need a glass wall between the snake and him, where the bet was whether the bloke could get the snake back into the pen from which it had been released without being bitten. But in such cases, the bloke had always been Aboriginal. Which I suppose goes to prove, she was now reluctantly forced to admit to herself, that all people *aren't* the same when it comes to snakes. Aussie blackfellas were born snake wranglers. Of course they have to be, don't they, she thought – they eat the bloody things.

Snake pens had been only one form of entertainment for the drunken miners in the godforsaken towns Val had worked. Hell, they'd bet on two flies crawling up a wall, she thought; grog and gambling, that's all they had. Those men stuck in that nowhere land were just begging for distraction. Which is what made my trade such a bloody goldmine!

Valda Joan Callahan, nee Hall, had led a tough life from the very beginning. Born in 1889, not fifty yards from a row of brothels and sly grog shops in Sydney's inner-city suburb of Surry Hills, her mother had been a prostitute and her father unknown. Val herself had entered the game, taking up her mother's trade as soon as she left the Bourke Street Public School at the tender age of thirteen. Five years, two abortions and a miscarriage later had seen her marry James Patrick Callahan, a miner from Broken Hill.

Theirs was a whirlwind courtship over one brief week, James sexually obsessed with the eighteen-year-old prostitute he'd discovered in a Riley Street brothel, and Val attracted to the idea of marriage as an alternative lifestyle. She gave up prostitution and accompanied her husband to Broken Hill, where in 1910 their daughter, Daisy, was born.

Daisy seemed to make a loveless marriage worthwhile, and Val would have been prepared to remain a faithful wife to a man who gambled his money away and who, in the drink, occasionally gave her a backhander. But in 1913, following a severe bout of diphtheria, little Daisy died, and something in Val died too. Marriage without Daisy was no longer worthwhile and she stopped even pretending it was.

James soon tired of his listless, depressed wife, and when war broke out a year later, he joined the Australian Army to seek adventure further afield. He didn't tell Val at the time. One moment he was there and the next he was gone, leaving her to fend for herself.

She had no alternative but to return to the only trade she knew well, so she bought a camper trailer from an English couple who intended to settle in Broken Hill and were no longer in need of a mobile home. Camper trailers were becoming quite popular among travellers, particularly in England and the United States. They were known to many as 'caravans'. Towing the vehicle behind her husband's second-hand jalopy, Val set off on her travels, trekking the mining towns and recruiting two other working girls along the way.

Word spread quickly, and 'Caravan Callahan' became a well-known identity, not only among the miners, but also the coppers, some accepting her bribe of money and turning a blind eye, others giving her half an hour to get her van and her girls out of town.

When she finally learned that her husband had been killed in Gallipoli at the Battle of Lone Pine, Val said to her girls, 'Luckiest thing that could have happened to the bastard – now instead of being remembered as a useless prick, everyone'll call him a bloody hero.'

By the end of World War I, having accrued considerable funds, Val decided to quit prostitution. She bade farewell to her girls and took her caravan north to Brisbane, this time not as a mobile brothel, but rather a mobile home.

Still a good-looking woman, it didn't take Val Callahan long to find a man. Thomas McIntyre was a publican with whom she lived and to whom she stayed faithful for a full five years. She worked hard, managing the bar, employing staff, keeping the books, and, with a sharp eye for business, was quick to learn the pub trade. But she made the mistake of letting her lover know she had money of her own, and within those five years McIntyre, another hopeless gambler, had spent every penny of it. Furthermore, once she'd served her purpose, not content with robbing her, he threw her out into the street. But Val still had her looks, and she still had her van. 'Caravan Callahan' was back in business.

Val had become attached to her caravan. She regarded it as the only real home she'd ever been able to call her own. And I'm bloody right, aren't I, she'd told herself any number of times – the only other homes I've had belonged to a couple of useless, bastard gamblers. God I can pick 'em!

She'd set out for far-off places in the remote north of Queensland, places where men needed the pleasures women could supply. And not just the sex. The role of a prostitute was not as simple as people supposed, in Val's well-informed opinion. Many of her clients were lonely men who craved not only a woman's body, but a woman's company. She could be a mother, a lover and a wife all in one; Val was very good at her job.

'Caravanning' from town to town, she'd made a bigger fortune than ever before, ending up in Mount Isa with three working girls she'd picked up on her travels. She even bought a second-hand car and another caravan for her team. She was a true businesswoman now.

In 1934 at the age of forty-five, Val decided to quit the game altogether. She handed over the business to her longest-serving girl and took off for Townsville, a place she'd visited and loved, and which, most conveniently, had a pub for sale. Now with money to burn, Val had determined to set her sights on the pub trade. And this time it would be without a man. She didn't need or want a husband, lover or partner. Val Callahan was more than capable of making it on her own.

And she had. She'd bought the pub on the corner of Stokes and Sturt streets, refurbished the main bar, introduced the snake pen and called it 'The Brown's Bar', and after that there was no looking back.

At first she'd thought about running a brothel upstairs, but it would invite too much trouble with the law, she'd decided, so, reserving several of the rooms as private accommodation and office space for herself and staff, she let out the others to guests. All but the larger room at the back, that is, the one that could be privately accessed via the hotel's rear steps. Here was the preserve of those trusted customers who wished to gamble – poker for the main part, although Baz had recently installed a blackjack table. Where he'd got it from Val had no idea and she had no intention of asking. Thirty-year-old Barry 'Baz' Taylor was the consummate con man and the restrictions of war seemed to work in his favour. A past master in the nefarious black-market trade, he acquired so many commodities denied to the general public that where they came from was anyone's guess. Fresh fruit and vegetables, butter, eggs and meat, even petrol, which was severely rationed. Val was one of the few Townsville citizens who still drove a car, all thanks to Baz. She could only presume the man had some inside connection with the Americans, who shamelessly flaunted the goods so readily available to them.

In any event, Baz had total charge of the Gaming Room, as it was known, and Val was happy to leave things that way. She didn't even care if he was robbing her on the side, as she suspected he was – the place was attracting a great deal of custom, and customers meant money. Particularly now with the Yanks in town.

She realised that once again it was quite possible she'd linked up with a gambler, for Baz himself was a regular at the poker tables. But if so at least this gambler was successful, and she was not personally involved with him.

Baz was merely convenient for business. At least that's what she told herself. Baz was actually indispensable for business.

The Gaming Room was of course illegal, but they kept it discreet, and Val had decided early on that gambling wouldn't be likely to cause as much of a problem with the law as prostitution.

These days, however, she'd changed her mind. Since the takeover of the town by the military, brothels were springing up all over the place, and despite disapproval from some local quarters, no-one was going to close them down. Certainly not the military, and therefore not the government. The military – who had the government in their collective pocket – were only too happy for troops to 'satisfy their basic male urges' with prostitutes rather than risk any form of emotional and lasting involvement with a woman, thereby losing focus upon the job at hand, which was to fight a war. The military, and most particularly the Americans, so far from home, were quite happy to have prostitutes available to service their men.

Val had wondered briefly about whether she should take advantage of this newfound freedom and the semi-official sanction afforded otherwise-illegal brothels. But no, she decided, those days were over. She liked being a publican.

Not that she was ashamed of her past. She didn't dine out on it, certainly, but nor did she bother hiding her background. Who cares, she thought. On the odd occasion when a man recognised her and made some intentionally smartarse, smutty 'Caravan Callahan' comment intended to humiliate, she'd come back with a riposte of her own.

'Oh, those were the days, mate,' she'd say with a friendly smile. 'Nice you remember me. Don't remember you, I'm afraid. You must have been a dud.'

Nope, Val thought, I don't care if there's big money to be had in brothels, I'll stick with my pub just being a pub.

She looked fondly at her girls, Betty and Jill. They were the daughters she'd lost all those years ago in little Daisy. They're my Daisy all grown up, she thought. Course they've got mums of their own, and bloody good mums at that, but no harm feeling motherly is there? And I wouldn't want one of my girls on the game. All the more reason for not opening a brothel.

She watched as Ben, having delivered the beers to his friends, returned to the bar, a bit of a swagger in his step, determined to chat up Betty. Betty kept working away, serving customers, wiping down the counter and transferring empty glasses to the sink behind her, all the while fielding his flirtatious chat with ease.

Val couldn't hear what was being said over the general noise of the bar, but she admired the girl's confidence. She always had. Betty fascinated her. Where did that slender little thing with the pretty fair hair and the blue, blue eyes get such strength, she wondered. Because Betty was strong, there was no doubt about that. In fact, she might even go so far as to call Betty tough.

She rounded the counter and headed for the stairs. She'd leave the girls handling things here and do some work in her office.

As she passed by Ben, who was lounging nonchalantly against the bar convinced he was making inroads, she heard Betty finally call a halt to the proceedings, and with such admirable aplomb.

'Sorry, Soldier Ben baby,' Betty said, flashing the young man a radiant smile and managing at the same time to look regretful, 'but I can't meet you after work. I'm afraid I'm taken.' Which was an outright lie.

Yep, Val thought, she's tough all right. Guts and charm. She'd have made a damn good hooker.

CHAPTER TWO

Betty wasn't really tough. But nor was her tough image really an act. Over the years, fiction and reality had merged into one as Betty had presented herself the way she wished to be perceived – a replica of the American movie stars she worshipped. The strong women of the screen had always been her favourites, and as a teenager she'd tried to model herself along the lines of Greta Garbo or Marlene Dietrich, both of whom had an austere authority she deeply admired. But Garbo and Dietrich hadn't worked for her – young Betty was too given to animation – 'stillness' was not her bag. So she'd turned her attention to the crisp wit of Katharine Hepburn or the tough-as-it-gets virago of Bette Davis, but she'd found these also to be a difficult balancing act. Eventually, she'd settled upon the good-natured, wisecracking style of Rosalind Russell and Carole Lombard, their frisky mix of humour and worldliness feeling more comfortable to her. The final result – which was actually a compilation of all the screen idols she adored – had become who Betty really was. And along the road of self-invention, she *had* toughened up. Beneath Betty's pretty façade there lurked a genuine rebel. She'd even sacrificed her virginity to the cause two months previously, just after her twentieth birthday.

This had been a conscious decision on Betty's part, and despite being a true romantic at heart, had had nothing at all to do with love. As a woman of the world, she had decided that twenty years of age was high time to lose one's virginity, and she'd gone about it in a very practical manner. She'd made her selection with care, a pleasant young Australian soldier who'd been pursuing her for several weeks, and she'd made sure he performed with a condom. The act had taken place in one of the hotel's little upstairs rooms, where she occasionally stayed when they were busy – as a rule she went home to her mother's house a twenty-minute walk away.

She'd not found the experience traumatic, but nor had she found it particularly pleasurable, so she hadn't considered a repeat performance necessary. What would be the point? The exercise had served its purpose – she knew what sex was like and she could now go back to simply having fun. Which she did, much to the confusion of the young soldier who'd been so sure they were about to embark upon a full-fledged affair.

Her return to 'simply having fun' was marred a week later, however, when Carole Lombard was killed in a plane crash in Nevada, USA, on 16 January. Betty went into mourning for a fortnight. Genuinely affected by the star's death, she wrote a letter of sympathy to Carole's husband and sent it to MGM in Hollywood. Poor, poor Clark Gable, her heart ached for him, the two had been so much in love.

Betty Francis was a well-brought-up girl from a typically middle-class family. Her father, George, was a policeman and her mother, Grace, a housewife, and little Betty was born in Brisbane. She was six years old when in 1928, upon her father's promotion to senior constable, the family moved to Townsville. Then one year later her baby brother, Tom, was born.

The family lived a comfortable life in the lazy, tropical township where nothing much seemed to happen. They even owned a weekender on Magnetic Island, a rustic little shack, certainly nothing fancy, but the childhood adventures shared by Betty and Tom in the idyllic setting of Arcadia were magical.

Everything proceeded as might have been expected. George became senior sergeant; Grace, whose mothering duties were now less demanding, became involved in charitable works; Betty entered her movie-obsessed teenage years, and young Tom proved a wily little manipulator with a good head for business.

Then the war came and turned things upside down.

For the Francis family, the upheaval of their life did not occur, as it did for most Townsville citizens, in 1942 following the fall of Singapore and the bombing of Darwin, but a full two years earlier.

It was in early 1940 that George Francis was approached by Lieutenant Commander Eric Feldt, who was based in Townsville to set up the HQ of Section C, Allied Intelligence Bureau, otherwise known as the Coastwatchers. George's early life and his knowledge of the South Pacific would be of great value to the Coastwatchers, he was told. A number of civilians as well as military personnel were being asked to volunteer and Lieutenant Commander Feldt was most eager to recruit him.

George, as it turned out, was more than willing to be recruited.

Both Betty and eleven-year-old Tom had been confused by the speed with which things had happened. As senior sergeant their father was one of Townsville's most prominent citizens, then all of a sudden he was gone and twenty-six-year-old Sergeant Bruce Desmond had been promoted to his position.

'It's because of Grandpa Albert,' their mother had patiently explained, which had only added to Betty's confusion. She'd met her paternal grandparents just once in her life when they'd paid a visit to Brisbane and she couldn't even remember what they looked like. Tom, who had never encountered his grandparents, was left even more in the dark. Then Grace had explained further.

Albert Francis had been employed as a teacher for the Australian Government Colonial Affairs Department and the family had travelled extensively throughout the South Pacific. George had grown up on the islands, living in Fiji, the New Hebrides, Bougainville and New Guinea.

'Your father's familiarity with the region will prove invaluable to the military,' Grace had said, and Betty had accepted the fact. She'd known her father had spent a great deal of time in the South Pacific as a child and also as a young man, so she supposed it made sense.

Tom, however, was not so easily satisfied. The freckle-faced, hyperactive and quick-witted boy had questions.

'But why has Dad disappeared so quickly,' he'd demanded, 'and why don't we know where he's been sent?'

'Your father is working in Navy Intelligence,' Grace had flatly answered in a tone that brooked no further discussion, 'they always keep things close to their chest.' And Betty and Tom had had to be satisfied with that.

Grace had carefully avoided throughout the conversation any mention of the Coastwatchers, for fear her children might discover the danger a Coastwatcher faced. In his lonely duty out there on those remote islands monitoring enemy activity, a Coastwatcher worked with virtually no backup support. Grace was not at all happy about her husband volunteering for such duty, despite his efforts to quell her fears.

'But it's not the Coastwatchers' duty to fight, dear,' George had said lightly. 'Indeed, the military doesn't want the Coastwatchers to do anything that might draw attention to themselves. All we're to do, I'm told, is to sit quietly observing and gathering information.' He'd smiled reassuringly, and even with a touch of humour, as he'd added, 'Feldt himself has code-named his organisation "Ferdinand" as a reminder of that very purpose. You remember the children's book *The Story of Ferdinand*, don't you? You read it to Tom when he was little.'

'Yes, of course I remember,' she replied, a brusque edge to her voice. 'Ferdinand was a bull who didn't want to fight. He sat under a tree and smelled the flowers instead.'

'Exactly.'

'But Ferdinand was not at war, was he,' she went on, the brusque edge now verging on acerbic. For a pretty and very feminine woman who had led a highly conventional life, Grace could at times display a surprisingly defiant streak. 'Ferdinand was not expected to enter an area of conflict and spy on the enemy.'

George had known at that moment there was no point in attempting to downplay the situation or mollycoddle her in any way. His wife was no fool, and he needed to be honest with her.

'I want to go, Grace,' he said. 'I *have* to go.'

Her stony expression said 'why?' so he continued reasonably.

'I can be useful, don't you see? I can serve my country.'

Still no reply.

'Oh, Gracie, I would have signed up to fight in this wretched war, but they don't take thirty-nine-year-olds.' His eyes begged her understanding. 'Can't you see, my love, this is the chance I've been waiting for, the chance I've been *longing* for. You *can* see that, can't you?'

'Yes,' she said quietly. 'Yes, I can see that.'

They hadn't talked any more on the subject, holding each other close instead, an action that spoke far more than words, but Grace hadn't felt any happier about the situation.

These days, when someone asked Betty about her father, as they occasionally did, she would reply in all honesty that she hadn't seen him for two whole years. 'He works in navy intelligence,' she would say. 'We don't know exactly where, but he's alive and well.'

That much the family did know. Feldt was a kind man. He kept Grace Francis well informed about her husband's state of health, even relaying messages between them from time to time, although never, never was she informed of George's whereabouts.

Young Tom's response to enquiries about his father varied somewhat from his sister's. 'Navy intelligence,' thirteen-year-old Tom would proudly boast. 'Top secret, sworn to silence, not allowed to say where,' he'd add as if he actually knew.

While still trying to come to terms with her husband's abrupt departure, and also to quell her constant worry for his safety, Grace had been faced with yet another dilemma. And this was Betty. For the past year, ever since leaving school, Betty had refused to undertake a course in shorthand and typing, which would qualify her for a secretarial career.

'It's what many young women are doing these days, dear,' Grace had suggested mildly, surprised that such a progressive girl as her daughter wouldn't want to follow the modern path.

'But I don't want to be a secretary,' Betty had insisted, 'I don't want to be locked away in an office. I want a social life where I get to meet people. I'm going to work in a shop.'

There was no budging the girl, and Grace could only hope it would be the right sort of shop, nothing too vulgar. Strangely enough, George hadn't seemed in the least worried.

'She'll be married in a couple of years, Grace,' he'd said airily. 'A girl as pretty as our Betty – crikey, she's already turning heads in the street. I wouldn't worry about what shop she works in, my dear, I'd worry about what bloke she chooses. We'll have to start vetting them carefully.'

The shop had proved to be acceptable – Mrs Bolton's tea rooms in Flinders Street, where many a nice family gathered for morning or afternoon tea, particularly on a Saturday. George had also proved to be right – there were many young men keen to curry favour with pretty Betty Francis. In fact, the young male clientele who now frequented Mrs Bolton's tea rooms showed a definite increase in numbers. Fortunately, Betty didn't appear to take any of them seriously, although it had to be admitted she was wickedly flirtatious. Grace didn't altogether approve of her daughter's behaviour, which was clearly influenced by a passion for American film actresses, but she was thankful nonetheless. Seventeen was far too young for any serious commitment that might lead to marriage.

Then all of a sudden things had changed. George was no longer at home monitoring the situation and Betty was eighteen. And Betty wanted to work in a *pub*! Not as a receptionist behind a counter welcoming the arrival of hotel guests, but in the hotel's *bar*! Which made it a *pub*! Which made her daughter a *barmaid*! Which was *unthinkable*!

Betty was not in the least fazed by her mother's outrage. 'Things are different now, Mum,' she said with an insouciant shrug. 'Since the war and all that, things have changed. Women are working all sorts of jobs these days.'

'Not my daughter, and not in a *bar*!'

Grace had remained adamant and Betty unfazed.

'It's a really good job Val's offering – pays twice as much as the tea rooms.'

Betty had been most impressed by Val Callahan. She'd seen the woman around town often enough – Val was difficult to miss, full-figured and bosomy, blonde-haired and red-lipped – but they'd never actually met until one day at the Roxy picture theatre when a friend of Betty's had introduced them.

'You look like Joan Blondell,' Betty had said admiringly.

Val had liked that. She'd been equally impressed by Betty. Pretty as a picture, but a bold, forthright young thing. 'You should come and work for me,' she'd said.

So Betty had gone to see her at The Brown's late the following day when she'd finished work at the tea rooms, and as soon as she'd walked into the bar she'd known this was where she belonged.

'At least come and meet Val, Mum,' she'd urged. 'You'll like her, honest you will. She's a really nice woman, down to earth, smart, too. At least come and meet her, *please* say you will!'

Grace did. Perhaps in order to keep the peace, or perhaps because she suspected that, with or without her permission, her daughter would accept this woman's offer. Better to know what I'm up against, Grace had wisely decided.

The moment she'd laid eyes on Val Callahan she'd recognised the woman's working-class roots. She'd recognised the woman herself – she too had seen Val about town. A common woman, she'd decided at the time, not without a certain flair some might find attractive, but hair obviously dyed; a bit 'mutton dressed as lamb'.

Now, upon chatting to Val in the upstairs office with Betty perched demurely on the sofa beside her, all three of them seated around the coffee table, cups in hand, a pot of tea having been served by young Jill, Grace was having second thoughts about Val.

Steel-grey eyes focused intently upon her and a no-nonsense voice speaking downright common sense, Grace was finding it difficult to make judgements. The blonde hair and red lips seemed somehow irrelevant.

'Don't you worry about your daughter, Grace,' Val said – right from the start she hadn't even bothered with a 'How do you do, Mrs Francis,' it was, 'Hello, Grace, I'm Val,' with a warm handshake that was as strong as a man's. Unconventional though the greeting was, Grace couldn't help feeling a little awestruck by the power of the woman's personality.

'Your girl will be well looked after working here with me,' Val now went on. 'You just met young Jill who served the tea. She's the same age as Betty and they're bound to become great mates. And while I know you're probably concerned about her working behind a bar where men are drinking and all that,' she continued seamlessly, 'well, don't be.' She gave a dismissive wave of her hand, although she knew that of course the girl's mother would be worried. Most mothers would be, especially a mother as conventional as Grace Francis in her neat little frock and her gloves and her handbag, and her carefully coiffed hair that really should be tinted where it was starting to show a bit of grey at the sides.

Val could see where Betty got her looks. Grace was a pretty woman, or she would be if she hadn't allowed herself to fade a little. So many women do around the forty mark, she thought critically. They slip into a drab middle age as if there's no alternative. What's wrong with a bit of colour, for God's sake?

'I don't allow drunkenness at The Brown's,' she went on, which was a lie. How on earth could one keep men sober when alcohol was to hand, and why should one try? Business was business after all. But she never allowed things to get out of hand. She kept a 12-gauge shotgun under the bar and had been known to march a trouble-maker out into the street on any number of occasions. And Baz was always there to act as a bouncer on Friday and Saturday nights when things tended to get raucous. Although she preferred not to rely too much on Baz, who carried a flick knife and could be unpredictable. Best not to tell Grace Francis all this stuff though.

'Besides, Betty will be doing a great deal more than serving behind the bar,' she continued, 'I intend to train your daughter in bookkeeping and general accounting right here in this office.' She gestured to the more austere end of the room, where a large desk was strewn with papers and ledgers, an authoritative carver placed behind it and two hardback chairs drawn up on the visitors' side. Very official, very respectable. 'She'll not only learn about office work,' Val said, 'she'll end up with an excellent personal reference from me – better than any business diploma.'

Betty had told Val that her mother wished her to do a secretarial course, and Val was painting the perfect picture for Grace. She was not lying, however. She had every intention of fully training the girl; it would be to her own advantage to do so.

'Nothing like getting experience on the job, Grace,' she said heartily, 'you learn far more than you do from books, I can assure you.'

Val drained the last of her tea and placed the cup and saucer on the coffee table with an air of finality. 'So what'll it be?' she queried, already confident of the answer, although she was intrigued by the way Grace Francis was studying her. Unflinchingly. It seemed out of character. 'Don't you worry about your little girl, love,' she said, 'I'll look after her.'

'Yes,' Grace replied, her gaze still unflinching, 'yes, I believe you will.'

Well, well, Val thought. There's a bit of spirit in our Grace after all. Good for you, love. She poured them a second cup of tea from the pot and they toasted the deal.

Now, two years later, Betty was an invaluable member of The Brown's team, and like family to Val, as was Jill. Grace had been right to trust Val.

As the end of March drew near, tensions continued to mount. Fear ran rife in Queensland, and most particularly in Townsville. The Japanese were advancing on Northern Australia through Malaya, the Dutch Indies and New Guinea, and Townsville had by now become the frontline hub for Australian and American forces. Troops continued to pour in, creating a garrison town, and over 7000 citizens had fled south. But many remained to confront whatever fate had in store for them. Including Grace Francis.

Grace had not once contemplated heading south, not while her husband still served with the Coastwatchers. When George returned – and she had firmly convinced herself he would – she would be waiting for him. George would come home to his wife and family.

She had briefly considered sending Tom to a school in Brisbane where he could stay with her sister and family. Christian Brothers, the school he attended in Townsville, was not one of those that had been closed, but situated as it was right on the coast, the Americans had fortified it with guns. Grace felt uncomfortable about her son being placed in such a vulnerable position.

Tom had strongly objected to both the idea and the reasoning behind it. 'What do you mean *vulnerable*!' he'd exclaimed as if she'd said something quite ludicrous. 'When they start dropping bombs the whole of *Townsville* will be *vulnerable*.'

Grace had felt a little foolish for having made the suggestion, and, as always, Tom had gone on to present a very persuasive argument.

'Besides, I'm serving a purpose here, Mum,' he'd insisted. 'I'm a runner for the Yanks, I told you that, remember?'

'Yes, dear, I remember.'

Tom was very proud of the purpose he served, which had started out quite innocently. In his inimitable style, he'd befriended a group of American soldiers for whom he'd run the odd errand, always receiving a generous gift in return, some article or food item unavailable to local citizens. He would dodge through the dense military traffic on his bicycle, delivering a message here and there, or fetching something, and he'd proved so efficient they'd now claimed him an official 'runner'. The term may have been applied to humour the youngster, but he was undoubtedly useful, for while many bicycles throughout Townsville had been requisitioned by the military, Tom had been allowed to keep his.

'I'm not just doing errands anymore, Mum, I can tell you,' he'd continued in all earnestness. 'I'm a real runner these days,' he'd said with pride. 'I'm serving my country, that's what I'm doing.'

Oh God, Grace thought, I might as well be listening to George.

The subject of Brisbane was not mentioned again.

Tom's commitment to duty actually set Grace thinking. There must surely be some purpose she too could serve, apart from the fundraising activities for the Red Cross with which she was currently involved. Her daughter's comment about women working all sorts of jobs now had also hit home.

They are, aren't they, Grace told herself; women are embracing all kinds of activities they would never have contemplated had it not been for the war. Working on the land and in munition factories, driving trucks, doing all sorts of men's jobs, even joining the army. There are the WAAAFs, and of course there are the nurses . . .

Well, she couldn't take on a career like that, could she, she reasoned, she did have a teenage son to look after,

much as he believed he didn't need looking after. And then
there was the house. She must take care of the house. The
house was of tantamount importance to Grace. George
must have a home to return to – a home and a wife and a
family. This was her principal duty.

It was in thinking of the family home that Grace hit
upon a possible answer. Of course, here was something
she could do. She could offer half her house as billet
quarters for officers. George would certainly approve. The
military were crying out for accommodation and there was
ample space. She had a spare bedroom, George's study sat
vacant, and she could clear out the music room, which was
rarely used these days with Betty so constantly working at
the hotel. In bygone times when they'd gathered together
with friends in the smaller of the house's two sitting
rooms, which had been designated 'the music room', it had
always been Betty at the piano leading the singalong. Betty
was a born musician.

'You're getting rid of the piano!' Far from being aghast
at the suggestion as Grace had expected she would be,
Betty was overjoyed. 'That's wonderful! I'll get Baz to
collect it and bring it to The Brown's. We'll have music in
the bar on weekends!' She swept a theatrical arc with her
arm as if envisaging the famous neon signs of Broadway.
'We'll call it *Saturday Singalong*.'

'Oh.' Grace was taken aback. 'Very well, dear.' She
hadn't mentioned 'getting rid' of the piano as such, she'd
only suggested they might store it away somewhere, but
the idea had been embraced with such gusto she now
supposed she must resign herself to its loss.

Tom had been equally enthusiastic. 'Clearing the decks
for an officer's billet, eh? Good on you, Mum, you're
doing your bit!'

Baz arrived, Betty in tow, the very next day aboard
a military GMC truck. They were accompanied by two
obliging American soldiers.

Things move very quickly when there's a war on, Grace thought, I suppose it's only natural they should. She felt a sense of regret as she stood on the pavement, Betty beside her, watching the soldiers load the small upright into the vehicle's open tray. The piano, with its pretty carved panels and moulded legs, symbolised the happiest of child-hoods. It had belonged to her grandmother, upon whose death her own mother had passed it on to her. She and George had had it shipped up from Brisbane. The piano was very much 'family'.

'Don't worry, Mum,' Betty whispered comfortingly. 'It's only on loan. We'll get it back when the war's over.'

And how long will that be, Grace wondered.

The piano was an instant hit at The Brown's, where it fitted perfectly into the corner of the bar. That night, when Betty sat down to play, they all knew it was destined to prove as great an attraction as the snake pen.

Baz stood nearby beaming, taking full credit and clapping along to the songs as if applauding himself, which of course he was. They'd never have got the thing here without his influence, would they?

Barry 'Baz' Taylor was a man who might be referred to by some as a 'spiv', while others might find him devastatingly attractive. He was to some a 'flashy dresser' – although never so flashy he couldn't go unno-ticed in a crowd if need be – while others might consider him 'stylish'. Whatever the opinion, Baz certainly knew how to turn on the charm. A clever manipulator, he was quick to recognise the main chance and knew how to turn things not only to his own advantage, but also to the advantage of those who were useful to him. Which was why someone as canny as Val Callahan had found herself reliant upon a man she actually didn't like, a situation she found at times irksome.

Baz, dark-haired and clean-shaven but for a neat Ronald Colman moustache – the fashion of the day – was good-looking, and popular with women. He appeared to have led a charmed life, but in fact he'd had a tough beginning. Born in Melbourne, the youngest of nine children, his father a waterside worker and opportunistic thief, his mother an obsessed Roman Catholic, who between giving birth spent every morning and evening at mass, young Barry Taylor's childhood had not been a particularly happy one. His older siblings either bullied him or failed to notice him altogether, he was never sure which galled him the most.

So Baz had rebelled. Following his father's example, he'd become a petty criminal, compiling a list of convictions in the Children's Court before being institutionalised at the age of twelve. He'd escaped Melbourne when he was fifteen, slowly travelling north to Sydney and committing ever-bolder crimes along the way, only to be once more hauled before the juvenile court system on breaking-and-entering charges. After being put into the boys' home, he'd managed again to escape, and at eighteen had been sentenced to three years in Long Bay Gaol for stealing and receiving stolen goods.

Upon his release, Baz had headed north and finally settled in Townsville, where nobody knew him. He'd lived in the same boarding house in Walker Street for the past nine years, always paying his rent up front and doing regular favours for his widowed landlady, old Mrs Cheetham, who considered him the nicest young man she had ever encountered.

Since arriving in Townsville, he'd given up petty crime as a career choice, although he'd continued to operate just a little outside the law, running a two-up school on a semi-regular basis and an occasional poker game. Oddly enough, despite the uncertainty of gambling, he'd miraculously managed to always stay in front. Lucky.

Then he'd met Val. Even luckier.

Then the war had engulfed Townsville. The Yanks had arrived, and the black market thrived. Luckier still. Baz was now in his element.

The mob in the bar was lapping up the music. It wasn't even a Saturday, but there was quite a crowd. People had flocked in off the street upon hearing the piano.

Betty had finished thumping out 'When the Saints Go Marching In', accompanied by a chorus of voices from those who knew the lyrics and hand-clapping from those who didn't, and now at a cry of 'Little Brown Jug' from one of the Yanks, she segued straight into the next number. She knew all the popular songs and could play them without sheet music. Who needed sheet music? Betty had an excellent ear and was a natural on the piano. She could play a song after hearing it only twice.

'Hey there, Doll Face, fancy a dance?' Baz had strolled over to the bar, where Jill was about to wash the glasses she'd collected. He gave her an enticing wink. 'Let's show 'em how we strut our stuff, shall we?'

He was referring to several days previously when, after the bar had closed, he'd taken twenty-year-old Jill to the Olympia just over the road, where they'd danced until midnight, much to Jill's delight. She absolutely adored Baz.

'Can't, silly, I'm working.' Jill flushed and cast a self-conscious glance at Val, who was also behind the bar serving some customers.

Val caught the girl's look, a mixture of pleasure and guilt, and she cursed Baz. She wished he'd stop flirting with Jill, who was vulnerable and highly susceptible to his charm. She tried to signal her feelings to him, but Baz was having none of it. Simply because Baz didn't care. Baz just wanted to dance.

'Oh, the boss won't mind if we take a bit of a whirl, will you, Boss?' he said in jocular fashion, flashing his most winning grin. 'You'll cut us some slack, won't you, Val? We need to celebrate the arrival of the piano after all.'

His tone unmistakeably implied 'you owe me', but that wasn't why Val gave in. Val couldn't give a shit about Baz. She knew full well that Baz Taylor needed her as much as she needed him. But she'd noticed how young Jill's foot had been tapping away to the music. The girl was just itching to dance. What a pity it had to be with Baz.

'Sure, Jill,' she said lightly, 'off you go. I'll look after things here.'

Jill's smile, as always, was captivating. White teeth gleamed in satin-brown skin and black eyes shone with pure joy. She was an unaffected and utterly disarming young woman.

Within seconds she was out from behind the counter and Baz was expertly steering her in a wild polka among the tables, men clearing the way for them and clapping along.

Val tried not to let her disapproval show. Everyone was enjoying the moment, why spoil the fun? But she was worried nonetheless. Baz laid on the charm with every young woman he met – with older women, too, for that matter – but Val wished he would concentrate on Betty. Betty was tough. Betty could play him at his own game and regularly did, matching him quip for quip, flirting with equal flair and at times just taking the piss out of the man. There was no pulling the wool over Betty's eyes. But Jill? Jill was a different matter altogether.

Val felt very much responsible for Jill, whom she'd known since childhood. Her relationship with Jill's mother, Aunty Edie, went back eight years and was special, for she and Edie Yiramba shared a secret from the past. A secret about which Jill knew nothing, and Val intended to keep things that way, but her knowledge of the girl's back-ground aroused in her a strongly protective streak.

'Little Brown Jug' came to a rousing finish and upon another yelled request Betty leaped into 'Chattanooga Choo Choo'.

Baz kept his arm around Jill and would have danced on, but she shook herself free and returned to the bar. Not that she wouldn't have loved to continue dancing, and particularly with Baz, but duty called. She would not overstep the mark.

Val had been growing more and more worried about Jill of late. The girl was a virgin, she was quite sure of it, there was an innocence about her that was eminently readable, and although the current situation was harmless enough – Baz's behaviour was instinctive, he flirted with every female in sight – she could tell that Jill was becoming besotted.

What if he decides to up the stakes, Val wondered. He'd lead her on to get her into bed, he'd tell her he loved her and the girl would most certainly crumble. But as soon as he'd had her he'd toss her aside. Baz Taylor was a thoroughly amoral bloke.

Yep, you're a right bastard, Baz, she thought as she watched him sidle up to the bar still laying on the charm. She could hear him asking Jill if she wanted to come out dancing after they'd closed.

Val decided there and then that she'd issue a warning. In fact, she'd make him swear an oath. He must solemnly promise not to seduce young Jill Yiramba, because if he did – well, bugger his worth to business, Val thought, he'd be out that door like a shot.

CHAPTER THREE

Rumours abounded. No-one knew exactly how they'd started or who had been first to spread the word, but by the beginning of April 1942, it was common knowledge the invasion of Northern Australia was expected within weeks. It was further told that in a memorandum to Federal Cabinet, the Chief of the Home Forces, Major General Iven Mackay, had stated that he did not intend to defend Townsville. He was even quoted as having written, 'It may be necessary to submit to the occupation of certain areas of Australia should local forces be overcome,' a prospect that was understandably worrying for the citizens of Townsville.

The rumours further went on to hint at a plan, emanating from Major General Mackay's suggestion, which would later become known as 'The Brisbane Line', wherein it was anticipated seven-eighths of the continent would capitulate to the enemy. This plan was to be enacted, or so the rumours said, in order to protect the south-east sliver between Brisbane and Melbourne, which was considered to be of the most military, economic and social importance. Where would that then leave those to the north? Were they to be deserted? Little wonder many felt a sense of betrayal.

As yet none of this was openly broadcast to the Australian people, but news had definitely been leaked from somewhere. The rumours continued to abound as rumours do, and there was every reason to believe them, particularly given the fact that preparations for a 'scorched earth' policy had already begun.

Small craft were to be removed from harbours and rivers; signboards had disappeared from railway stations and roads; people were requested to destroy road maps in case they fell into enemy hands; and those considered 'aliens' were being moved into internment camps. Massive cattle musters were organised too, thousands upon thousands of beasts shifted vast distances in order to prevent the provision of fresh meat to the Japanese should they successfully invade. Things were becoming decidedly ominous.

War had without doubt changed the face of Townsville. The once-gracious beachside walk down The Strand, where across the water Magnetic Island beckoned, was now a coastal mess of barbed wire and gun emplacements. The Kissing Point Fortification at the rocky northern end again served the purpose it had during World War I, a combined army barracks and battery of vital strategic value; and any number of buildings along The Strand had been requisitioned for military use. The Seaview Hotel was now an Australian Officers' Club; St Patrick's convent served as accommodation for the Women's Auxiliary Australian Air Force, its students, along with those from several other schools, having been evacuated to Ravenswood; and at the southern end of The Strand, where Wickham Street led up to Flinders and the main hub of Townsville, the magnificent two-storey Queen's Hotel, embracing the entire corner virtually a block each way and considered the finest hotel in the whole of Northern Queensland, now housed the American Officers' Club.

In the town's centre, the grand boulevard of Flinders Street still boasted many fine, colonial buildings, including the post office, although the imposing clock tower was in the process of being removed for fear it would serve as a beacon for Japanese bombers. There was much impressive architecture in the other broad streets that formed the core of Townsville, too – hotels and public buildings for the most part – but it was difficult to get a perspective. In whatever direction one looked, the eye was distracted by the seething mass of military activity.

Over the Victoria Bridge that crossed Ross Creek to South Townsville, the bedlam was even more evident. Here the military appeared to have blanketed the land. Seas of tents formed army barracks where once there had been parks, massive transport and munitions stores had sprung up everywhere, and all was interwoven with traffic; the endless, heavy-duty traffic of army trucks and machinery. Since the arrival of the Americans, the entire town seemed to have disappeared beneath the weight of war.

This very fact, however, was a comfort to many. The Americans were a price worth paying in these frightening times when invasion threatened. Their presence made people feel safe. Even the shortage of produce and general supplies – fresh fruit and vegetables, meat and eggs, dairy products and, surprisingly, rice, the majority being gobbled up by the American military – this too was a price worth paying. The lack of petrol and tyres for privately owned vehicles was also suffered, the people of Townsville accepting the fact they must travel in buses – roofed and open-sided single deckers that invariably chugged along at less than a walking pace – or weave their way through the congestion on bicycles. All of these deprivations were worth the presence of the Americans, for the Americans were here to save them.

There was one element though that was not as welcoming of the Americans as the citizens of Townsville. The Australian soldiers felt a strong antipathy towards their

American counterparts. The comic taunt that was applied to GIs – 'over-sexed, over-paid and over here' – did not have a humorous ring to the ears of the Aussie troops, who suffered deprivations similar to those of Townsville's civilians. Unlike the Americans, they couldn't devour huge feeds of steak and eggs every day of the week! Nor could they readily avail themselves of transport for personal use! After a night out in town, there was no hopping aboard a military Willys jeep or GMC truck. They had to walk back to camp or, humiliatingly, beg a lift with the Yanks.

The Aussies were paid a pittance in comparison, their uniforms looked shabby next to the smart outfits of the GIs, and they had no ready supply of nylons and chocolates and cigarettes to offer as gifts. Little wonder the Yanks were winning all the girls.

The Australians were angry. The imbalance was grossly unfair. They were here to fight a war, too!

'They've been at it again, Baz,' Ned complained, 'those bastard Aussies, I'm sick to death of 'em.'

Forty-year-old Ned Parslow was an out-and-out Aussie himself. He would never have thought he'd hear himself bellyache about his fellow Australians, particularly those who were fighting for their country, but he'd had enough.

'They raided the chook house last night,' he went on, 'third time in a month. I don't know how they do it, my Maxie's a bloody good guard dog, but I didn't hear a peep out of 'im. I reckon one of 'em must have a real way with dogs.' He gave a snort of disgust. 'Probably a bloke from the land, a bloody farmer just like me. Well, I'm gonna keep watch from now on, and I tell you if I spring 'im I'll blow 'is bloody head off!'

Baz nodded sympathetically, knowing it was a load of hot air and that Ned was just letting off steam. He'll run out of puff soon, he thought.

They were sitting in the kitchen, Ned's hard-working wife, Vera, having poured them a strong brew of Liptons before leaving them alone to chat while she tended to the children's tea – the Parslows had a son and a daughter, twelve and ten years old respectively. The kids would be home from school soon, riding their bikes the five miles from town.

Ned wasn't the only farmer who was fed up with Australian soldiers raiding properties, stealing vegetables from their crops, fruit from their orchards, and most particularly eggs from their henhouses.

'Ratbags, they are,' Ned grumbled, already starting to run out of puff. 'I wouldn't mind pissing off south, to tell you the truth.'

'What, because of a few ratbag Aussie soldiers?' Baz grinned. 'Bit drastic, wouldn't you say?'

'Nah, nah, not just because of them,' Ned admitted, 'but all this stuff about invasion and that, bit scary with the kids, you know. I'm wondering if I shouldn't take the family down south.' He shrugged. 'But then who'd look after the farm? Johnno wouldn't be able to manage things without me and Vera.' Johnno was the hired help.

'Oh, I think you're being a bit premature, mate,' Baz said, 'it's just talk at the moment, that's all it is.'

Baz would find it most inconvenient if Ned upped and left. The two of them had come to an excellent arrangement. The farm, a small family-run affair of three acres that didn't yield enough to be of interest to the military, was ideal for Baz's purposes. It was on the outskirts of town, just five miles south-west near the banks of the Ross River, an easy drive in Val's car, and he would regularly deliver petrol in exchange for eggs, fruit and vegetables. Ned Parslow was a perfect source of supply. If the man was to leave, Baz would have to find another small-time farmer whose produce wasn't sold directly to the Americans, and even if he found such a farmer, the property was bound to be a good deal further from town.

'I'd stay put a while if I were you,' he said comfortingly.

'Yeah, well,' Ned agreed, 'don't really have much option, do I?'

Later that same day, early evening just before they opened the bar, Baz sold a sizeable portion of the fresh produce to Val – for 'mates' rates', naturally – the rest he kept in reserve to be sold the following day at exorbitant prices to those he knew could afford it, or to those who could offer good barter in exchange.

'Only scored you a half-a-dozen eggs this time,' he said, 'the Aussies raided Ned's chook house again.'

'A half-a-dozen's fine,' Val replied.

As she counted out the money, she decided now would be a good time to issue the warning she'd planned. They were alone upstairs in her office.

'There's something I want to talk to you about, Baz.'

'Right. I'm all yours. Fire away.' He pocketed his earnings. 'What can I get you, Boss? Something you want? Name it and it's yours.'

'Nope. Nothing I need.'

'Ah. A bit of a chat then, eh?' He waited for her to offer him a drink or at least ask him to sit down, but no, they remained standing. And she had a funny look in her eyes. 'So what's up?'

'It's about Jill.'

'Oh yeah?' A touch of bewilderment. 'What *about* Jill?'

'I want you to leave her alone.'

Distinct puzzlement. 'What do you mean leave her alone? I haven't touched her.'

'Not yet you haven't.'

A definite warning. 'Oh come off it, Val, Jill's not my type, you know that. I like them a bit *flashier* than *Jill*,' he scoffed, as if pretty young Jill was downright plain.

Val felt a surge of something far stronger than annoyance, but she couldn't allow her anger to show. 'Then why do you keep flirting with her?' she said coldly.

'Can't help who I am, love,' he said with a careless shrug. 'You know that. I'm just being me.'

Yes, she did know that, just as she knew he was right. She could expect no change in his behaviour and it would be wrong of her to ask. But she could extract a promise. That much she could most certainly do.

'I want you to swear an oath to me, Baz,' she said solemnly, 'an oath that you'll keep your hands off Jill.'

'Sure, Val, no worries.' He made a gesture of mock surrender; it was an easy promise. But he was intrigued nonetheless. That had been the funny look he'd seen in her eyes, he realised. Something really serious was troubling her. But Jill? Why Jill? He couldn't help asking, 'What's the problem with Jill?'

'She's infatuated with you, that's the problem,' Val snarled. 'She's putty in your hands and you bloody well know it.'

'Oh.' He hadn't known it actually. He hadn't really taken much notice of Jill, apart from the fact she was a good dancer. 'Well, so many girls are, aren't they,' he said with a rakish grin. 'I can't be blamed for that, can I?'

Val wanted to slap his smug face, but she controlled the urge. 'I'm warning you, Baz,' she said evenly, 'if you fuck that girl, then you fuck any business you and I might have. You'll be out of here like a shot. Do you get my drift?'

'Yep. Sure do, Boss.' His smile remained. Val didn't frighten him. In fact, he rather liked goading her from time to time. 'And I promise, no bedding the little brown girl, cross my heart and hope to die.' With his finger, he made the sign of a cross on his shirtfront. 'Can I go now?'

'Yeah, piss off.'

Baz gave a cheeky wave and left. He would honour the promise, simply because his deal with Val was too valuable to risk. And it would be no hardship. Jill had never featured as a prospective conquest. He was interested to learn of the girl's infatuation though. If he'd registered that himself he probably would have bedded her, just for a bit of fun; it was nice to be adored. The warning had been timely.

He couldn't help wondering why Val was taking such a profound interest in Jill's sex life. Sure, she was motherly towards her 'girls' as she called Betty and Jill, but they were twenty years old, for God's sake! And they worked in a bar! They'd know the score. And if they didn't, it was about bloody time they did.

Jeez, you can't tell me Betty hasn't been around a bit, he thought. Shit, I wouldn't half mind bedding *her*!

Why the interest in Jill, he wondered. What's the connection?

Val's connection to Jill was stronger than even Jill herself was aware, despite the fact the two had known each other since she was a child. Val was her mother's best friend who had seen them through hard times and Jill loved her. Val was like a second mother. To Jill, the connection was that simple. But Jill didn't know the depth of the bond that existed between Val Callahan and Edie Yiramba.

The two had first met in 1934, six months after Val's arrival in Townsville and two years after Edie had been released from Palm Island, together with her ten-year-old child. Edie's daughter had been the result of a rape she'd suffered by a white man during the early days of her twelve-year incarceration, and she'd named the child Jill, after the kind, white nurse who ran the female dormitory. Jill knew nothing of all this. But Val did. Edie had told Val everything.

Edie Yiramba had been born shortly after the turn of the century – she was not sure which year exactly – in the Kuranda area of far North Queensland. At the age of fourteen she'd given birth to her first child, and her second had been born two years later. Edie had loved her children, a son and a daughter, but the white administration considering her little more than a child herself, in her mid-teens and with no husband, deemed her immoral and incompetent as a mother. Her children were taken from her, she was separated from her adult family, and in 1920 she was sent to Palm Island.

An idyllic setting forty-five miles north of Townsville on the Great Barrier Reef, Palm Island had been the choice of Queensland's Chief Protector of Aborigines in 1916. He had considered the remoteness of the place highly suitable as a reformatory for individuals who needed to be punished. Here, those Aborigines who threatened to cause trouble could be successfully isolated.

By the time Edie arrived in 1920, Palm Island was rapidly on the way to becoming the largest Aboriginal settlement in Queensland. Throughout the state, people were being removed from their tribal groups and sent to Palm Island, and often for the most innocuous and incomprehensible of reasons. Included in the infringements that led to this penalty was: being 'disruptive', falling pregnant to a white man, and being of 'mixed blood'.

Despite the administration's insistent use of the term 'Palm Island Mission', Aboriginal people used another term. They referred to the place as a 'penal settlement', and they were right.

Over time the population on Palm Island grew, but only because of the large numbers sent there. In actual fact, the death rate on the island was higher than the birth rate, due to the squalor and deprivation that prevailed. People were constantly hungry. Rations were never generous, and for those who didn't line up for parade or work allocation, the punishment meted out was always the denial of food.

Segregation in all forms was strictly observed. On arrival, children were separated from their parents and then segregated by gender. There were men's and women's dormitories, and boys' and girls' dormitories, and all Aborigines were forbidden entry to those zones deemed 'white'. All Palm Island Aborigines were furthermore forbidden to speak their own languages.

It was no doubt the mutual hardship they suffered that bonded the people of Palm Island, but the denial of their various tribal languages without doubt sealed that bond. Palm Islanders invariably referred to themselves as Bwgcolman people. And they said it with pride.

'I'm Bwgcolman,' they'd declare – *many tribes* – *one people* – a true statement of solidarity.

The forbidden entry to those zones deemed 'white' didn't work in reverse, even when it came to the women's dormitory, as Edie was soon to find out. She'd been on Palm Island barely six months when, upon returning from the ablutions block one evening, she was dragged around the side of the women's dormitory block, thrust up against the wall and brutally raped.

She knew who her rapist was. Even in the gloom of the night, she could make out his face in the flickering light that shone through one of the block's windows. She didn't know his name, but she'd seen him often enough. Crikey, she'd seen him on a daily basis – he was one of the guards who stood by every morning as the administrators doled out the work allocation. A bully of a bloke, nobody seemed to like him, not even the other white fellas.

She didn't scream, knowing she'd get into trouble if she did. He'd say she led him on, and she knew they always believed the white blokes. So instead, teeth gritted, she silently endured the searing pain of his thrusts and his animal grunts. Pig, she thought, pig.

Then the bell rang and the lights went out and she knew it was nine o'clock. They always rang the bell and turned off the electricity at nine o'clock. That was why she'd been hurrying from the ablutions block – she'd wanted to get back before it was dark – she'd be in trouble if she was found outside the dormitory after curfew. They'd cut her food rations.

The sound of the bell and the sudden blackness didn't halt him; his grunts were louder and faster now. He was nearing his climax.

And then it was over.

He shoved her aside, pulled up his trousers and disappeared into the night. Apart from his grunts he hadn't said a word.

Edie made her way along the side of the block, feeling the wall as she went, turning the corner, arriving at the main door. Thankfully, it wasn't locked yet. She opened it and slipped inside.

But only seconds later, as she started to cross the muster room, the door that led to the dormitory itself opened and the beam of a torch hit her in the face.

'What are you doing out of bed, Edie?' a voice asked. Despite its edge of authority, the voice was attractive, with a soft Irish lilt. 'You know you shouldn't be outside after lights-out.'

Nurse Jill Delaney quietly closed the door behind her so as not to wake those who were sleeping, although she knew once the door was closed most of the women would resume the chats they'd been having before she'd done her nine o'clock nightly round.

'Come along now,' she crossed to the girl, the beam of her torch still focused on Edie's face, 'what have you been up to?'

'Had to go, Missus,' Edie said, her eyes downcast, avoiding the white woman's gaze. 'Had to go toilet.'

'You should have gone earlier,' the nurse reprimanded, 'you know that, don't you. You should have gone before it was dark.'

'Yeh.' Edie shuffled her feet nervously, eyes still fixed on the floor, or where the floor would be if she could see it. The dazzle of torchlight rendered everything black. 'Yeh, yeh, I know that.'

Jill Delaney could see that the girl was shaken. Something's happened, she thought. 'What is it, Edie? What's wrong?'

'Nothin', Missus. Honest. Nothin'.' Edie looked up, an earnest plea in her eyes. 'I shoulda gone earlier, that's all. Got caught out. All my fault. I know I done wrong.'

'It's all right, Edie, it's all right.' The nurse lowered the torch. 'You won't be punished.' She directed the beam of light towards the dormitory door. 'Go to bed now, there's a good girl.'

Edie obediently headed for the door, breathing a huge inward sigh of relief. She'd been so sure she was in trouble. Crikey, if they knew what happened out there I would be, she told herself.

Jill Delaney watched as the door quietly closed, and when it had, she stood for a moment or so in the dark. It's him, she thought. He's been at it again, the filthy, bloody animal. She knew the guard. A regular rapist, he kept a lookout for any new young arrival who might take his fancy, biding his time, waiting for the perfect opportunity. Just the once, no repeat offence with the same girl. How she wished she could catch him in the act, but she never had. He was too cunning. And if she were to confront him with no proof he would naturally deny it. The only thing she had to go on was her own knowledge of these women for whom she cared; the furtive, fearful looks on their faces when they were in his presence – he of course ignoring them altogether – hardly evidence. And the truly wrongful part is, she thought, he's not the only guilty party. Rapes are not uncommon here. Any number of white men on Palm Island seem to think that the women under their care are fair game. It's sickening.

Jill Delaney felt personally responsible. She tried always to keep the young ones in view, particularly the new arrivals, but she'd let Edie down. She was very, very sorry about that.

She was even sorrier several months later when Edie was found to be well and truly pregnant. The poor, unfortunate girl, Jill Delaney thought. How unlucky could she be!

Edie didn't consider herself unfortunate. Nor did she consider her pregnancy unlucky, or even unusual. She'd always been fertile. Even a one-off, unwanted coupling was more than likely to prove fruitful. And Edie wanted this child. She missed her babies. She knew she'd never see them again. They'd been taken to somewhere far away and she'd have no idea where to find them. But no-one was going to take this baby away.

Not this baby's fault its father's a pig, she'd think as she paraded her swollen belly with pride, boldly meeting the eyes of her rapist. And Missus Jill, she help me keep this baby, 'cos Missus Jill know I want this baby. Missus Jill know who done it, too. She don't say so, but she know all right.

When the child was born, delivered by none other than Nurse Jill Delaney herself, Edie was so glad it was a girl.

'I'm namin' my baby after you, Missus Jill,' she said.

Many years later, when Edie told Val her story, the figure of Nurse Jill Delaney featured prominently.

'She got a real pretty voice that Missus Jill,' Edie said. 'Kinda sing-song, you know? She tell me it's the Irish in her.

Her proper name Delaney, but I call her Missus Jill 'cos we was real good friends her and me. She help me keep my baby.'

And Jill Delaney had. She'd not filled out the reports that would have seen the little girl taken from her mother. And although, at an early age, Palm Island children were removed from their parents to live in separate dormitories, she'd ensured mother and child saw each other regularly. She'd even assigned the little girl to work in the laundry alongside her mother.

'She save our lives, that woman,' Edie declared. 'A right angel she is, that Missus Jill. And Missus Jill, she know who raped me. She never tell me she knows, but I know she knows. And that bloke, that pig guard, he long gone by the time my Jill's askin' about her dad.' Edie's face broke into the broadest grin. She'd thoroughly enjoyed unburdening herself to the best friend she'd ever had. She'd never unburdened herself before and she'd found the experience most liberating.

'And then we come to Townsville, my little Jill and me,' she said. 'And then we meet you. And now all goin' good as good can be.'

That was the secret Val and Edie shared – a past unknown to young Jill. Not only the rape, but the whole of Edie's life. Edie had painted a past for her daughter that was sheer fantasy.

'No kid of mine gonna know she been fathered by a bastard pig rapist,' she'd vehemently declared. 'Sure, my Jill gotta know her dad was a white fella,' she said, 'sure, anyone can see that. But she don't need to know the truth. Nobody need to know the truth, and that's a fact.'

'So what did you tell her?' Val asked.

'I tell her that her dad's name was Reginald Smith.' Again that infectious grin of Edie's. 'I know a bloke called Reginald once – that a real nice name, I like that name.

And Smith,' she gave a shrug, 'lot of white fellas called Smith. I tell her my man Reginald real proud to have a pretty baby girl,' she shook her head sadly, 'but poor bloke, he got killed in an accident, run over by a truck out in the bush. And then I got sent to Palm Island. Not for anything bad, mind,' she added hastily, 'just to be looked after, you know? I don't tell her I got knocked up when I was about her age. No good tellin' her that sorta stuff.'

'Right,' Val nodded, albeit a little sceptically, 'and she accepted all of this, did she?'

'Why not? She's five years old when I tell her.'

'Of course.' Edie's logic was inescapable. 'And she never questions why she's not called Jill Smith?'

'Ah, that the best part, see.' Edie was particularly pleased with this bit. 'I tell her I give her my tribal name because I want her to be proud of who she is. And that the truth, Val, I swear, honest it is. Besides,' she added after a moment's thought, 'Yiramba much fancier name than Smith. Sounds a whole lot better, don't you reckon?'

'Yes,' Val agreed with a smile, 'yes, it does.'

This conversation had taken place after Val and Edie had known each other for only six months. Having opened her newly acquired pub, Val had hired the Aboriginal woman who'd walked into the bar, marched straight up to the counter and demanded employment.

'You hire me, you get best-ever laundry,' the woman had declared, 'me and my girl, we the best in Townsville.'

The woman's boldness had struck an immediate chord with Val and, upon hiring her, she'd found Edie was not lying. She and twelve-year-old Jill were experts at their trade. In fact, Edie Yiramba, Val discovered, was well known around Townsville, having worked as a daily domestic and laundress in a number of households and establishments for the past two years, ever since her arrival from Palm Island.

The situation was not uncommon. Most young Palm Islander women gravitated to Townsville and many were employed as domestics or chambermaids or such. They were discovered to be pleasant and well behaved for the most part, but not particularly reliable as after a while they were prone to go walkabout. Perhaps due to a sense of captivity or claustrophobia, no-one really knew the reason.

It hadn't taken long for Val and Edie to become the closest of friends. To others they appeared chalk and cheese, a fact that was regularly commented upon, but in actuality they were two of a kind. Bold to the point of brash and utterly candid, they recognised in each other a kindred spirit.

Val was always the boss, certainly, Edie the first to acknowledge her own subordinate position – it had taken Val a degree of persuasion to stop being 'Missus Val' – but there were some occasions when Edie stalwartly refused to budge, thus rendering Val powerless. The principal of these was the 'live-in' situation. Val simply could not understand why Edie, while retained as a full-time laundress and chambermaid, would not live on the hotel premises, but chose instead to arrive early in the morning and leave late in the afternoon – exactly to and from where, Val had no idea.

'I always do daily,' Edie replied upon first being queried, 'never live-in.'

'Why?'

'Don't like live-in,' Edie said. 'Too locked up, like bein' back on Palm Island.'

Time and again Val would try to insist Edie take one of the upstairs rooms, but the answer was always the same.

'No, no, need more space. I like space.'

'So where the hell are you living, then?' Val demanded. 'Are you camping out in the bush or what?'

But the more demanding Val became, the more lacka-daisical was Edie's response. She would just offer an unconcerned shrug.

'For God's sake, woman,' Val would insist, exasperated, 'you have a child! You can't just live blackfella style when you have a child.'

'Why not? My Jill, she blackfella, too. And we like our "freedom of lifestyle", we do.' Edie eked out the phrase. She'd heard it only recently and she relished the sound of it.

'Jill needs to go to school, that's bloody well why not. Christ alive, she's nearly thirteen years old!'

'She can read and write.' Whenever Jill's name came into the argument, Edie would get defensive. 'They teach her on Palm Island.'

'She needs more than that and you bloody know it! If you won't send her to school, then I'll teach her myself.'

Edie finally gave in on that one, allowing Val to tutor her daughter several times a week, Jill even staying overnight at the hotel on occasions – Val was already the girl's second mother, so where was the harm? But Edie steadfastly refused to stay at the hotel herself.

Val had resolutely avoided intruding upon her friend's privacy, but having decided the time had now come, she had no difficulty discovering Edie's chosen 'freedom of lifestyle' location. A few queries around town provided the answer. Everyone seemed to know where Edie Yiramba was shacked up.

'So are you going to show me this boatshed of yours?' she asked one day.

Far from being confronted, Edie just grinned cheekily. 'Took you long enough, eh?'

And later that same day, Val stood towards the southern end of Rose Bay surveying the dilapidated boatshed that had been home to Edie and her daughter since their arrival from Palm Island.

The boatshed was one of two, about twenty yards apart, and Edie had strung up a clothesline between them. Val was surprised to note that, for a derelict wooden shed, it appeared structurally sound, as did its partner. There was a small water tank standing beside it, too; someone had obviously lived here in the past. She wondered how long these two sheds had been vacant, and who owned them.

'Could do with a coat of paint,' she said critically.

'Yeh,' Edie replied, 'yeh, been meaning to get around to that.' She hadn't, but it now seemed like a good idea. 'C'mon inside, Val, I'll make you a cuppa tea.'

Inside was cosy. Cosy and clean. Edie took pride in her home. A kerosene lamp dangled on a chain from the shed's central beam, the only lighting provided, but obviously ample. There were no actual bedsteads and no actual chairs, but areas were allotted for specific purposes. The bedding in the far-left corner of the shed was neat and inviting, and the central mat where she and Jill sat to eat their meals immaculate – Edie regularly hung it on the clothesline and bashed it with a broom handle. There were just two items of furniture. In the far-right corner, next to the kerosene stove on the floor, was a small set of shelves housing kitchenware, and beneath one of the side windows an old wooden bench was built onto the wall. Val rightfully supposed it had been there when Edie had first moved in. On top of the bench was a large tin tub, over which sat a tap, its pipe leading through the wooden wall to the 100-gallon water tank outside.

The tin tub served multiple purposes, the bathing of bodies and the washing of crockery certainly, but above all, this was a laundry tub. During her early days in Townsville, Edie had brought laundry home from the houses she serviced. Her modest shack had proved quite a successful small business, enough for her own needs anyway.

Edie enjoyed her work. She liked everything about laundering. Seeing clothes and bedlinen come up spotless was a joy to her. But most of all she loved being the best at her trade.

'Runnin' water, see?' she boasted to Val as she held the kettle under the tap. 'Got all I need here.'

'It's nice, Edie.' Val gazed about approvingly. 'It's really nice. You've done a beaut job.'

Edie beamed. Val's approval meant a great deal to her. 'Used to run a laundry from this place, I did. Lug the linen and stuff home and do it right here in this tub. Worked real good, too.' She crossed to the kerosene stove, knelt and lit it, placing the kettle on top, then stood. 'Wanna come out and look at the view while she boils, eh?' she asked.

'Sure, why not?'

They stepped outside to the pristine beauty of Rose Bay, to the endless stretch of white beach and the stark blue of the ocean and the differing greens of the trees, of native gums and palms that formed a backdrop to the two lone boatsheds that sat there. As far as the eye could see, there was not another soul in sight.

'I'm happy here, Val,' Edie said. 'Feels like where I belong, you know?'

'Yep.' Val nodded slowly. 'Yep, I think I know.'

They stood for some time enjoying the view until Edie broke the silence. 'Come on inside, she'll be boilin' by now.'

Squatting by the stove, pouring the water into the teapot, Edie apologised. ''Fraid you'll have to sit on the floor, sorry about that.'

Val didn't say a word, but just plonked herself down.

'S'pose I'll have to get a chair if you're gonna come visitin', eh?' Edie asked as they sat side by side waiting for the tea to draw.

'Yes,' Val said. 'Yes, you certainly will.' She looked around the hut, her gaze coming to rest on the tub. 'You used to run a laundry service from here, you said?'

'Yeh. Yeh, that's right.'

It was a comparatively early stage in a friendship that they both knew was destined to prove lifelong, but a vague plan was already forming in Val Callahan's mind.

CHAPTER FOUR

Val followed through with her plan, the first step of which was much easier than she'd anticipated. Enquiries at the local Lands and Title office revealed that the owner of the boatsheds was long deceased and that he'd never owned the land anyway, it belonged to the council. He'd been a squatter. No-one knew exactly which year the sheds had been built, but it was not long after the war, Val was told, 'say around 1920'.

'Seems he built one to live in and the other one to house his boat and tackle,' her informant said. 'He was an old bloke, I believe; a retired local fisherman who lived a hermit existence and everyone turned a blind eye.'

A survey had been conducted and Val had purchased from the council a twenty-year lease on the quarter acre of land that included both boatsheds, with the proviso she be responsible for their maintenance. It had been that simple.

The next step had proved not quite so simple, because it involved Edie.

'What do you mean I *own* this place?' Edie had asked, confused, when Val had paid her an unexpected visit. 'This mine already,' she said, looking around at the boatshed where they sat drinking tea from enamel mugs. The shed now boasted two upright chairs. 'Me and Jill, we bin living 'ere for years.'

'Yes, I'm aware of that, Edie,' Val had patiently replied, 'but without actually *owning* the boatshed, you've always run the risk of being chucked out.' As her friend continued to stare at her blankly, she went on to explain. 'You know, if the owner turned up and wanted to have it back.'

'Yeh.' Edie nodded slowly. She'd never really thought about this before. 'Yeh, I s'pose you're right there. That why these blokes bin out 'ere, measurin' things up, then, is it?'

'That's right. You can't be chucked out now, you see. I bought the sheds, both of them, and I'm giving them to you. They're yours. You own them.'

'Oh.' Edie looked more than confused, she looked positively puzzled. 'That real nice of you, Val.'

If Val was expecting a 'thank you' she was destined for disappointment. Edie's expression clearly said, *Why?*

'They wouldn't let me buy the land though, I could only lease it,' Val went on, 'so you don't actually own the land.'

That part to Edie was abundantly clear. 'Course I don't own the *land*,' she said as if speaking to a simpleton, 'nobody own the *land*. The *land* own *us*.'

'Yes, of course,' Val replied. Blackfella logic, she thought, you've got to respect that.

'Why you doin' this, Val?' Edie finally blurted out what was uppermost in her mind. 'Why you buyin' me these sheds?'

'Because I want to.'

'I don' need charity, you know.' The suspicion that had lurked in her shrewd, black eyes was now replaced by a touch of belligerence. 'I don' take hand-outs from no-one. Not even from you, mate.'

'I'm not offering you charity, Edie.' Having suspected things might possibly go in this direction, Val had a strategy in place.

'Then why you do this?' Edie demanded.

There was so much Val could have said, so much she would like to have said. *Because of the bastard of a life you've had, Edie . . . Because you're a bloody good woman . . . Because you deserve better . . . Because you're my friend . . .*

But she didn't say any of those things.

'It's a business proposition, Edie,' she said. 'A business proposition between you and me. We're going to run a laundry. A proper laundry.'

Val's proposal was simple. She'd have the pub's old wood-heated laundry tub transferred to the boatshed – they needed a new copper at The Brown's anyway – and she'd have a brick kiln built to house it, and a chimney that would lead outside.

'You'll need to move into the other boatshed, you and Jill,' she said, 'this one'll have to be the laundry because of the water tank.'

Edie didn't say anything, she just let her mate rattle on, but eagle eyes trained on Val, she wasn't missing a trick.

'And the sheds'll need to be smartened up,' Val continued. 'We have to be responsible for their maintenance. I'll arrange for the materials to be delivered and you and Jill can sand everything back and whitewash the both of them. What do you say?'

'Where does the laundry come from?' Edie got straight to the point.

'From The Brown's to start with,' Val said, 'you can do the pub's laundry here. I'll get Baz to deliver it and collect it once a week.' Baz had recently joined the ranks at The Brown's and was bound to prove invaluable throughout the exercise, Val thought, he seemed to have contacts everywhere. 'And then we'll spread the word around. "Best-ever laundry in Townsville",' she concluded with a true salesman's pitch. 'People always want the best, Edie, as you and I both know.'

Edie liked the sound of that, but she didn't want to be seen as giving in too easily. 'And who'll do the rooms at the pub like I do 'em now?'

'I'll hire a young Palm Island girl as a chambermaid,' Val said, 'there are plenty around seeking employment.'

'Yeh,' Edie approved of that idea, 'good to hire a Palm Island girl.'

Val dumped her empty mug on the floor and stood. 'Partners, then?' She held out her hand.

'Yep.' Edie stood and they shook. 'Partners.'

Val's principal aim had been to keep Edie secure in her 'freedom of lifestyle', but as they shook hands she couldn't help thinking that perhaps this might even prove a workable investment.

The plan was quickly and smoothly put into action, all thanks due to Baz. Having joined forces with Val Callahan several months previously and having recognised her value, Baz Taylor was only too keen to prove his worth and cement their relationship.

'Sure, Val,' he said, embracing the laundry idea whole-heartedly, although to him it sounded damn stupid. 'I can line up the kiln for you. Got a builder mate who owes me a favour.'

The favours Baz called in and the barter deals he made were invariably an exchange for gambling debts that had got out of hand. He knew how to play the mugs who attended his two-up school and poker games.

So the brick kiln was built – the copper tub fitting perfectly in the centre – and the chimney that led outside was constructed. And Baz's mate built another chimney also, to accommodate the potbelly stove that had miraculously appeared from nowhere.

'A bloke I know's upgrading his kitchen,' Baz said. 'Got himself a brand-new Metters, doesn't want the old potbelly.'

The old potbelly stove would prove a godsend to Edie. It was bound to be handy for cooking, certainly, but of far greater importance was how perfect it would be for heating up the two flat irons she'd brought with her from The Brown's. With no source of electricity, the iron Val had recently purchased for the pub would be useless, but Edie never used it anyway. She eschewed the newfangled electric things. She didn't even like using the petrol-fuelled irons favoured by most. She'd been trained with flat irons on Palm Island and flat irons remained her instrument of choice.

The day finally came.

'All set now, Val,' she said proudly, 'we ready to give best-ever laundry in Townsville, eh.'

'We sure are, Edie,' Val agreed as they stood together one Saturday afternoon, young Jill, now fourteen, by their side surveying the newly whitewashed boatsheds. 'You two have done a bloody good job. You should feel very proud of yourselves.'

Mother and daughter exchanged smiles. They did. All the laborious sanding back and painting they'd done themselves; working around the clock, refusing assistance from others who'd offered. This was their home, and they felt inordinately proud.

The laundry was slow to take off, but word did get about, and gradually new customers came on board as regulars. Each week, Edie would walk the three miles from her boatshed to The Brown's and present Val with a half-share of the takings. Baz delivered and collected the pub's laundry on a weekly basis, it was true, but for some strange reason Edie didn't quite trust Baz with money. He was smart and he was handsome all right, but she found him a shifty kind of bloke. Anyway, she liked to walk. She could walk a whole day without stopping, and did every now and then. Deciding occasionally to take a day off, she and Jill would go walkabout far into the surrounding bush. The two would walk for miles, leaving at dawn and not returning until nightfall. Edie Yiramba had determined her daughter should always be aware of her heritage and her connection with the land.

Edie actually had no cause for worry as far as Baz was concerned. The pittance the laundry made was of no interest to him.

Nor was the sum delivered of any worthwhile value to Val, who had tried to dissuade Edie from what she obviously saw as her weekly obligation.

'Why don't you leave it until business has picked up a bit, Edie,' she'd suggested.

'No way, can't do that,' Edie had said with a vigorous shake of the head. 'We partners, you and me, Val. Partners, they share down the middle.'

Val could do nothing, aware this was a matter of pride. And more often than not, along with the money Edie would deliver a gift of fresh fish. Whenever Edie wasn't laundering or going walkabout she was fishing – Edie just loved to fish. She would refuse payment from Val, despite the fact that she sold much of her catch to others.

'That a present from me to you,' she'd say, offended when Val offered money. Aware she was powerless to help, Val quickly realised any offer to do so was unnecessary anyway. Edie may be poor, but she was blissfully happy.

Time ultimately solved any worries Val may have had, however, for within several years Edie's laundry business was successful enough to require the employment of a young Palm Island woman.

'Me and Jill need someone to lend a hand, Val,' Edie said, 'and good we give work to a Palm Island girl.'

Well, blow me down, Val thought, the investment's proved workable after all.

Then the following year, 1940, Jill was turning eighteen and keen to get a proper job – 'out in the real world', as Edie said. A problem easily solved.

'She'll come and work for me,' Val announced, 'I'll teach her all about the real world, Edie, I can promise you that. And she'll be safe in my hands, you know she will.'

So Edie employed a second Palm Island girl and Jill went off to The Brown's.

Over the following year or so, further changes occurred. The laundry sustained a modest income and could be considered moderately successful, but Edie's boatshed had by now become more than just a laundry, and Edie herself more than just a laundress. To the Palm Island girls who came and went, working for a while, then going walkabout, then more often than not returning, the boatshed was a gathering place. A place where they felt welcomed and at home. Whether they worked there or not, the girls gravitated to the boatshed, and above all to the matriarch who presided there. Aunty Edie.

Now in her early forties – or thereabouts, she was never quite sure – Edie had earned the title, which had been bestowed upon her as a measure of respect. She'd become Aunty Edie to all who knew her. To the Palm Island girls though, Aunty Edie was particularly special, for she was one of them. Aunty Edie was Bwgcolman.

But the biggest change of all was yet to come. And not just for Edie, but for the whole of Townsville. The army was about to arrive.

When the invasion of military took place in North Queensland, particularly the arrival of the Americans, Edie's business, like all those in Townsville, changed overnight. And her laundry just happened to be conveniently close to Kissing Point Fort and Jezzine Barracks.

First of all it had been several Allied officers who'd turned up.

'Heard you do a good job,' the Aussie lieutenant had said.

'Yep, best in Townsville,' Edie had replied, she and her girls accepting the bundle of uniforms that were handed over; the trousers, the shirts – they could easily manage this lot.

But then it had been a bunch of Yanks, eight of them in all, arriving in two jeeps. The American military had taken over the Townsville Steam Laundry, which was the only outlet capable of handling large quantities of linen, and these enterprising officers had decided to seek out their own personal laundress nearby.

Edie accepted their initial delivery, but she could foresee a problem lurking if this Yankee mob were to become regular customers. She visited Val.

'We gonna need more water,' she said. 'Our tank too small.'

Val immediately referred the matter to Baz, and a week later a 500-gallon corrugated-iron water tank was delivered to the boatshed.

'Above and to Betsy,' Edie breathlessly exclaimed as she watched Baz and his two mates unload it. A mixture of 'heavens above' and 'heavens to Betsy', this had become her favourite phrase when awestruck.

Upon being informed of the acquisition, Val was equally impressed. 'Fell off a truck, did it?' she enquired, aiming for cynicism, but secretly lost in admiration.

'Well, it fell *on* a truck actually,' Baz replied, 'then it fell *off* at Edie's place.'

They siphoned the water that was left in the old 100-gallon tank and luckily several heavy downpours followed over the next few weeks, but Edie knew they couldn't rely upon rain. Val was quick to point out also that water restrictions were bound to come into place.

Edie therefore had a word of advice for the American officers. 'If that gets empty,' she warned them, jabbing a finger at the tank, 'you Yankees have to fill it up or no more laundry, you understand?'

'Sure, Aunty, we'll look after you,' they assured her. Even the Yanks called her Aunty.

And now Edie's business was thriving. The Americans paid handsomely, at least four times more than the Australians. Sometimes they'd even hold out a wad of notes and say 'Take what you want, Aunty,' but she never abused their generosity. And she still laundered for the few Aussie officers who came to her, maintaining it was only right that she should. Mind you, she preferred the Americans' uniforms, their trousers in particular.

'Zips much better than buttons,' she told Val. 'Zips don't come off in the wash like buttons. Easer for ironin' too,' she added. 'Aussie pants a right bastard to iron, all them bloody buttons. Why can't they give the Aussies zips like the Yanks?'

The burgeoning fear of invasion was accompanied by another unpleasant aspect of war, also induced by fear. North Queenslanders were becoming increasingly wary of those they perceived to have sympathy with the enemy, and the fact that the government was introducing alien internment camps only inflamed their anxiety. Normally peaceful citizens were beginning to turn on their neighbours. Germans were seen as Nazis and Italians as fascists, even those who'd been settled in the country for years – those who were naturalised and whose children had been born on Australian soil.

The situation was becoming preposterous, so much so that on one occasion Townsville's deputy mayor, the colourfully charismatic, bicycle-riding, blatantly outspoken Tom Aikens, called a public meeting at the Theatre

Royal in order to discredit some of the ridiculous stories circulating about the 'disloyalty' of the local Italian community. In his inimitable style, his address was both scathing and humorous.

'I had two of Townsville's most prominent businessmen come to see me and complain that one fellow was out in Ross Creek in a rowing boat sending Morse-code messages to Japanese submarines!' he announced derisively. At the same time he was careful to avoid any specific names, aware it wouldn't do to publicly humiliate men of standing in the community.

Aikens had made the accusation sound as ludicrous as it was for he was very much against the xenophobia currently running rampant throughout Northern Queensland. Furthermore, as he'd openly stated from the outset, he considered the internment of aliens and naturalised British subjects to be the 'most putrid scandal associated with the war'.

The powerful influence of Tom Aikens may possibly have helped prevent the internment of the Baldinis, no-one could tell, but it did not prevent the alienation they experienced from a number of the town's citizens.

Tony Baldini and his wife, Elsa, had emigrated from Northern Italy to Australia in 1919 as young newlyweds intent upon rebuilding their lives following the devastation of World War I. After settling in Townsville, they'd bought land and prospered, working hard on their small market garden, expanding it over time and finally owning and operating a fruit-and-vegetable shop in Flinders Street, where they sold their own produce.

They'd become Australian citizens, and along the way they'd had three sons and a daughter, all born in Australia. Salvatore (Sal) was now twenty, Matheo (Mat) eighteen, Luca (Lucky) sixteen and young Sophia was fourteen.

For the past several years, the older boys had worked and lived on their father's five-acre market garden near the western fringes of Mount Louisa, young Lucky recently joining them, having just finished his schooling, while Sophia lived in the shop premises with her parents, serving behind the counter when she wasn't at school. The Baldinis were a close-knit, hard-working family, well known around town and well liked by all.

The patriarch, Tony, now in his mid-forties, was a flamboyant man, robust and vital with a love of good food and wine, a true *bon vivant*. His sons having taken over the hard manual labour, his once well-honed body had become stout, but he was nonetheless strong, and although not tall, he gave the impression of being a big man, no doubt due to a larger-than-life personality.

Tony's accent had never lessened over the years, and nor had that of his resilient wife, Elsa, a stocky, capable woman who had single-handedly managed the business while bringing up a family. The heavy accents of the two were hardly surprising as neither had been able to speak a word of English upon their arrival in the country.

Their children were 'dinky-di Aussies', as Tony was proud to claim, and they certainly sounded that way, particularly the boys, who had the broad accents of true North Queenslanders. But each of the children spoke fluent Italian, the family conversing at home in their mother tongue. Tony was as proud of his heritage as he was of his adopted country, and he wanted his children to be too.

Something else of which Tony was inordinately proud was his talent as a winemaker. He was self-taught, it was true, but his talent was innate, and he had a definite flair. Tony's wines were not only drinkable, they were downright delicious. And they were varied. For years now, any of the fruit that didn't sell he would reserve for the making of wine, his motto being '*lo spreco non vuole non*' – waste not, want not. But it wasn't really practicality dictating, it was the sheer love of producing wine.

Tony didn't market his wines, they were for home consumption only, and on Sundays when the boys came into town and the family gathered, there would invariably be several added guests at the huge dining table in the living quarters at the rear of the shop. Mates of Tony regularly turned up on a Sunday afternoon eager to get stuck into the latest batch of fruit wine that their host considered ready and right for opening. And if the mates arrived while lunch was still underway, they were always invited to join the table. Elsa kept a huge pot of bolognaise meat sauce simmering at all times for this very purpose – easy to boil up extra pasta according to the numbers that needed to be fed.

The Baldinis were generous to a fault. Their home was open to all, and their food and wine was there to be shared. And there was never a shortage of those eager to accept the hospitality on offer. The Baldinis were popular.

So why all of a sudden were they vilified? Why was there talk among some that Tony Baldini should be sent to an alien internment camp? And perhaps also his two older sons?

Was it just their Italian-ness? Was it because they ate spaghetti bolognaise and made their own wine? Was it because their home was always ripe with the pungent smell of freshly cooked garlic? Was it because of Tony Baldini's flamboyance, and his accent, and the fact that his children, despite having been born in Australia, spoke Italian?

Yes, it was all of this. It was every one of these things, and nothing more. There were some among the peaceful citizens of Townsville who suddenly feared those who were no longer merely colourful, but threateningly different.

And there were other citizens who were outraged by the injustice.

'Have you heard the latest?' Pete Vickers of the *Townsville Daily Bulletin* stormed into his editor's office fuming with rage. 'They're talking about sending Tony Baldini to an internment camp! And his sons, too! For God's sake, Tony's been here forever and his bloody sons are as Australian as I am —'

'Yes, yes,' his boss, Jim Burnet, said, cutting Pete off mid-stream. 'I've heard the word going around, I know there are a few out to cause Tony trouble, but —'

'Some bastard stuck a sign on his shop window last night saying, *Lock up the fascists!*' Pete exclaimed in utter outrage. 'Tony! A fucking fascist! They've got to be joking!'

'All right, mate, all right. Calm down.' Jim was accustomed to dousing the flames when it came to young Pete Vickers. Twenty-five-year-old Pete was a volatile bloke. Idealistic, ambitious, passionate about his work and the true purpose of journalism, all of which meant he was a bloody good reporter. But Jim, seasoned newspaper man that he was, recognised a renegade side. The kid has to learn to roll with the punches, he thought.

'Don't get yourself too worked up,' he said.

Seated comfortably behind his desk, Jim watched Pete stride about the office, his awkward gait reminiscent of a restless colt with an injury. He was a gangly young man always on the move, his clubfoot not in any way a disability, but rather lending him something between a limp and a lurch of which he seemed quite unaware.

'It won't come to anything, I'm sure,' Jim went on. 'Tom Aikens is sympathetic to the cause, he won't let them take Tony away . . . Or Tony's sons for that matter,' he added as Pete threatened once again to explode.

But Pete Vickers was in no mood to be placated. 'And in the meantime,' he said, planting his hands on his boss's desk and leaning forward in order to punch every point home, 'the man's character is being assassinated, his reputation besmirched, his family slandered. It's a bloody disgrace.'

Realising little was to be gained by further interruption, Jim said nothing, better to let Pete get things off his chest. '*Besmirched*', he mused, what an interestingly old-fashioned choice for a young bloke. But then he's a writer, and a talented one at that.

Pete took the older man's silence as a sign of encouragement and, raking a hand through his unruly hair, he plonked himself down onto one of the two hardback visitors' chairs. 'I want to write a feature about this kind of discrimination, Jim,' he said earnestly. 'As a matter of fact, I want to make it a bloody *exposé*! The treatment of Tony is only the tip of a very large iceberg that a lot of people don't know about.'

'Oh yes,' Jim said warily, he could see where this was leading.

'It's going on all over North Queensland, this sort of thing,' Pete continued. 'And the Northern Territory, too. Decent people being treated like the enemy, dragged away from their families, shoved in internment camps for no reason at all. The government has no right to do that!'

Jim wanted to say, 'Well they do, actually,' but resisted. 'I agree it doesn't seem fair, Pete,' he said instead, 'but in actual fact there *is* a reason. This country's on the brink of invasion and we here up north are at the very coalface. The local population's justifiably terrified. They want to see their government take every precaution possible. And you've got to understand also that the government has to be watchful for any potential collusion with the enemy. They can't afford to take chances. They need to be wary.'

'They don't need to be bloody *inhumane*!' Jim's attempt at reasonable argument had only reignited Pete's rage. 'The ignorance of the government and the military – *and* therefore, might I add, the general populace over whom they hold domain – is beyond all belief!' he exclaimed. 'Did you know that after Darwin was bombed, all full-blooded Aborigines were rounded up and moved into army camps to be used as labour and kept under observation?'

Jim didn't say a word. Yes, he had heard that.

'The government and the military apparently believe that if we're invaded, Aboriginal sympathies will lie with the Japanese rather than with white Australians. Now how fucking stupid is that!'

Jim remained silent. Which only egged Pete on.

'And did you know that right here in Townsville, Colonel Murray of the Volunteer Defence Corps ordered that in the case of invasion, Aborigines were the first ones to be shot!'

Still Jim said nothing. Yes, he'd heard that, too. He had to admit he'd been shocked himself, but he hadn't really taken the quote seriously. Just some loud-mouth military bigot blowing off steam, he'd thought.

'It's more than stupid,' Pete said, 'it's bloody criminal! When the nation's leaders spread racism and ethnic hatred, the whole population follows suit. We'll end up just like the dictatorship we're currently fighting! A case of follow-the-fucking-leader and kill everyone who's different.'

Oh dear, Jim thought, he's getting passionate, and it's dangerous territory. I'll have to nip this one in the bud.

'I intend to do a feature on the whole sordid business,' Pete declared, by now so carried away that he'd convinced himself Jim's silence was some form of tacit agreement. 'I'm going to write about the injustice being done to Tony Baldini and all the other innocent Aussies labelled enemies because of their ethnicity! And I'm going to write about the potential bloody genocide threatening our Aboriginal men!' He gave the desk an emphatic thump with his fist. 'I'm going to write a bloody exposé, Jim,' he concluded defiantly.

'No you're not.'

Halted in his tracks, Pete stared back wordlessly at his boss.

'You can't do that, mate, and you bloody well know it.'

'Why not?' Pete demanded.

'The censors, that's why not,' Jim replied curtly. 'If I printed an article like that they'd close the paper. We have to abide by the dictates, Pete, you know it as well as I do. We're to "*maintain high morale on the home front*" at all times, and print what the Department of Information wants us to print.'

'Which means we're just a fucking propaganda machine,' Pete growled.

'There is that aspect, yes,' Jim agreed, 'but wartime censorship serves a purpose. The government wants to avoid any unrest or panic on the home front.'

'Which is why the true number of dead in the Darwin bombing was misreported,' Pete interrupted.

Jim ignored the remark. 'And they want to prevent any false impressions of Australia overseas.'

'Or maybe any *true* impressions,' Pete said scathingly.

Jim ignored that remark, too. 'All of which is totally understandable,' he went on. 'Best to toe the line, Pete,' he said calmly, as if stroking an agitated puppy, 'no point in making waves, mate.'

Christ alive, Pete thought, two clichés in one sentence, he's outdoing himself today.

Jim and Pete got on well as a rule. Jim recognised the talent of the new kid on the block and Pete respected the older man's experience in the field. Jim Burnet's tendency to favour clichés did occasionally get on Pete's nerves, however.

How many times do I have to hear 'roll with the punches', 'toe the line', 'don't make waves'? he thought. But then old newspaper hacks are all the same. To them, clichés are par for the course.

Pete Vickers was an ambitious young man. He didn't see himself as a 'hack' like Jim Burnet, nice though the man was. Pete saw himself as an investigative journalist with a true duty to serve. And that duty was, above all else, to inform readers of the truth and to expose injustice.

Much of Pete's passion was due to the birth defect of his clubfoot, these days more than ever. During his youth, he'd managed to disguise his condition as well as was possible, wearing a slightly built-up right shoe, never appearing in shorts even during the hottest of summers, teaching himself to walk with a minimal limp, and upon reaching adulthood he had not considered himself a man with a disability. He hadn't even considered himself a man with a limp. No, no. He was a journalist, a man with a duty. But things had changed lately. Lately he'd been forced to admit that, yes, he *was* a man with a disability, which was why he could not be accepted as the war correspondent he so desperately longed to be. The army would never send a journalist deemed to be a cripple into a conflict zone. He'd tried. He'd begged. The answer had been a resounding no. So Pete had decided he'd be a war correspondent working from the home front instead, exposing the wartime truths that people needed to be told. These days Pete's passion burned with fresh fervour.

'I'm sorry, mate,' Jim said. He could see Pete felt let down, but the bloke's request had been totally unrealistic, he must surely realise that. 'Exposés aren't on the menu these days, I'm afraid.'

'Yep.' Pete nodded. He knew his idea was futile. He'd known from the outset, he supposed – he'd just let himself get carried away.

'I tell you what I'll do though,' Jim suggested. 'You write me a personal piece on Tony Baldini. You know, human-interest stuff, his background, his length of time in Australia, his family born here, and you bring up the threat of his internment. You get some quotes from Tom Aikens, too. Tom's already gone public with his views on the internment of aliens, particularly those with Australian citizenship. I could print a piece like that.'

Pete smiled gratefully, aware there was nothing more Jim could do. 'Thanks, mate,' he said. 'That'll help, it really will. In fact, I reckon it'll do the trick. For now anyway,' he added drily, 'who can tell what's going to happen further down the track? And at least it'll stop those pricks harassing the poor bastard.'

Both men recognised a truce had been called, as it always was when Pete went off half-cocked or pushed things too far. Jim was very good at his job.

It'll have to do for now, anyway, Pete thought as he walked out of the office, we can't risk giving the government an excuse to close the *Bulletin*. But the time will come, he told himself. I'll write the article I want to write one day, and if Jim still can't publish, then bugger Australia's bloody censors, I'll send it overseas where it really *will* be an exposé. I'll show up all the nasty things they're so determined to hide.

Deep down, Pete Vickers' sense of injustice still raged. You don't have to be at the battle front, he thought, to see there's more than one ugly side to war.

CHAPTER FIVE

Fear continued to escalate during the early days of April as Townsville prepared itself for the air attacks that would precede the imminent invasion of Australia.

'Brownouts' had been in place since the bombing of Darwin, an order that hadn't been taken altogether seriously, but given Townsville's current situation, it was warned that blackouts were soon to be imposed. Street lights would no longer be operated and citizens would be ordered to erect blackout curtains, or to paste black paper over their windows or, as some were to do, simply paint their window panes black. If chinks of light were visible, it was warned those who had neglected to carry out their duty would quickly be paid a visit by the air-raid warden.

Ugly concrete bomb shelters had now popped up all over town; dugouts had replaced landscaped back gardens; ditches with sandbags lined many a street; and slit trenches sat beside most of the houses. The once-pretty face of Townsville was ravaged by unsightly growths and ulcerations.

Yet still there were those who managed to have a good time, as people so often do in the face of adversity, and the presence of the Americans provided ample opportunity for enjoyment of one sort or another. In fact, many young women, both in the services and in civilian life, found themselves living a far more social existence than they had prior to the arrival of the military. Movie theatres remained immensely popular, concerts were regularly performed at various venues, and dances were held in hotels and clubs. The military, and most particularly the Americans with troops so far from home, were intent upon keeping their men happy at all costs.

And there was the seedier side, too. The town's 'red-light district' was situated a little to the south on the other side of Ross Creek. Here in Ford Street, behind the Causeway Hotel, was a line of timber 'workers' cottages', nine in all, where sexual services were provided to both American and Australian troops. Given the antipathy that existed between the two – although any show of aggression was invariably sparked by the Australians – this could at times lead to trouble. But there was yet a further complication. The brothels also catered to black servicemen. It seemed the prostitutes, who were mostly white, had no problem at all accepting black men as clients. To many white Americans, particularly those from the south, this fact rankled deeply.

And aggression was not limited to the red-light district. Given the vast numbers of servicemen from differing backgrounds who flooded the streets night and day, displays of hostility were becoming more and more evident even in the relatively innocent parts of town.

'You niggers get back where you belong!' the young American snarled.

His buddy immediately joined in. 'Yeah, you two got no right dancing with white gals!'

Betty Francis and Jill Yiramba froze right where they stood on the footpath of Denham Street just outside the Australian Workers' Union Hall. They exchanged a look of utter amazement, incredulity even; they'd thought they were in the company of two young, southern gentlemen. Betty just adored the way these boys spoke. Why, only an hour previously, she'd whispered to Jill that Josh and Beau were straight out of *Gone with the Wind*.

'Thorough southern gentlemen, Ah do declare,' she'd whispered, adopting a Scarlett O'Hara accent that had given Jill the giggles.

It was eleven o'clock at night and they'd been to the dance at the American Red Cross Canteen and Recreation Centre, the organisation that had appropriated the AWU Hall. Both girls had felt quite safe accepting the young soldiers' offer to walk them the several blocks home to The Brown's. The men were rank and file, admittedly, but they were certainly not roughnecks. These boys were absolute gentlemen. Now, however, it appeared to the girls that these boys were anything *but* gentlemen.

They're just a couple of bloody thugs, Betty thought. She wasn't in the least frightened, there were far too many people milling about in the street, but like Jill, she was shocked by their belligerence.

'You shouldn't even be this side of the bridge,' Josh said accusingly, 'niggers belong on the south side of the creek.'

'We're allowed to come over here,' the bigger of the two black soldiers firmly replied, standing his ground, although his friend quite obviously wanted to clear off.

'And just who the hell do you think you are,' Beau sneered, 'we seen you in there, dancing with white gals. You got no right.'

He and Josh hadn't dared cause a scene in the hall, which might have landed them in trouble, but out here in the street was quite a different matter.

'We're allowed to do that as well,' Percival Summers answered, 'ain't no law here says we can't. And *we* get invited to the Red Cross dances, too, you know.'

Perce stood his ground boldly, his voice disdainful. Twenty-two-year-old Perce was from the north; he wasn't about to be bullied by these southern boys who looked even younger than he was. 'You ain't in Alabama now, kid,' he said.

Beau appeared as if he might turn apoplectic with rage. 'You don't speak to *me* in that tone, nigger. I'm *sir* to you, you hear me, boy?'

'Why?' Perce asked in all innocence. 'You ain't no officer. You're a plain GI just the same as me.'

At that Beau lost it altogether. 'You listen to me, you fucking piece of nigger shit . . .'

Josh reined him in at this point. 'Hey, come on now, Beau, that'll do, ladies present and all.'

A group of several Aussie soldiers, also rank and file, had just emerged from the dance hall and couldn't resist a comment in passing. They hadn't actually heard the exchange, but they recognised there was some sort of altercation between the white and black Americans.

'That's what you get for going out with *Yanks*,' one of them sneered to the girls, although the remark was intended for the Americans, 'bloody racists, the whole lot of them.'

'Yep, serves you girls right,' another agreed, 'you should give the *paw paws* a miss and stick to the Aussies.' *Paw paws* was a particularly insulting – and utterly groundless – term the Australians had adopted when referring to the Yanks – *green on the outside and yellow on the inside*.

The others laughed and the group walked off down Denham Street.

Perce's mate, Selwood, who found this sort of confrontation very scary, now piped up. 'Come on, Perce,' he urged, 'let's go.' Selwood was from the south, and he expected any minute they'd be attacked.

But Percival Summers continued to stand his ground, saying nothing, not seeking conflict; just making a statement by being there.

'Sorry, ladies,' Josh said, ignoring the Negroes and concentrating upon the girls, keen to make amends for his friend's appallingly bad language. 'Beau normally don't swear like that, and he meant no offence, I promise. It was just seeing those blacks dancing with some of you white gals back there, you know? That's not right, that's not natural. We couldn't help being affronted, Beau and me, it's downright wrong!'

Betty was about to offer some scathing remark, but surprisingly enough it was Jill who piped up.

'Why?' she asked. 'You two have been dancing with a black Aussie girl for the past hour.' She glanced from one to the other; she'd danced with both young men. 'You got a different set of rules about that, have you?'

'Oh.' Josh was stumped for an answer. He looked at Beau, who appeared equally stumped. They'd both thought the pretty, olive-skinned girl was something exotic, or at least that she hailed from somewhere exotic, way down here in the Southern Hemisphere. They'd even shared whispered guesses about where this exotic place might be. 'A South Sea island?' they'd wondered. 'Tahiti perhaps?' 'Yes,' they'd finally agreed, 'I'd say she's Tahitian.' Josh and Beau had never travelled far from home.

Their obvious bewilderment delighted Percival Summers, who threw back his head and let out a hearty laugh.

Betty joined in the man's laughter. Then she crossed to him. 'I'm Betty, that's Jill,' she said. 'We only live a few blocks away, would you boys mind walking us home?'

'My pleasure, ma'am,' Perce answered, and Betty took the arm he offered.

Selwood's eyes darted nervously from his friend to the white soldiers, but he was given no time to object. Jill's arm was suddenly tucked into his and the four of them were walking away, leaving Josh and Beau standing in the street at a loss for words.

The following day, Betty recounted the story to Val. 'You should have seen their faces,' she laughed, 'they didn't even know they'd been dancing with a black girl. Talk about naïve! And you should have seen Jill, too. Bold as brass she was. God, you would have been proud!'

Yes, Val thought, I've no doubt I would have been. But there's still a word of advice that needs to be offered. 'You make sure you two stick together when you go to these dances, Betty,' she warned, 'you look after Jill.'

'Course I will,' Betty scoffed, 'I do every time. Safety in numbers and all that, we know the score. You don't need to worry about us, Val, we're safe as houses, Jill and me.'

You are, Val thought, yep I'd put money on that, but I'm not so sure about Jill. 'Good girl,' she said. No point in voicing her misgivings.

Val was actually grateful for Betty's influence upon Jill. The shy, reclusive Aboriginal girl who had first come to work at The Brown's had blossomed over the past two years, gaining confidence and social skills she'd never possessed. Val was convinced this was due to the strong friendship that had been forged between the two girls. Betty's mere presence was liberating and instructive; she was the perfect example of a strong, accomplished young woman who knew how to handle herself in these modern times.

But Jill? Jill was different. Jill was a true innocent, born of another culture and completely without guile. Jill was a girl who lived between two worlds.

She's at the mercy of any creep who might want to take advantage of her, Val thought. Someone like Baz, for instance. It was obvious that Baz, as promised, had made no advances, but it was equally obvious Jill remained infatuated. And if it's not Baz, Val thought cynically, then it could be any one of how many others? There are countless men like Baz. Particularly right here and right now with troops all over town and a war on our front doorstep. These are volatile times and women are at their most vulnerable.

Val Callahan was not the only woman who worried about the volatility of the times.

'I feel so terribly *vulnerable*,' Amelia Sanderson admitted to her good friend Grace Francis as they sat in the back room of the AWU wrapping up Red Cross parcels, a duty the two shared every Saturday afternoon.

'The house is so big and so empty and there are so many soldiers outside in the street night and day,' she said, 'I just don't feel *safe* somehow.' She smiled a little shame-facedly. 'That sounds awfully indulgent of me, doesn't it? Good heavens above, on the brink of invasion, who *does* feel safe!'

Amelia pushed back a lock of fair hair that threatened to impede her vision and focused her attention on the string she was tying around the parcel she'd just completed packing. She used to be so very deft with string, but her hands these days were a little shaky.

'And Martin's been gone for over a whole year now,' she went on, trying to sound practical, but her voice becoming tremulous, 'you'd think I'd be accustomed to living in an empty house, wouldn't you?' Her attempt at bravado was definitely crumbling. 'But I'm not, Grace, I'm not at all accustomed to the empty house. I'm nowhere near as accustomed to it as I used to be for some strange reason.'

She pulled herself together, once again painting on a brave face. 'I suppose it's just the growing turmoil that surrounds us, but I do seem to get so very nervous these days.'

'Of course you do,' Grace said sympathetically, 'it's perfectly understandable and you're not sounding indulgent at all.'

Grace felt immensely sorry for the younger woman. The fact that both she and Amelia had husbands missing had certainly formed a bond between them, but thanks to the messages relayed by Lieutenant Commander Eric Feldt, Grace at least knew her George was alive. She didn't know exactly where, but George Francis still served as a Coastwatcher, and given the heightened presence of the Japanese in the Pacific, his duties were now more valuable and more dangerous than ever. Grace prayed constantly for his safety and blessed Eric Feldt for the assurances that her husband lived. Twenty-eight-year-old Amelia Sanderson had received no such verification of her husband's existence. She had been informed that, following the fall of Singapore, Lieutenant Martin Sanderson was not registered among the thousands of Allied soldiers captured and imprisoned by the Japanese. Amelia's husband had been reported 'missing in action'.

'It's the not knowing,' she'd sobbed when she'd first heard the news barely a month previously. 'Oh, Grace, it's the not knowing. I think that's even harder than . . .' But she hadn't been able to go on.

These days, Amelia chose to adopt the 'stiff-upper-lip' approach when in the company of others, but it was obvious the poor young woman was torturing herself. No wonder she's nervy all alone in that big house, Grace thought.

'I tell you what you must do,' she said brightly, aware that Amelia didn't want any show of heartfelt concern. In fact, too much sympathy might well shatter the façade she took such care to present. A practical solution was of far more value.

She poured them both a fresh cup of tea from the large pot that sat on the table. The brew would by now be less than lukewarm, but Grace felt such an act of normalcy was important.

'You must offer part of your home as an officer's billet,' she said as she poured. 'I did, and it's working remarkably well. We're billeting a very pleasant American officer at the moment, he's an absolute gentleman.'

As she said it, Grace wondered why the idea hadn't occurred earlier, either to herself or to Amelia, or even to the military, who had been requisitioning properties all over Townsville. 'Hayden House', an attractively designed Queenslander that had belonged to Amelia's parents, was a sizeable property in Mitchell Street, parallel to The Strand and just one block back, very conveniently positioned.

'I don't know why I didn't think of it earlier,' she went on, passing Amelia her tea, 'it's a marvellous idea. You'll feel a lot safer with an officer about the house, and to quote Tom, you'll be *doing your bit*. He was so proud of me when I did mine,' she added with a smile.

'Doing *what* bit?' a boy's voice demanded from the door, and as if somehow conjured up by the mere mention of his name, Tom bounded into the room. He dumped the Red Cross collection box he was carrying onto the large trestle table behind which the women were seated.

'Good crowd this arvo,' he said, 'the blokes were pretty generous, particularly the Yanks, but then the Yanks always are.'

Tom had been making the rounds on his bike, calling in at a number of inner-city pubs collecting Red Cross donations. He'd managed to tie up other bits of business along the way, as was his custom. Tom was ever efficient. He'd dropped off a few frogs and mice to Val at The Brown's and he'd delivered a package for his new buddy, Frank, to the American Officers' Club, which was housed in the Queen's Hotel.

'So what particular *bit* will you be doing, Mrs Sanderson?' he asked, grabbing an Anzac biscuit from the plate that sat beside the teapot.

'I haven't really decided yet.' Amelia looked from mother to son, a little flustered.

'Just an idea, Tom, nothing more,' Grace said briskly, aware Amelia was feeling cornered. 'I suggested Mrs Sanderson might think of billeting an officer at her house, that's all.'

'Great idea,' Tom agreed enthusiastically through a mouthful of biscuit, 'you should give it a go, Mrs Sanderson.' He was about to enthuse further, but catching a warning glance from his mum, changed the subject instead. 'Hey, these are really beaut biscuits, I bet they're homemade.'

Grace smiled. It was an unwittingly perfect call. 'Yes, they are. Amelia . . . Mrs Sanderson baked them herself.'

'Well, they're great,' Tom said, 'really great!' Influenced by his new American friends, '*great*' featured equally alongside '*beaut*' in Tom's vocabulary these days.

Amelia looked pleased, both by the compliment and the enthusiasm displayed by the person who had made it. She very much liked young Tom. 'They're not quite as good as they should be,' she said, not self-deprecatingly, but rather critically for she was proud of her baking skills. 'I had a can of golden syrup but very little sugar, so the balance of sweetness in this batch isn't quite right, I'm afraid.'

'Probably what makes them spot on,' Tom said, his freckle-faced grin cheekily disarming, 'but I'll get you some sugar, Mrs Sanderson, don't you worry about that. Easy as pie.' And it would be. He'd get a bag of sugar from Baz – he ran errands for Baz as well as the Americans, and Baz always gave him a fair exchange of favours. In his own innocent way, young Tom Francis was as much a profiteer as Baz himself.

'Want me to give you a hand?' he asked, the question appearing rhetorical for he was already dragging another chair up to the trestle table.

'Yes, thank you, dear, how nice,' his mother said.

Tom stayed with them for over an hour, packing boxes, wrapping parcels, tying string, and chatting on entertainingly all the while.

Grace was glad of his presence, knowing her son's buoyancy was relaxing Amelia. She chastised herself for having been overly pushy with the poor woman. She certainly hadn't intended to be. It had just seemed like a good idea at the time, but she wouldn't bring up the subject of billeting again.

'I think that's it for the day,' she said, checking the clock on the wall. They'd completed their customary four-hour stint. 'Tom, dear, would you mind accompanying Mrs Sanderson home —'

'No, no,' Amelia hastily interrupted, flushing as she did so. How embarrassing that her complaints of nervousness should make Grace feel she needed to be shepherded about town. 'That's not necessary, Grace,' she insisted firmly, 'that's really not necessary.'

'I know it's not,' Grace countered with equal firmness, 'but you have a bag of groceries that Tom can carry on his bike, so it seems only practical to me. And Tom doesn't mind, do you, dear?'

'Nup.' That grin again. 'Happy to be of service, Mrs Sanderson.'

'That's settled, then,' Grace rose to her feet, 'off we go.'

As she sailed out the door, the others obediently following, Grace couldn't help but reflect upon the apparent change in her own character, or rather in the way she must surely be perceived by others. Not long ago it was she who would have been seen as the weaker woman in need of support, and yet here she was taking on the leadership, being the strong one.

I suppose war does that to people, she thought. Although she had a sneaking feeling her strength had always been there, lurking beneath the surface. Well, it would certainly remain with her in full force until George came home.

Barely fifteen minutes later, after strolling companionably side by side, Amelia and Tom came to a halt outside the attractive Queenslander house in Mitchell Street.

'Thank you so much, Tom,' Amelia said as he lifted her string bag of groceries from his bike's rear pannier, 'it's very kind of you.'

She was about to take the bag from him, but he kept hold of it. 'That's OK, Mrs Sanderson,' he said – '*OK*' was another adopted Americanism of which Tom had become extremely fond – 'I'll take it upstairs for you,' and propping his bike against the railings, he started bounding up the steps two at a time.

The Queenslander, on stilts roughly six feet above ground and painted white with green-trimmed windows, was pleasantly designed. Two white wooden staircases, running parallel to the building itself, led up from either side to converge at a covered front porch supported by slender pillars, giving the house a well-organised and slightly 'regal' look. It had been built by Amelia's parents, Dr Robert Hayden GP and his wife, Anthea, in the early 1920s and they'd considered it just that little bit different from the average Queenslander being built at the time, most of which had a central set of stairs and sprawling front verandahs.

Amelia followed the boy up the steps to where he was waiting on the front porch. 'Come in, Tom,' she said, leading the way. 'I'll get us a cup of tea and some more Anzac biscuits, what do you say?'

'Great,' he replied, 'but no tea for me, thanks, just the biccies'll do.'

They walked down the passage that led from the front door, and along the way Tom had a bit of a 'stickybeak', as his mother was wont to say. Doors led off from either side of the passage, two of them open and both revealing sitting rooms, one on each side. If the other closed doors were bedrooms, he thought, then the house appeared to be split into two. Great for an officer's billet!

They arrived at the large, roomy kitchen, where he dumped the string bag of groceries on the wooden table in the centre.

'This is a really beaut house, Mrs Sanderson.'

'Thanks, Tom,' she said as she filled the kettle. 'I've lived here for as long as I can remember. My mum and dad built it when I was about six years old.'

'Looks like it's been split in half,' he commented, unashamed for having so blatantly 'stickybeaked'.

'Yes, you're quite right, it has been,' Amelia admitted, taking no umbrage; he was just a curious boy. 'When Martin and I married we moved in here with my parents, who were very keen for us to do so. They had the rooms redesigned so that we could share the house amicably, all four of us. It worked very well, too.'

'That's what'd make it a great officer's billet,' Tom said eagerly. 'I reckon my mum's idea's a real beauty, Mrs Sanderson! You should give it a go.'

'I'll think about it, Tom.' Amelia smiled. She didn't feel cornered this time, or pressured in any way. The boy meant only to be helpful, just as his mother had. She really must stop letting her nerves get the better of her.

She lifted out the biscuit tin, opened the lid and set it down in front of him. She wouldn't bother with a plate. 'Help yourself,' she said, smiling once again as his hand immediately dived in.

'Wow, thanks!'

Tom sat at the table and watched her as she went about making the tea. She'd be pretty if she wasn't so sad, he thought. And when she smiles she doesn't even look old. Twenty-eight, to Tom, was nearly thirty and therefore virtually middle-aged. He understood *why* Amelia Sanderson was sad, of course. His mum had told him.

Poor Mrs Sanderson, he thought, *missing in action* really means *presumed dead*, but they don't tell you that for ages. They just make you wait. Must be awful for her.

'We've got this really beaut American bloke billeted at our place,' he said enthusiastically, determined not only to entertain but also to convince her she should give his mum's idea a go. 'He's not all that old, somewhere in his twenties, and he's a captain. But I'm allowed to call him Frank,' he added proudly. 'Anyway, I lent Frank my bike the other day,' he went on as she brought the teapot to the table and joined him. 'He wanted to go for a ride, said it made him feel like a kid again.'

'Oh yes?' Amelia put the knitted tea-cosy on the pot and gave Tom her full attention as she waited for the tea to draw.

'Yeah. And you know the way they say you never forget how to ride a bike?'

Amelia nodded. 'That's what they say all right.'

'*He* forgot, that's for sure, he came the most awful cropper. Rode out of town and came back an hour later soaking wet.'

'Really, my goodness, what happened?'

'He was riding down the hill, the big one just out of town, and he reckons the brakes jammed, but I tell you, Mrs Sanderson, there's nothing wrong with my bike. I keep it in top condition.' Tom grinned conspiratorially. 'I'd say Frank was embarrassed and covering his tracks.'

'Sounds like it to me,' she agreed.

'Turns out he steered the bike into the creek so he'd make a soft landing. Crikey, he even sounded proud of himself when he told me, but I ask you, how dumb is that!' Tom let out a huge hoot of laughter. 'I didn't have the heart to tell him there are crocs in that creek.'

Amelia laughed also and, mission accomplished, the boy felt rightly proud of himself.

She finished her tea and poured a second, he ate another two biscuits, and they talked for a further twenty minutes, or rather Tom did, eliciting an occasional smile, which pleased him immensely. Then it was time for him to go.

She put the remaining Anzac biscuits in a paper bag and insisted he take them with him.

'OK,' he agreed, 'and I'll bring you a bag of sugar, that's a fair deal.'

'It is indeed.'

She walked with him to the front door.

'This'd be a great officer's billet,' he said once again, determined to push the idea a final time, 'honest it would.'

'I'll think about it, Tom,' she said. 'I really will think about it, I promise.'

When he'd gone, Amelia returned to the kitchen table and poured herself a third cup of tea, which she knew she wouldn't drink. The house was once again big and lonely. She'd enjoyed the boy's company, and now she was left with her thoughts as always. The ones that tormented her. *Is it possible Martin's alive? And if he's not, how did he die? Was he alone? Was he in pain? Did it take long?* The questions were always hanging there in the recesses of her mind, resurfacing like a ghastly mantra whenever she was alone.

Perhaps young Tom's right, she thought. Perhaps I should offer half the house as a billet. Perhaps I need a distraction, a duty, at least some presence in the place.

The noises from outside in the street, the churn of heavy traffic, the stamp of men's boots and the bark of their voices now infiltrated the house, personally assaulting her, ringing jarringly in her head. Yet she hadn't even noticed them when the boy had been here.

But surely that's understandable, she thought, trying to reason with herself, I've only felt this way since I received the news. Before then, I was never frightened being here alone. The house didn't seem so big then. And during all those months he was away, I didn't even particularly miss Martin, which is a terrible thing to admit.

If only we'd had a child, she thought, perhaps a boy who might have grown up to be like Tom, cheeky, funny. But there probably wouldn't have been much chance of that.

For some inexplicable reason, Amelia began to cry.

I *did* love him, she told herself. I loved him very much and he loved me, I know he did, but it was my fault our marriage wasn't right. It was all my fault.

The tears kept flowing, silently, painfully.

Amelia had always blamed herself for the lack of sexual intimacy she and her husband shared. They'd had intercourse a number of times, it was true, but living in her parents' house had come at a price. Martin was a private man and clearly uncomfortable making love in the home of his parents-in-law. She should never have agreed to such an arrangement. At least that was the conclusion she'd come to in hindsight. And she'd only been gifted with hindsight on that night. That terrible night, which nobody talked about, that night when it had become so clear to her that it was all her fault. Everything. Poor Martin. How she had deprived him.

The ghastly mantra of queries about her husband's death . . . The jarring noises that came in from the street . . . The turmoil of guilt that plagued her constantly . . . There were times when Amelia felt she must surely be going mad.

*

Several days later, the violence that had threatened the streets of Townsville finally erupted, and as was perhaps to be expected it happened in the red-light district.

Things started out in the usual way. Around eleven o'clock, as men left the brothels of Ford Street to return to their respective barracks before the midnight curfew, there arose the customary show of hostility. A number of white Americans picked on a group of black Americans, and a couple of Aussies joined in under the guise of standing up for the black soldiers, but in reality relishing the opportunity to have a go at the Yanks.

A melee ensued. Just voices raised to start with, insults exchanged, men goading each other, egging mates on. Then the more aggressive among them started throwing punches and before long it had become a real free-for-all brawl.

A further group of white American troops appeared from the Causeway Hotel, drawn by the noise. The pub was closed, but they'd been having their own private party in the back room and the illicit liquor they'd consumed saw them right in the mood to join the fray.

By now there were twenty or more men kicking and punching and headbutting each other, some locked together on the ground, wrestling in the dark and dusty street, none of them with any idea what the fight was specifically about, apart from a release of ever-present hostilities and prejudice.

But it was one of the two Australians who was first to recognise the true danger at hand; this was no longer just a brawl.

'That bastard's got a knife,' he yelled to his mate. 'Come on, Mick, we're out of here.'

The Aussies disappeared into the night, leaving the Americans at it, and the fight progressed. Now, it seemed, in deadly earnest.

Before long and inevitably, the Military Police arrived, twelve American provosts in all, and the ruckus was quickly brought to a halt.

'Back up! Back up!' the MP sergeant ordered as his team steadfastly trained their .30 calibre semi-automatic rifles on the group.

But as men dragged themselves from the ground, bloodied and battered, one soldier remained where he lay.

The troops obeyed orders, backing off to stand a respectful distance away, but still the man on the ground did not move.

Stepping forward, the sergeant knelt to examine him. There was no pulse. He examined the wound. The soldier, a Negro, was dead. He'd been stabbed in the heart. The sergeant stood, quickly ordering one of his privates to notify HQ, and within minutes a jeep arrived with Major Hank Henry, the US Provost Marshal for Townsville.

'What's all this, Sergeant?' Hank Henry demanded, climbing from the jeep, a brisk nod to his driver to wait nearby. 'What's going on?' He was a big man, a tough, brash man, good at his job and feared by many.

'I'm afraid we have some trouble, Major,' the sergeant said as Hank Henry joined him. He looked down at the Negro soldier. 'This man is dead.'

Hank Henry knelt beside the body, made a cursory examination only, then stood and barked a command. 'This man is not dead,' he said, 'order an ambulance immediately and take him to the military hospital.'

'But, sir . . .' The sergeant was at a loss for words, his incredulity even causing him to stammer a little. 'But, sir . . . he has no pulse. He's dead! He's been stabbed in the heart.'

'You heard me, Sergeant,' Hank Henry barked for all to hear, 'order that goddamned ambulance immediately.' He then lowered his voice to a whisper. 'Would you like to be the one to explain this man's death to General MacArthur?' he queried scathingly. 'The killing of an American soldier by another American soldier on friendly foreign soil? That sort of publicity would not go down at all well here, Sergeant. And back home it'd cause a fucking furore. This business will be kept strictly under wraps.'

He turned heel and with a wave to his driver, strode off towards the jeep.

The sergeant's incredulity was shared by several of his subordinates, who, although not within hearing of the major's whispered exchange, had gathered the gist of what was going on. And the general feeling among them was, 'Would this death be kept a secret if the soldier was white?'

The men were shocked. But little did they know, this was nothing compared to what lay ahead.

PART TWO
THE SOLDIERS

CHAPTER SIX

The 96th Battalion US Army Corps of Engineers (Coloured) arrived in Townsville aboard the 12,000-tonne SS *Santa Clara* on 10 April 1942.

The men, over a thousand in all, had embarked upon their voyage in Brooklyn, New York, sharing the supply ship with the 576th Dump Truck Company and around 200 doctors. Travelling to Australia under escort via the Panama Canal, they'd arrived in Brisbane on 6 April.

The doctors had disembarked in Brisbane and the vessel had remained in port for several further days while cargo was unloaded and restacked. During this time, the 96th Battalion's white officers were able to take leave in shifts and go into the city, but the black troops were not granted any such R and R rights. The black troops were ordered to remain on board at all times, and were taken ashore only for heavily regimented, cross-country hikes, carefully avoiding the city. Whether these cross-country hikes were for the purpose of physical-fitness training or in order to distract the men from the injustice being served upon them was anyone's guess, but the tack did not work psychologically.

'Do you think they're trying to tell us something, Rupe?'

Nineteen-year-old Private William Parker was hanging over the railings of the *Santa Clara* with his good buddy, Rupert Barrett. It was their first day in port and the men had been informed only an hour or so previously that shore leave would not be granted. The two, like so many others lined up along the ship's decks, were gazing down longingly at the busy docks; at the bustling humanity that beckoned and the trucks and jeeps that were transporting people to the city only several miles away. Emotions were mixed. The view was simultaneously tantalising, teasing, insulting and hurtful.

'I'd say they're telling us something loud and clear, Willie,' Rupe agreed, 'though it's hardly surprising when you think about it.'

'Yeah? In what way?'

'Well, they killed off most of their own blacks years ago, they'd hardly want *us* here would they,' Rupe said, not cynically, just stating the facts as he'd heard them.

'Oh. I didn't know that.'

Willie admired Rupe. Rupe was older and from New York City, and he knew a whole lot of stuff that was really interesting, but he never showed off about it and he never treated you like you were a mug for not knowing stuff yourself. He was a really great guy, Rupe.

They were joined by young Kasey Davis, who'd come up on deck specifically to seek out his buddies. Kasey was also a private and also nineteen, but quite a deal more worldly than Willie, who hailed from South Philadelphia. Athletically gifted, Willie had encompassed nothing but baseball for the whole of his relatively short life.

'Might as well be home in South Carolina,' Kasey remarked, the perfect mouth in his perfect face twisting into a sardonic smile. 'I sure am being made aware of my place.'

'Rupe says they killed off their own coloured folk years ago and that's why they don't want us here,' Willie piped up.

'Oh, that right?' This was news to Kasey, also.

'Yep, believe so, killed off most of them anyway,' Rupe replied with a careless shrug of huge shoulders.

'Well, they can go get fucked as far as I'm concerned,' Kasey snarled, the light of rebellion flashing in his piercingly green eyes. 'We travel all this way to help people who don't even want us to set foot on their soil! Fuck 'em, I say! Fuck the whole damn lot of 'em.'

'Hey, calm down, buddy.' Rupe smiled benignly, aware his diplomatic skills were once again being called upon. Kasey was so darn good-looking he was often underestimated. People assumed someone that pretty was a bit of a girl. But they were wrong. Young Kasey was a real firebrand.

'We're not exactly embraced back home, Kase,' he went on, his smile broadening into a good-humoured grin, 'you of all people should know that . . . *southern boy*.'

Kasey relaxed and returned the grin. Rupe was always a calming influence. A big, powerfully built man, mild in temperament, a gentle giant; all the younger ones looked up to Rupe.

At twenty-six, Corporal Rupert Barrett was senior to his newfound buddies in both years and rank, but it made no difference to Rupe, who just took people as he found them. He liked these two boys. But then he liked most of the guys who served in the 96th Battalion's Company C, those he'd come to know anyway among the close to 200 in number; the troops had bonded during their month-long voyage to Australia. Many of the younger ones had only recently joined up, but this was Rupe's sixth year of service with the US Army and he felt kind of responsible for the new kids on the block.

'Yeah, you're right,' Kasey acknowledged, 'we *southern boys* should be used to feeling inferior, shouldn't we?'

The cheeky wink he gave Rupe clearly signalled he was joking; Kasey Davis felt anything but inferior. 'I guess *all* we boys should be used to it,' he said with a gesture that encompassed the entire ship and therefore the entire battalion. 'Hell, the army don't even tell us what we're going to be doing. They don't even give us weapons.'

Kase was suddenly no longer joking. 'I mean, we're supposed to be fuckin' soldiers and we don't even have a fuckin' gun,' he went on, 'that don't seem right to me.'

'Take it easy, Kase,' Rupe once more came to the rescue. 'We'll find out what we're going to be doing all in good time. You've just got to learn to go with the flow.'

He looked out over the railing at the view below. 'Hey, there goes our favourite man,' he said by way of distraction and he pointed at the figure walking down the gangplank. 'At least we'll have a rest from our buddy Chuck for a couple of hours. That's something to be grateful for.'

'The prick,' Kasey said, 'hope he goes to a brothel and gets a massive dose of the clap!'

Willie laughed. He often found Kase funny when Kase was actually being deadly earnest.

Each of the companies constituting the 96th Battalion was commanded by two white officers, and none of the men from Company C had any time for Captain Charles Leroy Maxwell, known to his fellow white officers as 'Chuck'. In fact, they despised him. Maxwell was a bully who'd made the lives of many insufferable during the long weeks at sea, and the principal whipping boy of his choice had been young Kasey Davis.

Like all bullies, Maxwell was also a coward, and he hadn't picked on Rupe for obvious reasons – not so much the man's size, for there were many big men among the black troops, but rather his professionalism – Corporal Rupert Barrett's military knowledge and experience rendered him virtually unassailable. The boys who were newer to the ropes, however, had been easy game, simple to find fault with, and Maxwell had appeared to take a great deal of pleasure meting out punishment.

'That's what the army is all about,' he would stipulate as he abused his men mercilessly. 'You niggers got to learn that the army is all about discipline! Particularly you, pretty boy,' he'd add when singling out Kasey.

The truth of the matter was, Maxwell's background did not make him an ideal choice to command a company of black soldiers. Twenty-six-year-old Charles 'Chuck' Leroy Maxwell III was born son of Sheridan Leroy Maxwell II, one of the wealthiest men in Alabama and fifth-generation owner of the Elliston cotton plantation. 'Daddy', as Chuck still referred to his father, was a member of the Alabama State Government and also the Exalted Cyclops ('president' to those unfamiliar with the term) of the Montgomery chapter of the Ku Klux Klan.

Chuck Maxwell's entire life having been one of privilege and assumed racial superiority hardly qualified him for his current position of command. But it appeared those allotting command weren't too fussy about the social niceties.

Rupe was all too aware of the demoralising effect Maxwell had had upon the young troops of Company C, particularly Kasey. Perhaps Maxwell had simply been relieving his boredom, Rupe had thought – hell, they'd all been bored throughout the month-long sea voyage. But if Maxwell continued his unnecessarily heavy bullying tactics when they were settled in Townsville, Rupe intended to seek the assistance of the company's other commanding officer. Captain Samuel Robinson was older, wiser and more tolerant than Maxwell, but most important of all he was not consumed by racial hatred.

'Ah well,' Rupe now said as the three of them watched Maxwell climb into a waiting jeep with another two white officers, young lieutenants, platoon commanders of Company C. 'There he goes, off for a good time.' Then, catching the scowl on Kasey's handsome face, he added, 'Don't worry, Kase, it'll be us in a few days' time. They can't keep us on this ship forever. We'll be landing in Townsville before long.'

'Oh yeah,' Kasey sneered, 'and what'll happen then? You think Townsville is going to be any different? I bet they'll head us right out of that place just as quick as they can.'

But Townsville *did* prove different. And young Kasey Davis was the first to acknowledge the fact.

'I don't believe this,' he said when, on the very first leave they were granted, he and Rupe and Willie headed straight into town. 'Where are the signs?' he asked, gazing about the streets; at a bus passing by, at the open doorways of buildings, of shops and bars. 'Where's all the "blacks only"? Where's all the "whites only"? There are no signs in this place.'

Kasey was amazed to discover segregation did not exist in Townsville. It astounded him to know that he could catch the same taxi as a white man; that he could travel on the same public transport as a white man; that cinemas and entertainment areas were open to both black and white. There were even hotels and brothels that catered for both, or so he was told. Admittedly, with the Americans in town, blacks and whites seemed to favour either one establishment or the other, he was informed, but this was by personal choice, not officially by law.

'And the people are so darn nice,' he said, 'I don't feel any hate.' His look to Rupe was one of puzzlement. 'So why did they kill off their own blacks?'

'I don't know,' Rupe said, 'just something I read somewhere.'

The 96th Battalion had set up camp at Farrington Farms about four miles south of Townsville, a makeshift camp to start with, one-man pup tents, while they settled in and were given their work orders. But the men didn't mind. This was a welcoming place and trips into town, to dances and concerts and pubs, and for those in the mood brothels, alleviated the boredom and dissatisfaction of their work.

And their work was certainly boring, offering little by way of personal satisfaction. It was also hard and exhausting. Extending the runways of Garbutt Airfield to accommodate the ever-increasing activity of American aircraft, particularly the massive B-17 bombers that were shortly to arrive in numbers, was an arduous task.

'I guess we found out what we're going to be doing,' Kasey complained as, side by side and in a long line of others reminiscent of a chain gang, he and Willie dug away at the ground with picks and shovels. 'We're going to be spending the entire war shovelling shit from one place to another.'

Willie, lanky, fit and with an easy disposition, gave a pleasant nod but made no remark. Accustomed to heavy-duty athletic training, he quite liked the mindlessness of hard physical work. And besides, Kase was just being Kase.

Aware he was going to get no backup from Willie, Kasey raised the complaint with Rupe later in the day as they queued up for lunch at the canteen tent.

'Downright slave labour it is,' he said. 'And what kind of soldiers does it make us anyway? I joined the army to fight, not shovel shit.'

But he wasn't going to get any backup from Rupe either. 'Seems we're a labour unit, Kase,' he said, 'I'm afraid you'll just have to learn to live with it.'

Maxwell didn't make things any easier either, particularly for Kasey, whose good looks and confidence continued to rankle with 'Chuck'.

'Hey, you! Pretty nigger! Put your back into it there.'

Kasey slowly straightened up – he'd been digging as hard as was humanely possible – this was the third time today Maxwell had singled him out from the twenty or so men in this particular work detail.

He didn't turn to face the captain who had arrived out of nowhere and was standing several paces behind him, instead taking a handkerchief from his pocket and wiping away the sweat that streamed down his face and neck. Then returning the handkerchief to his pocket, he resumed digging.

'I said you!' Maxwell yelled. 'You! Pretty nigger!'

Kasey continued to ignore the man and just kept digging.

The black sergeant overseeing the detail stood awaiting orders from his captain while the surrounding men, Willie among them, continued to make a pretence of working, but twenty sets of eyes were darting in Kasey's direction.

Maxwell, infuriated, strode the several paces forward to Kasey and shoved him in the back so forcefully he fell to the ground. 'Did you hear me, boy,' he screamed, 'I'm talking to you!'

Kasey rose to his feet slowly. 'I'm sorry, sir,' he said, 'I didn't know you meant me.' Of course he knew – he was always 'pretty nigger' to this bastard. He looked Maxwell directly in the eyes, bold and unwavering. 'I didn't realise it was me you were talking to, sir.'

Maxwell drew his Colt semi-automatic pistol from its holster and held it to Kasey's head. Where he came from, no nigger dared look a white man directly in the eyes, and certainly not the way this pretty nigger was doing right now.

'I could have you shot for this, boy,' he said menacingly.

Kasey felt fear, but he didn't show it. He didn't even flinch. 'Have me shot for what, sir?' he asked innocently.

The surrounding men were making no pretence of work now, and Maxwell, realising he was the full focus of their attention, lowered his weapon. 'For your insolence, boy,' he said. 'The army will not tolerate insolence among the ranks, do I make myself clear?'

'Yes, sir.'

'Carry on, Sergeant.' Maxwell gave a brisk nod to the sergeant who hadn't moved a muscle. Then he turned heel and marched off.

'You niggers heard what the captain said,' First Sergeant Walker 'Strut' Stowers roared, ensuring Maxwell was still well within hearing range. 'Get your lazy black asses back to work.'

Forty-year-old career soldier Strut Stowers, streetwise and rat-cunning, had gravitated through the ranks to First Sergeant by giving his senior white officers exactly what they wanted from him. Strut knew how to work the system to his own advantage, and did so at all times.

At the end of the day's labour Willie couldn't wait to relate the drama to Rupe, but he didn't get very far.

'I know,' Rupe said, 'I heard.' And he had. He'd heard every single detail from any number of men, as word had quickly got around. Maxwell's set against Kasey, for whatever reason it may be, was obviously not letting up. The man needed to be reined in.

Rupe had already decided to report the incident directly to Captain Robinson. There was no point in trying to elicit the assistance of Sergeant Strut Stowers, whom Rupe knew from the past to be a nasty piece of work who'd sell his own kind down the river. And regularly did. He'd seek out Robinson on his own.

The following day at lunchtime, he paid a visit to the Company C officers' tent, aware that he might well find both commanding officers present, in which case he'd have to request a private meeting with Robinson, which could be awkward. However, as luck would have it, Maxwell was not there. Nor were any of the four young lieutenants who served as Company C's platoon commanders. They were all in the officers' mess tent having lunch.

Rupe was relieved to discover that, apart from Robinson, the only other person in the tent was Private Percy Owen, seated at the small desk in the corner tapping away at his typewriter. Young Percy Owen had been allotted clerk duty due to the literacy skills he possessed, a cushy job that made him the envy of the buddies he'd made in Company C, many of whom were illiterate.

'What can I do for you, Corporal?' Robinson asked after Rupe had saluted and presented himself.

As he listened, Samuel Robinson showed little reaction, which was not unusual for he was a self-contained man who rarely displayed emotion, but it was clear Rupe had his full attention.

'So what exactly is it you're after, Corporal?' he asked finally, the dark eyes in his chisel-boned face keenly seeking an answer. 'Is this an official report you're making? Do you want it to go further? Do you want to see action taken?'

Robinson, an experienced officer thirty-two years of age, was not taunting Rupe in any way, but rather offering a warning. Both men respected each other and both knew the futility of the outcome should Rupe's answer be 'yes'. Any complaint a black soldier lodged against a white officer was not only doomed to failure, but doomed to dramatically backfire on the complainant and probably upon the troops themselves.

'No, sir,' Rupe said, 'I just want Maxwell to lay off a bit, that's all. He comes on way too strong at times.'

'I know.' Robinson's nod might have appeared sympathetic if he'd allowed his true feelings to show – he was fully aware of Maxwell's shameful bullying – but he maintained his façade. Much as Samuel Robinson despised Chuck Maxwell and others of his ilk, it was imperative for morale and discipline that officers be seen to stick together at all times.

'I know Maxwell's a hard bastard, Corporal,' he went on, 'but the army needs hard bastards to do the hard jobs, as I'm sure you're aware.' Samuel even allowed himself the faintest smile as he added, 'And at least the man's consistent, you'd have to admit that. At least he's tough on *all* of the troops.'

'Not the way he is with Kasey, sir,' Rupe interrupted with some force, which was unlike him, but he wasn't going to leave without making his point. 'Maxwell's got a set on Kasey Davis. I don't know exactly why, but it's not healthy. Private Davis has become a regular scapegoat, sir. Yesterday's incident was only one of many.'

'I see.' Robinson gave a brisk nod, signalling the interview was over. 'Thank you for informing me, Corporal, I shall look into the matter.'

'Thank you, sir.'

Rupe was about to salute and take his leave when Captain Chuck Maxwell bowled in, coming to an abrupt halt when he saw the two of them together.

'My, my, my, isn't this something,' he jeered, 'a nigger in the officers' tent. And cosying up to an officer what's more. You want to watch you don't catch something nasty, Robinson – these boys carry all kinds of disease.'

'That's enough, Captain,' Samuel snapped, 'Corporal Barrett was just leaving.'

He nodded once again to Rupe, who snapped a salute and left without so much as a passing glance at Maxwell. Although, as he spun on his heel he did catch sight of young Percy Owen. Percy had stopped typing, probably for fear the noise would attract attention to him. But Percy wasn't watching the white officers. His gaze was firmly and subserviently focused upon the report that sat on the table before him, the report he was pretending to read. Rupe left the tent with the image of Percy in his mind.

This was one of those rare occasions when Samuel Robinson failed to disguise his feelings, or rather when he refused to even try. His look to his fellow officer was one of disgust. 'You really are some piece of work, aren't you, Chuck,' he said with loathing.

'What's your problem, Robinson?' Maxwell responded with equal disdain. Nigger lovers like this man disgusted him. 'We have to work with them, we don't have to like them. You hang around niggers too long and get too close the smell's bound to rub off, and that's the truth. Why, if we were back home you'd be in a world of trouble right now.'

'But we're not back home, Maxwell, that's something you need to recognise.' Samuel's tone was brusque. Time to drum some sense into this spoilt young prick's head. 'We're not back home and you're not on your daddy's plantation. The rules are different here.'

'Bullshit. The rules never change. When it comes to niggers we *wrote* the goddamned rules.' Maxwell was irritated. Samuel Robinson might be older, but he was inferior in every way. How dare he patronise. 'And I'll tell you something else, which I'm sure you know only too well,' he smiled spitefully, twisting the knife, intent upon hurting, 'the same rule applies to *Jews*!' He spat out the word as if it were something foul, which to him it was. 'What's your *real* name, Samuel? Come on now, do tell. It sure as hell isn't Robinson, is it?'

Samuel Rabinowicz was accustomed to Jew-baiting, just as his Eastern European parents had been when they'd arrived in New York City forty years previously, which was why they'd changed their family name. But the change of name hadn't really worked for any of them. They were still Jews, and Samuel had suffered accordingly. From school bullies to university bullies, from a successfully stifled career in civil engineering to a military career that had seen little promotion, Samuel Robinson had been discriminated against his entire life. He was by now thoroughly immune to cheap taunts from the likes of Chuck Maxwell. But there was no way he was going to let the prick get away with it.

'Have you ever stopped to wonder, Chuck,' he said slowly, as if the thought might just have occurred, 'why you and I are here at the ass-end of the world in charge of a non-combat black battalion? I mean, let's face it, this is a shitty detail. Sure, we both know why *I'm* here. I'm a New York Jew who isn't allowed to mix with the colonel's country club buddies. But *you*, Chuck? Why in God's name are *you* at the very bottom of the barrel? Well now, let's see.'

Samuel paced around a little, hand thoughtfully and theatrically to chin as if trying to figure out such an anomaly. 'You could be here because the army doesn't consider you capable of handling a combat role, which would make sense to me,' he went on, 'but there's another possibility, too. Your appointment to a non-combat battalion might have been specially arranged by your daddy, who wants you kept safe till the end of the war.'

'You leave my daddy out of this.' Robinson's needling was having the desired effect. Maxwell was more than irritated now, he was fuming.

'Of course your daddy would want you home to take over the family plantation one day,' Samuel continued, 'but your daddy might also know you're really not cut out for combat duty. He might feel his baby boy needs protection, that little Chuck must be looked after.'

'I said you leave my daddy out of this!' Maxwell raised his fist threateningly. 'One more word and I'll break your filthy kike nose.'

'Go on,' Samuel urged, 'do it! Strike a brother officer. You'll be court-martialled so fast your head will spin.'

They stood facing each other off for several seconds, then Maxwell lowered his fist.

'That's sensible,' Samuel said. 'Now I tell you what you're going to do, Chuck.' Being senior, if not in rank, then in age and experience, Samuel spoke to Maxwell as he would to a junior officer. 'You're going to stop bullying Private Davis the way you have been.'

'Why?' Maxwell demanded belligerently. 'Nothing personal to it, I treat him same as I do all the others.'

'Oh yeah? You don't think putting a gun to the boy's head was coming on a little heavy?'

'I was teaching him a lesson, that's all. Not as if it hasn't been done before! Hell, I'm not the first to shove a gun at a nigger's head! These boys have got to know who's boss, and scaring the shit out of them works a treat.'

'There are other ways to discipline,' Samuel replied coldly. 'I'm telling you, Maxwell, you're to lay off Davis, because if I hear you're still riding him, I swear I'll report you myself.'

Once again they stared each other down.

Then, 'Nigger lover,' Maxwell hissed before marching out of the tent.

Percy Owen resumed his typing.

Life continued on a more even keel after Rupe's visit to the officers' tent. The men didn't know why, or what had taken place, but Maxwell, although still the pig that he was, didn't seem to favour a particular kicking boy. His malice was directed equally to all, or so it seemed.

The work remained heavy-duty and boring, and for those among the troops who had anticipated combat duty, extremely frustrating. But it was offset by the R and R pleasures Townsville offered. And for a number of men from Company C, the principal pleasure was music.

It had been a mutual love of music that had bonded Rupert Barrett and Kasey Davis from the moment they'd first met. Between the two of them, they'd provided the main form of entertainment for the troops of Company C aboard the *Santa Clara*, Rupe on harmonica, Kasey singing the vocals, and both men playing guitar.

Music was in their blood. Rupe came from a professional background, his father, Albert, being a jazz piano player of considerable note in New York. But despite formal training and the ongoing encouragement of a master musician, Rupe had not attempted to emulate his father's career. Realising he would never attain Albert's brilliance, he'd joined the army instead.

Kasey's background was altogether different. There was no music in Kasey's family. He was a born natural who just loved to sing. He'd started out in talent shows as a ten-year-old, then he'd taught himself to play the guitar. He would like to have taught himself to play the piano, too, if his folks had been able to afford a piano, but no-one in their neighbourhood had a piano so that option was out the window. When at the age of sixteen he'd been convicted of robbery and sent to a juvenile detention centre, he'd volunteered to sing in their gospel choir and had relished every moment of the experience. So much indeed that upon his release he'd joined a semi-professional gospel group, augmenting the pittance he earned from his job as a janitor at the local school.

During the whole of his life, it had never once occurred to Kasey that his musical talents might earn him a living. He just wanted to sing and be around music. And Rupe, despite his musical training, was willing to take a second seat to this young man, who'd never had a lesson in his life and whose talent was truly prodigious.

It wasn't long before Rupe and Kasey discovered The Brown's. They'd heard of the bar with the snake pen immediately upon their arrival, and also the fact that the pub welcomed both blacks and whites, but it was the music that attracted them. They'd heard also that The Brown's had a piano and a girl who could really play the thing.

'Do you know "Amazing Grace"?'

'Course I do,' Betty said, looking up at the big black serviceman who towered over her where she sat at the piano.

'Do you want to hear it sung the way it's supposed to be sung?'

'Sure.' She smiled at the man's cheeky arrogance. Given his size and the depth of his voice, he was bound to be a baritone rather than a tenor, and 'Amazing Grace' was more suited to a tenor, in Betty's opinion anyway. The bar was busy, too, and there was even a couple dancing over in the corner they'd lately reserved as a pocket-sized dance floor, hardly the time for a solo performance, and a hymn of all things. But what the heck, she thought, everyone's bound to join in. They all like a good singalong.

She played the introduction, not adjusting the key to suit a baritone, but sticking to the way she always played it. She didn't need sheet music for this hymn, which was a popular choice among all Americans, both white and black.

'*Amazing grace, how sweet the sound . . .*'

But it wasn't the big Negro who sang. He'd stepped aside to reveal one of the most beautiful human beings

Betty thought she had ever seen. And the perfection of his voice equalled his physical beauty.

The Brown's Bar came to a breathless standstill. No-one joined in, not a murmur was heard; people even stopped drinking. The moment seemed frozen in time as the young man's voice soared effortlessly about a room that only minutes earlier had been loud and chaotic.

Rising to the occasion, Betty played as she'd never played before, her eyes occasionally meeting those of the young black man, both aware of the loveliness they were creating.

There was a moment's silence when the song came to an end. Then followed a deafening round of applause.

'See?' The big man leaned down and flashed her the broadest grin. 'What did I tell you?'

'Yep,' Betty agreed, 'that's the way it should be sung all right.'

'You play a mean piano, too,' Rupe said, 'that's a great touch you have there, little lady.'

'Thank you.'

'Name's Rupert,' he held out his hand, 'Rupe for short.'

'Betty. G'day, Rupe.' They shook.

'Mind if I have a quick tickle of the ivories?' he asked.

Betty stood. 'Be my guest.'

The big man seated himself on the piano stool. 'A taste of New Orleans for you, Betty,' he said, 'from the greatest of the great, Jelly Roll Morton,' and he leaped straight into 'Jelly Roll Blues'.

Betty found herself standing beside the beautiful young man. 'He's good isn't he, your mate Rupe,' she said, watching the big man's fingers fly about the keyboard.

'Yep.' Kasey nodded. 'You're pretty good yourself. Can I buy you a drink?'

Kasey was aware of scowls being cast in their direction from a group of white American soldiers standing nearby.

Those same white soldiers had thoroughly enjoyed his rendition of 'Amazing Grace', but performance over, he was now supposed to know his place. No talking to the white girl. What the hell, he told himself rebelliously. This is Townsville, not South Carolina, not Georgia, those rules don't apply here.

'Come on,' he urged, 'let's go to the bar.'

Betty hesitated. It seemed rude to walk away while Rupe was playing.

'Don't worry about him,' Kasey said, 'he won't even notice we've gone. He never cares if anyone's listening, he just wants to play piano.'

They went to the bar where they seated themselves and Val served them a couple of beers, refusing to take payment.

'For a song like that, lovey, it's on the house,' she said, moving off to serve someone else.

'What's your name?' Betty asked.

'Kasey. Kasey Davis,' he answered. 'What's yours?'

'Betty Francis.' She took a sip of her beer. 'I've never heard anyone sing like that,' she said, thinking how very young he looked.

'I like to sing.' Kasey downed half his beer in one go.

'How old are you?' she asked.

'Nineteen.'

Betty gave a Veronica Lake flick of her head that effectively set an unruly lock of fair hair back in its place. 'That's awfully young to be so talented,' she said, 'where did you train?'

'I didn't. How old are you?'

'Twenty.'

Kasey grinned, a devastating flash of white teeth, green eyes dancing. He had this girl's number. She liked to play it tough, but she was really a country girl at heart. 'Twenty, going on thirty-five, eh?' he said. 'I like older women.'

Betty threw back her head and laughed. A big, unaffected laugh, aware that her intention to patronise hadn't worked. This beautiful young man was no innocent, he was as worldly as she was.

'So where do you come from, Kasey?' she asked.

'Elko, South Carolina,' he said, 'that's where I was born anyway. When I was ten we moved to Augusta, Georgia.'

'And you never had any training?'

'What, singing, you mean?'

She nodded.

'Nope. Started out when I was ten in talent shows. First time was the Augusta Variety Talent Spectacular of 1934.' He downed the remainder of his beer. 'I sang a blues ballad and ended up winning the show. Judge said I was a child prodigy. I had to look up what that meant,' he added with a grin. 'I been singing ever since. Do you want another beer?'

'No thanks. I'll have to get back to work in a sec.'

'But Rupe's happy. He'll play for as long as you want him to.'

'No, I mean behind the bar.' She leaned forward conspiratorially. 'I'll let you in on a secret,' she whispered, 'I'm not really a piano player at all.'

'You could have fooled me.'

'I'm a barmaid,' she announced with pride, then she gave him a cheeky wink, 'and a bloody good one if I say so myself.' She jumped eagerly to her feet. 'Tell you what though, while Rupe's playing, why don't we have a quick dance? Just one number, what do you say?'

She noted the dubious look he cast at the group of American soldiers who were still glowering in their direction.

'Oh, don't mind them,' she said dismissively, 'Val's got a shotgun under the counter, she'll make them leave if they cause any trouble.'

She took his hand, and as they weaved their way through the crowded bar to the pocket-sized dance floor, Kasey marvelled at this slender young woman, so blonde, so pretty, yet head held high, defying the animosity he could feel in the room. She might be a country girl, he thought admiringly, but she really *is* tough.

Kasey had never known anything quite like this.

CHAPTER SEVEN

The Brown's Bar, during the limited hours of its opening anyway, continued to be a favourite haunt of Rupe's and Kasey's – and also of Willie's because Willie went wherever his two best buddies went. But it was evident to a number of onlookers that young Kasey Davis was drawn to the place for more than the music.

'You think perhaps you should practise a little caution, Kase?' Rupe couldn't help offering a gentle word of warning. 'You think perhaps you might be getting a little close with this gal?'

'No, no,' Kasey replied with an airy wave of his hand. 'We're just friends, that's all. Friends who like music, simple as that.'

The observation was not one-sided, and Rupe wasn't the only person offering a word of warning. Although Val's initial approach was more brutal.

'You're not leading this boy on, are you?' she demanded. 'Because if you're playing some sort of game you could get him into real trouble, you do know that, don't you?'

Betty took umbrage. 'I'm not leading him on at all,' she responded with icy dignity, 'Kasey and I are good friends who just happen to share a love of music.'

'Fair enough.' Val backed off immediately. 'But watch out, lovey,' she said, her tone gentle now, 'you don't want to get your*self* into trouble.'

So the friendship between the two continued. And it did genuinely appear to be the music causing it to blossom the way it was, for when Kasey sang and Betty joined him on piano it was as if the two were making love. Which was of course why Rupe and Val had felt it necessary to issue a warning, which both had realised was of course destined to go unheeded.

One late Saturday afternoon, when the queue of drinkers had poured into the bar and Betty had started up on the piano, there turned out to be a surprise arrival.

'Well, well, they were right, you really do make some beautiful music in this place.'

Samuel Robinson had stood quietly by the door watching as Betty and Kasey performed 'Fascinating Rhythm' to an appreciative audience that was astoundingly quiet for a room full of servicemen. Now, at the conclusion of the song, as the crowd gave a rapturous round of applause, he walked up to them and made his presence known.

'Even better than aboard ship,' he said to Rupe, who was propped beside the piano.

'Yes siree, Captain,' Rupe agreed with a nod to Betty, 'and all due thanks to this young lady.'

'Indeed. Well played, Miss . . . ?'

'I'm Betty.' Betty jumped up from the piano stool, hand outstretched. She'd heard all about the men's commanding officers from Kasey. This was the nice bloke, the one who liked music, the other one was a right prick. 'Betty Francis.'

'How do you do, Betty.'

They shook and he introduced himself. 'Captain Samuel Robinson,' he said, thinking how amazingly confident the girl was for one so young. He turned to Kasey. 'Another spot-on Gershwin rendition, Private,' he said with a smile. Samuel had hugely enjoyed the impromptu entertainment aboard the *Santa Clara*, which had not unsurprisingly endeared him to his men.

'Thank you, sir.' Kasey returned the smile. 'We do a lot of Gershwin, Betty and me. She knows them all. Don't even need the sheet music.'

'It's Rupe's turn now though,' Betty interrupted, 'I have to give Jilly a break at the bar. You don't have a drink, Captain,' she continued without drawing breath, 'come and I'll serve you, what'll it be, a beer?'

'Yes. Thank you.' He followed her meekly.

Rupe took a seat at the piano and leaped straight into a lively version of 'At the Woodchopper's Ball'.

Upon arriving at the bar, Betty told Jill to take a break. 'I know you're dying to have a dance,' she said, 'and just look at Willie over there, he's straining at the leash.'

Barely a minute later, as she delivered Samuel Robinson his beer, Betty was pleased to see that Jill and young Willie Parker were already throwing their bodies around on the minuscule dance floor. Willie had taught Jill to jitterbug just the previous week, and Jill, who adored to dance, was a very quick learner.

'They're good, aren't they?' she said, noting the strumming of the captain's fingers on the bar top while he watched the dancers.

'Eh? Oh, yes,' Samuel agreed as she nodded in the direction of the dance floor, but he hadn't really been watching the pair at all, he'd just been grooving to the beat. God he loved jazz.

'So you heard we make beautiful music in this place?'

'Sorry?' he queried, unsure of what she'd said, he'd clocked out of his surrounds and on to the beat once again.

'That's what you said,' she prompted, 'that you'd heard we make beautiful music in this place.'

'Yep, I sure did.' The girl was interested in small talk so it was only polite to oblige. 'And I must say I was delighted to discover the music's been coming from our own Company C boys.' He gave her a friendly smile. 'Makes me feel darn proud.'

'Yeah, Rupe and Kasey are talented all right.' Betty could tell the captain didn't really want to talk, but she didn't care. She felt as though somehow she knew him – well, just a bit – from what Kasey had told her. This bloke was a jazz freak, Kasey had said, 'Not a nigger hater like the other bastard,' had been his exact words. 'This guy really loves music. That makes him one of us, you know?'

Betty didn't dare let on that Kasey had spoken so intimately about his commanding officer, it might get him into trouble, but she wanted to make contact with this man. She could report whatever she learned back to Kasey. The two of them talked about absolutely everything.

'So if you didn't hear from your own blokes,' she queried, 'who was it that told you about our place?'

'A couple of officers from Kissing Point Fort,' he replied dutifully. 'I'm billeted down that way, a private house in Mitchell Street.'

'Oh really, which one? Whose house?'

The girl wasn't going to give up. She was extremely distracting, and Samuel tried not to sound just a little testy. 'Hayden House, it's called, the owner's a very nice lady —'

'Amelia Sanderson,' Betty said with a distinct ring of triumph.

'Yes, that's right. Mrs Sanderson is —'

'She's a close friend of my mother's,' Betty trumpeted with an even greater ring of triumph.

'Really.' Samuel tried to appear as if the fact held even the remotest shred of interest.

'Yes, everyone knows everyone in Townsville.'

'Apparently.' He smiled in a way that he hoped was warm and pushed a note across the bar. 'Keep the change, Betty, and thank you for your excellent Gershwin.'

'Golly,' she picked up the one-pound note, it was an excellent tip, 'thanks.'

By now, Rupe had segued into Duke Ellington's 'I Ain't Got Nothin' But the Blues'.

'Enjoy the beautiful music,' she called as Samuel, beer in hand, walked off to stand near the piano. Betty knew she'd been a source of irritation to the captain, but she wasn't in the least bothered. She only regretted that she hadn't been able to glean a little more inside information to share with Kasey. No matter, she'd be able to make a funny story about how annoying she'd been to the poor man, 'When all he wanted to do was groove to the music,' she'd say. She loved making Kasey laugh.

She caught Kasey's eye now and they exchanged intimate smiles, a language of their own. He'd be waiting for her when she knocked off work in a couple of hours – the bar was never open for very long – and they'd go for a walk. Their relationship had escalated dramatically over the past days. But all love-at-first-sight relationships do, don't they, Betty thought knowingly.

Not for one minute did Betty question what she felt was true love. Nor did she question the degree of Kasey's love. They were both head over heels and they both knew it. This was undoubtedly the real thing. They'd even shared a kiss during their last walk – down by the creek, away from the crowds – it had naturally been she who had initiated the kiss.

'Nobody's watching,' she'd whispered. She could tell he was guarded, wary – because she was white, of course. For all Kasey's boldness, he was very conscious of the looks people gave them. No doubt on her behalf. But he needn't be. She didn't care what people thought.

So they'd kissed. The perfect kiss. Tender, loving, everything she'd imagined a perfect kiss would be. She'd been transported. Yes, this was definitely the real thing, she'd thought. And that very same night, lying in bed, reliving the moment, she'd made a plan.

Betty intended to tell Kasey all about her plan later today, in the early evening when they went for their walk. She'd leave it until after they'd kissed though.

Over the next half hour or so, as she continued pulling beers, pouring drinks and flashing pretty smiles at customers, even exchanging flirtatious repartee, Betty was really working on automatic pilot.

Her mind in full romantic mode, her glance happened upon the captain and she couldn't help but think of poor tragic Amelia Sanderson. Still young. Well, relatively – Amelia must be close to thirty, she thought. Still attractive – well, sort of, perhaps a bit colourless. But so sad. Ever watching, ever waiting for a husband who would never return. How wonderful if poor Amelia could accept her widowhood and find a new love in Captain Robinson. Who isn't really bad looking, Betty thought – in an older-man, craggy sort of way.

Amelia Sanderson was actually quite taken with Captain Samuel Robinson, although certainly not in the manner about which Betty fantasised. Amelia considered the captain a real gentleman and she felt much safer with his presence in the house. She admitted as much to her good friend Grace as they sat side by side in the back room of the AWU packing their Red Cross parcels.

'You were quite right, Grace,' she said, 'I do feel safer, just as you said I would, which is odd really, because Captain Robinson is not even there most of the time. I suppose it's the fact that an officer is seen coming and going from the house that makes me less jumpy about the thought of those rowdy hordes out in the street breaking down the door and . . . well, it's just nerves, of course.' She broke off, embarrassed. 'Silly of me I know, but this past week with Captain Robinson there, the noises out in the street don't seem nearly as frightening as they were.'

'And you're *doing your bit*,' Grace said encouragingly, delighted that her advice had proved so helpful.

'Yes, as a matter of fact I am,' Amelia replied with surprising eagerness, 'but not just in providing an officer's billet. I've agreed to teach some of the soldiers under Captain Robinson's command.'

'Really? How wonderful.' Grace was impressed.

'Yes. Quite a number of them are illiterate, you know.' Amelia smiled. She actually smiled. A pretty smile, a genuinely happy smile, and one not seen for such a long time that, rather than surprise, Grace's reaction was closer to astonishment.

'I shall teach them to read and write,' Amelia went on. 'Just the basics. And I shall help them write a simple letter home, one that can be read out to their family. I think that would be a fine thing to do.'

Amelia was to meet her first pupil the very next day. She was looking forward to teaching again. Captain Robinson's idea had rather taken her aback, but now she embraced the prospect of serving a purpose. It seemed such a very long time since she'd served any form of purpose at all.

'I was a primary school teacher before my marriage,' she'd told Captain Robinson as she'd poured them tea in the sitting room that had once been her parents'. This was the sitting room to the right of the house; the left side of the house had always been hers and Martin's. Strangely enough, when her parents had moved to Sydney, leaving her the house, she and Martin had never availed themselves of the right-hand side, which had always sat vacant, accusingly so, as if it was blaming them for something.

'But I gave up teaching after I married. We so wanted a family,' she continued, 'but sadly I'm afraid it was not meant to be.'

She passed the American his cup of tea. This was the first time they'd met. She'd given him a guided tour of the house before serving tea, accompanied naturally by a plate of her Anzac biscuits.

'I must say I rather miss teaching,' she said. She found Captain Robinson very easy to talk to; there was an aura of 'calm' about him that was somehow relaxing. 'Would you like a biscuit?' She proffered the plate.

'I would, yes, thank you,' he said, taking one. 'Primary school, you say.' He seemed very interested. 'That would be what we would term "elementary school", I take it?'

'I presume so, yes.'

'You'd be accustomed to teaching elementary reading and writing, then?'

'Oh yes, indeed.'

'I have an idea,' he said. And then he'd gone on to outline his suggestion of a possible one-on-one lesson with a select few of his men. 'I would personally choose which men and with great care, of course,' he assured her. 'And they would attend their lesson at a time when I'm here in the house. I wouldn't wish you to feel in any way threatened.'

'Well . . .' Amelia was hesitant.

'They're nice boys, many of them young, barely twenty, and many of them illiterate or semi-literate. They get their more educated friends to write letters home for them. I think it would be nice if they could learn to write one of their own, don't you?'

The idea sounded most appealing. 'Yes,' she said, 'I agree that would be very nice indeed.'

'I need to tell you though, Mrs Sanderson, just in case you don't know,' he went on, 'that the men under my command are coloured.'

'Oh.' She *hadn't* known that.

Samuel bit into the biscuit he'd forgotten he was still holding. 'By golly these are good,' he said, munching away.

A decision seemed to have been reached and Amelia worried that there might be no turning back. 'I spend an afternoon each week wrapping Red Cross parcels for the troops,' she said, chatting on needlessly and just a little nervously now, 'but I have been wanting to do more to help. Perhaps this might be a possible way I could contribute, although I'm really not sure . . .' She trailed off.

'Oh, it most certainly would be an excellent contribution,' Samuel assured her. 'You'd be offering a great service to these men, I can promise you that. Anyway, Mrs Sanderson, you just have a think on the matter and we'll talk about it a little way down the track. May I have another biscuit?'

'Please do.'

Amelia had known deep down that she'd already accepted the challenge, and in doing so she felt immensely daring.

And so on a Sunday, just the day after she'd been chatting to Grace in the back room of the AWU Hall, she was introduced to Anthony, whom she'd been informed by Captain Robinson was semi-literate.

'This is Private Anthony Hill,' Samuel said.

They were gathered once again in the sitting room to the right of the house, the one that was reserved for Samuel himself. They had agreed there would be no intrusion upon her personal quarters.

'Private Hill, this is Mrs Sanderson, who has agreed to give you some lessons. What do you say?'

'Thank you kindly, ma'am.'

Twenty-year-old Anthony Hill was a gawky young man. Relatively tall and obviously fit, he was lean and seemed all arms and legs. He also appeared painfully self-conscious, and was reluctant to look her in the eye, shuffling his feet and gazing down at the ground.

'How do you do, Private Hill,' she said.

'Yes, ma'am. How do.' Still no direct eye contact, just a flicker of a glance up and then back to the floor.

Amelia thought she'd never seen anyone so black. Not up close anyway. But of course she'd never personally met a Negro.

'Private Hill is from Louisiana,' Samuel said. 'He can read a little, and he can write his name, but that's about it. Isn't that so, Private?'

'Yes, sir.'

'I see.' Amelia realised in the pause that followed that Captain Robinson didn't intend to offer anything further. 'Let's get started, then shall we?' she said with a positivity she didn't feel.

'Excellent,' Samuel agreed, 'I'll leave you to it,' and he marched out the open door, heading for the kitchen, where he'd make himself a cup of tea and settle down with the newspaper while the lesson was in progress.

Amelia sat on one of the two hardback chairs that were pulled up either side of the card table, which they'd placed in the centre of the room. On the table was a miscellany of pencils and paper and a large notepad, together with a well-worn copy of Rudyard Kipling's *Just So Stories*. It had been Amelia's favourite book as a small child.

'Do sit down, Private Hill,' she said, indicating the other chair.

'Yes, ma'am. Thank you.' Like an obedient child, he sat, eyes still downcast.

'Captain Robinson said you can read a little?'

'Yes, ma'am. Some. Not much.'

'Very well, then.' She opened the book at the first story and pushed it across the table to him. 'Read from there for me,' she instructed, pointing at the page, 'starting with the title at the top.'

'Yes, ma'am.' Haltingly, his finger tracing each word, he started. '*How . . . the . . . Whale . . . Got . . . His . . . um . . .*' He faltered.

'Throat,' she said.

'Yes, ma'am. Throat. Thank you, ma'am.'

'Go on,' she prompted, 'how does the story begin?'

Very slowly, eyes and finger focused upon every word as he went, he continued. '*In . . . the . . . sea . . . once . . . upon . . . a . . . time . . .*' He looked up, confused. 'That's not a word,' he said, 'that's just a letter O, a big letter O.'

'Yes, that's correct. Go on.'

He looked down once again at the book and struggled on. '*O . . . my . . . best . . . um . . .*' Then he halted altogether.

'Beloved,' she said, 'yes, that's a difficult one. "O my Best Beloved" is how Mr Kipling refers to his readers.'

'Oh. Yes. Sorry, ma'am.' Again he averted his gaze guiltily, as if somehow it wasn't right to make eye contact with her.

Amelia found the young man's insecurity disconcerting. He simply could not relax in her presence.

'Don't be sorry, Private Hill, you're doing very well.' She really must do something to put him at his ease, she thought. 'May I call you Anthony?' she asked, willing him to look at her.

He did. And when she smiled reassuringly he nodded. Clearly he didn't mind at all, but he seemed nonetheless tongue-tied.

'Is that what your friends call you? Anthony?'

He shook his head.

'So what do they call you?'

'Ant,' he said, forgetting to add the 'ma'am'. 'My friends call me Ant.'

'Ant Hill.' She gave a light laugh. 'What an excellent nickname. May I call you Ant, then?'

'Yes'm.'

Well, she supposed the shortened version of 'm' was a progression from 'ma'am'.

'Go on, Ant,' she said, 'read me some more. This is a very good story.'

'. . . There . . . was . . . a . . . Whale . . . and . . . he . . . ate . . . fishes.'

For a page or so, they read on together with Amelia taking over from him during the difficult bits, particularly when the 'Stute Fish gave directions as to where and how the Whale might find the shipwrecked Mariner.

By the time they got to the part where the Whale swallowed the Mariner, Ant was thoroughly lost in the story. He couldn't wait to find out what happened next. When he arrived at a passage he could see was beyond him, he simply pushed the book across to her and when she'd read out the passage she pushed it back to him and on they went.

'So he said to the 'Stute Fish,' Ant read, barely hesitating now, 'This man is . . .' Then he turned the page, and there was the picture. He stopped and stared down at it, utterly transfixed. Here was the mighty Whale, his massive jaw wide, and here was the Mariner on his raft, swirling in the black, black water that gushed into the giant mouth and down into the giant throat. The Mariner was in the very act of being swallowed. Ant had never seen such a magnificent picture.

'Yes, that's the reward,' Amelia said, smiling, feeling rewarded herself. His reaction was exactly the same as hers had been when she'd been taught to read from this very book. 'You mustn't peek ahead and look at the pictures, Amelia,' her mother had reprimanded when she'd tried to do so, 'the pictures are a reward when you get to them.'

She stood, circling the table to stand beside him. 'I'll read you Mr Kipling's description of the drawing,' she said. 'All of his pictures have wonderful descriptions and they explain the story in great detail.'

She proceeded to do so, while Ant traced with his finger each feature mentioned, from the Mariner's jack-knife to the buttony-things on his suspenders. He laughed when she said the Whale's name was *Smiler*.

Then they went on to finish the story, Amelia reading to him the description of the second illustration also. 'Each story has two pictures,' she told him. This was the one of the Whale looking for the little 'Stute Fish who was hiding under the Door-sills of the Equator, and Ant studied it with equal wonderment. And then they came to the end.

'. . . *And that is the end of* that *tale*,' Ant read before looking up at her victoriously.

'Well done, Ant,' she said. 'That really was excellent.'

'Can we read another one?' he asked.

His eagerness delighted her, but she remained in schoolteacher mode. 'No, not until next time,' she said firmly. 'We'll practise some writing now.' She stood, moving her chair around the table to sit beside him. 'We'll write some words from the story, shall we?'

'Yes'm,' he said, taking the pencil she handed him.

Whatever inhibitions Ant had had upon his arrival had well and truly disappeared. He was perfectly comfortable now. Mrs Sanderson was his friend. And Mr Kipling was too.

Betty's plan was put into action on that same Sunday, the last Sunday in April. She and Kasey both had that Sunday clear, which meant they'd be able to get an early start. And they did, boarding the first ferry that morning bound for Magnetic Island.

A rough, choppy crossing of one hour, the wooden ferry called in to Picnic Bay and Nelly Bay and finally Arcadia, which was their destination.

She'd told him previously of her childhood school holidays spent in the family's shack at Arcadia. She'd talked of the island's beauty, of the magic of the place and the swimming and the fishing, and she'd told him also of the Aboriginal family she and her brother had befriended.

'When Tom and I were kids, we'd play with Big Bill's kids. His mob lived in bark lean-tos up in the bush not all that far from our place. We'd watch Big Bill spear fish. Gosh, he was good. He'd stand in the water still as a statue, spear raised, like this,' she demonstrated, striking a pose, 'and he'd stay dead still for as long as it took. Then *whoosh*, lightning-fast, the spear was gone and when he picked it up again there was a fish on the end.' She laughed. 'I remember the time when he tried to teach Tom how to do it – Big Bill was Tom's absolute hero – but Tom turned out to be utterly hopeless. Understandable, I suppose, he was only ten at the time.'

Betty had appeared suddenly regretful at that point. 'Come to think of it, we haven't been back to Arcadia since Tom was ten,' she said. 'We didn't go to the shack the summer before Dad left – we spent the school holidays with friends at Port Douglas instead – and now, ever since he's been gone, I don't think Mum wants to go there without him.'

Kasey had found Betty's recounting of her childhood both fascinating and enlightening. He'd never spoken so intimately with a white woman, and he wondered now whether perhaps Betty's early contact with Aboriginal people might account for her apparent lack of concern about the colour of a person's skin. Betty really didn't seem to care whether someone was black.

In actual fact Betty's, and also Tom's, acceptance of racial difference was a direct result of their father's early life spent among Pacific Islanders.

'Colour is only skin deep,' George Francis was wont to say, quoting his own parents as he did. 'People are people, good, bad or indifferent. Make no assumptions until you get to know the person inside the skin.'

Now, as the ferry approached the alluringly pretty island with its vivid turquoise water and immaculate sandy beaches, they leaned over the railings, admiring the view.

'I wonder if Big Bill's still there,' Betty said thoughtfully. But they both knew they weren't going to hike up into the bush to find out.

There were quite a few servicemen aboard the ferry; Magnetic Island was a popular choice for an R and R day trip. Along with the beautiful swimming beaches on offer, the major bays boasted a number of social gathering places in the form of picnic reserves, bars and tea rooms.

Upon disembarking, however, Betty and Kasey headed for none of these. Their intention was neither to swim, nor to socialise.

'Are you sure?' he'd asked her.

She'd been extraordinarily bold, indeed forward, when she'd proposed her plan during their walk on that evening barely a week ago, and he'd wondered if she'd thought it through properly. The prospect had excited him of course, it had excited him immensely and it still did. But much as he wanted her, he hated to think she might end up with regrets.

'Yes, I'm quite sure,' she'd said. 'We love each other, Kasey, we both know we do, and this is the natural progression of love.' She'd sounded very worldly, which was exactly her intention because she knew she was right. 'We'll take precautions though,' she'd added, 'you'll look after that side of things, won't you?'

Not only bold, not only forward, but practical also. There was obviously no point in wondering whether she might live with regrets. Betty knew exactly what she was doing.

That same night, before he returned to camp, Kasey had paid a visit to one of the many outlets, which were always lit by blue lights to ensure they were easily discernible. Venereal disease by now being rife throughout Townsville, condoms were readily available to servicemen.

Slinging her bag over one shoulder, Betty set off. 'Only about half a mile,' she said cheerily.

Hoisting his own kit bag over his shoulder, Kasey followed, and together they hiked along a track that led across the boulder-strewn headland, arriving ten minutes later at a picturesque bay with a pristine beach.

He could see several small buildings dotted about here and there, but trekking along the sand she led him past these, finally turning off the beach and up a narrow track to arrive before a cottage that had been barely visible where it sat among the trees and coastal vegetation.

'Here we are,' she announced, 'the family mansion.'

It was a modest wooden shack with a tin roof, a water tank on a stand beside it and several steps leading up to a tiny front verandah, but it looked so pretty amid the surrounding terrain of rocky outcrops and scrubland and tropical greenery.

'Why now, that is truly beautiful,' he said admiringly.

'Yes, isn't it,' she agreed. 'Come on, I'll show you around – all three rooms,' and she trotted up the steps, opening the front door, which was never locked.

Inside, they explored the house briefly, all three rooms as she'd said – the general living room and a small bedroom each side, one for the parents and one for the children.

'It was all right when I was a kid, but I hated sharing with Tom when I was a teenager,' she said, 'that was the only bad part.'

They dumped their bags on the table that sat in the very centre of the shack and she unpacked her towel, bathing togs and the sandwiches she'd brought, chatting all the while.

'There's no bathroom,' she explained, 'just a shower that comes off the water tank, but when we were here during the holidays we'd swim every day, so most of the time we'd stay salty. Well, Tom and I would anyway.' She walked to the back door and threw it open. 'And of course there's the dunny way up there,' she said, pointing to the outhouse among the trees twenty yards up the slope.

She rejoined him at the table, where he hadn't unpacked his own kit; his bathing costume and towel, and the bottle of champagne he'd purchased from a black-market contact and brought along as a special surprise. He was simply standing there, watching her every movement.

'Do you want to go for a swim?' she asked.

He thought she seemed to be talking a lot and he wondered whether she might be nervous, or perhaps even regretting her decision. 'Not really,' he said. 'Do you?'

'No.'

They stood motionless, looking at each other, both wondering who would make the first move.

It might have been presumed that Betty would be the bold one, it was she who had initiated their first kiss after all, and the consummation of their love too had been her idea. But she remained frozen. She didn't quite know why. She wasn't nervous. She knew what to expect of sex. She wasn't regretting her decision either. So why was she hesitant? Perhaps it was the awful possibility that she might be disappointed, that making love with Kasey might be the altogether forgettable experience it had been with the Australian soldier to whom she had surrendered her virginity. What if her romantic dream was on the verge of being shattered?

So Kasey made the first move. He kissed her. Not with burning passion, nor in a sexually explorative way, but as he had before, tenderly, lovingly. Then taking her in his arms, he whispered, 'Let's dance.'

And they did. In perfect unison. The dance was a foxtrot, but performed very, very slowly as they circled about the table of the little wooden shack.

'Can you hear the music?' he murmured, his lips brushing her ear, his breath fanning her neck.

'Yes,' she whispered, 'oh yes, I can.' She could hear the music with utter clarity, the piano, the string section, a full orchestra. Betty was in heaven.

They circumnavigated the table three times before he danced her into one of the bedrooms, she didn't know which one, and they kept swaying to the music while they kissed and slowly undressed each other. Then as they made love, still slowly to start with, romance steadily grew to become passion, Betty giving herself to him with a fervour that matched his own. And the music was still there, the brass section now joining in, louder and louder and bolder and bolder, rising to an almighty crescendo.

Betty's first orgasm did not disappoint.

As they lay naked side by side, breathing deeply and looking up at the exposed wooden beams of the ceiling, she realised they were in her parents' bedroom. Just as well, she thought vaguely, the bed here's bigger than the ones in our room.

Then out of the blue she heard herself say, *'Those who dance are thought mad by those who can't hear the music.'*

Kasey turned to face her, a query in his eyes.

'It's a quote my dad cut out of something and stuck up on the wall of his study years ago,' she said. 'He told Tom and me it actually means that people reject other people they don't understand. But I think it's a whole lot simpler. I think you either hear the music or you don't.'

'We sure as hell do,' he said, rising on one elbow and kissing her gently. 'We hear the same music, you and me, Betty. We're in each other's blood.'

She cuddled up to him. 'Tell me something about yourself that I don't know, Kasey,' she said. They'd talked so much, about so many things and so intimately. She knew his mother had left the marriage when he was a child, that he'd been shunted around among various aunts, and that he'd been in trouble with the law as a juvenile. But she wanted to know more. She wanted to know everything about him. 'Tell me something special,' she begged, 'something nobody else knows about you.'

'Well, for a start my name's not Kasey.'

'What?' She sat bolt upright. 'You've been lying to me?'

'No, no, I swear. My name is Kalvin Chester Davis,' he said in all seriousness. 'When I was a little boy my momma called me KC and that became Kasey and then it kind of stuck. After she left, I stayed being Kasey and I've been Kasey ever since. To everyone. Nobody except you knows, I promise.'

'Good.' She smiled happily. 'I consider that special.'

'Hey, I got a present for you.' Jumping from the bed, he crossed to the table and took the bottle of champagne from his kitbag. 'What do you say we toast to us?' he said, holding it aloft.

'Most definitely.' She jumped up herself and fetched two glasses from the cupboard over the sink. Champagne, how suitably romantic. She should have thought of it herself; she could easily have scored a bottle from Baz. But then, probably not a good idea. Baz would have twigged.

'I don't know how cold it'll be,' he said as he popped the cork.

'Who cares,' she replied.

They sat cross-legged and unashamedly naked on the bed as he poured the champagne into the cheap glass tumblers she held out to him.

'I'm sorry I don't have proper glasses,' she said.

'Who cares,' he replied.

They toasted each other and drank a full tumbler each, which on empty stomachs went straight to their heads. She offered the sandwiches, but they didn't get around to eating them; they made love again instead. Then they finished the champagne, while discussing how they would continue their affair. They didn't have regular whole days off for trips to Magnetic Island. But there was the little upstairs bedroom where she often stayed at The Brown's, she told him.

'You can reach it via the back stairs that lead to the gambling room,' she said.

Problem solved, they made love again.

They ate the sandwiches on the late-afternoon ferry back to Townsville.

CHAPTER EIGHT

The first days of May saw Townsville vibrate ever louder with the rattle of war as US and Australian forces assembled in the Pacific, preparing to halt the enemy advance. The Japanese had continued their expansion south, their aim being the invasion of Port Moresby, but they would be met by fierce opposition from the Allied forces. The Battle of the Coral Sea was to be the first naval conflict fought entirely by carrier-borne and land-based aircraft. It was also to prove the most significant naval battle ever fought off the coast of Australia.

Aunty Edie didn't know where the planes were coming *from* or where they were going *to* – some said New Guinea, some said islands in the Pacific, but she knew for sure there were plenty of them and they flew so bloody low they nearly clipped her boatsheds.

'Right over me head,' she'd say. 'Above and to Betsy, I reckon if I stuck a broom up in the air they'd hit it.'

She was exaggerating, as she tended to do when something impressed, but her boatsheds were certainly situated beneath a major flight path to and from nearby Garbutt Airfield, so, dependent upon the prevailing wind, aircraft did fly very low over her domain.

'And all *sorts* of planes, too,' she'd say, 'big ones, little ones, crikey some of them are *monsters*.'

She was right. The American bombers were massive aircraft. As many locals commented, 'It's difficult to imagine how they can get up in the air.'

But get up in the air they did. They came and they went, and very soon Aunty Edie lost all interest. She no longer looked up and exclaimed, 'Above and to Betsy!' She just went on with her work, and if she was chatting with one of her girls, as she so often was, she'd simply stop until the roar of the engine had died away enough for her to be heard and then pick up from where she'd left off. Edie never liked to yell.

Of far greater concern to Edie than the planes overhead was the water shortage that threatened. Indeed, water was becoming a matter of concern to the whole of Townsville. The wet season of 1941–42 from November to April had provided the customary tropical downpour, but water supplies were already threateningly low, and with the month of May heralding the start of the dry season, there was talk of restrictions being set in place.

'It's all you Yankees,' Aunty Edie said accusingly to her American officers when they delivered their laundry. 'You're the ones usin' up all our water. Well, don't you come cryin' to me if I can't do your laundry, 'cos if we run dry it'll be all your fault.'

'Don't you worry, Aunty,' the captain promised her, 'we'll keep your tank topped up. Can't risk losing the best laundry service in town, can we,' he added, giving her a wink that he shared with his buddies. They all liked Aunty Edie.

The captain was true to his word – her tank was topped up regularly. Edie was grateful. But it didn't stop her being critical of the situation.

'Too many people, not enough water,' she said. 'Simple as that. They're nice boys them Yankees, but too many of 'em. Too many of 'em all in one place.'

Edie was right about that, too. The population of Townsville had already doubled and was rapidly on the way to tripling in number. With such a vastly expanding populace, the town's water supply was under tremendous strain. And adding to the strain was ignorance.

From the outset, the American military had demanded clean, fresh water for its troops and it was up to the Townsville City Council to provide and regulate the supply. But the American troops had no idea of the value of water or the need to employ its use economically. In many a military barracks ablutions block, men simply dumped their clothes on the floor and turned on all the showers as a method of laundering. The City Council not unsurprisingly determined to bring this practice to a halt, and regular inspections of military camps came into play, with fines imposed upon offenders. The American Command, by now aware of the problem, supported the TCC and helped enforce the penalties incurred by its troops, but the water supply continued to be an ongoing problem, and was destined to become even more so.

'The council's approached the *Bulletin* with the idea of running daily water-usage tallies,' Pete Vickers confided to his good mate Bruce Desmond. They'd met up at the magnificent Queen's Hotel on The Strand, home to the American Officers' Club, and a popular watering hole for many when its bar was operating.

'A copper and a journo walk into a bar . . .' Bruce had said as they'd entered the place. It was a running gag between them, originally demanding a witty response, but these days producing no more than a shared smile. Both of them were Townsville boys born and bred, and now in their mid-twenties were well-respected identities in their home town. Having grown up together, Bruce and Pete were the firmest of friends.

They'd settled themselves at the bar with their beers, Senior Sergeant Bruce Desmond in civvies, having come off duty after an eight-hour shift, and Pete Vickers having left the *Townsville Daily Bulletin* offices for the day. Not that Pete had stopped work. Far from it. The American Officers' Club was a favourite hangout of his, even when the bar wasn't open. He'd hang around the lounge, drinking cups of tea and eavesdropping for any piece of inside information he might glean. And he gleaned quite a bit, although to his constant chagrin there was very little his editor would agree to print.

'You can go ahead and write it, Pete,' Jim Burnet would say in his infuriatingly placid way, 'but you'll be wasting your time. It won't see the light of day.'

And Pete would heave a weary sigh. 'Yeah, yeah, wartime censorship, I know, I know.'

'Afraid so, mate,' Jim would reply with a nod intended to appear sympathetic, although he was simply stating the case as it was. 'Got to toe the line.' And that's when Pete would want to clock him.

'So I suppose that'll soon be my job,' he now whinged to his mate as they sat at the bar, 'a daily report on bloody water usage.'

'Oh, come off it,' Bruce countered, 'they wouldn't waste their top-gun journo on a daily tally report.'

Pete's response was no more than a snort, followed by a hefty swig of his beer.

'I read your piece on the water situation,' Bruce said, 'on why it's come about, future weather predictions and how it's bound to reach a crisis point. I thought it was a hell of a good article.'

'Yeah, that's all I'm allowed to report on these days,' Pete growled. 'There's a bloody great war raging in the Pacific and I'm told to write about the level of the Ross

River weirs, a burgeoning military population and the city's bloody water supply.'

Jeez, he's in a foul mood, Bruce thought. 'Well, you've got to admit it's worthwhile, mate,' he replied in all seriousness. 'If the situation's as drastic as you said in your article then people need to be told.' Responding to Pete's further scowl he signalled the barman. 'I'll get us another beer.'

The water problem was not drastic for Aunty Edie though, thanks to her valuable connections among the American military. Edie's laundry continued to operate as always, her girls doing their daily chores, washing and ironing and hanging out clothes while aircraft roared low overhead.

Amid the ever-present backdrop of war with all its resultant privations and fears, not the least being the ominous threat of invasion, it was bizarre how everyday life did go on.

Despite restricted operating hours, The Brown's Bar continued to function as normal, the snake pen attracting punters just as it had during its pre-war days. And young Tom Francis, in between his bicycling duties as a runner for the Americans, could still be relied upon to catch and deliver frogs and mice for Val's snakes as he had done since he was ten.

And as for Amelia Sanderson, well, strangely enough, life seemed more 'normal' than it had for a long time. She was a teacher again. After years of feeling suffocated by guilt and an overwhelming sense of purposelessness, it was as if she was finally able to breathe.

Following the success of Private Anthony Hill's first lesson, Samuel Robinson had lost no time introducing Amelia to two new students from Company C. Aged nineteen and twenty respectively, young Privates Leopold

Smith and Robert Symonds, like Anthony, were to attend one-on-one classes each Sunday when Samuel could be present in the house, reading his paper over a cup of tea in the kitchen.

Sunday for Amelia promised to become a very busy day, and already she was loving every minute of it. She loved too her preparation for each pupil. Leo was completely illiterate, so she would need to approach his lessons as she might those of a five-year-old, with ABC pictures of apples and bananas and carrots. Robbie, like Ant, was semi-literate, so she intended to rely once again on the magical works of Rudyard Kipling. Her decision proved a wise one; Robbie's very first lesson was just as fulfilling as Ant's had been. The story of the Whale, the 'Stute Fish and the Mariner was a great success.

Now, after just two Sundays, Amelia no longer noticed that her students were black. She was a teacher and these her pupils, and her pupils were responding to her instruction, they were learning; this was the purpose she'd craved.

She had determined not to have favourites, but she couldn't help herself. Ant remained special. During his second lesson, they'd read Mr Kipling's next *two* stories (she hadn't been able to resist his request for another): 'How the Camel Got His Hump' and 'How the Rhinoceros Got His Skin'. Each story with its attendant pictures produced the same reaction in Ant – utter enchantment. And he shared his delight with her unashamedly. She would catch his intense gaze when she looked up from a difficult section she'd read out to him, or he would smile at her in triumph as he looked up from a piece he knew he'd read well, on all occasions meeting her eyes directly. And when they studied the difficult sections, analysing the words, writing out the letters together, Ant copying her hand, they would sit huddled side by side, so close their bodies would occasionally make contact – unconsciously – the slightest touch of a shoulder, an arm or even a thigh, which did not in the least bother either of them.

The difference in Ant mystified Amelia. He was two different people. In the company of Captain Robinson, he was just as he'd been when she'd first met him – withdrawn, insecure, eyes focused on the ground – different altogether from the animated, endearingly childlike creature who related to her so intimately in private. She could only presume his subservient manner was because Captain Robinson was his commanding officer. But this, also, she found odd. Samuel Robinson was always cordial to his men, at least he was in her company. Neither Leo nor Robbie appeared to find him overly intimidating. Was there a problem? Was something going on, something ugly? Did Ant possibly live in fear of his commanding officer? Could Samuel Robinson, who appeared a kind man, be bullying young Anthony? Amelia longed to find out, but dared not ask.

From the sheltered existence of her twenty-eight years in Townsville, from a childhood ruled by over-protective parents followed by a dysfunctional marriage, Amelia Sanderson could have had no idea of Anthony Hill's background and the world he came from. She could never have known she was the only white person in whose company Ant had ever relaxed, and that this was principally due not only to the joy of learning he was currently discovering, but to the fact she was a woman. Had he been introduced to the magic of Rudyard Kipling by a kindly male teacher with the best of intentions, just as Amelia's were, his reaction would not have been the same. Ant could relate to no white man on a personal level. It was not the way he'd been brought up. It was not the way his parents had been brought up, nor his parents' parents. Ant came from a very long line of subjugated Negroes, as did so many of his friends back home.

Amelia was correct in her surmise, however. Ant *did* have a problem and he *was* being bullied. The problem and the bully both came in the form of Captain Charles 'Chuck' Maxwell.

Since his altercation with Samuel Robinson, Chuck Maxwell had stopped singling out Kasey Davis. In Chuck's mind, this was not because his fellow officer's threat to report him had instilled fear, no, not at all. Robinson was a dirty kike who should never have attained officer rank in the first place. But Chuck was aware of his own personal trigger points and above all his level of tolerance. The anger Kasey Davis aroused in him was dangerous. The pretty nigger was far more spirited than any black had a right to be. In fact, the pretty nigger was downright insolent, and if Chuck was pushed too far he might well kill the bastard.

God Almighty, he thought, if we were back home on the plantation, it'd be my bounden duty to teach that boy a lesson he'd never forget. But here in the army it seems a nigger's allowed to show disrespect to his racial superior. It's a downright disgrace! My daddy wouldn't stand for it!

Chuck knew that if he *was* pushed too far, and if he *did* happen to kill Kasey Davis, he really *would* be in trouble. He needed a more pliant kicking boy, one who knew his place. And that boy was Private Anthony Hill.

Samuel Robinson's words had continued to rankle with Chuck, or rather the inference of Samuel Robinson's words. '*Your daddy might also know you're really not cut out for combat duty. He might feel his baby boy needs protection, that little Chuck must be looked after.*'

How could the dirty kike know it was Daddy who'd arranged his appointment to the 96th Battalion? And how could the dirty kike possibly know the goddamned reason?

'You'll be safe there, Chuck,' Sheridan Leroy Maxwell had promised his son, 'I've made sure of that. You'll see no conflict. The 96th is a non-combat battalion.'

Daddy had always looked after things. For as long as Chuck could remember, it had been Daddy who had paved the way. When, upon attending the University of Alabama, he'd failed both academically and in the field of sports, Daddy had pulled every string possible to arrange his entry to and graduation from an expensive military school in Virginia.

Back then, neither of them had anticipated he might actually be sent off to war. But when the time had arrived, Daddy had successfully looked after that, too.

'You're going to come home in one piece, Chuck, don't you worry yourself now.'

Chuck had been deeply thankful. He'd tried to pretend he was quite prepared to go into battle. He'd be happy to fight for his country, he'd declared, although the mere thought terrified him.

And Daddy, in turn, had pretended to believe him. 'I know you would, son, of course you would. But I will not have my boy put in harm's way.'

Sheridan Leroy Maxwell had tried in the early days to toughen up his only son, to instil in him the leadership qualities required of a powerful man destined to become the sixth-generation owner and ruler of the vast Elliston cotton plantation and family business. But it had soon become apparent the boy didn't have what the old man had, so the only option was to look after him. A damn shame, Sheridan had thought, that one of his two daughters wasn't a son – both girls were tougher than their brother.

'Your daddy might feel his baby boy needs protection, that little Chuck must be looked after.'

Samuel Robinson's words had cut far deeper than he could possibly have imagined. What had been intended as a patronising dig at a coward and a bully had struck to the very heart of the truth.

Chuck Maxwell had spent his entire life trying to be a copy of his all-powerful, dominant father, but he was a mere shadow, blurred at the edges, constantly trying to prove himself. And the easiest way to prove himself was to bully those who would never answer back.

So having decided Kasey Davis presented a threat to his personal level of tolerance, the obvious choice was Anthony Hill. A nigger aware of the rules. A nigger who knew that the bottom of the pecking order was his rightful place in life.

Chuck proceeded to make the young man's life hell, but he was careful not to be too public about it. Never in the presence of the young Lieutenant Platoon Commanders, precious northern boys all four; he wouldn't want word getting back to the dirty kike. And he was wary also of the interfering corporal who'd obviously reported the gun-to-the-head episode with pretty-boy Davis.

Funnily enough, the one person Chuck fully trusted happened to be a black man – First Sergeant Strut Stowers. It was no real surprise, at least not to Chuck, for here was another nigger who knew his place. *Always give the white boss what he wants*. The sergeant had the right idea. They made a good team.

By the 8th of May, the Battle of the Coral Sea was over. It had lasted just five days. The Japanese had won a tactical victory, sinking more ships than their enemy, but strategically the triumph belonged to the Allies. Port Moresby had not been taken, and, for the first time since the start of the war, the US and Australian forces had halted a major Japanese advance.

With the conflict resolved and a certain amount of detail released by the military, particularly the proud report of a victory in halting the Japanese advance, Pete Vickers was given the go-ahead by his editor to write a feature on the battle. So long as he stuck to the guidelines provided by the Department of Information, of course.

Pete did as he was instructed, and in abiding by the rules found it not much more exciting than writing about the water crisis, but by now there was a topic of even greater interest, at least to the locals. While war had been raging out in the Pacific, mayhem had erupted in the streets of Townsville. Although, sadly, Pete Vickers knew he wouldn't be allowed to report openly and honestly on this particular subject either.

It had happened only several days previously. The burgeoning unrest that had been threatening for weeks – the fights outside pubs and brothels and in backstreet alleys – had finally come to a head at the railway station. No-one knew exactly how or why the violence had broken out. A troop train had arrived from the south, nothing new about that, and soldiers, both black and white, were swarming the station when out of nowhere all hell broke loose. Perhaps it had originated from a mere passing insult or a shove in the back, who could tell, but all of a sudden and without warning, hostility was running rampant like a virus unleashed.

Amid the chaos, a number of white troops drew guns from holsters and shots rang out; in retaliation, black troops drew knives from sheaths, defending and attacking simultaneously; men fell to the ground, some shot, some clutching at stab wounds; the battle was on.

Civilians passing by in the street, including a couple with young children, ran screaming from the area; those troops with sense enough to realise the danger of the situation, both physically and from a disciplinary aspect, also beat a hasty retreat. But many remained locked together in brutal combat, shooting and stabbing and wrestling each other on the dusty railway platform.

It wasn't long before a team of US Military Police stormed the scene, their chief officer, Major Hank Henry, Provost Marshal for Townsville, barking orders and in full command.

Within minutes, Hank Henry had the situation under control, all rebellious weapons had been dropped and his men's semi-automatic rifles remained trained on the principal troublemakers. But to Hank Henry, of even greater importance than breaking up the fight was the need for the surrounding vicinity to be cleared of all civilians. There must be no witnesses to the aftermath of such blatant insubordination.

When, very quickly, the area had been cleared of prying eyes, he ordered those troops whose weapons had been drawn transported to the stockade for interrogation and appropriate disciplinary action. Those lying on the ground, wounded, bleeding or unconscious, he ordered be taken by ambulance to the military hospital.

'Regardless of their condition,' he added to his sergeant in a tone that defied any form of reply apart from a salute, a 'yes, sir', and a carrying out of the order. Hank Henry was concerned. This could well be worse than the brawl he'd attended in the red-light district a while back.

If there are any dead among these numbers, he thought, and there's bound to be, we'll have to keep it quiet. I guess we can only hope there're no white fatalities. Harder to keep a white man's death secret.

Pete Vickers had not been witness to the event. Not many civilians had. But he'd certainly heard the shots coming from the direction of the railway station, as had any number of other citizens. He'd even tried to get there, weaving through the crowded streets and ducking the traffic, his lurching gait proving no impediment, but he'd been unable to gain entry, the whole vicinity having been cordoned off by the military.

He'd wasted no time asking around, however, seeking those who might have been in the area, and he'd found several who'd witnessed at least the start of the fight before running for their own safety.

Tony Baldini had proved his most valuable find. Tony had been passing by the station and had stayed to watch from a block or so away, interested in the outcome, content in the knowledge that his wife and daughter were safely at home well out of harm's way.

'Is terrible, Pete,' he said in his ludicrously butchered, Italian–Australian accent as they sat drinking wine in the back room of his shop that night. 'The white soldiers they start the fight with their guns. The black soldiers they defend with their knives. Men they is fall to the ground. They is shot and stab, they is bleeding. Is terrible, I tell you. Some dead I think,' he said with a woeful shake of his head.

'What did the MPs do?' Pete asked.

'I don' know.' Tony shrugged. 'I don' see. Nobody see. They make all people go away. When I try to stay – you know, to see what happen – very quick I is order to leave. By golly, I tell you, Pete,' he added with dramatic emphasis and a theatrical eye roll, 'they don' just *order* me, they *march* me *off* like I have no *right* to be there.'

'Yeah, of course.' Pete nodded. 'Of course that's just what they'd do.'

And of course he brought up the subject with Jim Burnet the very next day.

'The *Bulletin* has to report *something*, for God's sake,' he said, 'there's been a bloody great fight in the centre of town between American servicemen. Shots were fired, some of the men are probably dead, civilians could have been killed or wounded, and we're supposed to say *nothing*?'

'Well, not exactly *nothing*,' Jim said in placatory fashion. 'Of course we must report there was a bit of a fracas. Far too many people are aware of the incident for us to ignore it altogether, but . . .' He left the sentence irritatingly dangling as if the answer was obvious, which to Pete it was.

'But there's to be no report of possible deaths or serious injuries.'

'Naturally. Even if such were the case, the military isn't about to release details; they want the whole business hushed up. Which of course is understandable.'

'Yes,' Pete sighed, 'understandable, of course. So I'm to write a piece saying there was a bit of a stoush, but the military has it all in hand.'

'Precisely. However, there is some further information you're permitted to report. In fact, they've asked us to publish it.'

'Oh yes?'

'Certain Negro troops will no longer be allowed into Townsville.'

Pete raised an eyebrow, but made no comment.

'Exactly,' Jim responded as if in reply to a question. 'There was some trouble with black soldiers in town several weeks back, do you recall? Close to a hundred men, I believe.'

'That's right. Unarmed troops, some of them having a brawl. I heard they were rounded up by white soldiers with fixed bayonets and loaded guns. But I wasn't allowed to report on that either, remember?'

Ignoring both the comment and the sarcasm, Jim carried on oblivious. 'It appears the same mob may be responsible for this latest disturbance, as a result of which the military has decided to take action and ban the entire battalion from the city.'

Bullshit, Pete thought, the military's decided it needs a bloody scapegoat! Blame the black troops for everything, easier that way. Bloody disgraceful.

'So we are to report,' Jim continued, 'that in the interest of keeping our streets peaceful, the coloured troops of the 96th Battalion are to be banned from Townsville.'

Aware of the anger simmering in his young ace reporter, Jim added a warning. 'The *Bulletin* is naturally to make no personal comment upon the matter.'

The American military's plan of action was put into effect as of that day. All coloured troops of the 96th Battalion were now barred from town. This did not of course apply to their white officers, who retained full access to the city. There were also changes to be made within the five companies of the battalion, including the relocation of Companies A and C, whose troops were to be immediately transferred to the Upper Ross area approximately fourteen miles south-west of Townsville, where they would be tasked with clearing and constructing three 7000-foot-long grass airfields at Kelso Field.

'I don't believe it,' Betty whispered, 'they can't do this.'

'They can and they have,' Kasey replied, also in a whisper, although being alone in the little upstairs bedroom, whispering probably wasn't necessary. 'We're banned from town, the whole lot of us.'

He'd gone AWOL in the afternoon, when after setting up camp at Kelso, the troops had been granted a meal break. He'd simply slunk away and hitched a ride into town with an obliging farmer, Willie having promised he'd do his best to cover for him. It was risky certainly, but Kasey was determined to see his girl.

'I know all about the ban,' Betty said. 'I read it in the paper, but I still couldn't believe it. You weren't involved in that fight at the station, were you?'

'Nope. I don't know anyone from our company who was. I can't answer for the rest of the guys, but I'm guessing they're using the 96th as a smokescreen so white troops won't get the blame.'

He kissed her, and as she returned the kiss they started undressing each other, slowly at first, but with increasing urgency.

'What'll we do, Kasey, what'll we do?' she whispered as, with a creak of bedsprings they lowered themselves onto the small single bunk.

'I'll find a way,' he murmured, 'don't you worry, I'll find a way.'

Since their trip to Magnetic Island, this was the third time they'd availed themselves of the little upstairs bedroom. Kasey and Betty were as hopelessly and recklessly in love as two young people could be.

'What'll happen if you're caught?' she whispered later as they lay in each other's arms, skin slick with sweat, bodies still entwined.

'I don't know,' he said, 'and I don't care.' He was only partly lying. He did know, or at least he had a pretty good idea; time in the stockade was downright nasty, everyone knew that. But he didn't care. This moment was worth whatever they threw at him.

He made it safely back to camp, hitching a ride halfway there in a US military supply truck, the two soldiers asking no questions despite the fact they were white. They were privates, both from the northern states, neither particularly fussed by the colour of a man's skin, and besides, they couldn't care less about orders that didn't apply to them.

The rest of the way, Kasey walked, sneaking undetected into camp just before nightfall. He was lucky to get away with it, he knew that, just as he knew he'd take the risk again as soon as he got the chance.

Betty was not the only person bemoaning the ban of the 96th Battalion's black troops, and surprisingly enough not the only white woman.

'So the men won't even be allowed to come into town for *tuition*?' Amelia was aghast.

'I'm afraid not,' Samuel said.

'That seems to me most unjust,' she replied, speaking her mind sharply, which was rather out of character, but Amelia had changed of late. She was stronger these days. 'That seems to me most unjust indeed.' She would sorely miss her students, particularly Ant, who had become very dear to her.

Oh poor Ant, she thought, poor, poor Ant, he'd been so looking forward to discovering 'How the Leopard Got His Spots'. Amelia was angry with the military for denying young men the opportunity to learn, yet at the same time she felt a strange urge to cry.

'I agree with you, Amelia,' Samuel said – they'd progressed to first names over the past week or so. 'I agree with you entirely. The military's decision is unjust on a great many levels, I fear.'

Already, Samuel Robinson was worried about the outcome of such a radical decision. His men's daily duty involved long hours of heavy physical toil. Their existence was akin to a prison sentence as it was – 'like doing hard labour on a chain gang', he'd heard some say, and they were right. Men working under such conditions needed something to look forward to, some form of pleasure; bars and alcohol, music and dance halls, brothels and women. To deny them all the city offered and keep them stuck out in the bush working like dogs was to invite disaster.

'Will you do me a favour, Samuel?' Amelia asked.

'Of course, if it's within my power,' he said.

'I'll just be a moment,' she promised, rising from her chair. They were seated in the kitchen having had a cup of tea. Samuel would be leaving shortly.

She disappeared, returning barely a minute later with a book in her hand. 'Will you give this to Private Anthony Hill, please?'

She sat, putting the book on the table before him. He saw that it was a copy of Rudyard Kipling's *Just So Stories*, an old copy by the looks of it, the dust jacket tattered and well-worn.

'Tell him it's a gift from me,' she said. 'Tell him he is to keep it.'

'Of course, Amelia,' he said, 'I'll be happy to do that.' He stood, picking up the book.

She stood also, her eyes remaining on the book as he tucked it under his arm.

Samuel found something very touching about her, something sad, regretful, as if she were saying goodbye to a part of her life, which perhaps she was. She'd enjoyed her return to teaching, he knew that much, she'd openly told him so. She looks as if she might cry, he thought, and suddenly he wanted to put a comforting arm about her.

'I'll see you next weekend, Amelia,' he said. With the company now based at Kelso, he would be returning to his city billet only on weekends.

Her eyes left the book to meet his and she gave him a bright smile. 'Yes, next weekend,' she said. 'I'll bake some scones to have with our tea.'

Samuel's worst fears were realised in no time at all. Discontent ran rampant throughout the base camp that had been set up by the banks of the Ross River. Even on the very first day, a powder keg of bitterness spewed forth as men protested their treatment. Why us, they demanded. What have we done? The trouble in town wasn't our fault, why should we be banned?

And then followed the work, which was more arduous than ever. The clearing of an airfield, 7000 feet long and 150 feet wide, was to be done virtually by hand with only the most basic of tools. No machinery was provided. And this was just the first of three such airfields. Morale was at its lowest point. Men were angry. The fuse had been lit.

'It's only a matter of time, Major.'

Samuel sought the assistance of Major Hank Henry in pleading the case for an alternative solution to the ban placed on the troops of the 96th.

'A cauldron of unrest is brewing out there at Kelso, and you can't blame the men. They're overworked to the extreme and then denied access to any sort of leisure that might relieve the tension. We have to provide them with some form of recreation . . .'

'And you expect the United States Army to set up a *brothel*!' Hank's expression was a mix of outrage and amusement, albeit of the sardonic kind. To him, the idea was preposterous. 'I grant you, a blind eye is turned in the interests of serving troops' basic male urges, Captain, but I hardly think the military will embrace the idea of going into the prostitution business itself.'

'Oh come on now, Hank.' Samuel dropped formalities. They were alone in Hank's office at the barracks and they knew each other well enough. Let's skip the sarcasm and get down to business, he thought. 'I didn't mean a brothel exactly, I meant a form of club on the outskirts of town, a place where the men can unwind with a beer, some music – some girls to dance with, yes, but not necessarily prostitutes. A place where they can relax, for God's sake.'

'You want the US Army to fund a club for non-combat Negro servicemen?'

'Exactly.'

'And you expect me to take this cockamamie scheme to HQ?'

'All I'm saying is it wouldn't hurt to ask,' Samuel replied tightly. 'We're inviting a whole heap of trouble if we don't do something.'

'Oh. *We* are, are we?' Hank sneered. 'You're speaking on behalf of the American military, I take it?'

'Yes, I believe I am.' Samuel met the man's gaze fearlessly. 'I believe we'll pay a price if we don't address the needs of these men.'

Hank couldn't help being just a little impressed. His aggression rattled people as a rule, but apparently not Samuel Robinson.

'Look, Samuel,' he said reasonably enough, 'I'm not going to take this idea to HQ – if I did they'd laugh in my face, but I'll tell you what I'll do. If you can get some local business to set up a place out of town – call it a club, call it a brothel, what you will – and if it's run in an orderly fashion, then I think I can assure you that *we* will turn a blind eye.' He smiled as he emphasised the 'we', but it wasn't a humorous smile. Hank Henry was not known for his humour.

'Well, I guess that's a start,' Samuel said.

'I must warn you though, Captain,' Hank continued, 'should you be able to pull off such an enterprise, *we* – and in this case I mean *I* – will be watching things very, very closely.'

'Of course.'

So where to from here, Samuel wondered as he left Hank Henry's office.

As it turned out, Rupe was the one who provided the answer. Upon his return to Kelso, Samuel summoned

Corporal Rupert Barrett to the Company C officers' tent in order to tell him the outcome of his meeting with the provost marshal. The two men had discussed the troops' predicament in some detail previously, the corporal having voiced his own worries about the men's morale. Both had agreed it would be an excellent idea if the military could be persuaded to provide some recreational centre for the troops of the 96th.

When Rupe arrived at the tent, young Percy Owen was tapping away at his typewriter in the corner, but Chuck Maxwell was nowhere to be seen. Samuel had known this would be the case; Maxwell was on duty out in the field. Indeed, had the man been present Samuel would have chosen to meet up with Rupert Barrett elsewhere. Any discussion of a solution to the current dilemma was met with scorn by Chuck Maxwell. A scorn that Samuel found disgusting.

'They're niggers,' Chuck had said when Samuel had first brought up the subject, 'they're here to work, that's what niggers are for.'

Rupe listened patiently as his commanding officer recounted the meeting he'd had with Major Hank Henry. Then he said just two words. 'Val Callahan.'

'What?' A pause. Samuel was confused.

'Val Callahan, she's the one you should see.'

'You mean the woman who runs The Brown's Bar?'

Young Percy Owen looked up from his typewriter. He knew The Brown's Bar and the snake pen and Val. He'd been there himself one night when she'd pulled a shotgun on a couple of troublemakers and marched them out onto the street.

'Yep, that's the one,' Rupe said. 'Val doesn't just *run* the place, you know, she *owns* it.'

'But The Brown's Bar's in town,' Samuel replied, still confused, 'off limits to our guys. What use could she be to us?'

'For starters, she'd be sympathetic to our cause. Val's a good buddy. But she wouldn't just be doing us a favour, I can assure you, Captain.' Rupe grinned. 'Val's first and foremost a businesswoman who knows a good deal when she sees one. Our guys have money, lots of money by Australian standards, and stuck out here in the bush like they are they got nowhere to spend it. I reckon Val would like the sound of that. In fact, I reckon if anyone could get a club up and going outside of the city limits, it'd be Val Callahan.'

'Then I'd better pay a visit to The Brown's Bar,' Samuel said.

'I think that would be a good idea, sir.'

Val was most certainly sympathetic to the cause. 'It's criminal,' she declared. 'To deny your hard-working men the pleasures they've rightly earned is downright bloody criminal.'

She also recognised in Samuel's proposition the possibility of a highly profitable business enterprise. 'Leave it with me, Captain,' she said. 'I'll see what I can do.'

'Thank you, Mrs Callahan.' He shook the hand she offered. 'Without sounding pushy,' he said apologetically, 'might I add that speed is of the essence. My men are going crazy out there.'

'Understood,' she replied. 'And call me Val. I haven't been Mrs Callahan for years.'

When he'd gone, she sent for Baz and immediately called a meeting in her office.

'You come too, Betty,' she said, leaving Jill in charge of the bar. 'I think you'll want to be in on this,' she added drily as they walked up the stairs.

When the three of them were settled, she told Baz and Betty of Captain Robinson's proposition.

'What a marvellous idea,' Betty exclaimed, her face lighting up, 'we'll take the piano to the club and I'll play for them.'

'Yes, that's what I thought you might say,' Val remarked, once again drily.

Betty just offered a radiant smile by way of reply.

Val knew exactly what was going on between Betty and Kasey. She was aware of each tryst they'd shared in the little upstairs bedroom and had made only one comment to the girl. 'I hope you're being careful, lovey,' she'd said. To which Betty had boldly replied, 'Course I am,' and they'd left it at that.

You can't stop young love, Val thought. There's no point in trying. She was actually pleased that if they could get this club going it would offer an opportunity for the lovers to meet. Better than Kasey going AWOL anyway, she thought. If the kid tries it again he's bound to be caught.

'We'll need to line up some girls as dancing partners for the men,' she said with a meaningful glance at Baz.

'Easy enough,' he replied with a cocky grin, 'a few of the girls who work at Edie's laundry'd be up for the task.'

'Yes,' Val nodded, she was aware some of Edie's girls moonlighted as hookers, 'but they don't all have to be on the game. We want this to be a legitimate club, not just a brothel.'

'Sure.' Baz's response held a touch of the 'nudge-and-a-wink'.

Betty's eyes darted between the two, although not wishing to appear naïve she was careful to disguise her surprise. So she'd be playing piano in a brothel. Goodness, she'd better not let her mum know. Then she smiled to herself. Mind you, there's a heck of a lot Mum doesn't know already, she thought.

'I mean it, Baz,' Val said in all seriousness, 'I want this club to be run along legit lines as much as possible. Good booze, good music, singing and dancing, a social club, you get my drift?'

'Of course,' Baz replied, matching her seriousness, although a slightly arched eyebrow was a bit of a giveaway.

'The main problem is the venue,' Val said with a frown. 'Where the hell are we going to put this club?'

'Don't give it another thought, Boss.' Baz leaned back in his chair, hands behind head, the picture of confidence. 'I've got the perfect place. Just five miles out of town. We'll need a hundred quid up front and it'll be ours for the taking.'

Baz had a plan.

CHAPTER NINE

'There you go, mate.' Baz slapped a wad of ten-pound notes down on the kitchen table. 'A hundred quid up front, more than enough to get you and Vera and the kids settled down south. What do you say?'

Ned Parslow stared at the money sitting on the scarred old wooden table. He and his wife rarely saw this amount in cash. The payments for their produce usually came in the form of a cheque, a long-overdue cheque at that, and after being banked the sum was immediately paid out to their various debtors with cheques of their own.

Vera, seated beside her husband, grabbed the notes. 'I'll look after that, love,' she said.

'No, no, hang on a minute,' Ned protested, but it didn't stop his wife clutching the wad of money to her chest. Vera wasn't about to give up easily.

'What are these people who want to hire the place gonna do with the actual property?' Ned asked Baz. 'You say they want to rent the buildings, but what about the farm? I won't have my place going to rack and ruin.'

'No, no,' Baz exclaimed, holding his right hand up in the air as if swearing an oath, 'the farm will be well looked after. The tenant will retain your hired help, Johnno, and pay him his customary wage.'

'Johnno can't run the farm on his own,' Ned said scathingly, 'Young Johnno's a moron. He can only take orders.'

'The tenant is prepared to pay an overseer's wage and also, if necessary, another worker,' Baz said smoothly. This was something he hadn't been prepared for, but upon quick consideration it was certainly worthwhile. It would be to his advantage to maintain the farm. 'You'll be receiving regular monthly rental payments, Ned,' he said, flashing a winning smile to Vera in the knowledge that he already had her on side, 'and by the time all this terrible threat of invasion is over, you'll come home to a flourishing farm, I can promise you. What's wrong with that?'

'Nuthin', Ned,' Vera broke in with the voice of authority, 'bloody nuthin'. We get the kids down to Brisbane right now, you hear me? Soon as we can, within the next couple of days. Let the Japs invade, let the yellow bastards do whatever they're gonna do, but our kids'll be safe.'

Baz left the Parslow property a half-hour later. It had been as easy as he had known it would be. But there was hard work to follow. As soon as the family had departed, there was a farmhouse and outbuildings that needed to be cleared, if not gutted, and adjustments made.

Val came out and inspected the place, she and Baz discussing in detail its merits and shortcomings. The positioning was ideal, just five miles from town and less than ten miles from Kelso, and the conversion was not impossible.

It was a fine autumn morning and the two of them walked about the property, which was attractively situated near the banks of the Ross River, examining the buildings and the layout.

The farmhouse itself, a rambling affair that had been passed down through several generations of Parslows before ending up with Ned, would serve as the club, they decided. Its rooms would be cleared and converted into bars and lounges. The floor of the large barn nearby would be laid with decking and the building converted to a dance hall. And the stables . . . well, the purpose the stables would serve was fairly obvious to them both.

The stables consisted of six conjoined stalls, and had been built by Ned's father in the days when horses had done all the work, but the Parslows hadn't kept horses for years, so the stalls had been used purely for storage.

'We clear out all the junk,' Baz said as they wandered the stables, closely examining every one of the stalls, 'give each a scrub-down, shove in some flooring and a bunk and . . . *voilà*,' he said with a theatrical wave of his hand.

'Not much privacy and hardly soundproof,' Val remarked, eyeing the wooden partitions that separated each conjoined stall, only around six feet in height and stopping well short of the stable's ceiling.

'So?' Baz grinned suggestively, 'some sound effects from next door might add to the eroticism, wouldn't you say?'

Val gave a mirthless snort. 'Yes, you might be right. I don't suppose soldiers after a quick fuck'll be all that fussy about privacy.'

And yet, she could well remember those shy boys, some of them virgins, whom she'd serviced all those years ago. They wouldn't have liked this set-up at all, she thought. God, they'd been sweet boys, those young ones. Several had even been brought along by their father, who considered it time they lost their cherry. She smiled at the memory; of course the dads had been clients of hers, too.

Ah well, she told herself, looking about at the stables, beggars can't be choosers. 'Yep, this'll do,' she said.

'And there are the bedrooms in the farmhouse,' Baz suggested, 'we can . . .'

'Nope,' she cut him short, 'they'll be reserved for poker. We'll get rid of the beds and set up a card table in each room. The brothel remains strictly out here, and we don't publicise it.'

'Why not?' Baz was puzzled. There was big money in brothels, as Val well knew.

'Because to publicise the place as a brothel would call a lot of attention from the authorities, both military and civic,' she firmly replied. 'Like I told you before, Baz, the club is to be legit, the hookers are a sideline. We'll have girls here for the men to dance with and there'll be a few of them willing to make themselves available if the blokes want to fork out a bit more for a fuck. Do you get my drift?'

'Sure, Boss,' he backed off immediately, 'sure, whatever you say.'

Under Baz's instruction, the team of workers he'd organised set about clearing anything and everything unnecessary from the house and the barn and the stables, the whole lot being unceremoniously dumped into the tractor shed.

Johnno, the young, ginger-haired, hired hand, looked on in horror. The whole place was being gutted – what would Ned say? But it wasn't up to him to interfere, he told himself. Baz had upped his wages, paying cash in advance what's more, and Baz had told him to employ another worker to help him. A worker who was to be paid the same wages he'd previously received himself as the hired hand. Which now made him the boss. A foreman no less.

Seventeen-year-old Johnno lived with his widowed mother and younger brother on the outskirts of town, travelling to and from the farm on his bicycle as he had for the past three years. He'd never before been given such responsibility, but he was determined to meet the challenge. He intended to hire his brother, Mick, who was fifteen and having recently left school was looking for work as a labourer. Mick was a very good choice, Johnno decided, because Mick wasn't afraid of hard yakka. And their mum'd be pleased too, another wage coming into the house.

Johnno was very happy with the current arrangement. He just wished they weren't wrecking the place. Ned could be scary when he was angry.

Upon being informed of the proceedings, Samuel Robinson offered Val the assistance of a work team from Company C, a work team comprised of those volunteers willing to offer their R and R time on a roster basis. There were many such volunteers as it turned out. The troops were only too keen to pitch in and help with the construction of a Negro Servicemen's Club. Besides, what else did they have to do with their R and R time?

Samuel was pleased. The creation of the club would give his men a sense of purpose and might hopefully defuse a potentially dangerous situation as tensions continued to mount at Kelso.

Chuck Maxwell did not in the least agree. Chuck Maxwell found the whole exercise intensely irritating.

'You're babying them, Robinson,' he sneered. 'Who the hell builds a country club for niggers! You're weak as piss, you really are.'

Samuel made no reply.

During his last weekend visit to town, as they'd sat eating scones and drinking tea in the kitchen, Samuel had been most gratified by Amelia's response to the note he'd promised to deliver.

'From young Private Hill,' he said, handing her the envelope, 'a thank you for the book you gave him, I believe.' That's what Rupert Barrett had said anyway when he'd delivered the note to the officers' tent.

'Oh my goodness,' Amelia exclaimed as she looked down at the envelope, upon which was very clumsily written, 'Mrs Sanderson'. 'Oh my goodness,' she repeated in breathless amazement, 'Ant wrote this himself.'

'So his corporal tells me, yes,' Samuel said.

She opened the envelope and took out the note. Watching her closely, he could see she was touched as she read its brief content, several times over, it seemed.

'How lovely,' she murmured finally. She looked up at him and smiled.

Such a sweet smile, Samuel thought. Then, looking down once again at the note, she read it out loud to him.

'*Dear Mrs Sanderson,*

'*Thank you for the book you gave me. I am reading "How the Leopard Got His Spots".*

'*Yours sincerely,*

'*Anthony Hill (Ant)*

'He wrote every single word himself,' she said, showing Samuel the note with its crude, half-written, half-printed scrawl. 'But the arrangement and the wording itself, particularly the "yours sincerely",' she added, 'how could Ant possibly have come up with that?'

'I believe he had some helpful suggestions from his corporal, Rupert Barrett,' Samuel said. 'In fact, Corporal Barrett told me he's helping young Anthony read the book, just as you did.'

'Oh how wonderful.' Amelia's smile this time was one of pure joy. 'How absolutely wonderful.'

'Yes, as I mentioned, the men often help each other,' Samuel said. 'Many of the educated write letters home for the illiterate and teach them how to sign their own names. It's most heartening to see.'

'I'm sure it would be, Samuel,' she replied, still with that joyous smile. 'I'm sure it would be most heartening to see, for I find it most heartening to hear of such a thing. Men teaching literacy skills to those less fortunate. How splendid.'

He found her pleasure unbelievably rewarding, which seemed to him rather strange.

The construction of the out-of-town Negro Servicemen's Club had not gone unnoticed by a number of prominent locals, including Senior Sergeant Bruce Desmond and his mate Pete Vickers.

'The old Parslow farm,' Pete said as they sat in their customary corner of the bar at the Queen's Hotel. 'Ned's taken his family and shot through to Brisbane and Val Callahan's converting the place to a club.' As usual, Pete had made it his business to find out all he could.

'Really?' Bruce was surprised. 'I presumed the US military was footing the bill.'

'No, no,' Pete scoffed, 'the military doesn't give a stuff about its black soldiers, that's why the poor bastards were pissed off out of town.'

'Well, maybe it was for the best,' Bruce said circumspectly. 'I mean, you know, after all the trouble there's been.'

'Don't believe that shit you saw in the *Bulletin*, mate.'

'Why not? You wrote it.'

'I wrote what I was told to write.' Pete downed the remnants of his beer and leaned forward, lowering his voice in conspiratorial fashion, but speaking passionately nonetheless. 'The military's putting the blame on the black troops as a scapegoat, Bruce. The whole thing's a cover-up to get their white soldiers off the hook. Christ alive, how I'd like to report that!'

Pete, as always, found immense relief in unburdening himself to his old mate, just letting it all pour out the way he knew he could. Bruce was the one person he could trust and with whom he could share the truth, or at least the truth as he saw it.

'I'm going to do it, you know,' he said, 'I've made a decision.'

Bruce was mystified. 'You've made a decision about what?'

'I'm going to report on the injustice being perpetrated upon the coloured troops of the 96th Battalion,' Pete announced grandly, although he was careful to keep his voice down. 'Bugger them all, I'm going to write the truth about what's been going on here. Men barred from town, deprived of their liberty, worked like bloody dogs, and all because they're black. The army wouldn't treat their white soldiers like this. It's bloody shameful.'

'If that's the case then I agree with you, Pete,' Bruce said, not doubting his mate's veracity for a minute, 'but who'd publish such a report?'

'OK, I'm going to *write* the report,' Pete corrected himself, 'but one day I'll get it out there, I promise you.' Even as he spoke an idea occurred. 'I might send it overseas, to England perhaps. War censorship laws aren't as strictly enforced in Britain as they are here. But it'll get out there, I'll make bloody sure it does.'

'Good on you.' Bruce admired Pete's principles, he always had. His principles and his passion and his pursuit of the truth. Pete was a bloody fine journo. 'Good luck to you, mate.'

Only several days later, something happened that rattled Bruce Desmond. And the first person he thought of was his mate Pete Vickers. This was surely something that should go in Pete's unauthorised report, he thought. If what Charlie said was true, then this was something the world should know about.

It was late afternoon when he phoned Pete at the *Bulletin*. 'Get yourself down to the police station,' he said urgently, 'and make it quick. I'm going to have to ring the US military, but I'll wait until after you've heard Charlie's story.'

'What's happened?'

'You reckon there's a cover-up with the black soldiers of the 96th? Just wait till you hear what Charlie has to say.'

Charlie Phipps, semi-retired, was a railway porter. A weathered man in his early sixties, he hadn't always been a porter. In fact, he'd once been assistant station master, but upon retirement he'd been so loath to leave his precious trains that the transport department had humoured him and kept him on as a part-time porter. So Charlie knew everything there was to know about trains and freight cars and the cargo they carried. And he knew how to use his knowledge to his own advantage.

Charlie had no trouble at all justifying his actions. His petty thieving was necessitated by war, and no more than anyone else would do under the current circumstances if they were offered half a chance. Given the drastic shortage of supplies in Townsville – for civilians anyway, everything being gobbled up by the American military – he considered it only fair to nick whatever possible in the way of tinned and packaged goods and any items that might fetch a price on the black market. He had his principles though. He only ever stole from US Army supplies and he was never overly greedy. The odd crate or box that disappeared from a freight car wouldn't be missed among the massive supplies that arrived and departed Townsville Railway Station.

He'd just knocked off work that afternoon when the train had arrived from Mount Isa. Only a few passengers alighted – it was principally a freight train – so he thought it might be worth taking a peek.

He waited until the coast was clear before sauntering up to one of the freight cars. He was still in uniform so his actions would hardly look suspicious. Sliding open the freight car's door, he stepped inside, took a quick furtive glance about the platform, then closed the door behind him.

It was dark inside the freight car, impossible to see a thing as his eyes adjusted from the glare of outside. But he turned on the powerful torch he always carried hooked to his belt and shone its beam directly onto one of the many long wooden boxes that were set out in a line.

Stamped on the top of the box, he could clearly make out the words, 'Property of US Armed Forces'. Excellent, just as he'd expected, an American shipment of supplies.

Then the realisation hit him. Good grief, he thought, it's a coffin. He looked about in amazement. They're *all* coffins. What on earth is the army doing with empty coffins, he wondered, are these being shipped off to some battle zone or something?

He kicked the nearest coffin with the toe of his boot, a healthy kick, but the sound that resulted was not what he'd expected. That thing's not empty, he thought. He kicked another one, and then another. The result was the same. They must be using these coffins to ship military equipment, he thought. Ammunition maybe. That's a bit odd.

Charlie wouldn't dare steal ammunition from the military, but curiosity got the better of him and he decided to take a look. Unsheathing the knife he carried for this very purpose, he put down his torch and set about prising up the lid, very carefully so as not to leave traces of damage. And when he'd successfully jimmied open the entire lid, he lifted it aside with equal care and placed it on the top of the next coffin. Then he picked up his torch.

'Oh, Jesus,' he breathed as looked back at his work, 'oh, sweet Jesus . . .'

In the beam of torchlight, he was staring down at a dead Negro soldier.

Charlie felt panic rise. 'Shit,' he muttered, 'shit, shit, shit.' He wished he'd never opened the bloody thing. But what was he to do? He had to tell somebody. He stared about the freight car, focusing his torch on coffin after coffin, the frantic movement of its beam mirroring his panic. Did all of these things have a bloody body inside? What do I do, he thought frantically, what do I do, who do I tell?

The coppers, he decided, I'll go to the coppers. He sure as hell wasn't going to go to the military, they'd twig he'd been tampering with their property. And the sergeant was a good bloke. Bruce Desmond would know what to do.

Charlie needed to get out of that freight car and as soon as possible. He left without even resealing the lid of the coffin, just slid it back on top, he didn't want to look at that dead bloke again. But he did think to slide the door closed behind him. Then he fled to the police station.

By the time Pete arrived, Charlie had calmed down. Bruce Desmond was a good cop, always a calming influence when panic threatened.

'Tell Pete what you told me, Charlie,' he instructed.

And Charlie did, although in a less hysterical manner than he'd recounted his story to Bruce.

Pete listened, fascinated, without saying a word. Then when Charlie had finished, the interrogation began.

'How many coffins were there?' he asked.

'Don't know,' Charlie said, 'didn't count.'

'And were there bodies in all of them?'

'Don't know,' Charlie said, 'didn't open them.'

'But they all seemed to be weighty,' Bruce chimed in. 'Charlie kicked several of them, and he reckons they weren't empty.'

'He said the train arrived from Mount Isa?' Pete directed the query to Bruce, but it was Charlie who answered.

'Isa, that's right, come in about forty minutes ago now.'

Pete nodded. There was a big contingency of black American labour troops in the mining area of Mount Isa. They were employed in the same thankless manner as the

96th Battalion, heavy labour, building airstrips and military installations. What on earth had happened, he wondered.

'I have to ring the military,' Bruce said to Pete, 'do you want to stick around?'

'Bloody oath I do,' Pete replied, 'they won't like it, but I'm not leaving until we've got a few answers.'

Bruce smiled. He'd known the response would be just that. 'You're here because we're mates and you just dropped in to see me,' he said warningly as he picked up the phone and dialled the office of Major Hank Henry.

'Naturally.' Pete returned the smile. 'Popped in to say hello, purely coincidental.'

As was to be expected, Major Hank Henry was not at all happy about the presence of Pete Vickers, whom he knew all too well to be a reporter with the *Daily Bulletin*.

'Sorry, sir,' Bruce apologised, 'but Pete was already here when Charlie arrived in an absolute panic and poured out his story. Didn't seem much point asking him to go now that he knows all about it.'

Gruffly accepting the premise, or rather unable to refute it, Hank listened as for a third time Charlie recounted his experience. Although this time around, Charlie was careful to leave out the fact that he'd prised open one of the coffins.

The major appeared a little thrown at first by the discovery not only of the coffins, but of the body that was apparently visible in one that had suffered damage. Quickly regaining his composure, however, he was in no mood to be messed with.

'You were not authorised entry to that freight car,' he said icily to Charlie. 'Those contents are the property of the US Armed Forces.'

'Charlie was only doing his job, Major,' Bruce came quickly and smoothly to Charlie's defence, 'checking the carriages for damage to cargo and the like.' He had wondered himself, as had Pete, what Charlie was doing opening one of the coffins, but he hadn't pursued that line and was not about to do so now.

Hank knew it was useless trying to bluff things out, so instead he barked an order to all three men. 'You will say nothing of this, not a word to anyone. This whole unfortunate business is a military secret, and in the interest of public safety and security it must remain so.' He looked at each one of them directly, his eyes boring into theirs. 'Do you understand me?'

The three nodded, Bruce answering for all. 'Yes, sir,' he said.

Hank turned to Pete. 'This applies particularly to you, Mr Vickers. You do realise, don't you, that if you attempt to print one word about this, the military will close down the *Daily Bulletin*.'

'Yes, sir, I'm aware of that. Just as I'm aware, should I write this story, my editor would refuse to publish it. The *Daily Bulletin* abides by the censorship laws at all times.'

'I'm glad to hear that.'

The major appeared about to leave, but Pete wasn't prepared to let him go without a few more answers.

'Off the record, Major, may I ask how these men died? They came from Mount Isa, I believe, but there's been no conflict in that area. Was there an illness, a contagion of some kind?'

Hank Henry seemed momentarily torn, as if he might like to respond, but was so unaccustomed to answering questions, he didn't quite know how.

'Was there perhaps some military accident, sir?' Pete asked, in all apparent innocence, but knowing it would pique the major. He was right.

'The military is in no way responsible for this unfortunate event,' Hank said brusquely, 'the men brought it upon themselves.'

'Which men, sir?' Pete asked the question gently, knowing the major was on the brink of telling the truth.

'The 610th Battalion, C Company.' Hank shook his head in genuine sympathy. 'Poor bastards.'

'What happened, Major?'

'Apparently, the men were making their own hooch, brewing it in disused drums that were surplus from the mines. They didn't know the drums had once housed cyanide that must have seeped into the seams. They were killed drinking their own home brew, Mr Vickers. A tragic outcome, but no fault of the military.'

'How many men?'

'I don't know to be honest,' Hank replied, 'I haven't been informed as yet. But we'll soon find out when I get the full report and when we count those bodies.'

'And what will happen to the men, sir?'

'The coffins will be unloaded from the train under the cover of darkness in order to avoid attracting notice,' Hank replied curtly. 'It is imperative for army morale that this whole sad, wretched business remains under wraps. Do I make myself clear?'

'Yes, sir,' Pete said. Abundantly clear, he thought. You know bloody well I wasn't asking about the coffins. I was asking about the *men*.

'That will be all, gentlemen,' Hank said. 'Bear in mind my instructions, not one word.' And he marched out of the police station.

All the questions he'd wanted to ask the major churned through Pete's brain as he sat in the lounge of the American Officers' Club, sipping his cup of tea, writing his unauthorised report and cursing the bar for having closed so early.

What is the US Army going to do with these men, Major? Are the bodies going to be buried here in Townsville's military graveyard? *Under the cover of darkness* of course. And he kept coming up with answers to his own questions. No, I doubt that, he thought. They'll be whisked away somewhere. But where, Major? Will the men's bodies be returned to their families? No, I wouldn't think so, he told himself, too much trouble when there's a war to be fought. Will they perhaps be taken to Hawaii and buried on American soil, is that the intention, Major?

Finally, he gave up torturing himself with questions. We'll never know, he thought. We'll never know how many of the poor bastards died, and we'll never know what happened to their bodies. But by hell, we'll know whose fault it was, I'll make sure of that.

From then on, Pete's pencil couldn't move fast enough across the page of the notepad he was scribbling on. One phrase of Hank Henry's echoed in his mind above all else. *No fault of the military*, Hank Henry had said. Well, bullshit, Major, Pete thought. The military is entirely responsible for 'this unfortunate event' as you call it. These men didn't bring this fate upon themselves. *You* did. The Army of the United States of America is directly responsible for the deaths of these soldiers.

You stick men out in the desolate region that's Mount Isa, an inland mining area, a desert of blistering heat and flies where insanity prevails even in peacetime, and you make them work like beasts with no reward for their labours. You give them none of the escape you afford your white soldiers. Under such conditions, why *wouldn't* they make hooch, for God's sake? Anything to alleviate the boredom and the misery. These men, suffering this miserable existence you inflict upon them, commit one small and totally understandable act that results in their deaths, and it's *not your fault*?

Pete's pencil was literally flying across the paper in an effort to keep up with his thoughts.

And the same thing's happening right here in Townsville. No, he corrected himself, not right here in Townsville. Right outside Townsville where you've marooned those men of the 96th Battalion, where you're treating them as something less than human. You're creating a potential disaster and when it blows up in your face, I presume that will also be *not your fault*!

The passion Pete was pouring into his 'unauthorised report', overly dramatic though it may have sounded, was very close to the truth. The frustration of the men at Kelso was reaching boiling point. The only thing preventing a total eruption was the creation of the Negro Servicemen's Club and the thought that when it was completed the men would have a place of their own.

With the renovations well underway, Baz set about lining up hookers. Val's idea that the club be legit and the hookers just a sideline didn't sit all that well with him. There was more money than ever in brothels these days, the Yanks' sexual appetites were insatiable and their cash supply endless.

Never one to openly disobey the boss, however, Baz was subtle in the way he went about things. He was lining up girls to dance with the troops, just as Val had instructed he should. But he was making sure that the girls he lined up were accustomed to going that step further and, if not already on the game, were those who could be easily enticed.

'Yeh, all right by me, Baz,' Edie said. 'Any of my girls wanna work after hours, no skin off my nose. So long as they get the laundry done before they knock off.'

Aunty Edie had been his first port of call. He and Val had agreed they'd seek brown girls as dance partners for the troops, and he also knew several of Edie's girls moonlighted.

As it eventuated, the other Palm Islander girls who

gathered at Edie's were also keen to sign up for the club dances. The idea of earning extra money for just dancing with soldiers was irresistible. Their innocence didn't bother Baz in the least. He didn't issue instructions, or even offer a warning. They'll make the jump, he thought, I'll bet my last quid on it. They'll take the lead from their more sophisticated black sisters and be on the game in a matter of days.

One of the most eager among the girls was Edie's own daughter, Jill. Jill wasn't even attracted by the money. Jill would have danced every single night of the week for nothing if she had the chance.

Val fronted Baz; she wasn't having a bar of it. 'Did you ask Jill to sign up for the dances?' she demanded.

'Nup,' Baz said, and he wasn't lying. He hadn't seen any value in approaching Jill. 'She must have heard about it from her mum. I've lined up a good team of Edie's girls.'

'Well, I won't have Jill being a part of it,' Val said firmly.

'Why not?' Baz decided to play her at her own game. 'You said yourself, the club's to be legit. Most of the girls will be there to dance with the men, that's what you said. The hookers are just a sideline.'

Val scowled. She knew what Baz was up to. I wouldn't trust you as far as I could spit, mate, she thought, you'd be quite happy to throw that girl to the wolves, wouldn't you.

'Jill's too young and too innocent,' she snapped.

'You're being a bit over-protective, Val.' For once Baz spoke his true mind. 'The girl's twenty, she's got to learn to fend for herself some time or other.'

'Oh yeah,' Val sneered, 'and you'd know all about that, wouldn't you, Baz.'

But strangely enough, when she sought out Edie's support, she was met with the same response.

'Girl's gotta learn,' Edie said with a shrug when Val insisted they forbid Jill from attending the dances.

'For God's sake, Edie, she's a *virgin*.'

'Yeh.' Edie nodded, unperturbed. 'In my day, girls is married at fourteen, fifteen, having babies at sixteen, just like me. Jill gotta learn someday.'

'But not this way, Edie. Not this way.' God, the girl could be raped by one of the Yankee soldiers, Val thought, or she might even end up on the game. Anything could happen.

'Whatever,' Edie answered with another careless shrug. She appeared not remotely concerned. Growing up, in Edie's mind, was something a girl simply had to do. Her Jill had had it pretty lucky so far.

Val was forced to give in. Jill would be permitted to attend the dances, a fact that delighted Betty.

'We'll watch each other's backs, Val,' Betty breezily assured her, 'we always do. It'll be great fun.'

Am I the only one out of step here, Val wondered.

At Kelso, the burgeoning unrest and dissatisfaction was taking its toll on one man possibly more than others. Chuck Maxwell did not have the incentive his troops had in the building of the Negro Servicemen's Club. In fact, the creation of the club was a source of such irritation to Chuck that he found himself plagued by an ever-increasing sense of injustice. How dare these niggers be offered the same rights afforded a white man! A club of their very own? Women to dance with? A brothel?

The more Chuck dwelt upon the subject, the more his irritation became anger and the more he seethed. He was witnessing the desecration of a system he'd known all his life, a system based upon racial superiority. Niggers were here to serve, not be pampered. This presumption of an equality that did not exist disgusted him.

And the greater the build-up of pressure in Chuck, the more he took it out on Private Anthony Hill. As if to preserve his very sanity, Chuck Maxwell needed the release of a whipping boy.

Kasey Davis was witness to one such episode. Coming upon the scene, he watched unobserved from some distance as Maxwell goaded Ant.

Having ordered him to stand to attention, Chuck was now physically circling the young man, calling him names, deriding him mercilessly. Nothing new about that, Kasey thought, Chuck Maxwell often addressed men this way, shaming them for some supposed misdemeanour, usually of his own invention. And Ant was taking it all, staring directly ahead, ensuring he made no eye contact with his white officer. Nothing new about that either, Kasey thought, most men reacted that way, particularly those from the south. It irked him to see Strut Stowers though, standing nearby, impassive; a traitor to your own kind, Kasey thought with loathing.

Then, having worked himself into a frenzy of vitriol, Maxwell shoved the young man in the back so forcefully Ant fell to his knees.

Just like the bastard did to me, Kasey thought. Any minute the gun will be drawn and held to Ant's head. He stepped forward. And that's when Stowers spied him.

Stowers didn't appear to say anything, but even from some distance, Kasey could see he'd sent a definite signal to Maxwell, probably just a look or a gesture, but warning enough.

Maxwell didn't turn to discover who might be watching. But he didn't lay the boot into Ant as had been his intention, and as Stowers had known he was about to do.

'Get back to work, nigger,' he said instead. Then he strode away without looking back.

Kasey reported the episode to Rupe. 'Maxwell's obviously chosen Ant as his next victim,' he said. Kasey couldn't help feeling guilty somehow, as if this was all his fault. 'It used to be me, but now Ant's the one copping it. And that's not fair, Rupe, Ant can't handle the pressure the way I could, it's just not fair.'

'I'll see if he'd like me to take some action on his behalf, Kase,' Rupe promised. But he already knew what the answer would be.

Reading the *Just So Stories* together as they did, and helping him write his letter to Mrs Sanderson, Rupe had come to know exactly the type of young man Anthony Hill was.

Early that evening after the meal break, he paid a visit to the four-man tent Ant shared with three others. Fortunately the others were not there, which was not unusual. Ant spent much of his time alone in the tent reading his book by the light of a torch, while most men preferred to socialise.

'Oh no, I don't want to cause no trouble, sir,' Ant said when Rupe suggested he might intervene on his behalf and seek the assistance of Captain Robinson. 'Oh no, sir, I wouldn't want that.'

Away from the parade ground and the call of duty and the work details to which they were assigned, the men of Company C knew Corporal Rupert Barrett as 'Rupe' and they addressed him as such. But not Ant. To Ant, the corporal was always 'sir', even when they sat huddled over the book sharing how the leopard got his spots.

Rupe had certainly come to recognise that for young Anthony Hill, there was something far more frightening than being bullied by a white man. Such bullying was no doubt something he'd suffered for so much of his life, it had become the natural way of things. The 'something else' Ant feared far more was being made the centre of attention among white men. The very thought of having his predicament reported to a higher authority terrified Ant.

'Very well, then,' Rupe said, 'you just tell me if things get out of hand, Private.'

'I will, sir,' Ant said, 'yes I will.'

But they both knew he wouldn't.

CHAPTER TEN

After several days of feverish labour, the Negro Servicemen's Club was about to become a reality. As a gesture of good will and a matter of courtesy, Samuel invited Major Hank Henry out to the property in order to make an inspection. That was if he was interested in doing so, the major was of course a very busy man. The major agreed.

Samuel's action was neither a gesture of good will nor a matter of courtesy. He was keen to remind Hank Henry of the arrangement they'd agreed upon. If a local business were to set up a place out of town with no cost to the military, then the military would turn a blind eye.

'So, as you can see, Major,' he said during their walk around the property, 'a great deal of work has gone into the place.'

'It certainly has,' Hank said, 'most impressive.'

'And at no cost to the military,' Samuel added meaningfully.

Aware of the blatant reminder, Hank's mouth twisted into a wry smile. 'And if memory serves me, Captain, I added the proviso that the club must be run in an *orderly* fashion. Any brawls or disturbances and I'll have you closed in an instant. I take it that's understood?'

'Indeed it is,' Samuel said with a confidence he didn't feel. The men have been cooped up for so long, he thought.

There'll be alcohol – the illicit booze Baz somehow conjures up from nowhere; how the hell does the man do it? And there'll be women; women vastly disproportionate to men in number furthermore; whenever this is the case brawls are inevitable. He intended to issue appropriate instructions, but under the circumstances he doubted they would be adhered to.

Samuel could only hope in desperation there would be no serious trouble, and that if there was they would be able to contain it.

'I'm sure you'll find the club will function in as orderly a manner as any other servicemen's club, Major,' he said calmly.

'I hope for your sake it does, Samuel.' Hank Henry's well wishes actually seemed genuine. 'But rest assured, as I warned you, I shall be keeping a very close eye on things.'

'Yes,' Samuel allowed himself a smile, 'yes, believe me, I know you will.'

And then came the big day. On Friday 15 May, in the early evening dusk of a perfect autumn day, truckloads of troops arrived at the old Parslow farm for the grand opening of the Negro Servicemen's Club. The excitement was palpable. They were all there to party, almost half the troops stationed at Kelso. In order to keep numbers manageable, the officers of Companies A and C had granted leave proportionately. The rest of the men would need to wait their turn until the following evening, but everyone had accepted their lot, there'd been no bickering or signs of resentment. The men finally had their special place.

The girls arrived in a truck of their own, which wasn't really their own of course, it was a US military transport vehicle. The same one that had transported the piano from The Brown's just the previous day, and driven by the same lieutenant whose considerable gambling debts Baz was willing to waive if he agreed to sign on as a regular chauffeur. This time around the truck was packed with Edie's girls, three of them laundresses and another nine Palm Islanders who regularly gathered at Aunty Edie's place, twelve girls in all, whom the lieutenant would willingly transport back to Townsville at the conclusion of the evening's entertainment.

Baz had driven out earlier in Val's car, accompanied by Betty and Jill, having faithfully promised the boss he would guard both with his life if necessary.

'Well, Jill anyway,' Val added caustically, doubting Betty would relish being saved from the assignation that awaited her.

The band was already setting up in the barn when they got there. The band was one of Baz's true 'coups', or so he boasted. 'Just wait'll you hear them,' he said to Betty and Jill, and also to Samuel, who'd been waiting to greet them.

A rather motley-looking five-piece group, with drums, piano, double bass, saxophone, clarinet and a male vocalist thrown in, the band played at a lot of the clubs around Townsville.

'They might not look all that much,' Baz admitted, 'but I swear to God you'll reckon you're listening to Glenn Miller's Big Band, they're that bloody good.'

Interestingly enough, every member of the band, including the vocalist, was white.

The barn where the four of them stood watching the band set up had been miraculously transformed into a dance hall, complete with a mirror ball and strings of fairy lights. Stepping inside, Betty and Jill had been instantly entranced. The effect was spectacular, and bound to become even more so as night descended.

But from the outside, the barn being windowless, the lights would remain barely visible, which had been a great relief to Samuel. The last thing he needed was a visit from the blackout duty inspectors. The same applied to the windowless stables, although the lights there would be dim anyway.

The club itself also observed the blackout laws; this was one area Samuel had determined they should not be called out on. The farmhouse windows now boasted lush curtains, which in a strange way rather complemented the stark stylishness of the place. The living room and dining room had been renovated by the Parslows long ago to form an open-plan design so the area had been large to start with, but all furnishings had been removed to create extra space, leaving only bar stools, the odd table, and of course the small upright piano from The Brown's, which sat in the corner.

Things got off to an excellent start.

Out in the barn, the band struck up 'One O'clock Jump'. No messing around with these boys; they leaped straight into big-band-style swing.

'You're right,' Samuel said to Baz, raising his voice in order to be heard. 'I might as well be listening to Glenn Miller's Big Band.'

Baz nodded smugly. 'Told you.'

Samuel had actually been joking. In fact, the band wasn't really good at all. But by golly, he thought, they sure as hell make a big noise, and that's just what the men want.

Inside the clubhouse, Betty was at the piano and Kasey was singing 'Smoke Gets in Your Eyes', a quieter start to the night, but one equally appreciated as men watched and listened in silent admiration. As always, the two were making love through their music, eyes locked, piano and tenor caressing each other, a precursor to the physical union that was destined to follow.

But the quiet appreciation of true musical talent didn't last long; it wasn't meant to. Betty quickly segued to more upbeat popular numbers and men joined each other in song, glasses raised and boots tapping to the rhythm.

As Betty played, she kept an eye out for Rupe. In half an hour or so, she planned it would be his turn at the piano. He wouldn't mind. Rupe loved every opportunity to 'tickle the ivories', and she had the key to the smallest of the four bedrooms, the one Val had agreed could remain a 'rest room' for staff.

Val hadn't gone into any further detail, but she had issued a brief warning to Betty. 'Be discreet, lovey.'

Val herself didn't intend to go out to the club. Being a busy Friday, she'd stayed back at The Brown's, so she'd felt it necessary to issue a further warning to Betty, or rather an instruction.

'And under no circumstances is Baz to hire out that room,' she'd said sharply. 'If the prick tries to, you tell him I'll have his balls.'

Betty and Kasey couldn't wait. Soon they'd be alone together. Soon. But where the hell was Rupe?

Rupe was out in the barn, enjoying the band. They weren't particularly good, but they were vibrant and the place was pulsating with the sound of swing jazz.

The dance floor had become a sea of energy, of vigorously executed jitterbug and jive; even those who couldn't dance were jigging about to the tempo infected by the syncopated rhythm and the 4/4 beat. The girls in particular were indefatigable, dancing from one man to the next, sharing their favours.

To Rupe, the image was extraordinary. All the people on the dance floor were black, or brown. And all those in the band, including the singer, were white. To him this was a phenomenon, something he'd not witnessed before.

He recalled the New York gigs where his dad used to play, the fancy supper clubs, the upmarket bars and late-night jazz venues. The band was always black and the audience white. Furthermore, the band always came in through the back door, usually via the kitchen, never through the main front door like the white folks. He remembered those back doors and kitchens vividly from the nights, when as a boy he'd accompanied his dad to sit and listen in the dressing rooms, or to watch so proudly from backstage.

How different is this, Rupe thought, marvelling at the scene before him. As far as he knew things hadn't changed at all back home. Black bands still played to white audiences and black musos still came and went via back doors. Only in Australia, he thought. Or perhaps only in Queensland. Or perhaps only in Townsville . . .

'Hey, Rupe.' It was Kasey who interrupted his musings. 'Want to come inside and play piano?' he asked with his most winning smile. 'I think Betty might be getting a little bit weary.'

'Sure, Kase, sure,' Rupe said, returning the smile. Then he added with a cod southern accent, 'I'll bet she's just plain tuckered out.'

They laughed and walked from the barn to the clubhouse, where the sound of the singalong vied in volume with the sound of the band. The whole night was alive with music and song. Finally liberated, the men were enjoying themselves.

Fifteen minutes later, to the strains of 'Blue Moon' with Rupe at the piano and the men giving voice, Betty and Kasey were making love in the small 'rest room'. With the door safely locked and the entire house a raucous cacophony of song, there was no need for them to practise their normal restraint, no need to whisper their endearments or stifle their moans.

Others too were satisfying their carnal lusts as business in the stables started getting underway. Baz had positioned himself by the door and was taking the money. He had staff at the clubhouse looking after the bar and alcohol trade; the brothel he entrusted to no-one other than himself.

There were three professional hookers and they were happy to perform 'quickies', with men queuing up for their favours. But Baz was pleased to note that, as he'd expected would be the case, several other of the Palm Island girls were already succumbing to the charms of the Americans. Perhaps it was the heat of the moment and the big handsome soldiers, perhaps it was the excitement of the dance floor and the heady pleasure of the music, or perhaps it was a mixture of all these elements that aroused them. Or perhaps, like the pros, the money was the attraction. The new girls took longer on the job, clearly proving they weren't as efficient as their more sophisticated sisters, but that didn't bother Baz. They'd learn soon enough that time was money.

'We'd better get back,' Betty said regretfully. How she longed to stay entwined like this all night, to fall asleep together as lovers do, to wake up and make love again, drowsily, languidly as if they had all the time in the world.

'Why?' Kasey argued. 'Rupe'll happily play all night, you know he will.' He drew her to him even closer. 'Why don't we just stay locked away in here until the very last minute? Why don't we do that?'

Betty laughed out loud. 'Because it's my job to play piano, that's what Val pays me for.' It had been liberating for them both to give voice to their pleasure, and for Betty, above all, to laugh out loud as she had any number of times just for the sheer joy of the moment.

'And besides,' she added in a more sober vein, 'I promised I'd look after Jill. Val doesn't trust Baz.' Was it Baz Val didn't trust, or Jill, Betty wondered briefly. Either way, she'd promised she'd keep an eye on Jill.

After checking to make sure the coast was clear, she gave Kasey the nod and, once he was safely gone, made a leisurely exit herself, closing the door behind her and pocketing the key. Just a member of the staff taking advantage of the 'rest room'. But she blessed Val. You're a bloody saint, Val, she thought gratefully.

Then, before taking over from Rupe at the piano, she popped out to the barn to do her duty and check on Jill.

Val's fears had obviously proved unfounded. Until now, anyway. Jill's hair was a tangled mess and her body glowed with sweat; the most indefatigable of all the girls, she hadn't once left the dance floor. And every second dance had been with Willie. She would have danced all night with Willie if she could; he was by far and away the best dancer and equally inexhaustible. But both she and Willie knew it was only fair they regularly let other guys cut in. There were so few girls to go around as it was, and with the night growing wilder several seemed to disappear every now and then.

Catching Jill's eye, Betty gave her a wave, Jill responding with a wave of her own and a radiant smile.

All was clearly going well, so Betty returned to the clubhouse where Kasey, determined not to let her out of his sight, was waiting beside the piano.

Back at Kelso, the half-deserted camp was eerily quiet. The majority of the men were gathered in the huge open-sided mess tent that served both as a canteen and social centre, but the customary sound of a musical instrument here and there, a guitar, a harmonica, a banjo or ukulele, invariably banding together for a singalong, was not evident tonight. Perhaps it was simply the dearth of numbers, or perhaps it was the absence of Rupe and Kasey, the true musicians among them who always led the troops in song, but there were many others who played instruments and many others who could sing. Tonight, for some reason, they chose not to. Instead they'd gathered in groups, playing cards or simply talking. There was no brooding resentment towards those of their buddies who were at the club, but everyone's thoughts were with them nonetheless. Here at camp there was a definite sense that the men were just biding their time.

Chuck Maxwell found the very quietness of the camp disconcerting. He'd expected some sort of trouble from these niggers who'd been denied the pleasures their friends were experiencing. He'd hoped there would be, for at least that would prove a distraction. Any troublemakers among them would give him a justifiable reason to vent his anger, but as things were he was powerless and growing angrier by the minute.

To Chuck's mind, the fact that a club exclusively for Negroes was operating right now, right out there in the bush barely ten miles away, was enough to drive any sane man crazy. Why, the very sight would sicken my daddy, he thought. This whole world has turned upside down.

He said as much to Stowers as together they embarked upon their rounds of the camp. He'd taken on the task of patrolling the camp himself, having dismissed young Lieutenant Stanley Hartford, who would normally have carried out the duty. The other three Company C platoon commanders were on supervision duty at the club, and just sitting alone with his thoughts was driving Chuck mad. He simply had to do something.

'Downright insane,' he now growled to Stowers as they left the officers' tent, 'setting up a social club for niggers. Downright insane! By hell, the 96th is a labour force, our niggers are here to work, not have a goddamned party!'

'Quite right, sir.' As always, Stowers was quick to agree. 'We gotta keep our niggers in line.'

'We surely do, Sergeant. Give your niggers too much freedom and you're just begging for trouble.' There were times when Chuck all but forgot Stowers was a nigger himself. 'That goddamned club will prove a disaster, I tell you.'

'Yessir,' Stowers echoed, 'a real disaster.'

Strut Stowers actually longed to be at the club. He had a strong link with the club's major mastermind, Baz Taylor, and knew exactly the delights the men would currently be experiencing, from the heady liquor, to the band and the girls in ready supply. Strut and Baz had been doing business ever since the arrival of the 96th Battalion. Over his years in the army, Strut had always been quick to suss out a good black-market contact keen for US military supplies unavailable to the locals, and a quick check around had proved that here in Townsville Baz Taylor was just the man. The connection had proved most convenient for both, and yet now, frustratingly, Strut found himself unable to openly embrace all he knew was on offer.

Strut hadn't been among those granted leave for tonight, having been ordered to remain on guard at the camp with so many men gone. Tomorrow night, however, if he put in a request, he'd have to be given leave to attend. No-one would deny him the right. But did he dare risk annoying Chuck Maxwell, with whom he had such a valuable relationship? Keeping on side with the captain worked very much to his advantage. He never saw the part he played as servile, but rather as teamwork that placed him in an eminently superior position. Was it worth threatening such a delicate balance? Strut was in a terrible state of indecision.

Apart from Chuck Maxwell, there was possibly only one other person in the whole of the camp who had no wish to go to the Negro Servicemen's Club, and that person was Private Anthony Hill.

Ant could have gone to the club with his buddies tonight, he'd been among those troops of Company C granted leave, but he'd chosen not to attend simply because such a night held little attraction for him. He enjoyed the company of his buddies to a certain extent, but he was unlike them. He didn't drink alcohol, he was painfully shy in the company of women and he couldn't dance. What would be the point? Instead, he relished the thought of a peaceful evening alone, curled up in the bunk of his deserted tent reading the next of his *Just So Stories*. He was about to embark on 'The Elephant's Child'.

Chuck Maxwell and Strut Stowers continued their rounds checking all was in order. The camp was lit by gasoline-powered electric generators that sat on concrete slabs housed in four electrical huts based at each corner of the camp's perimeter. Electric wiring ran overhead from poles made of local timber, and as the two men walked among the rows of four-man tents, Chuck searched hopefully among the lights that criss-crossed the camp for something untoward, something suspicious.

There would surely be some thieving nigger taking advantage of the semi-deserted camp and robbing other men's tents, he thought, none of the bastards were to be trusted. But he was disappointed. All was in order.

He was further disappointed as they passed by the general mess tent for rank and file, where he'd hoped that by now there might be some unrest demanding of attention. But no, the mess tent, where well over a hundred men were gathered, remained unusually quiet. All was in order.

They passed by the other mess tents, one for white officers, the other for black non-commissioned officers, or NCOs, closer to the border of the camp where slit trenches had been dug in preparation for attack from the air, and they came to the armoury where two troops stood on guard. Apart from the four makeshift electrical huts, the quonset hut housing the armoury was the only solid structure in the camp. All else was a sea of tents.

The two guards saluted. The captain returned the salute. All was in order.

They continued on to the next block of four-man tents, walking up and down between the rows that looked for all the world like streets in a town of khaki canvas, which indeed they were. The rows appeared deserted in the gloomy overhead-generated light. There were no men going back and forth as was customary, and the tents themselves appeared in total darkness, the single light that dangled from the central pole inside obviously not in use.

Then Maxwell halted abruptly, a signal to Stowers beside him who also halted. Up ahead towards the end of the row was a tent with a light inside. But it was not the overhead light. Someone was using a torch.

Chuck Maxwell drew his Colt semi-automatic pistol. He'd been right, some thieving nigger was at work. He couldn't wait to make an example of the bastard.

With a quick nod to his sergeant, Maxwell crept quietly towards the tent, Stowers obeying orders and following in silence.

When he reached the front flap he threw it aside and stepped briskly into the tent, handgun at the ready, Stowers right behind him.

Startled by the unexpected intrusion, Ant dropped his torch, which fell to the ground, shining directly on the boots of Captain Maxwell. He jumped from his bunk where he'd been reading by the torchlight and stood to attention. He must have been doing something wrong, but he couldn't think what. One thing he was sure of, though. He was about to pay the price.

With the torch still shining on his boots and the tent now in virtual darkness, Chuck didn't know the identity of the man he'd sprung. 'What you doing in here, nigger,' he demanded, 'you stealing from your buddies?'

'No, sir, no,' Ant protested.

Maxwell bent down and picked up the torch. 'Then why're you here in the dark?' he asked. Pistol still threateningly in hand, he shone the torch's beam on Ant's face. My, my, he thought with a sense of satisfaction, just look who we have. He tossed the torch onto the bunk. 'Why didn't you turn on this here light?' he said, pulling the string that turned on the central overhead, illuminating the tent in a dull yellow glow. 'You got to be up to no good not doing that, creeping around in the dark like you were.'

Ant's eyes flickered to Stowers, seeking support. The sergeant knew this was his tent. But Stowers said nothing.

'I wasn't creeping around, sir,' he said, still at attention, gaze now trained to the front, avoiding eye contact with the captain. 'This is my tent. I was on my bunk, reading my book. I use the torch 'cause the light's better that way.'

'*Reading*, were you,' Chuck taunted, pretending to be impressed. 'Oh my! A nigger who can *read*. Well now, that really is something, wouldn't you say, Sergeant?' His eyes didn't leave Ant, even as he addressed Stowers. Chuck had found his whipping boy and was in fine form.

'Yessir.' Strut beamed, white teeth flashing in the blackness of his face. He enjoyed being part of the captain's game. This was the teamwork they shared, the teamwork that made him superior. 'A nigger reading, that sure is something.'

'And exactly what were you *reading*, boy?' Chuck picked up the book that remained open where it sat on the bunk. He balanced it in the palm of one hand, riffling clumsily through its pages with the muzzle of his pistol as if the book itself was an enemy that needed to be threatened.

Ant's eyes were no longer trained to the front. He watched his precious book with breathless anxiety, unable to respond.

'Looks to me like a valuable book,' Chuck said, still playing with the pages, 'wouldn't you say so, Sergeant?'

'Yessir, I would,' Strut agreed, 'that's one valuable book, all right.'

'Where'd you get this, nigger?' Chuck slammed the book shut. 'Who'd you steal this from?' he barked. The game was about to turn serious. He could physically punish this nigger for theft, he'd have every right to do so. He could order Stowers to beat the shit out of him.

'I didn't . . . I didn't steal it, sir, I swear . . . I swear I didn't steal it.' Ant faltered over each word, stuttering in his anxiety. He wished the captain would put the book down. He wasn't fearful for himself, he was fearful for his book. Put it down, his mind begged; please, please, put it down.

Chuck was interested in the reaction. This young nigger who took everything he dished out, who never looked him in the eye, who always stood to attention, was now totally focused upon the goddamned book that he held in his hand. This book was obviously something of great value to the boy. Chuck decided to extend the game a little further.

'So where'd you get this from, nigger?' he asked, carelessly waving the book about, watching as the boy's eyes nervously followed its path through the air. 'If you didn't steal this here book, then where did you get it?'

'A gift . . . it was . . . a gift, sir,' Ant stammered, his mind pleading, *Give it back, give it back . . .*

'A gift.' Chuck pretended once again to be impressed. 'My, my, a gift indeed.' He made a further pretence of examining the book. 'Yep, sure looks valuable to me, an old book, I'd say.'

'Yes. Yes, sir, it is.' Ant was thankful he'd stopped waving the book around.

'And who would give a nigger like you a valuable book like this, I wonder.'

'A teacher, sir, a teacher in town, a lady called Mrs Sanderson.'

'A lady, you say?' Chuck's voice now had a distinctly dangerous edge. He didn't like the sound of this. 'You mean a *white* lady?'

'Yes, sir.'

'You been messing with a white woman, have you, boy?'

'No, sir, no . . .' Ant protested. He was desperate now, forgetting to avoid the captain's eyes, appealing to him directly, begging him.

'A white woman gives a young nigger like you a gift? Only one reason I can see why that might happen, boy. You been messing with white trash.'

'No, sir, I swear. She's a teacher lady, like I said. She was teaching me to read.'

'White teacher lady or white trash, makes no difference to me,' Chuck said, opening the book and grasping a half in each hand. 'I'll show you what I think of a white woman giving a gift to a nigger.' And ripping through the central binding, he tore the book in two. It wasn't a difficult feat. The book was old, and the binding came apart with relative ease.

Ant let out a howl. Instinctively, he launched himself forwards to grab at the severed halves of his precious book as they fell from the captain's hands. But he was not successful. The butt of Chuck Maxwell's pistol smashed into the side of his skull with such force that his head whipped back and he fell to the ground, landing right beside the two halves of Rudyard Kipling's *Just So Stories*.

Chuck waited a moment or so before prodding the young man's body with his boot. He hadn't thought he'd hit the boy all that hard, but he was lying very still, and his head seemed to be at a weird sort of angle.

'You saw that, Sergeant,' he said to Stowers, 'this nigger was attacking me. You saw that, didn't you?'

'Yessir, I sure did,' Strut said dutifully, automatically, although he wasn't at all happy about the situation. That had been one hell of a whack the captain had given the boy, and there were no witnesses to prove he'd acted in self-defence. No witnesses except me, Strut thought.

'Check him out,' Chuck ordered, 'is he dead?'

Strut knelt and checked the young man's pulse, but from the angle of the head they both knew already what the answer would be.

'Yessir,' he said, 'this man is dead.'

Chuck's mind instantly sprang into action. Even with Stowers' support as a witness, making this a case of self-defence could prove tricky. Far better to avoid an investigation altogether.

He clicked off the overhead light, but from the bunk the torch's beam still shone upon the canvas wall of the tent. He quickly picked up the torch and turned it off. 'Check all's clear outside, Sergeant,' he hissed.

Stowers did so, peering through the tent flap. All remained as deserted as it had been when they'd first arrived.

'Yessir,' he reported, 'all clear outside.'

'Right. Get a jeep back here at the double. Take this nigger somewhere and dump him, you got that?'

'Yessir.'

'You make it look like an accident. We know nothing about this. There'll be no official investigation. The boy just met with an accident, you hear me?'

'Yessir, I hear you loud and clear. An accident.'

'You get going now, Sergeant. I'll check things are all in order here.'

Stowers dived out of the tent and set off as fast as he could without drawing attention to himself. He was relieved Captain Maxwell had decided upon this course of action. In obeying any order the captain might issue, as he always did, Strut Stowers would vastly prefer to stage an accident than to act as a witness in a military investigation.

Alone in the tent, Chuck switched on the torch, this time pointing it to the ground, shielding its beam. He checked the butt of his pistol. There was no sign of blood. He holstered the weapon and checked the tent's ground cloth. Tossing the two halves of the book onto the bunk, he knelt and closely examined the area around the young man's head. No blood. He examined the young man's skull where he'd struck him. No blood there either.

Well, well, Chuck thought, switching off the torch and rising to his feet. How downright lucky. No mess at all. This nigger didn't die from a smashed-in skull. This nigger died from a broken neck.

Chuck left the tent feeling satisfied with the outcome. Stowers could look after things from here on in. And if the sergeant, through some clumsiness of his own doing, should be discovered dumping the body, which was highly unlikely, for the man was very efficient, it would have nothing whatsoever to do with Chuck Maxwell. A nigger's word would never be taken against that of a white officer.

When Stowers returned to discover his captain had not waited to assist him, he was not in the least surprised. It was exactly as he'd expected. Captain Maxwell trusted him implicitly, and it was only right that he should, for Strut was loyal. He obeyed his captain's orders to the very letter, and this occasion would be no different from any other. The loyalty they shared was what made them such an excellent team.

Late that night, given the extended curfew that had been allowed for the opening of the Negro Servicemen's Club, truckloads of troops were transported back to camp in various states of disrepair.

The three men who shared Ant's tent didn't even notice he wasn't there. He was so quiet anyway, they barely noticed him when he *was* there. Now, like so many around the camp, with bellies full of beer and other forms of illicit alcohol, they fell happily into their bunks and were asleep within minutes.

It was only in the morning they noticed he was gone. They noticed he didn't front up to the canteen for breakfast either. And he didn't report for work; he'd been on roster that Saturday morning.

As the day wore on, Private Anthony Hill was reported missing. Questions were asked. Had he gone AWOL? Doubtful, most replied, very unlike Ant, who always stuck to the rules. Had something untoward happened while so many of the troops had been at the club? Had anyone witnessed anything? No. No-one had seen Anthony Hill since the early evening meal the previous day.

A small search party was sent out to scour the local area and they found him within an hour. His body was barely one mile from the camp, on a steep track that led down to the river. His neck was broken. He must have tripped and fallen down the embankment, a tragic accident.

The men were dismayed to hear the news, for Ant, although a bit of a loner, was liked by all. A nice young man, how sad, they thought, what a terrible thing to have happened. But there was no reason to query the cause of his death. Ant was known to go for walks on his own.

One anomaly, however, raised a question among the three men who shared his tent. They had discovered Ant's book torn in half on his bunk. Ant would never destroy his book, which they knew to be precious to him. Had there been a fight of some kind? They decided to report their find to Corporal Rupert Barrett that very morning, and they took the book along to show him the evidence.

'We never really knew Ant all that well,' their spokesman, Private Amos Cole, a huge, beefy soldier in his late twenties, said, 'he kept to himself. But we sure as hell knew that he treasured this book.'

'Yeah, yeah,' the others agreed, nodding vigorously.

'We wondered whether there might have been a fight or something,' Amos went on, the bass baritone of his voice matching the size of his body. 'Young Ant would never have ripped that up,' he said, pointing to the book Rupe held in his hands.

'I know.' Rupe gazed down at the two halves of *Just So Stories*, remembering the reading sessions he'd had with Anthony Hill, the introverted young man who always called him sir, even off duty. As they'd shared 'How the Leopard Got His Spots', that boy had come to life. He'd been animated, joyful even. That boy would never have destroyed this book.

'I know,' he said once again, 'thank you for bringing this to my attention, Private Cole. I shall look into the matter, I assure you.'

During lunchbreak, Rupe sought out Kasey and took him aside, explaining the situation. The book, its destruction and its background importance.

Kasey was the one who said the words out loud. Or rather just one word to start with.

'Maxwell.' Then, 'It would have been Chuck Maxwell ripped that book up.'

He wasn't saying anything that hadn't already occurred to Rupe. In fact, he was echoing Rupe's very thoughts.

'Chuck Maxwell bullied that kid to death,' Kasey said.

'He fucking killed him, and I'll bet fucking Stowers was in on it, too.'

Kasey, quick to fire up at the best of times, was seething with anger. And his anger was founded upon something that felt strangely like guilt. If he'd remained Maxwell's whipping boy this wouldn't have happened, he was sure of that. He could have withstood whatever Maxwell chose to dish out, but Ant couldn't. And Ant had ended up paying the ultimate price.

But the guilt Kasey suffered was nothing compared to that of Rupert Barrett. Rupe cursed himself, the sudden rush of guilt that consumed him born of a deep-seated regret. I should never have listened to Ant's plea not to intervene, he thought. I should have reported Maxwell's bullying to Samuel Robinson. If I'd done that, and if by any chance Kase and I are right, Anthony Hill would be alive today.

Rupe knew if they were to seek justice, however, common sense must prevail.

'We're just surmising, Kase,' he warned, 'we can't prove a thing. Keep your mouth shut for now and don't talk to anyone about this. If you do, word's bound to get back to Maxwell. We'll ask around quietly, see what we can find out.'

Rupe decided nonetheless to pay a visit to Samuel Robinson. He would make no mention of his suspicions, but he would show Robinson the book. Captain Robinson, above all others, knew the value Anthony Hill placed on his copy of *Just So Stories*. Surely the destruction of something so precious to young Ant would point to possible foul play. And then perhaps this might lead to some form of investigation, Rupe thought, or at least to some questions being asked, instead of the complacent acceptance by all that Anthony Hill's death was no more than an unfortunate accident.

But Captain Samuel Robinson was not to be found. At the Company C headquarters tent, young Percy Owen said he'd left for town just half an hour ago.

Captain Samuel Robinson had been called into the city for an urgent meeting with Major Hank Henry. A meeting where an announcement was to be made that would ultimately alter the course of history for the men of the 96th Battalion, or at least those of Companies A and C who had been posted to Kelso.

CHAPTER ELEVEN

'What do you mean the club's to be closed?' Seated opposite the major in the provost marshal's office, Samuel couldn't believe what he was hearing.

'Just that,' Hank Henry replied. 'The troops of the 96th are to remain barred from town and there is to be no club outside the city limits. It's back to scratch, I'm afraid.'

There was just the vaguest hint of apology in Hank's tone, or at least of regret. Hank Henry was not given to apologies of any kind, and certainly not for circumstances that were beyond his control.

'But why,' Samuel demanded, 'tell me why? For God's sake, what possible reason could there be?' The normally implacable Samuel Robinson was having trouble controlling his anger, which was steadily on the rise. 'The club was run in an *orderly* fashion as stipulated,' he emphasised, 'there were no brawls, no disturbances, just as we'd agreed. Give me one good reason for its closure.'

Hank heaved a sigh that seemed to say *here we go*. 'There have been complaints,' he said with a touch of world-weariness.

'From whom?'

'From local farmers in the vicinity.'

'Complaints about what?'

'Noise for one thing . . .' He shrugged as if aware the explanation was a lame one.

'Of course there was noise,' Samuel said, exasperated, 'there was always going to be noise. It's a club, there's a band, there's singing and dancing. The farmers were told about that, weren't they? And besides, their properties are miles away, it's hardly as if they're cheek-by-jowl neighbours.'

'It's the wives rather than the farmers themselves,' Hank admitted, aware he'd have to get to the point. He might as well have come out with it right from the start, he thought. 'You're right, the farmers were told there was to be a servicemen's club set up at the old Parslow property, but the wives say they weren't told exactly what *sort* of servicemen's club.'

'Ah,' Samuel said slowly, the truth dawning, 'I see.' And he did. 'A *Negro* servicemen's club, you mean.'

'Exactly. They've lodged a formal complaint with the US military. They feel their children are not safe with so many soldiers nearby, particularly on premises where alcohol is available —'

'So many *black* soldiers, you mean,' Samuel interrupted with uncharacteristic force, 'they'd have felt perfectly safe if the soldiers had been *white*.'

'Exactly.' Hank decided to stop pussyfooting around. Robinson had every right to be riled up; he'd stuck to the rules and done a damn good job with the club. 'That's it in a nutshell,' he admitted. 'The farmers had been quite happy to have a servicemen's club a few miles down the track. Hell, one of them even asked if there'd be girls there,' Hank's smile was sardonic, 'maybe he liked the idea of popping in for a quick poke.'

Samuel didn't return the smile, which didn't matter, Hank had not intended to be humorous.

'Anyway,' he continued, 'seems around dusk a few of the local kids were out riding their bikes when a load of army trucks passed by. The kids followed the trucks and watched them pull up at the Parslow place. Said they saw blacks, hundreds and hundreds of blacks, exaggerating, you know, the way kids do.' Hank shook his head dolefully. 'Well, the wives didn't like the sound of that at all. Told their husbands they wouldn't stand for it. The safety of their children is threatened, they say, and they won't have a bar of the club. So the farmers have lodged a formal complaint.'

Hank Henry went on to sum up the situation in his customary blunt manner. 'It's a complaint we can't ignore, Samuel, we need to take immediate action. The club will be closed as of today. We can't afford to offend the locals.'

'But what's wrong with these people,' Samuel protested, 'why this over-reaction to the presence of Negroes? Surely they know there's a huge labour force of black soldiers camped five to ten miles down the road from wherever their farms happen to be.'

'That's precisely why we must be seen to take immediate action,' Hank explained. 'The Australian Government was reluctant to accept Negro soldiers from the outset. MacArthur himself vowed to respect this country's racial views, and our own military has been ordered under no circumstances to offend the locals. A complaint like this has to be taken very seriously.'

Recognising defeat, Samuel felt himself slump a little, despair engulfing him. The Negro Servicemen's Club had been the perfect answer to the troop's justifiable frustration at being banned from town. Now the club was to close its doors, and after just one night. How was he to face his men? What was he to tell them? That they were too black for this country? They'd felt so welcomed in Townsville.

'So it seems racism is as alive and well here as it is back home,' he said drily. He expected no response. In fact, he'd made the remark more to himself than Hank Henry. But the reply that came back surprised him.

'It would appear so, yes,' Hank said, not without the strangest element of something that could have been interpreted as sympathy, one would never know.

The meeting was over.

After leaving the military barracks, Samuel headed straight for The Brown's. It was nearly two o'clock in the afternoon; Val and Baz needed to be told the news as soon as possible.

'Oh for fuck's sake,' Val said disbelievingly, 'they want to close us after just one night! What's the problem? Baz here said everything went smooth as clockwork.'

'It did,' Baz declared. 'It did, I swear it did.'

'So why?' she demanded aggressively, hands planted on buxom hips, steel-grey eyes smouldering with righteous anger. 'You tell me bloody well why.'

Samuel stared her down for a moment. 'There were complaints from some of the locals,' he said meaningfully.

'Oh?' Val held his look, aware he was signalling something.

'The soldiers weren't the right colour.'

'Oh.' A nod. 'Gotcha,' she said. 'Fucking shame.'

Samuel left only minutes later. Conveying the news to his men wouldn't be quite so simple.

At The Brown's, Val and Baz discussed the situation. The girls would be disappointed of course, particularly Betty – 'she'll be bloody ropeable,' Val said – but the principal topic was what to do with the premises after all the expense and hard work that had been put in. Baz, as was to be expected, came up with the perfect answer.

'We'll get all our dough back from the US military,' he said. 'Given time, we'll end up making a damn good profit.'

'Oh yeah?' Val knew better than to sound overly sceptical, more often than not Baz's ideas were spot on. 'And how do you propose we do that?'

'We shove all the furniture back into the farmhouse and hire the place out to them as an officers' billet – the Yanks are just begging for accommodation. Come to think of it, we can hire the barn out to them, too. Excellent storage space.' Baz was not in the least unhappy with the situation.

'And the liquor,' Val said, 'we spent a good deal on heavy-duty hooch. I can't sell it here at the pub.'

'Don't give the hooch a second thought, Boss,' Baz assured her, 'no worries there.'

This was the part of least concern to Baz. The considerable supply of illicit liquor he'd laid in would actually fetch a higher price on the black market than it would have at the club. Hell, his first clients would be the deprived troops at Kelso, where he had the perfect contact in Sergeant Strut Stowers. A simple phone call would suffice. Val didn't need to know about that part though.

'I'll get a good price for it, I promise you.'

Yeah, I'll just bet you will, Val thought, and I can guess from where, too – those poor bastards out at Kelso. But she made no comment. There were some things it was best she didn't know about.

'Not sure what we can do with the stables,' he concluded, 'but give me time, I'll come up with something.'

'Rightio.' Val nodded. She had no doubt he would. He's a right prick, she thought, but Christ he's good.

Samuel briefly considered paying a visit to Amelia Sanderson to tell her about the tragic accident that had led to the death of young Anthony Hill. She would be devastated by the news, he was sure. He'd promised he'd see her this weekend, too. But of course he wouldn't call upon her. He knew he was only seeking a means to delay the inevitable.

He must get back to camp and inform the men of the club's closure, and as soon as possible. The mere thought of what lay ahead left a bitter taste in his mouth, as bitter as the way in which his news would be received, no doubt.

The men's reaction was varied. At first they were shocked, then mystification quickly followed. Why, they all asked. Why in God's name was the club to be closed? What had gone wrong? There'd been no trouble the previous night. Not at the club anyway. The only trouble had occurred back at the camp with the sad death of poor young Ant, a subject that was currently on the lips of many. They'd been told nothing more than the fact that, due to complaints from locals, the military had ordered the instant closure of their club. *What* complaints?

Samuel had wisely opted to provide no further detail. It was not his job to do so, after all. These were his orders. Due to complaints the club was to be closed, simple as that. The men would no doubt work things out for themselves.

They did. Gathered in groups, first voicing their bewilderment, then repeating their questions, some among them insisting upon answers. They'd form a group, they said, and they'd demand from their commanding officers an honest explanation for the closure.

But there were those others among them who quickly came to the obvious conclusion.

'It's because we're black,' they said. 'You remember when the *Santa Clara* was docked in Brisbane . . . ?'

'Yeah, we wasn't allowed into the city . . .'

'That's right, we stayed on board that ship . . .'

'. . . And all because we was black . . .'

'. . . They don't want black folk in this country . . .'

The word quickly spread. It was only then that the bitterness set in. And it set in with a vengeance.

The only person who appeared unmoved by the closure of the Negro Servicemen's Club was Captain Charles

'Chuck' Maxwell, who had positively gloated when Samuel had informed him of their orders.

'Told you no good would come from a social club for niggers,' he'd said smugly.

To which Samuel had retorted sharply, 'We must inform the men, Maxwell,' he said, 'no further comment is necessary.'

Chuck had informed the men as briefly and succinctly as Samuel had, but he hadn't bothered to disguise his satisfaction in communicating the news.

Apart from personal malice, Chuck Maxwell had further reason to welcome the closure of the club. Here was the perfect distraction. The men would now be talking of nothing but this, the death of their young friend bound to take a back seat conversationally. Not that Chuck didn't feel safe from the threat of last night. The ever-reliable Stowers had carried out his orders unobserved, the body had been discovered and a case of accidental death had gone unquestioned. He could now put the whole episode behind him. The boy was just another dead nigger about whom no questions would be asked.

But Chuck was wrong.

'The guys who shared Anthony Hill's tent brought this to me this morning,' Rupe said, handing the mutilated book to Samuel.

It was well after the evening meal break and Rupe had been careful to seek out the captain alone in his tent. He'd deliberately chosen not to approach him at the officers' tent for fear of bumping into Maxwell, and he'd also taken care to carry the book concealed in his kit bag. As far as Rupert Barrett was concerned, the destruction of this book was positive evidence of foul play.

Samuel felt much the same way. Simply seeing the copy of *Just So Stories* savagely ripped in half, and knowing how valuable it had been to Anthony Hill, Samuel knew in an instant that something was wrong.

'I feel it's my duty to tell you, sir,' Rupe said, 'that Captain Maxwell had been bullying young Ant something terrible. Same way he was Kasey Davis a while back.'

The two men's eyes locked. Both understood exactly what was being implied.

'Kasey himself told me about the bullying,' Rupe went on, 'said he'd witnessed an incident and felt that the captain had found another whipping boy in young Ant. I asked Anthony if he'd like me to intervene on his behalf. I was prepared to come to you, sir, just like I did with Kasey. But Private Hill didn't want me to do that. In fact, he was very much against it. He didn't want to cause any trouble.' Rupe's eyes flickered away and he stared at the ground, feeling wretched. 'I wish to God now I hadn't listened to him,' he said, 'I wish to God I'd come to see you instead.'

Samuel felt sorry for Rupert Barrett. A big man, a strong man, yet he looked so helpless, so vulnerable. It was clear he felt guilty, but he had no cause. He was a good soldier who cared for his men.

'This whole tragic affair is not your fault, Corporal,' he said. 'You mustn't blame yourself, you're hardly the guilty party.' Samuel stopped short, not prepared to name out loud who they both believed was. 'Besides, you've come to me now and I'm glad you have. We must get to the bottom of this.' He gazed down at the book in his hands. 'That is if it's at all humanly possible,' he added. 'I'm afraid this discovery of yours is hardly solid evidence.'

'Yes, sir, I'm aware of that.'

'Perhaps some discreet enquiries around the camp,' Samuel suggested, 'and perhaps with the help of Private Davis?'

'Oh yes, sir,' Rupe instantly responded, 'Kase is right with me on this. He feels as strongly as I do that Ant's death was no accident.'

'Good. Well, let's see what the two of you can come up with. Maybe someone witnessed something unusual, perhaps you can discover some sort of link.' He didn't mention a link to whom. Once again, his fellow officer's name went unmentioned.

Samuel knew what he was doing was highly unethical according to the military code of allegiance among officers, but he didn't care. The customary bond shared by white commanding officers meant nothing when one was dealing with a man like Chuck Maxwell.

He hefted his kit bag onto his bunk. 'Leave this with me,' he said, tucking the book well inside, 'and keep me posted, Corporal.'

'I will, sir, yes.'

Rupe was fully aware of Samuel Robinson's powerlessness to offer any practical assistance at this stage, but that didn't bother him. He felt buoyed by the knowledge that he had an ally, and a powerful one at that if he and Kasey could come up with some form of evidence against Maxwell.

Over the next several days, the two of them set about sleuthing, and they did so with the greatest of care. It was important they arouse no hint of suspicion that might reach Maxwell's ears, thereby giving him warning to further cover his tracks. As it turned out, they met with no problem. The troops openly answered any query put to them, with no responding query of their own as to why they were being asked. Everyone was too busy talking about the closure of the club.

One of the search-party members who had discovered Ant's body told Rupe of the exact whereabouts, and he and Kasey examined the scene. Nothing untoward to report there. The narrow track that led from the road to the river's edge was steep; perfectly believable a man could trip and fall down the embankment, breaking his neck. There were numerous vehicle tyre tracks along the dirt road, but these too signified nothing. The road had been created by the military and was one of many such roads linking the camp to various work sites.

They asked around among the men whose tents were in the same section as Ant's, but those troops housed nearby had all been at the club that night. Ant was the only one who had chosen not to go.

Questions asked of men who'd remained in camp, however, proved far more revealing. The two troops on guard at the armoury had seen Captain Maxwell and Sergeant Stowers on patrol that night. Others who'd been gathered at the mess tent playing cards or just talking were of even greater interest, articulating their opinion in no uncertain terms.

'Maxwell, he was on the prowl, I tell you,' one said, 'couldn't believe why we was so quiet when our buddies were at the club.'

'Yeah,' another agreed, 'that fucker was aching to find trouble so as he could lay into one of us. The son of a bitch just hated that we had a club of our own.'

This confirmed their suspicions. Maxwell had killed Anthony Hill. But such talk was useless, no more than conjecture; it offered no proof. They'd reached a stalemate. In typical fashion, Kasey was quick to give vent to his fury.

'I'm gonna kill that no good piece of white shit,' he said, pacing about the clearing well away from the camp where they'd retired to discuss their findings. 'And I'm gonna kill that no good piece of nigger shit, too. Stowers is covering for the prick like he always does. I'll just bet it was Strut-fucking-Stowers who dumped the body.'

Rupe agreed entirely with the theory, but he didn't dare fuel Kase's rage. Kasey Davis was a ticking time bomb. Frustrated and angered beyond belief that he was now to be separated from Betty, Kase was prepared to stop at nothing. If Maxwell became the full focus of his fury, Rupe feared the outcome.

'Take it easy, Kase,' he warned, 'going off half-cocked won't serve our cause. You know I'm right, buddy, so you just calm right down. That's an order now, you hear me?'

Kasey had stopped his pacing. 'Yeah, I hear you,' he said, 'I hear you loud and clear.' Rupe's authority and plain common sense had its usual pacifying effect, but this time only to a certain degree. Anger still burned in young Kasey Davis.

Rupe reported their findings, or rather their lack of findings, to Samuel Robinson, recounting the men's very words.

'Nothing concrete to go on I'm afraid, sir,' he said, 'although what the guys say seems to confirm our suspicions.'

'Yes,' Samuel agreed, 'no direct link, though, nothing that provides us with proof.'

Again so much was left unsaid. But they were both speaking exactly the same language. And they were both feeling equally thwarted, equally powerless.

'Leave things with me for now, Corporal,' Samuel said, 'I'll make a couple of enquiries of my own.'

'Yes, sir. Thank you, sir.' Rupe was intrigued. Enquiries, he thought. Enquiries about what and of whom? The captain surely wasn't going to confront Maxwell.

But Samuel was, and did. In an indirect way. Early the following morning, he took the mutilated book with him to the officers' tent, where he placed it beneath the papers on his desk and sat awaiting the arrival of Chuck Maxwell.

'Morning, sir.'

Young Percy Owen, punctilious in his duties, was surprised to find Captain Robinson had preceded him. Percy always arrived well before his commanding officers to ensure the work rosters were neatly drawn up and waiting, despite the fact he'd addressed all the necessary detail the previous day.

'Morning, Private.' Samuel gave a brief smile and returned to the pretence of work. He wasn't bothered that Percy would be present during his questioning of Maxwell. Indeed, should there be any particular reaction of note, he rather hoped the boy would be paying attention.

Chuck arrived fifteen minutes later. Offering no more than a perfunctory nod by way of acknowledgement to Samuel, he was about to proceed to Percy's desk in the corner, but Samuel rose to greet him.

'Morning, Chuck,' he said pleasantly enough. 'Just before you head off, there's something I'd like to run by you, if you wouldn't mind.'

Chuck made no reply, but halted and stood waiting with an expression that clearly said, *All right, get on with it.*

'You and Sergeant Stowers carried out a patrol of the camp on Friday night, did you not?'

'You know damn well I did,' Chuck sneered, 'I was doing my job while you were partying on with your nigger friends at their fancy club.'

'And that was the same night Private Anthony Hill met with his accidental death.'

'Correct. But, like everyone else, I didn't see or hear anything.'

'Yes, so you've said, and so has Sergeant Stowers, but something has come up since then and I wondered if you knew anything about it.'

'Oh yeah, and what would that be?' Chuck's tone was impatient more than anything. He had no fear, no anxiety.

It was Tuesday, four days since the boy's death, the body had been taken away for burial or shipment God only knew where, all the necessary questions had been asked and adequately answered; he was quite safe.

'The men who shared Private Hill's tent found this the day after his death.' Sweeping the papers on his desk to one side, Samuel picked up the two halves of the book. As he held them out for Chuck Maxwell's inspection, he studied the man closely. 'This book was of great value to Private Hill,' he went on, 'but as you can see it's been destroyed. The men who shared his tent wondered whether perhaps there might have been a fight of some kind.'

Chuck didn't miss a beat. 'Not to the best of my knowledge,' he said, 'but I can tell you who ripped that thing in half.' He looked Samuel directly in the eyes. 'I did.'

'Why? Why would you want to do a thing like that?'

'Lazy nigger didn't jump to attention when I entered his tent, just sat there looking at his goddamned book. Niggers like that got to be taught a lesson, Robinson, so I tore up that there book. Then I got on with doing the rest of my rounds.'

'Yes,' Samuel said with weary loathing, 'of course you tore up the book. It's just the sort of thing you *would* do, Maxwell.' He dumped the book back on his desk, feeling utterly helpless. The confrontation had gone nowhere.

'Got to teach these boys respect, you know, got to teach them their place,' Chuck said smugly. 'Now is there anything else I can help you with, Captain?' Chuck was congratulating himself on his quick thinking. He felt more than smug, he felt positively triumphant. Why would he deny destroying the book? If in the unlikely event it proved to be an object of importance and they chose to run tests, his fingerprints would be all over it.

Samuel couldn't bring himself to look at the man. 'No,' he said, 'nothing else you can help me with. Not yet anyway,' he added in an attempt to sound ominous, but the words were empty and he knew it.

So did Chuck, who smiled as he crossed to the clerk's desk to collect his paperwork.

That night after the evening meal, Samuel went into town, intending to stay at his billet, despite the fact it would mean a very early start the next morning, returning to camp to report for duty. He felt guilty escaping as he was, guilty for exercising the freedom not allowed his men, but he simply had to get away from the camp, which was now seething with an undercurrent of resentment he was powerless to control. He had to escape the presence of Maxwell, too, and the numbing sense of his own inadequacy. He couldn't bring himself to face Rupert Barrett with the news that, in confronting Chuck Maxwell, he'd only succeeded in shoring up the man's alibi. Rupert Barrett had been convinced the destruction of Anthony's book might somehow prove as evidence of foul play, but Maxwell had outsmarted them both.

It was after dark when he pulled the jeep up outside Amelia Sanderson's house. He let himself in with the key she'd provided, and very quietly made his way down the passage towards the kitchen. The light was on in her quarters, but the rest of the house was in darkness, so he took care not to disturb her in case she'd retired early for the night. He would make himself a cup of tea and retire early himself, he decided, although his head teeming with thoughts as it was, with self-recrimination and guilt and blame, he was sure sleep would be impossible.

But he'd barely finished filling the kettle before she materialised.

'Hello, Samuel,' came her voice from the door, 'I thought I heard you arrive.'

'Hello, Amelia,' he said as she entered the kitchen, 'I'm sorry if I disturbed you, I tried very hard to be quiet.'

'You didn't disturb me at all,' she replied with a smile, 'I was reading. Good heavens above,' she said, joining him at the sink, 'you look terrible. What's happened?'

'Nothing.' He attempted a reassuring smile. 'Just a bit of pressure out at camp, some recent happenings, nothing that need concern you. Would you like a cup of tea?'

She was not in the least reassured. 'I'm sure you could do with something a little stronger than tea,' she said briskly. 'I have only sherry, I'm afraid, will that do?'

'That'll do perfectly, thank you.'

She lifted a near-full bottle from the pantry. 'It's for cooking, I'm afraid, so I'm not sure of the quality,' she said, pouring him a healthy measure in a tumbler.

'I wouldn't know a good sherry from a bad one.'

She handed him the glass and they sat opposite each other at the four-seater table.

'I missed you at the weekend,' she said, 'we were going to have tea, remember? And I made a batch of scones.' There was no recrimination in her tone. She was merely making light conversation as she studied his face, wondering what on earth could be wrong. He looked so worried and drawn.

He took a huge swig of the sherry, which rasped his throat, yet felt extremely gratifying. 'I'm sorry, Amelia, really I am, but so many things have happened, and —'

'I can see that. You need to eat.' She wanted very much to do something practical. 'Let me get you —'

'No thank you,' he said, 'I had a meal back at camp.'

'Not even some scones?' she asked hopefully.

'No. Sorry, not even that.' He took another swig of the sherry.

'What is it, Samuel? Please tell me. It might do you good to talk.'

Fuelled by the sherry and grateful for her company, he decided to break the news to her, the news about Ant. She had a right to know.

'I'm afraid I wasn't altogether truthful when I said the happenings at camp were nothing that need concern you. There is some news that I know will affect you . . .'

'Oh yes?' she said encouragingly as he halted.

'It's about Anthony Hill.'

'Young Ant, yes, has something happened?' She was immediately anxious. 'He's not got himself into trouble, surely? The poor boy's so shy he could never cause a problem.'

'No, no, nothing like that,' he said. She wasn't helping at all, he probably should have just blurted it out. 'There was an accident, you see . . .'

'Oh dear,' a hand fluttered to her throat, 'he's hurt.'

'No. Worse. He's dead.' The words came out far more brutally than he'd intended.

There was no reply apart from a sharp intake of breath. Eyes wide, she stared at him in shock. The hand that had fluttered to her throat was joined by her other hand, the fingers of both now tightly laced, knuckles rapidly whitening as if she was praying she'd heard incorrectly.

'Several nights ago, he went for a walk on his own apparently, a track that led down to the river,' Samuel explained. 'It was dark, the track was steep and he fell. His body was discovered the following morning.'

Her breath was coming in a series of barely audible little gasps now. Rather like the panting of a distressed puppy, he thought, feeling oddly detached. And her eyes, still focused upon his, were welling with tears. He didn't like to see her so distraught.

'I don't believe he would have suffered throughout the night, Amelia,' he assured her, trying to ease her torment. 'His neck was broken. Death would have been instantaneous.'

At which point Amelia gave in to her shock and anguish. Tears flowing freely, she buried her head in her hands.

'Oh that poor boy,' she wept, 'that poor, poor, dear, sweet boy.'

He stood and, circling the table, sat beside her intent upon offering comfort. He put his arms around her and she accepted the embrace, her cheek resting damply against his, her hands on his chest, clinging to the cloth of his uniform as if she daren't let go.

'There, there,' he whispered, 'there, there now. Young Anthony would have felt no pain, you mustn't distress yourself.'

Gradually her sobs subsided, but she remained clinging gratefully to him, as if his support were some sort of lifeline.

'That dear boy,' she whispered, 'why him? Why him?'

Why him indeed, Samuel thought.

As she clung to him, he found himself equally grateful for her support, as if somehow she were also a lifeline to him. And indeed she was. They both needed a friend.

Very gently he took her face in his hands, and very gently he kissed her. A comforting kiss, a kiss shared between friends, no more than that. Or at least that's what he intended. But as he was about to break from the kiss, something happened. The hands that, in her grief, had been innocently and desperately clutching the cloth of his uniform, were now linked behind his neck, drawing him closer. Her lips were opening, demanding his do likewise. He could taste the saltiness of her tears. She was offering herself to him.

He drew away, shocked. Had she misread his intentions? Was it he who was at fault? Had he misguidedly signalled an interest that was sexual?

He stood. 'I must leave, Amelia,' he said.

'Yes,' she replied in barely a whisper, 'yes, of course you must.'

She remained sitting, staring down unseeingly at the wooden surface of the table, unable even to apologise.

She wanted to beg his forgiveness. 'I'm sorry, I'm so sorry,' she wanted to say, 'I don't know what came over me.' But she was too humiliated, too mortified, too altogether horrified to say anything at all.

She remained as she was, hearing the sound of his boots as he walked down the hall, hearing the sound of the front door closing behind him. What had she done!

Amelia had never before experienced any form of sexual desire. She had presumed she was one of those women medical experts referred to as 'frigid'. She had sought no advice, naturally, and had discussed her suspicions with no-one, but she had heard of this term and had presumed it must apply to her.

She had had sexual relations with her husband, although admittedly not often, but she had never experienced personal pleasure in their coupling. She'd always had the feeling that Martin, too, despite achieving his release, had not found the act particularly pleasurable. But this she'd put down to the fact they were living in her parents' house, making love furtively and silently in the dark as if it were something shameful.

Amelia blamed herself for everything, including her infertility, but most of all she blamed herself for that night. That night when she'd realised that her sexual inadequacy had, in effect, ruined her husband's life.

And now here she was behaving like a bitch on heat, offering herself to a man she barely knew. What had aroused in her this terrible lust? Little wonder Samuel Robinson had fled into the night.

What in heaven's name is wrong with me, she agonised.

On the drive back to camp, Samuel was feeling equally mortified. His behaviour had been shockingly inappropriate.

Inappropriate? What a very kind word, he chastised himself, disgraceful would be more fitting. Amelia

Sanderson is a married woman. She's lonely, she's vulnerable. She must surely feel betrayed, preyed upon by a man she'd presumed was a friend.

But she misunderstood me, he told himself desperately, I wasn't preying upon her at all, I wasn't trying to seduce her . . .

His self-justification didn't quite ring true, however. He did find Amelia Sanderson attractive, and the comfort he'd offered could most certainly have been interpreted as a sexual invitation, particularly to a lonely and vulnerable woman. He wondered how he'd ever be able to make amends.

Samuel didn't much like himself at that moment. Tonight, a night when he'd simply wanted to escape the hideousness that surrounded him, had become a night that was only serving to compound his woes.

CHAPTER TWELVE

Wednesday. Only five days since the closure of their club, but every single one of those days had seen a radical increase in tension among the troops of Companies A and C of the 96th Battalion. To the men it seemed that each new day their work grew harder, and each new day they became ever-more keenly aware there was no reward in sight, that their lives were no more than an endless existence of exhausting and thankless drudgery. Admittedly, the promise of four crates of hard liquor that now awaited them at the end of the work day acted as a salve of sorts, but tempers were nonetheless simmering closer to boiling point.

The deal between Baz Taylor and Strut Stowers had been seamlessly sealed over one quick phone call several days previously. Baz had needed no sales pitch at all; Strut had recognised in an instant the profit that was to be made from his own troops and also those of Company A. There was barely a man among the lot of them who wouldn't be willing to pay top dollar for the sort of heavy-duty hooch that would alleviate their boredom.

'You can add your own agent's commission of course,' Baz had said after naming his price.

And of course Strut had. He'd also added the commission he intended to pay the four corporals who would act on his behalf, two men from each company. They would collect the money from the troops and deliver it to him. One of them would then collect the four crates of liquor that Baz would leave stowed in the stables of the old Parslow property on Friday afternoon.

Strut had been selective in his choice of deputies, opting not only for men with an eye to the main chance, but those who would recognise his gratitude if they kept his involvement to themselves. He didn't trust them, Strut Stowers trusted no-one, but as a powerful figure who worked the system to his own advantage, there were always those who knew how very useful he could be to them, and alternatively what a threat he could prove to those who crossed him.

'All the boys know the booze comes from Baz Taylor,' he'd said with a smile that was a mixture of friendliness and threat so typical of Strut, 'no need for any further information to get around.'

The transaction had gone very smoothly. Strut was in possession of the money that had been collected, a sizeable amount indeed, half of which would duly be delivered to Baz, and the liquor supply had been picked up by one of the Company C privates, who, under Strut's own orders had been sent off on a transport-delivery errand. The four crates of hooch were now sitting well out of sight under canvas tarpaulins in the corner of the rank-and-file mess tent.

The knowledge that a supply of hard liquor awaited them that night may have been enough to help some through yet another interminable day, but others were not so easily mollified.

Kasey Davis gazed across the vast, flat landscape at the army of men wielding shovels and picks; hundreds of troops clearing the land, grubbing out tree stumps, levering rocks from the earth and digging up clumps of hardy scrub. Leaning his weight against the handle of his own pick, his light-khaki shirt drenched in sweat just like the shirts of all the other men, he found the sight sickening. Look at us, he thought. We might as well be working a southern plantation a hundred years ago; black slaves, that's what we are, and that's just how the army sees us.

All the men were angry, but none more so than Kasey, who was now doing his best to incite his fellow troops. Rebellion, that's what Kasey wanted.

He'd always been a firebrand, always the one to agitate, right from the outset, right from the moment when he'd first recognised the immensity of his disillusionment. Perhaps his anger had been directed at himself for having been naïve enough, or even downright stupid enough, to have expected anything different.

'You join up to fight a war and you're not allowed to carry a gun,' he'd regularly growled as he'd laboured beside his fellow troops with pick, axe and shovel. 'We supposed to call these things weapons, are we? I tell you right here and now, these are the tools of slaves. Those fuckers even title us a *non-combat* battalion. We're not here to fight a war, we're just here to do the shit work so as white soldiers don't have to soil their hands.'

And in the several days since the club had been closed he'd upped the pace, stirring ever-more strongly and along ever-more personal lines, aiming to further inflame his fellow troops.

'Not allowed to fight and not allowed to fuck,' he'd snarled, his handsome face twisted with bitterness. So consumed was he with his fight for justice that even Betty had become a symbol of the rights denied him. 'Shit, not allowed to go into town and buy ourselves a beer, that's what the army thinks of us. To those fuckers, we're not even human.'

By this stage, all the soldiers were feeling exactly the same way. Even those accustomed to the denial of equal

rights back in their home country were not prepared to
have their liberty curtailed altogether. Being banned from
town, and now having their own club denied them, was
wrong. Men needed some form of recreation, particularly
men being worked as hard as they were.

But today things had taken a further dramatic turn
for Kasey. The moment Rupe had muttered the news to
him as they'd been about to set off on their march to the
work site, Kasey's agenda had changed. When Rupe had
told him it now appeared glaringly obvious the death
of Anthony Hill was to go unavenged and that Chuck
Maxwell was to walk away scot-free, Kasey wanted one
thing, and one thing only. He was on the warpath now.
He wanted revenge.

Samuel had called Rupe to the Company C headquarters tent early that morning. The four lieutenant platoon
commanders were not present, having already embarked
upon their duties, and the moment Chuck Maxwell had
collected his paperwork and left, Samuel had sent off
young Percy Owen to summon Corporal Barrett to the
tent. Upon the pair's arrival, he hadn't even cared if Percy
Owen, from the little desk where he sat in the corner,
had overheard his admission. As if to punish himself for
his failure, Samuel felt compelled to admit to his botched
attempt in confronting Maxwell with the mutilated book.
He couldn't allow Rupert Barrett to live with false hope a
minute longer, it simply wasn't fair.

'I'm sorry, Corporal,' he said in conclusion, 'I've let
you down, you and Private Davis. The book you gave
me can serve no purpose now. Maxwell has covered his
tracks perfectly.' This time, throughout the brief telling
of his story, Samuel had named the name he'd previously avoided. 'There appears nothing else we can do,
I'm afraid.'

He'd spoken so softly that Percy Owen had heard very little and understood nothing. But the young private's ears had pricked up at the several mentions of Maxwell's name, and each time without the rank that should have preceded it. A most unusual discussion it would seem between a black soldier and his white commanding officer, Percy had thought.

Throughout the whole of that work day, the knowledge continued to plague all three men, Samuel Robinson, Rupert Barrett and Kasey Davis. Chuck Maxwell had literally got away with murder and they were helpless to do anything about it.

But Kasey had decided to use this news to further incite the men, to set them on the path of rebellion. He began spreading the rumour right there and then, starting with big Amos Cole and the other two men who had shared Ant's tent. Amos and his buddies were in the same working party, so it was easy to wend his way over to where they were, even under the watchful eye of Strut Stowers, just so long as he kept wielding his pick.

'You remember that book of Ant's that you gave to Rupe,' he muttered to Amos as they laboured side by side.

''Course I do,' the big man replied.

'We know who ripped it in half.'

'Oh yeah? And who'd that be?'

'Captain Chuck fucking Maxwell.'

'Hah.' Amos raised his pick high, brought it crashing down into the earth and levered up a good-sized rock. 'That'd be right. Just like that peckerwood to do a shit thing like that.'

'Yeah.' Kasey kept labouring away with his own pick, although not as effectively as Amos. 'Maxwell ripped up the book all right.' Another blow with the pick followed by a telling pause for effect. 'And then he killed Ant.'

The big man abruptly came to a halt. Standing straight and tall, all six-and-a-half feet of him, he looked Kasey in the eye. 'You sayin' what?' he asked.

Kasey met his gaze directly, although he had to look up quite a bit. 'I'm saying Maxwell murdered Ant. We can't prove it, mind, but we know it for a fact, and that's the truth, I swear.'

'You two lazy niggers move your asses,' Stowers' voice rang out from some distance off. 'You ain't here to chat.'

Amos and Kasey got back to work as ordered, but it didn't stop their further muttering.

'We reckon on him being in on it, too,' Kasey added with a jerk of his head in Stowers' direction. 'We reckon it was Stowers dumped Ant's body, made it look like an accident.'

'Yeah, makes sense,' Amos agreed, 'that nigger would shit on command if Maxwell told him to.'

'Like I say, we can't prove it, but pass the word on down the line,' Kasey said, 'tell everyone Ant's death weren't no accident, that Maxwell murdered him. The guys got the right to know the truth.'

'They sure have, Kase, they sure as hell have. Don't you worry, me and my buddies, we'll get the word out there.'

As big Amos Cole, now stern-faced and purposeful, worked his way towards his tent buddies only a few paces from him, Kasey felt satisfied that the wheels had been successfully set in motion.

Over the next two days, it certainly appeared he was right. By Friday morning, word had spread surreptitiously throughout the camp and men were talking of little else. The subject of Anthony Hill's murder at the hands of Chuck Maxwell was discussed with as much furtive fervour as the closure of the club and the deprivation of liberty. In fact, these topics were by now so intertwined as to become one in the eyes of men whose anger seemed to grow hourly.

Although the troops were careful to keep their whispers to themselves, well away from those with any form of rank, word of the rumour that was spreading reached the ears of Rupert Barrett. Men tended to be a little slack around Rupe, who, despite his seniority, always seemed 'one of them'. He confronted Kasey at the canteen tent early Friday morning.

'A word with you, Kase,' he said pleasantly enough while forcefully hauling him from the queue that was lined up for breakfast.

'Hey . . .' Kasey tried to object, but Rupe wasn't in the mood to listen, and by now they were a good ten yards from the others.

'Did you put out the rumour that Maxwell killed Ant?' Rupe hissed.

'It's no goddamned rumour,' Kasey hissed back, breakfast queue forgotten, 'and you damn well know that.'

'But there is no *proof*,' Rupe insisted, curbing his annoyance, trying to talk sense into his young friend. 'We can't bring him to justice, Kase, and you know it. You're only causing trouble for both yourself and the rest of the men. You're fuelling their anger, can't you see that?'

Kasey wanted to say, *Of course I can see that, why do you think I'm doing what I'm doing*, but he didn't. He wanted to say, *Fuck justice, Rupe. If we can't get justice I'll settle for revenge*, but he didn't. If he was to incite a rebellion as he intended, it would be unfair of him to involve Rupert Barrett, a professional soldier and a man of integrity. Any involvement would cost Rupe his career.

'I'll have to go to the end of the queue now,' he said sulkily, indicating the long line snaking its way to the canteen serving station.

Rupe shook his head as he watched Kasey walk off. He felt distinctly uneasy. He loved that kid, but that kid was a real worry.

*

Like all the other white officers, Samuel had heard nothing of the rumour going around. No whisper had been allowed to reach the ears of white men. But anyone could sense the growing frustration and unhappiness that permeated the camp.

And who can blame them, Samuel thought as he watched the troops march back after their long day's work, and others arrive by truck from further afield, all of them dispirited, all of them weary, with nothing to look forward to. Hell, who can blame them, of course they're unhappy, they're being treated like animals.

Unable to remedy his men's situation, Samuel felt equally unhappy. He'd been rendered utterly powerless. If only the club hadn't been closed, he thought, the club had been the answer, the club would have solved everything; but the more he dwelt upon the club, the angrier he became. He cursed the locals, he cursed the army, he cursed Australia's racial policies, but above all he cursed himself. His anger turning to guilt, he cursed himself for his apparent failure on all levels. He'd not only failed his men, he'd failed in his pathetic attempt to expose Chuck Maxwell, and he'd failed Amelia Sanderson, whose trust he'd betrayed.

But as he pondered his own inadequacy it occurred to him that perhaps he was not powerless to rectify just one of these failures. He must at least try. He would go into town tonight, he decided, and he would ask Amelia Sanderson's forgiveness.

He didn't stay for the evening meal, which was always served early in order to accommodate hungry working men, but left the camp while it was still light, just as dusk was starting to fall.

After their meal, in the rank-and-file general mess tent, men set about the serious business of hard drinking.

This was a Friday and under normal conditions they might have headed into town for a social night on the drink, or a night at a brothel, or a night simply of dancing and music. But as conditions were not normal, tonight was to be a night when they would get thoroughly drunk on the booze provided by Baz Taylor instead. Nobody cared who the middle man might be, nor did they query, they'd simply forked out their money, grateful for the opportunity to get their hands on hard liquor. And Baz's booze certainly packed a punch.

'Worth every cent,' Amos Cole said after swigging back half a mugful of cheap, rough whisky that tore at the throat.

'Just as well,' replied Bernie, one of his tent buddies, a nuggetty twenty-two-year-old from Chicago, smaller than most of the men, but streetwise and tough. 'The guy's sure slugging us enough for the stuff. We're paying twice what we did at the club that night.'

'So?' The big man gave a careless shrug. 'What else we goin' to spend our money on?'

The others agreed, Amos was right, of course, and disgruntlement set in as they drank not for pleasure, but simply in the knowledge there was nothing else to do.

Willie was into the rum, or at least they'd been told it was rum; the bottle was unlabelled. Thick, dark-brown, treacly stuff that had nearly caused him to gag when he'd taken his first mouthful. Willie wasn't used to heavy liquor. But Kasey was urging him on and Willie was rapidly coming to the conclusion that it wasn't really that bad after all.

No-one knew exactly where Baz Taylor got his liquor supply, but it certainly had the desired effect. Men were becoming drunker by the minute.

*

Amelia was busying herself getting the tea, bustling about the kitchen, filling the kettle, putting it on the stove, lifting the teapot from the cupboard together with its cosy, and the cups and their saucers, the teaspoons, the sugar, the milk, setting things out on the table, focusing upon anything that might prevent her eyes meeting his.

She hadn't been able to believe it when he'd arrived at the front door. He hadn't used his key, he'd rung the bell instead.

'May I come in?' he'd said.

'Yes, of course,' she'd replied, averting her eyes and opening the door wide, presuming that he'd come to collect his things.

But as she'd closed the door behind him he hadn't disappeared into his quarters, he'd waited patiently in the hall instead, as if he were a visitor, as if this weren't his billet at all.

'Any chance of a cup of tea?' he'd asked, which again had surprised her. This was his official place of residence after all, the US Army paid his rent; the kitchen was as much for his use as it was hers. 'That is if you have the time,' he'd added as she'd hesitated, and she'd realised he was suggesting they have tea together.

'Yes, of course,' she'd answered once again, and she'd led the way down the hall to the kitchen.

Now as she busied herself, assiduously avoiding any form of eye contact, she wondered what in heaven's name she was expected to say by way of apology. How humiliating this was.

Why is he just standing there looking at me, she thought, why can't he talk about the weather or something? Surely if we're to continue any form of social contact he might at least have the good grace to pretend Tuesday night didn't happen.

Then all of a sudden . . .

'I'm sorry, Amelia,' Samuel said. 'I can't begin to tell you how sorry I am, please forgive me . . .'

He was apologising to *her*? Why? For the first time she met his eyes, but she couldn't reply, she was dumbfounded.

Samuel felt guiltier than ever. She looked so confused, so helpless somehow. 'I overstepped the mark,' he said. 'I meant only to comfort you, truly I did, but my behaviour was improper and I sincerely apologise.'

You're apologising to *me*, she thought. But you were consoling me the other night, Samuel. You were consoling me and I behaved shamelessly. Dear God, like a bitch on heat, she thought, shuddering at the memory. Why do you feel the need to apologise?

His apology seemed to be confusing her even more, so Samuel felt compelled to go on. 'I betrayed your trust as a friend, Amelia,' he said. 'You're vulnerable, you're living alone, I invaded your privacy . . .' He was fumbling for words now, and she was looking at him most strangely. 'I should not have behaved in such an intimate fashion,' he said, 'it was wrong of me. You're a married woman, you have a husband . . .'

'I do not have a husband, I'm a widow. My husband is dead.' Where had she found the strength to bark those words at him so harshly? To even say the truth out loud, the truth she'd been denying herself for months? But after the sleepless nights she'd spent analysing what had happened, seeking some form of excuse, or at least some explanation for her appalling conduct, she had no wish to be patronised. Nor did she want his sympathy. Did he seriously consider her behaviour justifiable? As the poor, lonely, husbandless woman he perceived her to be, did he find it excusable that she should offer herself to him sexually? Such a suggestion was not only patronising, but an insult of the basest kind.

The kettle was on the boil now. She poured water into the teapot, swirled it around and emptied it down the sink.

Samuel watched her ladle several spoons of tea from the canister into the heated pot. He was at a loss for words. Until finally, 'I'm sorry, Amelia,' he said, watching as she filled the pot, continuing her tea-making duties with the utmost efficiency. 'I didn't know . . . About your husband, that is. I thought . . .' He paused. He wasn't sure what he'd thought. She'd never said anything about her husband, though he'd been informed by others he was a soldier.

'Yes,' she said briskly, putting the cosy over the teapot and bringing it to the table. 'The fall of Singapore, reported missing in action over three months ago.' Again she sounded uncharacteristically harsh, surprising even herself. 'So by now presumed dead, of course.'

She turned the pot three times, and leaving the tea to brew fetched the biscuit tin housing the scones, together with side plates and some butter and jam.

'I presume you will have scones with your tea?' she asked, setting everything out on the table.

'Yes, that would be lovely, thank you,' he said.

'Good.' She sat. 'Do please sit down, Samuel,' she said as she picked up the pot and started to pour.

Amelia felt a renewed sense of confidence. She had taken control, and things were back on an even keel. They could put Tuesday night behind them now.

Back at camp, things were starting to get a little out of hand. Baz's booze was working its magic and men were becoming louder, bolder, some unruly, others simply wanting to make the night a party.

'Come on, Kase,' several urged, 'give us a song.'

'Yeah,' one man started strumming his guitar, 'come on, buddy.'

Another took his harmonica from his pocket. 'Let's get hold of Rupe and make it a real party,' he said. Rupe, who was in the NCOs' mess tent along with the other officers, was by far and away the best guitarist among them and often joined his men for a night of song.

'No,' Kasey snapped an immediate order. 'Don't get Rupe, don't be crazy!'

They were still sober enough, all of them, to recognise the danger. Popular as Rupe was with the men, he was still a corporal, and if he were to discover them drunk he'd have to report the fact.

'OK, OK,' the man with the harmonica backed down immediately, 'but give us a song anyway, Kase.'

Rebellion on his mind, Kasey wasn't in the mood for song, but he obliged anyway, embarking upon a rousing version of 'Up a Lazy River', which he was aware they all knew and would sing along to while they kept happily drinking. It was barely seven o'clock, plenty of time to agitate for some action. There were many others, he knew, who were just like him, angry and aching for trouble. All it would take was a few more drinks.

But as things turned out, it took less than a few more drinks. In fact, it took less than a few more songs before something happened that brought about an instant mood change.

In the officers' mess tent, Lieutenant Stanley Hartford of Company C returned from having completed a round of the camp with one of his fellow platoon commanders, Lieutenant Thomas Woods, fondly known as Woodsy. Neither Stan nor Woodsy had any wish to spoil the troops' fun, but diligent young men both, they felt obliged to report their findings to their senior officer.

'I do believe the men are getting drunk, sir,' Stan said to Captain Maxwell, with a confirming nod from Woodsy.

'We think they may have a liquor supply in the rank-and-file mess.'

Captain Mick O'Brien of Company A, an amiable Irish–American from Los Angeles, gave a humorous snort. 'I thought they were sounding a bit happy,' he said, 'Christ, the poor bastards haven't got much to sing about. Wonder where they got the booze.'

They could all hear the raucous rendition of 'Lulu's Back in Town' ringing loud and clear across the camp. The men certainly sounded drunk.

The other officers, nine in all, seated at several tables playing cards and indeed drinking themselves, appeared equally unfazed. But not Chuck Maxwell, who rose instantly to his feet.

'Did you see evidence of a liquor supply?' he demanded of Hartford.

'Well, um . . .' Given the general good-natured reception from the others, particularly the two commanding officers of Company A, Stan and Woodsy rather wished they hadn't brought up the subject, but neither was prepared to lie. 'Yes, sir,' Stan said, with another confirming nod from Woodsy. 'We think we saw the odd bottle being passed around.'

'Right.' Chuck marched towards the tent entrance, pistol in hand. 'Come with me, Lieutenant,' he ordered, 'you too,' he said to Woodsy. 'We'll sort these niggers out once and for all. I won't stand for this kind of shit.'

'Hang on a minute, Maxwell.' Mick O'Brien stood, calling Chuck to a halt. 'Let's go about this peaceably,' he said.

Mick didn't approve of Maxwell's antagonistic attitude, but then he didn't approve of Maxwell himself. Nor did Biff Baker, his fellow commanding officer of Company A. Both wondered why a man like Chuck Maxwell had been appointed to such a position in the first place, and both sympathised with Samuel Robinson for having to share the command with him.

'Sure, sure,' Mick now went on in his easygoing manner, 'we need to sort out the problem, can't have the boys getting drunk in camp, but no point in riling them any further than necessary. Let's face it, they've been having a rough trot of things lately.'

A rough trot of things? Chuck could barely believe he'd heard a white man say that. 'What's going on out there is trouble in the making,' he said with a superior sneer. O'Brien was another of those ignorant northerners who didn't understand nigger mentality. 'What's going on out there,' he repeated pedantically, just to drum the point home, 'is about to turn right nasty, I can tell you that here and now. Niggers and liquor, they just don't mix.'

'Yeah, yeah, I'm sure you have a point, but let's you and me address the situation together and as peaceably as possible.' Mick exchanged a telling glance with his fellow officer. Neither he nor Biff Baker wished their men to be addressed at all by the likes of Chuck Maxwell.

Ordering two of his lieutenants to accompany him, Mick joined Chuck – much to Chuck's chagrin, for Chuck would vastly have preferred to confront the men on his own – and together all six officers left the tent.

By the time they reached the general mess tent, the men had segued onto 'Minnie the Moocher', yelling the lyrics at the tops of their voices, the clapping of hands and drumming of tin mugs on wooden tabletops all but drowning out the accompanying guitars and harmonicas, of which there were now several.

Hi-De-Hi-De-Hi-De-Ho . . . The men swayed drunkenly from side to side as they screamed out the scat line.

Both captains, flanked by their junior officers, stood no more than a dozen or so yards from the open-sided tent surveying the scene, apparently unobserved. Which to all, seemed a little strange.

Or, Chuck thought, if we *are* being observed, apparently none of these drunken niggers gives a damn. Either way, the sight annoyed the hell out of him. If they're going to flout authority you'd think they'd keep a lookout, wouldn't you? But no, they're too damn dumb for that. And if some of them *have* seen us, he thought, standing right here where we are out in the open, lit clear as day by the camp lights, then why the hell aren't they shitting themselves?

The officers stood there for a good minute or so, which to Stan and Woodsy and the other two lieutenants seemed a very long time. They too wondered why the men hadn't cottoned on to the fact they were there.

Mick O'Brien, however, had a feeling that some, perhaps those not as drunk as others, were aware of their presence, but were not communicating the fact to their buddies. In which case they're making a definite statement, he thought, and that's a bit of a worry. We'll have to go about this carefully. I reckon we just leave it until the end of the song before we call attention to ourselves. He drew his pistol from its holster and cast a look to Maxwell, which said as much, Maxwell returning a brief nod that Mick took as agreement.

Captain Mick O'Brien was right in his assessment. A number of the men were fully aware of their presence. Kasey had seen the officers from the moment they'd arrived. And several others among the troops had too, but they'd only raised their voices louder and smashed their mugs harder by way of thumbing their noses at authority. Their attitude gave Kasey immense satisfaction.

When they came to the end of the song, the men burst into a raucous round of applause, and as mugs were refilled, requests were yelled out for which song Kasey should lead them in next.

Then above the hubbub two shots rang out.

Everyone fell instantly silent and all turned to where Captains Maxwell and O'Brien stood, both with pistols raised high overhead.

Mick O'Brien holstered his weapon. He would rather have called attention to their presence in a less aggressive fashion, but the action had nonetheless been necessary. He stepped forward and addressed the troops.

'You men are in direct contravention of US Army Standing Orders concerning the possession and consumption of alcohol,' he announced. 'Now before this matter gets any further out of hand —'

At that point, Maxwell, still with his pistol held high, dived in. 'The next shot don't go up there,' Chuck announced, and arm fully extended he lowered his firearm, pointing the muzzle directly at the densest part of the gathering. 'Next shot goes right where I'm aiming, you understand me? And the shot after that, and the one after that, too. I don't care if I have to kill every goddamned nigger in this here tent. You scum are disobeying army orders and where I come from that's mutiny.' Chuck allowed himself a smile. Now that he had the men's full attention, he was rather enjoying himself. 'Surely even you niggers can grasp the fact that mutiny calls for a firing squad. And I'm more than happy to be that firing squad.'

Mutiny? Mick O'Brien was taken aback. The situation was hardly a mutiny. Did the man have to be so overly dramatic? He considered Maxwell's threat unnecessarily belligerent, and perhaps even provocative, but he had to admit it appeared to have had the desired effect. Many of the troops were clearly cowed by his warning, while a number of others, although still appearing rebellious, had been brought under control.

He tempered his own address, while still maintaining the utmost severity, aware he and Maxwell must be seen to work as a team.

'We will need to confiscate the liquor you men have acquired,' he ordered, wishing like hell Maxwell would lower his pistol, which remained steadfastly pointed at the crowd. 'So you will place your supply on the tables for collection.' A short pause followed. 'Immediately,' he added, and while men dumped bottles on tabletops, he further added, 'and I mean your *entire* supply,' as he spied several ill-concealed crates tucked about the tent.

He nodded a command to his lieutenants and Chuck did the same.

'Collect the liquor,' Chuck ordered Stan and Woodsy, who breathed a joint sigh of relief. They'd both been praying Maxwell wouldn't order them to turn their own weapons upon the men in the pretence of forming a firing squad.

The four lieutenants went among the men collecting all the bottles they could find and placing them in the crates from which they'd obviously been taken, Chuck remaining all the while with his pistol trained upon the troops.

'A full report will be filed on each and every one of you,' he announced, 'and there will be punishment meted out, you can be sure of that. The US Army will not tolerate rebellious behaviour of any kind, particularly not from the likes of you niggers. You boys got to learn your place, you hear me.'

When the three crates, which had been discovered by the junior officers, were placed on the ground before the two captains with some bottles empty, some half full, some unopened, Mick O'Brien was about to order they be taken away, but once again Chuck Maxwell got in first.

'Empty them,' he ordered Stan and Woodsy, 'empty those bottles right here and right now.'

Mick O'Brien had no option but to order his own lieutenants do likewise; he could not counter-command a fellow officer. He stood by and watched as the bottles' contents, four at a time, were steadily poured out onto the ground, and the animosity from the men as they too watched the liquor glug its way into the thirsty earth was palpable.

Maxwell's a damn fool, Mick thought, this is only exacerbating a volatile situation.

Chuck didn't think so, however. As they marched back to the officers' mess tent, Chuck Maxwell was thoroughly satisfied with the way he'd handled the episode, which could quite easily have got out of hand. Trouble in the making that was back there, he thought. Yes siree, trouble in the making. One of Daddy's first rules – never let your niggers get a hold of hard liquor. He congratulated himself for having well and truly 'nipped things in the bud' as his daddy would say.

But Chuck Maxwell had unknowingly left behind him a festering sea of trouble beyond his comprehension.

'The man wants a mutiny,' big Amos Cole snarled, 'let's give him a mutiny.'

'Yeah, why not,' his tent buddy Bernie agreed, 'that's the fucker who killed Ant. He'd kill every one of us, too, if he had half a chance.'

Many of the men were backing away, prepared to call it a night, not willing to push things further, but others were muttering rebelliously.

'He stole our liquor . . .'

'Fuck US Army Standing Orders, we paid good money for that . . .'

'He's got no right . . .'

Their reaction pleased Kasey no end. He didn't need to sow the seeds of rebellion; Chuck Maxwell had successfully done it for him. In fact, it was just possible

Chuck Maxwell had successfully dug his own grave. Kasey certainly hoped so.

'Drink up, Willie,' he said. Willie still had half a mug of rum. So did many of the others. The officers hadn't collected the mugs. Little did the officers know too that hidden under the tarpaulin in the corner of the tent was another whole crate of hooch. The men dug out fresh bottles, tin mugs were refilled, and they continued to scoff down yet more liquor while feeding their ever-increasing desire to rebel.

Those in the NCOs' mess tent, which was closer to the general mess tent than that of the officers, had also deduced the troops had alcohol. Stowers and his four corporals were in the know from the outset of course, but well before the white commanding officers had been informed by their lieutenants on patrol duty, the NCOs had gathered from the boisterous singing that the men must be liquor-affected. After all, the sergeants and corporals knew only too well that their black brothers had little cause to rejoice.

They'd talked among themselves, aware the booze must have come from Baz Taylor's supply for the club, and some comments had been made about how the troops might have acquired it, but nobody really cared. For the most part, they hoped the men were having a good time, in the knowledge that it wouldn't last long, particularly with the racket they were making.

First Sergeant Strut Stowers, top-ranking officer among all twenty-four present, was not in the least concerned he might be implicated, but he was cursing the men nonetheless. Dumb young niggers, he thought, how stupid to get so fucking drunk and so fucking loud so fucking quick; they'll have their booze taken off them before they've drunk even half of it. Ah well, none of my business and not my fault. Strut wasn't fussed. He had their money and that's all that mattered.

'Well, I guess that's that, then,' he said when they heard the shots and watched from their mess tent as the officers collected the bottles and emptied the liquor out onto the ground. 'A good time, but a short time.'

Much as Rupe detested Stowers, he'd actually been thinking along the same lines. How downright dumb of the men to put on such a show, he thought. But then it occurred to him, perhaps that's what they're after, some of them anyway. Perhaps they're making a statement.

Following the confiscation of the liquor, it soon became apparent the problem had not been resolved, that if anything it had worsened. The boisterous singing had stopped, certainly, but the men were just as loud, louder even, and now in their rowdiness aggression could be heard. There was the shattering of glass as a bottle was smashed against a tent post, and angry protests at the fact that it hadn't even been empty, a waste of good liquor. A scuffle broke out, some of the men taking sides. 'Fight, fight!' they called, egging each other on, demanding entertainment.

Quite obviously, they had more booze, and were getting drunker.

It was decided in the NCOs' tent that Sergeant Reed of Company A, together with Rupe and two other corporals, would pay a visit to the men and try to talk sense to them.

Stowers thought this an excellent idea, although he wasn't going to go himself, considering it might be a bit risky under the circumstances. Besides, he knew he was unpopular with the troops – which given his seniority he considered only proper – and his presence might rile them further.

'You're the best bet, Barrett,' he said, 'you're the men's favourite.' His voice laced with sarcasm, it wasn't a compliment. 'They just love your kind of big-brother soft touch. You could maybe take your guitar along.'

Rupe didn't deign to answer, but followed Reed and the other corporals outside.

Upon their arrival at the general mess tent, Sergeant Reed, a strict but well-respected officer, tried to call the troops to order.

'You men need to stop this here and now,' Reed yelled in the powerful voice that had rung clear as a bell across many a parade ground.

They heard him all right, but his air of command didn't have its customary effect. They kept drinking and jostling each other and jeering at the mere presence of authority. They really didn't seem to care.

'You're drunk and disorderly,' Reed yelled, 'call it a night, all of you! Disband and go to your tents.'

But a voice answered back as loud and clear as Reed's stentorian tones, a young voice, bold and challenging. 'You here to take our booze off us, too, are you, Sarge?'

It was Private Kasey Davis at the forefront of the mob, standing defiant and unwavering, confronting his senior officers. And standing right beside him, equally defiant, clearly offering his support, was big Amos Cole.

'I'm here to talk sense to you, son.' Reed addressed young Kasey directly, but in registering the two ringleaders were from Company C, he gave a nod to Rupert Barrett that said, *Over to you.*

Rupe stepped forward. Surely if anyone could get through to Kasey it was him. Come on, Kase, his mind pleaded, it's me, buddy, it's Rupe, you've got to stop this, you know you do. Listen to me, buddy, please listen to me.

His eyes said it all as he met Kasey's gaze, but already he could tell Kasey wasn't getting the message. Kasey's own eyes, a penetrating green and normally so full of life, were clouded over. Possibly with alcohol, but no, Rupe thought, there's something else, something much stronger. And then he realised what he could see was dull, murderous revenge.

Oh dear God, he thought, this is what the kid's been aiming for all the while. He's been inciting the men to riot – why the hell couldn't I see that?

'You've got to stop this, Kase,' he said quietly. His eyes quickly roamed the gathering, then returned to Kasey, willing him to listen. 'You've got to call a halt to all this, you know you do.'

'It's too late for that.' Kasey's voice was as dead as his eyes.

And behind him, the men kept drinking.

Sergeant Reed and Corporal Barrett reported their findings to their commanding officers.

'We think there's trouble brewing, sir,' Reed said, addressing both Captains Maxwell and O'Brien. 'Corporal Barrett and I attempted to communicate with the men, but neither of us seemed to get through. The troops have more booze and they refuse to stop drinking.'

At that point he handed the floor over to Corporal Barrett, the ringleaders being from Company C and obviously well known to him.

Rupe also addressed both captains, although he focused principally upon O'Brien, preferring to ignore Chuck Maxwell, despite the man being his own commanding officer.

'The men are certainly drunk and disorderly, sir,' he said, 'and under normal circumstances it might be best to just let them get completely out of it, sleep it off and address the issue in the morning . . .'

He ignored the derisive snort from Maxwell and concentrated solely upon O'Brien, who had his full attention.

'. . . But I do believe things have gone beyond drunk and disorderly,' he went on, 'and that we may have some sort of riot on our hands.'

'I agree with you, Corporal,' O'Brien said. 'In fact, we've already taken precautions. HQ has been informed of the situation.'

He cast a brief glance at Maxwell, and from the reaction between the two white officers, Rupe deduced there had been some form of altercation.

'I agree with you also,' O'Brien continued, 'that under normal circumstances it might have been a good idea to let the men drink themselves into a stupor and sort out the whole mess tomorrow morning. However, these are not normal circumstances, and there are too few of us to contain a riot if, God help us, things should deteriorate to that extent.'

They were virtually the same words he'd spat at Chuck Maxwell when they'd arrived back at the tent after the booze had been poured out on the ground and the troops had been left palpably fuming.

'You do realise you've all but incited a riot, don't you,' he'd hissed out of hearing of the junior officers, but in the presence of Captain Biff Baker. 'And you do realise that if the men choose to make trouble there are too few of us to control them.'

Maxwell's reaction had been typically arrogant, typically dismissive. 'Rubbish,' he'd scoffed, 'they know who their bosses are. They'll bellyache for a while, sure, but they're niggers, they'll end up doing what they're told.'

When he'd been proven wrong and the white officers, like the NCOs, had deduced the matter had not been settled at all, Maxwell had been all for a further confrontation. He'd been quickly howled down by his fellow officers, however, who this time hadn't bothered to hide their disdain from the lieutenants.

'For God's sake, man, leave it be,' Biff Baker had snarled, 'these guys are soldiers, not slaves on some goddamned cotton plantation.' Biff didn't even know Chuck's background and how very close he was to the truth. He did wonder though, given the man's attitude, what idiot had placed him in command of a black labour force.

'We'll need to inform HQ,' Mick O'Brien had said briskly, not even bothering to address Maxwell. 'Radio Hank Henry,' he'd ordered his lieutenant.

Now, upon this visit from his NCOs and upon receiving the report of their findings, O'Brien was further reassured he'd taken the right action. NCOs like Reed and Barrett, who knew their men so well, would not tend to be alarmists unless the situation called for it.

'Things have certainly gone too far, Corporal,' he said, 'and I can assure you the provost marshal has been alerted. A unit of MPs will shortly be on the way to offer assistance if necessary and the major is arranging further precautions in case of other contingencies.'

Hank Henry was indeed taking no chances. He'd already warned the Commander of the Australian 51st Regiment based at Mount Louisa to stand by in the unlikely event there was any form of breakout.

'I guess all we do now,' O'Brien summed up, 'is we play the waiting game. Perhaps,' he added with a smile to Rupe, 'we hope they all drink themselves stupid, pass out and wake up with a hangover.'

'Yes, sir,' Rupe agreed, 'that would be the ideal outcome.'

But as he walked out of the tent with Sergeant Reed, Rupe doubted very much this would be the outcome. As did they all. There's going to be a whole heap of trouble, Rupe thought.

He wished Samuel Robinson was here. Captain Samuel Robinson was the one white officer who'd shown true compassion, who'd set up the Negro Servicemen's Club, who'd recognised the needs, and the undeniable rights, of his men. Captain Robinson might have been the one white officer who could have controlled the troops, particularly those of Company C who appeared so fired up by young Kasey Davis.

But Captain Samuel Robinson was elsewhere, unwittingly becoming a part of another problem altogether.

CHAPTER THIRTEEN

'That's the first time I've ever admitted to Martin's death,' Amelia said.

They were speaking more intimately now. After the niceties had been exchanged about the scones, Samuel's compliment upon her baking, her apology for the lack of whipped cream to go with the jam, Amelia herself had changed the tone of the conversation.

'I must admit it was something of a relief to say the words out loud,' she said. 'I've known for some time that of course he's not alive, but "missing in action" is a hideously indefinite phrase, isn't it?' She was not speaking emotionally, but in a very matter-of-fact fashion, again rather surprising herself. 'The term is neither black nor white, but an awful shade of grey, leaving one open to such torment.'

'I agree,' Samuel said in an equally blunt fashion, 'far better to be told a loved one is dead, I would think, rather than missing in action.'

'Precisely. And there's also the fact that, with no witnesses to the death, one spends so much time wondering whether one's husband suffered much pain. One hopes it was quick, but one can't help . . .' She stopped abruptly. He was looking at her with such compassion, so much care was reflected in his eyes, and yet she hadn't been seeking sympathy at all. She'd simply been speaking her thoughts out loud, thoughts she'd never shared with anyone. She'd found the exercise most liberating admittedly, but she didn't want him to misunderstand, to misread her motives as a bid for his sympathy.

'Ah well,' she said with a smile, 'so many other women have suffered, and are sadly yet to suffer, I'm sure, the same fate. Wives, mothers, daughters, sisters . . .' She shook her head. 'War is such a terrible thing, isn't it?' Then without even giving him time to answer . . . 'Would you like another cup of tea?'

'Yes, I would very much. Thank you, Amelia.'

He passed her his cup and saucer, and as she took them from him their fingers inadvertently touched. No more than the slightest split-second contact of skin on skin, but enough to completely undermine her newfound confidence.

Amelia picked up the pot and poured the tea a little shakily. She had recognised in that very instant that she could not put Tuesday night behind her, that just the touch of his fingers was enough.

The men were rapidly becoming discontented with their own company, the ringleaders among them wanting a change of scene. And besides, big Amos Cole was getting sick of the hooch.

'This is dog's piss,' he said, having drained the last of the rotgut whisky directly from the bottle, which he threw to the ground, where it crashed among several other empties. 'I suggest we go into town and buy ourselves a few real drinks, what do you say?'

'I say yeah, that's what we do all right.' Tough little Bernie punched the air with his fist in a show of aggression. 'And we don't let nobody stop us. We get hold of some weapons from the armoury, too, just in case, just to let 'em know we mean business.'

'Sounds like a mighty fine plan to me,' big Amos agreed, turning to the others and rousing them along, 'who's up for it, eh?'

Several men nodded and raised their hands immediately. Amos Cole, with a voice as big as his stature, was a natural leader.

'Count me in, too,' Kasey said, as if this hadn't been his plan right from the start. 'You up for it, Willie?'

'Sure thing, Kase.' Befuddled with rum, Willie wasn't sure what he was 'up for' at all, which was probably the case with most of the others. But Willie was happy to go along with whatever Kasey wanted. Kase was his buddy.

More men started raising their hands, urging their buddies to do the same, calling them into action. Numbers were growing. The next stop, it was agreed, would be the armoury.

As many of the troops – angry, defiant – continued muttering rebelliously, others – perhaps those who were not so very drunk or at least had sense enough to recognise the danger – cleared off to their tents, wanting no part of an action that would surely spell disaster.

There was no holding back those bent on rebellion, however, and barely ten minutes later there must have been well over a hundred men approaching the armoury. No-one counted, so no-one could be sure. Most were drunk, some angry and feeling justifiably so, and some perhaps joining in for the adventure, not altogether sure of what they were doing apart from defying orders and going into town.

But the leaders were committed, and none more so than Kasey Davis.

'We'd ask you guys to step aside if you wouldn't mind,' Amos Cole said to the two men on guard outside the armoury, 'after you've opened up the doors for us that is.' He sounded very polite and appeared not in the least drunk, but then it took a lot of liquor, even of the rotgut-whisky variety, to render big Amos Cole noticeably intoxicated.

The two guards cast a brief, uncertain look at one another.

'There's a lot of us here,' Amos said, 'and we got no beef with you guys, we don't want to do you no harm.'

The guards downed arms, opened the doors and stepped to one side.

The majority hung back, awaiting further orders as they were accustomed to do, while the ringleaders and a dozen or so more adventurous men entered the armoury in order to select their weapons of choice.

'Go fetch the Jimmy's,' Amos instructed several men, 'I'd say we'll need three in all.'

'Sure, Amos.' The men left on the double for the camp's transport area where the GMC trucks were housed, and Amos joined the others in the armoury.

Their selection of weapons was varied. Many chose M1 Garand carbines, the standard US Army Infantry–issue rifles, while several others armed themselves with Browning 9mm handguns, but tough little Bernie's choice was far more exciting.

'Well, look what I got me here,' he said, picking up a Thompson .45 calibre machine gun. 'I got me a real-live Chicago Piano.' Bernie felt extra tough brandishing the machine gun, which he knew to have been the favoured weapon of Chicago gangsters. 'This'll sure as hell frighten the shit out of them.'

'That's not a bad idea, Bernie,' big Amos said, selecting a machine gun of his own, 'we'll put on a show, give them a real scare. They won't open fire on us if we're carrying a couple of these.'

'Yeah, damn good idea, Bernie,' Kasey agreed, trying to make the comment sound casual, and he too chose a

Thompson. But Kasey was not out to scare, Kasey had already determined his weapon would not be for show. Every fibre aquiver, Kasey was poised for revenge.

The men were all riled up by now, even those who'd awaited orders outside the armoury. The sight of their buddies stepping out into the night armed to the hilt excited them. They were going into town come hell or high water and just let anyone try to stop them.

The sight and the sound of the trucks arriving riled them up even further, and they let out whooping cheers of triumph as the Jimmy's came to a halt before them in a swirl of dust.

Men clambered eagerly into the open trays and stood holding onto the overhead steel frames, which supported the canvas when the vehicles, usually due to inclement weather, were covered. But despite the approach of winter, covers were not in play on this crisp, still night of 22 May, and the image of the mutinous men, some of them armed, was clearly visible to all.

Kasey climbed into the first truck, machine gun at the ready, Willie beside him with a standard army-issue rifle. Like many of the others, Willie wasn't sure what he was supposed to do with the rifle, apart from look as if he really meant business, but that didn't matter. They were on the rampage and going into town.

In the second truck, it was Bernie, proudly displaying his Chicago Piano, who chose to lead the mutineers, and in the third truck big Amos Cole took the helm, also with his Thompson machine gun. All in all, as others kept clambering in after them, they presented a formidable sight.

For a while now, in the officers' mess tent where they awaited the arrival of the MPs, the captains and lieutenants had been commenting on how much quieter things seemed to have become.

In the NCOs' mess tent, too, the sergeants and corporals had been remarking upon the comparative silence. And looking out towards the rank-and-file mess some distance away, the huge tent appeared to be half-deserted. Had the men simply decided to call it a night?

Now, the very silence upon which they'd all been commenting was suddenly broken by the sound of trucks and the voices of troops whooping in drunken triumph. What the hell was going on?

Quickly arming themselves, the officers raced from their respective tents to discover pandemonium.

Several hundred yards away, outside the armoury, were three GMC troop-transport trucks. Their engines were being revved up and they were starting to circle, the drivers with the clear intention of heading for the major dirt road that led out of the camp. Men were still clambering aboard, many of them armed, at least it appeared so.

'Shit, they've got machine guns,' Stan said to Woodsy.

'What the hell do those boys think they're up to?' Mick O'Brien yelled angrily, brandishing his pistol. He wasn't having any of this sort of insubordinate nonsense. 'Damn them, what kind of dumb show are they putting on!'

Under normal conditions, Chuck Maxwell might have come up with a smug *I told you so*, but even he recognised this wasn't the moment. In heading for the road out of camp, the trucks would pass right by the officers' mess tent. There was no time to lose if they were to stop these drunken troops, who were obviously bent on having a good time.

The trucks were underway now, in single line all three, and as they passed the NCOs' mess, Rupe, who had raced outside with the others, saw Kasey in the first vehicle, machine gun at the ready.

Oh dear God no, he thought, the kid's aiming at a full-on mutiny, he's going to get himself killed. He yelled out to

Kase and the troops, but to no avail, his voice useless above the melee, and then the trucks were approaching the officers' mess, where men waited, weapons poised.

The commanding officers bellowed orders to halt and their lieutenants stood with rifles threateningly raised, but the trucks didn't stop.

Mick O'Brien fired a warning shot in the air, as did Biff Baker. Chuck Maxwell would have preferred to have taken aim directly at the mutineers, but for all his earlier bravura, he was aware that shooting one or two, even under these conditions, might get him into trouble. At this stage of the proceedings, they were just drunkards showing off and out for a joy ride.

He raised his pistol, about to fire his own warning shot, and that's when he realised the Thompson machine gun in the first truck was sighted directly upon him.

Kasey had been searching for Maxwell among the officers gathered, and in spying the man and realising he had a clear shot, he'd decided this was the moment.

The action was instantaneous. The rapid fire of the machine gun cracked the night. Maxwell ducked behind the nearest man, and as young Woodsy took the bullet intended for him and fell to the ground, Maxwell raced inside the mess tent, the crack of machine gun following, 600 to 800 rounds per minute, shredding the canvas. Then he dived into the slit trench on the other side of the mess tent and the rain of bullets came to a halt.

Kasey's heart was racing, adrenaline pumping. Had he killed the man? Surely yes. No-one inside that tent could have survived. He rejoiced in the thought. Maxwell was dead and Ant's death avenged. To Kasey, now in a state of madness, this was war and not for one minute did he regret his actions, nor did he care what the outcome might be for him. A pity the lieutenant had to cop it, he thought, although he could see now that the young man was stirring, not dead. But so what if the guy dies, he told himself, a casualty of war, that's what he is. And as a show of triumph, Kasey released another round of machine-gun fire into the air.

He was not the only one. Incited by the Thompson's *rat-tat-tat* and the sense of battle that surrounded them, others were firing weapons indiscriminately. Not taking aim, not with the intention to kill, but revelling in their power. No longer slave labour, but soldiers with firearms, they were letting loose in every direction, displaying no concern for ricocheting bullets that might cause harm. Particularly Bernie. Bernie was exulting in the sheer might of his Chicago Piano.

And those unarmed, intoxicated by both the liquor and the heightened thrill of the moment, yelled encouragement, urging their buddies on as the trucks drove out of camp and headed for Townsville, leaving behind them utter chaos.

The Commander of the Australian 51st Regiment based at Mount Louisa was alerted immediately, and the militia unit known as the Far North Queensland Regiment was informed it was no longer on 'standby', that its young troops, principally national servicemen called up for the defence of the north, were now ordered into action. But against who? Not the Japanese. The heavily anticipated invasion had so far not occurred, yet their orders were 'shoot to kill'. Kill who? The answer appeared insane. American soldiers. Troops of the US 96th Engineers, a Negro labour battalion camped out at Kelso. Kill them! Why?

'A mutiny they say, some sort of riot. They're heading into town.'

'But why do we have to kill them?'

'I dunno.'

Two companies of the 51st Battalion were hurriedly deployed to block off the approaches into Townsville and halt the Americans, who were apparently armed. Already awaiting their arrival at the designated rendezvous points would be several units of US Military Police. Should the Negro troops not surrender peaceably upon command, the operational orders were undeniably clear – 'shoot to kill'.

'Jeez, who was the prick who came up with the code name *Operation Black Buck*?' Private Frank Midgely queried his fellow two-man crew as their Bren Gun Carrier trundled its way to the road-block point. 'Bit disrespectful, don't you reckon,' he said, eyes trained on the dark track ahead, now eerily illuminated by the carrier's spotlights. 'Downright bloody rude when you think about it.'

'Nah, just some clown of an officer trying to be funny,' his gunner mate Paddy Sullivan assured him, 'probably didn't mean to offend. Anyway, they've shortened the code name to *Buck*, so no harm done.'

'Yeah, don't lose any sleep over it, Midge,' Ron Kibbey, the third team member said. Midge, although undoubtedly the leader of the three, was a bit of a softie, always aware of other people's feelings, which was why his mates liked him.

'*Buck*'s still rude though,' Midge wasn't budging from his argument, 'kind of patronising, you know? Sort of putting them down. I've met quite a few of these Negroes in town and they're really nice blokes.'

'Too right they are,' Paddy agreed, 'a helluva lot nicer than the white Yankees, I'll give them that much.'

'Yeah,' Ron agreed once more and this time with a grin to Paddy. 'Pity we haven't been ordered to shoot *them* instead,' and both young men laughed.

'You're just jealous, that's your problem,' Midge said, not unpleasantly, simply stating a fact. 'All the Aussies are jealous of the Yanks, and that's understandable, but jeez, it's not the Yanks' fault they get paid more than we do.'

Ron and Paddy exchanged a look. Sometimes Midge could be too nice for his own good. Besides, Midge had it easier than most. From a well-off, middle-class family and with a steady girlfriend, Midge had extra money and no desire to compete with the Yanks for women. Despite this seeming advantage, though, neither Ron nor Paddy bore Midge any form of true grudge. To the contrary they respected him. All three privates were twenty-year-old 'nashos' from North Queensland – 'chocolate soldiers' to the enlisted men who didn't hold them in high regard, a term which most found galling. Ron and Paddy reckoned that, as such, you really had to give it to Midge. Midge had been two years into his university course in Brisbane when he'd been called up, and as a uni student he could easily have deferred his national service. But he hadn't. Born and bred in Cairns, he'd headed home to defend the north, believing it his bounden duty to do so. Midge didn't give a shit about being called a 'choc'. Midge had his principles.

The radio crackled. The password *Buck* sounded. Orders were coming through. They were on the Ross River Road now and had reached the junction where the road block had been formed. Armed troops were already there waiting, along with a unit of US Military Police. They must now take up position, their Bren machine gun and the carrier's spotlights trained steadily upon the road ahead awaiting the arrival of the mutineers.

'Crikey, Midge, what'll we do,' Paddy muttered as he stood by ready to man the machine gun. He wasn't really asking a question, more voicing the thoughts of his mates. None of them had killed before, but they'd thought if they were called upon to do so their target would be a Jap, not a Yank.

'We'll await orders,' Midge said, sounding far calmer than he felt – sounding in fact like the fine officer he would have made had he sought a military career.

A further road block had been set up near Corbeth's water hole on Ross River, another Bren Gun Carrier, together with troops and MPs with live ammunition trained upon the approach to Townsville. And the conversation among these soldiers, too, particularly the three-man crew of the carrier, was along very much the same lines.

'Shoot to kill,' the gunner said tremulously to the carrier's skipper, 'do you really reckon we'll have to, Vince? Do you reckon they'll make us do that?'

'Just got to wait for the sergeant's order, mate,' Vince replied. He'd been thinking the same thing himself, hoping he'd be able to tell his gunner to fire over their heads. Doesn't seem right to shoot blokes who've come here to fight a war with us, he thought.

Then the gunner voiced his thoughts right out loud, practically word for word. 'Can't see the sense in shooting our own allies,' the gunner said.

Nor can I, mate, Vince agreed, nor can I. But he didn't say anything.

The front doorbell rang.

'Who on earth could that be,' Amelia said, 'and at this hour?'

She and Samuel were having a cup of hot chocolate in the sitting room on his side of the house. She had insisted upon cooking him a meal, which they'd shared in the kitchen, and then they'd adjourned to the sitting room and the comfort of armchairs for what Amelia had referred to as a 'nightcap'.

He'd never had Milo before.

'So soothing,' she said, 'I find it the perfect bedtime drink. Although why I don't know,' she added with a light laugh, 'it's pure chocolate and malt, and promoted as an energy booster, so . . .' She shrugged. 'Psychological, I suppose, just the taste of hot chocolate.'

'It's delicious,' he said in all honesty.

'Yes, very popular with Australians.'

Then the sound of the doorbell.

Even as she rose to answer it, the bell was followed by a thunderous knocking on the front door, the urgency of which signalled cause for alarm.

Samuel stood. 'I'll go,' he said, 'you stay here.'

She didn't stay, this was her house after all, but she remained a little distance behind him as she followed him down the hall.

Samuel opened the front door to reveal Major Hank Henry standing on the porch, together with a young lieutenant.

'Captain Robinson,' the major barked, 'you're needed back at camp.'

'What's up?' Samuel asked, mystified.

Hank's eyes flickered to Amelia, who remained several paces away down the hall. He was relieved to find the captain at his billet – he hadn't relished the prospect of searching Townsville's night spots – but he didn't need to announce the severity of the situation to the man's landlady. He lowered his voice.

'There's been a riot, Samuel,' he muttered, 'in fact, there's been a goddamned mutiny. The troops at Kelso have armed themselves with machine guns and turned on their white officers.'

'Good God.' Samuel stared back at Hank Henry in shocked amazement.

'We don't know how many there are, possibly hundreds, but I'm told they're heading into town by the truckload,' Hank said. 'The Australian 51st have set up road blocks to stop them and if they don't halt peaceably we've issued orders "shoot to kill".'

Samuel continued to stare at the major, stunned by what he was hearing. How had it come to this? He'd expected trouble somewhere along the line, certainly – brawls, insubordination from frustrated, dissatisfied men – but mutiny? Murder? And if the situation was as dire as Hank Henry was saying, what on earth was personally expected of him? Mingled with Samuel's shock was a sense of bewilderment.

'The ringleaders appear to be from Company C,' Hank went on to explain, 'and one of your NCOs informs us you're possibly the only officer who might be able to reason with them. From what I hear, I'd say it's way too late for that myself, but we can't afford not to give it a chance.'

'Of course. I'll get my gear.' Fired into action, Samuel quickly disappeared to his quarters.

Amelia Sanderson and Hank Henry were left to contemplate each other in silence. Neither made any attempt to speak, although Amelia longed to enquire further. She'd edged just a little closer, trying desperately to hear what was going on, and indeed she'd heard enough to instil in her a deathly fear. The words 'shoot to kill' had been *more* than enough. Captain Robinson was being ordered into what seemed to be a battle zone.

Samuel reappeared in the hall only seconds later, strapping on his belt and holster with a .45 calibre Browning, and as he was about to pass her, she couldn't help herself.

'Samuel . . .' She placed a hand on his arm, and he halted briefly. 'Take care,' she said, 'please take care.'

'I will, Amelia.' He patted her hand, fleetingly but reassuringly, 'I will, don't worry yourself,' and then he was out the door.

The exchange, brief though it had been, had not gone unnoticed by Hank Henry, to whom it had spoken multitudes. So the two are having an affair, he thought disapprovingly. I wouldn't have expected such behaviour of an officer like Robinson who knows the military's view on relationships with local women. No emotional involvement, that's the rule, Samuel. Far too much of this sort of thing going on. Damn it, man, what do you think we have brothels for?

Hardly the time to be handing out lectures on love affairs with locals though, he told himself as they marched to the waiting jeep, he and Samuel climbing into the back seat, the lieutenant taking the wheel.

'Let's hope you can pull a miracle out of the hat, Samuel,' he said gruffly as the lieutenant revved up the jeep's engine and the vehicle roared down Mitchell Street, heading towards the town centre and Victoria Bridge. 'Let's hope we get there before it's too late and all hell breaks loose.'

The three trucks carrying the renegade troops of the 96th Battalion careered along the road towards Towns-ville, the Jimmys' headlights dimly lighting the way. The men on board were now more drunk with reckless freedom than they were with Baz Taylor's hooch. Several of those bearing weapons still fired sporadically into the surrounding darkness, Bernie letting loose now and then with a quick burst from his Chicago Piano, the others following up with a rifle shot, ensuring the level of excitement was maintained.

No-one was thinking of what might be waiting for them up ahead. No-one was thinking of anything much apart from the thrill of the moment.

Then as the trucks rounded a bend, they were hit with a stern reminder of reality. A hundred yards away, blocking the road, were bright lights that momentarily blinded them. The trucks slowed down, and as the men's vision adjusted they could clearly make out the Bren Gun Carrier and the silhouettes of armed troops beside it lined up ready for battle, all weapons focused upon them.

The drivers brought the trucks to a halt. The men were shocked into a state of sobriety. Silence reigned. No-one moved.

The young troops of the Australian 51st Regiment, particularly those in the Bren Gun Carrier, and even the well-seasoned soldiers of the US Military Police, breathed a collective sigh of relief. Good. They wouldn't be required to shoot to kill.

The silence was broken by the voice of authority calling out loud and clear from beyond the glare of the lights.

'I am Lieutenant Stanwick of the US Military Police,' the voice commanded. 'You men of the 96th will divest yourselves of any weapons in your possession. You will throw them onto the ground well clear of the trucks. You will then turn the trucks around and return to Kelso Camp immediately. Failure to do so will result in your arrest for . . .'

But a voice interrupted him. The voice of Kasey Davis.

'We're going into town,' Kasey yelled, and several of the mutineers, big Amos Cole and Bernie in particular, gave a cheer of support just by way of bravado.

'We'll give you the weapons,' Kasey yelled, 'but let us pass.'

The murderous madness had left Kasey and, bizarre as it seemed, he was actually trying to reason. He considered he was the one who should do so. Having killed Maxwell as had been his plan, it was he who would suffer the full wrath of the military. God only knew what they'd do to him – firing squad maybe? He didn't care, although he'd like to have let Betty know why he'd done this. But the others shouldn't be made to pay. The others should be granted their liberty and allowed into town.

'Give us back our rights,' he yelled. 'Let us go into town —'

He got no further than that.

'You will consider this an order of the Provost Marshal General of the United States Army,' the voice of the unseen Lieutenant Stanwick continued. 'Failure to comply forthwith will result in your immediate arrest and —'

A sudden rush of anger consumed Kasey. 'Let us pass!' he screamed, and raising his Thompson machine gun, he released a burst into the air.

That was the moment all hell broke loose. The moment when the stillness of the night was rent asunder by a cacophony of gunfire.

The first casualty was Kasey Davis. He'd been a dead man from the moment he'd opened his mouth; nervous young soldiers and seasoned MPs alike setting their sights on him. Nobody talked back or attempted to negotiate with the US military. One brief burst from the Thompson was all it took; war had been declared and the orders were 'shoot to kill'.

Kasey fell from the truck, hitting the ground heavily. But he felt no pain. His body riddled with bullets, he was already dead.

Bernie was next. Bernie, another mutineer in control of a machine gun, had also been targeted, despite the fact he hadn't aimed his Chicago Piano at his assailants. He hadn't aimed it anywhere; it hung limply by his side. Whether he would have fired the weapon no-one would ever know, because he hadn't had the time. Bernie too felt no pain.

Others about him did though. As men jumped from the trucks and fought to flee, the hail of bullets intensified, smacking into human flesh and bone.

In the third truck, big Amos Cole was the obvious target, even as he threw his Thompson machine gun to the ground. Amos had no intention of doing battle. Like the others, he would happily have surrendered, but as he leaped from the vehicle he was hit in the shoulder. The bullet didn't stop him though. For a giant of a man, and a wounded one at that, he moved with great speed, fleeing into the shadows of the surrounding bush.

A number of men made a similar escape, while the rest were surrounded and quickly succumbed, all of them terrified by the outcome of their drunken escapade.

'Cease fire!' came the order.

The men stood with their hands in the air, those who'd been armed, barely one-quarter in all, having dropped their weapons right from the start. Many lay on the ground wounded, some motionless, several obviously dead. Willie was there on the ground, on his knees. But he wasn't wounded. He was kneeling beside Kasey.

Why, Kase, he was thinking, why did you have to do that, buddy?

The acrid stink of cordite hung in the smoke-filled air, and apart from some moans of pain here and there silence once again reigned.

This was the scene that greeted the arrival of Hank Henry and Samuel Robinson.

'Holy fuck,' Hank muttered as the lieutenant pulled up the jeep. All three had heard the gunfire just minutes previously, but had hoped it had been only scare tactics. Hank had said as much to his junior officer and Samuel.

'Hope to hell they're firing over their heads,' he'd said drily, 'we're in a whole heap of trouble if they're not.'

Samuel had simply prayed for the safety of his men.

They climbed out of the jeep and surveyed the mayhem, Samuel noting the several bodies of those obviously dead, Kasey Davis and young Bernie in particular, both riddled with bullets. Surely they didn't deserve this, he thought. What did they do? Did they fire upon the white troops? Why would they do that?

Lieutenant Stanwick was immediately by Hank Henry's side. 'A number of men fled into the bush, sir,' he said, 'and I'm just about to radio the Medical Corps for the transfer of the dead and wounded.'

'No, no,' Hank swiftly corrected him. 'Ambulances will be ordered to collect the wounded only, there are no dead here.'

Samuel's eyes met Lieutenant Stanwick's, a briefly shared flicker of mystification, then both looked away, aware of what was about to follow.

'The dead will be transported by truck to the stockade, Lieutenant,' Hank ordered crisply, although he kept his voice down, 'and have the bodies covered in a tarpaulin. No-one must know what took place on this night.'

'Yes, sir.'

And what will happen to those bodies, Samuel wondered. No doubt they'll be stored in some prison cell for collection, but to be taken where? And to whom? Will their families be informed, and if so of what? How did their sons die? Samuel was aware similar secrecy measures had been observed in the past, but never on a scale such as this.

Hank's orders continued, brisk and businesslike. The riot was over, the mutiny quelled, now the task at hand was how to deal with the aftermath.

He was quick to dismiss the troops of the Australian 51st Regiment, who were to return immediately to their base at Mount Louisa. The sooner all witnesses were out of the way the better.

The Australians withdrew as ordered, grateful to be released, thankful they were not required to view the carnage surely wrought on this fearful night. To the young troops, the episode, in its shocking brevity, already held a nightmare element, as if perhaps the horror hadn't really taken place at all.

When Lieutenant Stanwick had contacted the Medical Corps and the ambulances were on their way, Hank had further orders for him, too.

'The identity of each and every man here, wounded or otherwise, is to be established, and these remaining troops are to be returned to Kelso,' he said, 'where investigations will be conducted into those principally responsible for this riot. A unit of ours is to accompany them in order to round up those escapees who no doubt intend to slip back into camp undetected.'

'Yes, sir.'

Lieutenant Stanwick immediately set about obeying the major's orders. An experienced and accomplished officer, he was only too thankful Major Hank Henry was in sole command of the night's aftermath. He'd found *Operation Buck* intensely stressful himself, a disastrous and harrowing state of affairs, and one that in his personal opinion should never have eventuated. But it was not his place to say so. He and his men would obey orders and maintain silence on the matter at all times.

Hank directed his attention to Samuel.

'You and I will go directly to Kelso, Captain Robinson,' he said with a nod to his driver, who was standing nearby awaiting instruction. 'Lord only knows what we'll find there,' he continued as they walked to the jeep and climbed into the back seat, the lieutenant already starting up the engine. 'Reports say the mutineers fired into the officers' mess tent. No white deaths were reported, which is a blessing, but we sure do need to get to the bottom of this whole goddamned business. Then,' he added, 'we need to make it go away.'

Big Amos Cole ploughed his way slowly and steadily through the bush. Unlike others who had escaped the mayhem, he was not crashing along in a blind panic, desperate to get back to camp as soon as possible, sneak in undetected and pretend to have played no part in the riot. Amos knew he was far too recognisable to avoid detection. He'd been one of those carrying a Thompson machine gun, he'd been targeted, and he had the wound to prove it. He'd be rightly picked as a ringleader and was prepared to face the consequences, but why, oh why, he agonised, had Kasey fired that goddamn machine gun! Poor little Bernie had copped it, too. But Bernie would never have turned his Thompson on those white soldiers! Never! Bernie was just a loud-mouthed little fucker who always played it tough because of his size. And Bernie was his buddy. Or rather, Bernie *had been* his buddy.

The catastrophe of the night had severely rattled Amos and he was plagued by guilt, the responsibility of his own actions weighing heavily upon him. None of this should have happened. But it hadn't been all Kasey's fault. Hell no.

I was the one who urged the guys on, he told himself. I was the one who said we should go into town and get ourselves a real drink. And I was the one who went along with Bernie's crazy idea of breaking into the armoury. Weapons. Just for show, that's all, but how dumb was that? Dumb enough to get men killed, that's how dumb.

He clutched a hand to his left shoulder to stem the bleeding. He hadn't felt much pain to start with, but it was hurting something fierce now. He wasn't too worried, he could move his arm; the bone wasn't shattered, a flesh wound only, but it needed attention. The medical orderlies would look after him back at camp.

He noted a farmhouse some distance ahead. The lights were on. Mighty late for folks to be up, he thought. He couldn't see his watch in the dark, but it had to be at least two in the morning, even later. Probably the gunfire that woke them.

He wondered whether he should call in at the farmhouse. They'd have bandages, most folks did; he could wash the wound, bind it, stem the bleeding.

Amos approached the farmhouse with caution, unsure what reaction he might get, hoping they wouldn't be hostile. He'd tell them he was American . . . an ally . . . there'd been an accident, and would they mind . . .

There were kennels near the farmhouse, two that he could make out, and he could see the flickering of a light beside them. As he approached, several dogs started barking, obviously sensing his presence. Then . . .

'Who's there?' a voice called. A woman's voice. 'Who's there?' she demanded. And suddenly, the beam of a torch was turned directly upon him.

Thirty-five-year-old Norma Hodgeman, farmer's wife and mother of two, was terror-struck. She let out an almighty scream. Right in front of her, looming out of the night, was a huge man, the biggest man she'd ever seen and he was coal-black, his sweat-glistening face caught in the fierce beam of her torch.

''Scuse me, ma'am,' Amos Cole stretched out a reassuring hand, 'I mean no harm, I just want . . .'

Norma screamed again. She was not normally a woman prone to panic, but the black man's *basso profundo* voice seemed to come from the depths of some demonic place, and the hand reaching out for her was bloodied.

She dropped the torch and ran for her life, the dogs behind her, still chained in their kennels, renewing their barking.

Amos clutched his shoulder once more and walked on, slowly, steadily.

By the time he finally reached camp, the other escapees had already returned. None of them had successfully sneaked in undetected, the MPs having been ready and waiting. Those involved in the mutiny were by now herded together and under guard in the general mess tent, where interrogations were being conducted by their NCOs to ascertain the leaders.

The arrival of Amos Cole lent just one more to their numbers and after half an hour with the orderlies who bathed and dressed his wound, he joined the others, arm in a sling, to become the instant centre of attention.

While the MPs had rounded up the mutineers, Hank Henry had requested Samuel join him as he questioned the white officers on the events of the night. As had been reported, there were thankfully no deaths, but two were wounded. A ricocheting bullet had glanced Captain Biff Baker's arm and young Lieutenant Thomas Woods had been hit in the side, a far more serious injury. Both had been tended by orderlies and would make a full recovery, but the Medical Corps had been radioed and an ambulance was on its way for Woodsy, who would need further treatment and hospitalisation.

'Could have been a damned sight worse, Major,' Captain Mick O'Brien said. 'Thankfully we were outside at the time, but as you can see by the damage all around you, one of the ringleaders fired right into this mess tent.'

'And I'll tell you exactly which one it was,' Chuck Maxwell sneered. He didn't address the major, his comment, which sounded more like a personal accusation, being directed to his fellow commanding officer, Samuel Robinson, instead.

'It was the pretty nigger, your favourite, Robinson, the one you told me to go soft on, remember? Kasey Davis? You recall that name, I take it?' Maxwell was gloating, as if he'd been proved right about something. 'That nigger was out to get me, I tell you, had me right in his sights. There's others who'll swear to it.' He looked about the mess tent, and several men nodded. No-one could refute him. 'If I hadn't dived into the slit trench out back I'd be dead meat by now,' he went on. 'That's one bad-ass nigger and always was,' he said triumphantly. 'I swear to you, Robinson, that boy's rotten to the core.'

'That boy's dead,' Samuel replied flatly.

Chuck would have crowed on longer, but was momentarily halted by the news. 'Oh, is that so,' he remarked as if disappointed. 'Well, too good for him, I say. He should have faced a firing squad.'

Samuel wanted to say, 'He did,' but out of deference to Hank Henry remained silent.

Upon the major's orders, Samuel was to join the NCOs in the general mess tent and assist with the interrogations.

'According to your own NCOs, the ringleaders were from Company C,' Hank said. 'And I'm told furthermore by one of your corporals that you're the only white officer they're likely to open up to.' Hank's tone held a measure of respect.

Samuel nodded. Yes, he thought, that would have been Rupert Barrett. He and Corporal Barrett certainly had a lot to talk about, principally the underlying reason for the men's rebellion. There seemed more to the mutiny than mere drunkenness. Could Kasey Davis's targeting of Chuck Maxwell have had anything to do with the death of young Anthony Hill? Could Private Davis have been seeking revenge? So many questions ran through Samuel's mind.

'There'll have to be an official investigation, of course,' Hank went on, 'and I'll have to write a report for HQ. But we want to keep the number of those brought into the barracks for further questioning to an absolute minimum. Just a few ringleaders we can throw the book at while keeping this whole business strictly under wraps.'

Hank Henry's further instructions were that they were both to remain at Kelso until the following afternoon, by which time Samuel would have selected the few men deemed responsible for the mutiny. Hank and his driver would then personally return Samuel to his city billet, where his jeep was still parked outside.

'You'll need to remain in the city over the next week or so,' he said. 'I'll want you present during the official investigation.'

The next day, which was a Sunday, in the late afternoon, the major dropped Samuel off at Amelia Sanderson's house in Mitchell Street.

Throughout the drive into town, they'd been relatively silent. They'd discussed the facts and figures that had come through, including the identities of those slain, and Hank had made a brief enquiry about the men Samuel had chosen for further investigation.

'Only two,' Samuel had replied, 'and one of them wasn't even a ringleader. He wants to plead the case for a friend of his who was. He wants to be heard.'

'How odd,' Hank had said, although he hadn't appeared remotely interested. It was not his intention anyone be given the chance to 'plead a case', or indeed even to be heard. All he needed was a couple of scapegoats.

'Yes, odd indeed.' Samuel had nodded as if in agreement, but he was glad Willie had volunteered to speak out. 'There were two other major ringleaders,' he'd added, 'but they're both dead.'

Hank had found that piece of information of far greater interest. 'How convenient,' he'd said, 'much easier for all concerned.'

After this short conversation they'd lapsed into silence, each preoccupied with his own thoughts.

Samuel was pondering how he might go about presenting the men's case to investigators, given all he'd learned from Rupert Barrett, Willie Parker and Amos Cole. He understood the US Army would want no publicity, and he respected the reasons why. But the situation is more complex than it appears, he thought, it's only right that voices should be heard by those in command.

Hank Henry's thoughts were running along vastly different lines. This riot, this rebellion, this mutiny, call it what you will, he thought, has to be sorted out as soon as possible and locked away forever to become something that simply never happened.

'I'll send off my basic report to HQ and get back to you first thing Monday morning,' he said briskly as Samuel alighted from the vehicle. 'In the meantime, it goes without saying, not a word to anyone. Understood?'

'Understood, of course.'

Hank didn't bother looking back as the jeep took off and Samuel walked up the steps to the front porch of the Queenslander. She'll be waiting for him inside, he thought with more than a touch of contempt, that mistress of his. What a goddamned fool. How an officer of Robinson's experience and professionalism can fall into such a trap is beyond me.

She *was* waiting for him inside. She'd stepped out into the hall the moment she'd heard his key in the latch.

'You're safe,' she whispered as she saw his silhouette framed in the doorway.

Amelia had been worried sick ever since the major's visit the night before last when she'd overheard those ominous words – 'shoot to kill'. Then today shopping in town, she'd heard the rumours. So many had, people were talking already. There'd been some terrible fracas out in the country near the army camps. Machine-gun fire in the dead of night. It wouldn't have been military training at that hour, people said. And when he hadn't returned that day and the whole of the following night, she'd lain awake fearing the worst, convincing herself that Samuel was dead.

'Thank God you're safe,' she whispered once again.

He closed the door gently behind him. 'Yes, I'm safe,' he said.

They drifted effortlessly and unconsciously into each other's arms.

Hank Henry, tough, no-nonsense military man though he was, critical and harsh to boot, was an excellent observer of human nature. Unbeknownst to themselves, Samuel Robinson and Amelia Sanderson had been in love for some time.

There was an inevitability about that late afternoon when they finally became the lovers they were destined to be.

PART THREE
THE POLITICIANS

CHAPTER FOURTEEN

Pete Vickers was in his customary state of frustration. Like many others he was aware of the rumours. A couple of farmers had heard the gunfire and spread the word, but nobody knew what had happened.

Being the hard-nosed investigative journalist he was, Pete determined to sniff out any leak he could find in order to discover the truth, despite his knowledge that whatever he managed to unearth was not likely to appear in print. Not in Australia anyway. But he would compile a report nonetheless that would one day be published, if not in his home country, then in Britain or America. Furthermore, he determined it would be published along with the other material he'd written, all of which had been smothered by army censorship.

Choosing as his first port of call the two farms where, independent of each other, both farmers swore they'd heard the sound of heavy gunfire, he rode his bicycle out to their farmhouses on Monday morning.

'Dunno what the heck was going on,' came the reply from the Wicks farm. 'Thought at first it was some sort of military training, but why the hell would they be training in the dead of night? Dangerous, if you ask me. Someone could've got hurt.'

There was a little more information on offer at the Hodgeman farm, however.

'Yeah,' Geoff said, 'me and Norma thought it was some kind of army drill using live ammo, heavy-duty stuff, too, machine-gun fire. Bit funny in the middle of the night we reckoned though, didn't we, love?'

'Too right we did,' his wife, a scrawny, tough outback woman in her late thirties replied. 'Wasn't bloody funny what happened after though,' she added, her tone dour, a scowl darkening her already weathered face.

'Yeah, you tell him, love,' Geoff urged, nodding at her over the kitchen table around which they were gathered. 'Go on, you tell young Pete here.'

Norma needed no encouragement. 'The din had got the dogs going,' she said, 'helluva racket, and even when it was over they wouldn't shut up. On and on they went. Got themselves all worked up, see, egging each other on, so I went out to quieten them down. Then soon as I had, they started up again. That was when I realised there was somebody there, sort of sensed it, you know? So I shone my torch on him . . .' She shook her head as if in a state of disbelief, which in a way she was. 'You wouldn't believe what I saw, honest to God you wouldn't.' She paused breathlessly.

'And that was . . . ?' Pete prompted.

'The biggest, blackest bloke you could ever imagine,' Norma said, reliving the moment, 'had to be about seven feet tall. And when he spoke his voice was like thunder rumbling out of this massive chest. God he was big.'

'What did he say?' Pete asked as she paused again.

'Dunno, can't remember, but he reached out to grab me, and his giant black hand was all covered in blood, and his arm, too, and his shirt, all drenched in blood.' She shook her head once again. 'Oh I tell you, I've never been so scared, I knew he was going to rape me.'

'So what did you do?'

'I screamed my lungs out and belted inside. Made Geoff lock all the doors and windows.'

'She was terrified all right,' Geoff said, 'never seen Norma like that. Never.'

'This black bloke, he was a soldier, I take it?' Pete asked.

'Oh yes, he was a soldier all right, a Yankee soldier in uniform. He'd be one of those Negroes from the camp at Kelso, you know the ones that are banned from town? The army tried to start up a club for them at the old Parslow place a couple of weeks back, but me and Mabel Wicks put a stop to that quick-smart. Can't have those big black bastards getting drunk and roaming about the place, not with little kiddies around.' Lips drawn in a thin, tight line, she nodded self-righteously. 'Just goes to show how right we were, doesn't it, eh?'

Pete chose to make no comment upon this particular topic. 'I presume you're going to report this incident to the US military, Mrs Hodgeman,' he said.

'*Going* to,' Norma replied with a touch of outrage, 'bloody well *have*! Me and Geoff went into town the very next day. We weren't going to wait around, were we, Geoff?'

'No way,' Geoff agreed – Geoff always agreed with Norma – 'not when your wife's been threatened like that.'

'And what response did you get?'

'The boss of the American Military Police,' Norma said, referring once again to her husband, 'you know, what's-his-name, the one we complained to about the club . . .'

'Major Henry,' Pete supplied the information, 'he's the provost marshal for Townsville.'

'Yeah, that's him. He saw us straightaway, didn't leave us hanging around for one sec. And so he should of course, I mean you can't have women being threatened by huge black rapists, can you?'

'What was the major's reaction?' Now we're getting to the interesting part, Pete thought.

'Oh, he was very concerned,' Norma said, 'very sympathetic. He told Geoff and me that all due action would be taken, didn't he, love?' A quick glance to her husband.

'He certainly did,' Geoff once again agreed. 'He's a good bloke, the major, has our interests at heart. Understands the locals.'

'Yeah,' Norma nodded, 'just like he did when me and Mabel complained about the club. He understood our concerns then, too.'

'So what exactly did he say?'

'He said *action will be taken immediately*.' Norma quoted the major virtually word for word, emphasising the parts she considered to be of the greatest importance. 'He said the Negro soldier would be *brought to task*, that he'd be easily identifiable because of his size and his injury, and that *full military justice would be served*, that he'd be punished and we had nothing more to worry about.' Norma's smile was triumphant. She was proud of the impact she'd had upon the major. '*The army will look after everything*, that's what he said.'

Yes, I'll just bet he did, Pete thought.

'I believe him, too,' she added vehemently. 'I mean, he sorted out that club business, didn't he? Closed the place down just the very next day. Like Geoff said, the major understands the locals.'

The major certainly does, Pete thought. The major also understands military policy and how to keep people quiet. 'Well, thanks very much, Mrs Hodgeman, Mr Hodgeman.' He nodded politely to both as he rose from his chair.

'You sure you won't stay for that cuppa?' Norma asked. She'd made the offer earlier.

'No thanks, Mrs Hodgeman,' he gave her a smile, 'got to get back to work.' Nothing more to be found here, he thought. 'I'll be moving on.'

They waved goodbye to him from the verandah.

'Nice young bloke, Pete,' Geoff said as they watched him stride awkwardly but purposefully down the path to the bicycle parked by the front gate. 'Polite, always was, even as a boy.'

'Yeah,' Norma agreed, 'who'd have thought a kid like that would have done so well for himself. 'Cept for that funny walk you'd hardly know he was a cripple, would you?'

As he rode the ten miles or so into Townsville, Pete's mind was sifting through the information he'd gleaned. The big Negro soldier, who'd obviously been wounded and was probably seeking help, poor bastard, would have been from the 96th Battalion based at Kelso. Norma Hodgeman, bigoted bitch that she was and always had been, would have been right about that much at least. And the troops of the 96th were the poor buggers who'd been used as scapegoats, blamed for all the racial trouble in town and banned from the city. So what had happened? Had there been some sort of uprising out at Kelso? And if so, had troops been called in from elsewhere to contain it? Heavy-duty machine-gun fire, both farmers had said. Well, the closest army camp to Kelso was the Aussie 51st Regiment based at Mount Louisa. Queensland boys for the most part. Nashos. Yep, they'd be the ones to talk to all right.

By the time he was crossing Victoria Bridge, weaving his bicycle through the endless military traffic that clogged the city's streets, Pete had a plan in mind for the next stage of his investigations. He'd need to wait until Friday, but he didn't mind. There was certainly no point in attempting to seek information through legitimate channels. A visit to

Hank Henry or any one of his MPs, or the commanding officer of the Australian 51st for that matter, would be useless, they'd all have closed ranks. No matter. Pete was prepared to wait for the right person . . . the right time . . . the right place . . .

Pete Vickers was not the only person who on that Monday morning was busily concerned with the events of Friday night. Samuel Robinson had been called into Hank Henry's office first thing; big Amos Cole and young Willie Parker had been transported to the stockade to await interrogation; Corporal Rupert Barrett had been ordered to report also to the stockade to assist with the interrogation; the purpose of all being the discovery of what exactly had led to the mutiny. Although the purpose in the minds of some varied just a little.

'What do you mean you've ordered Corporal Barrett to assist with the investigation?' Hank Henry demanded. 'He wasn't part of the mutiny, we can't throw the book at him.'

'He'll be of great value in discovering the reason *why* the troops mutinied, sir,' Samuel answered with care, 'he knows the men really well.'

'And so do you, Samuel,' Hank responded with equal care, 'or so I've been led to believe. And by none other than Corporal Barrett himself.'

'Yes.'

The two studied each other shrewdly, both aware of unspoken agendas that might possibly differ.

'Yes, I know the men,' Samuel said. 'But I'm not black.'

'There is that, of course,' Hank Henry allowed himself one of his brief and rare smiles, albeit wry, 'there is always that.'

Samuel returned the smile. Different though they were, the two men understood and respected each other.

Hank's smile was the first to disappear. 'You do realise we need this business sorted out and filed away as soon as possible, Captain,' he said crisply. 'The longer the case lingers the more talk gets around.'

'Yes, I understand,' Samuel said, 'just as I fully understand why secrecy is of tantamount importance. But there are certain complications I believe should be brought to the attention of High Command. The specifics of these complications would remain strictly confidential, I can assure you, Major.'

'Very well.' Hank Henry leaned back in his chair, elbows on armrests, hands raised in front of him, fingertips tapping as he appraised Samuel thoughtfully. 'You may be right to follow through on this in a little more detail than I would normally have advised.'

'Oh?' Samuel was surprised. Such a statement from Hank Henry was most unusual.

'According to HQ anyway,' Hank admitted drily. 'Following the report I submitted, I've been informed a member of MacArthur's staff will be arriving in the next day or so, a Lieutenant Colonel John Carter.' Hank didn't appear too happy about the fact. 'I'm not sure whether Carter's being sent to ensure we keep this successfully under wraps, or whether he'll wish to conduct his own investigation, but either way it would seem you'll have the attention of High Command.'

'Good,' Samuel nodded, 'that's good.'

'Well,' Hank rose from his chair, meeting over, 'we'll see about that, won't we.' He clearly didn't think it was such a good idea himself.

Samuel was pleased to discover he would have the ear of an officer from HQ staff, and therefore a direct link to General Douglas MacArthur. Perhaps something could be learned from this whole shocking business. He intended to call attention to the lack of rights accorded the Negro troops of the 96th Battalion, the loss of their liberty being a key factor to their rebellion. The bullying, too. The death of young Anthony Hill. A case of murder could not be proved, of course, but according to Rupert Barrett, the men believed Hill's death was linked to the bullying he'd sustained, and revenge had certainly been uppermost in the mind of Kasey Davis. Perhaps, Samuel hoped with a deep sense of irony, this might draw attention to the appointment of which particular white officers should, or should not, be given command of a Negro company. Chuck Maxwell was certainly not the right man for the job.

Samuel had learned so many things himself that night, although by then it would have been the early hours of Saturday morning as he'd sat in the general mess tent with Rupert Barrett, listening to the men pour their hearts out, most of them only too eager to speak.

But today, before he reported to the stockade to start his official interrogation with an MP lieutenant in attendance as clerk noting every word that was said, he had one other private matter to address. He must honour the promise he'd made to Rupert Barrett.

'Please, sir,' Rupe had said as they'd talked privately in the early hours of Saturday – it must have been around four by then. 'I know it's a lot to ask, and believe me I'd be willing to do it myself, except as you know I'm banned from going into town. But someone has to tell her. Betty has to know that Kasey's dead.'

'Betty?' He'd been bewildered.

'She works for Val at The Brown's, plays the piano.'

Of course, Samuel remembered, the pretty fair-haired girl who'd so beautifully accompanied Kasey Davis as he'd sung in that gloriously God-given voice of his. He recalled seeing them perform on several occasions at The Brown's, and also the night of the ill-fated club opening, and each time had been a magical experience.

'She and Kase were lovers, sir.' Rupe was very blunt as he looked his commanding officer directly in the eye. This was man-to-man time now, he was speaking intimately and he didn't care if in doing so he was out of line. Besides, he trusted Samuel Robinson.

'Sure, their relationship flouted every military rule,' he went on, 'and sure it would have met with disapproval from everyone for all the obvious reasons, but the truth is they loved each other. It wasn't just an affair, sir. There was a bond between them, they truly loved each other. If Kasey Davis's death is to be covered up, as I'm sure the military intends it to be, along with the deaths of the others who rebelled, then Betty will be left believing he deserted her. That he just walked away and didn't care. But Kase would never, ever have done such a thing. Far better she knows he's dead, wouldn't you agree? Far kinder.'

Samuel Robinson's reluctance was readable, and Rupe understood why. It was a very big favour he was asking of a man in Robinson's position.

'She wouldn't need to be given any detail, sir,' he urged. 'Just an act of kindness, that's all. She could be told Kasey's death was an accident, no more than that. And you wouldn't need to see Betty herself. Just Val . . . Val knew about them . . . Val would realise you were doing a personal favour, she wouldn't spread the word around . . . And Val would know how to break the news to Betty in the right way.'

'OK, OK.' Samuel couldn't bear it any longer, the man was by now virtually begging. 'OK, I'll tell Val, I promise.'

Samuel's agreement was a measure of the contract that had been reached between the two men that night. They were about to embark upon something each saw as some sort of crusade. To both, the mutiny was to serve a purpose, rather than an ugly military incident to be hidden away for all time. Surely informing a young woman of her lover's death was incidental to the main objective.

As was to be expected, the bar was closed when Samuel arrived at The Brown's; like all of Townsville's hotels, its operational hours were limited. But the main door was unlocked, allowing access to the several guests accommodated in the upstairs rooms. Upon entering, Samuel encountered young Jill, the Aboriginal girl who worked for Val, sweeping the tiled floor of the reception area.

'Hello there,' he said, thankful it wasn't Betty he'd bumped into. 'I'm after Val, is she around?'

'Oh hello.' Jill smiled, recognising the captain, who they'd all agreed was a really nice bloke. 'Yeh, she's up there in her office.' She indicated the stairs with a jerk of her head. 'Top of the stairs, door on the left. You want me to announce you?' she asked, thinking he might like that; he was an officer after all.

'No, I'm fine, thanks.' As he mounted the stairs Samuel prayed Betty wasn't in the office with her boss.

Val, thankfully, was alone. She opened the door herself in response to his knock.

'Well, well, g'day, Captain, to what do I owe the honour,' she said heartily, ushering him inside and closing the door. 'Pull up a pew. Would you like a cup of . . . ?'

'No, thank you,' he replied, 'I only want a minute of your time.'

'Oh.' She halted halfway to her desk, turning back with a look of concern. 'Something's wrong.'

'Yes.' He told her exactly as Rupe had instructed he should, and he didn't mince words. There'd been a tragic accident. Kasey Davis was dead. Betty needed to be told.

A pause followed as Val absorbed the facts. Then, 'You knew about Kasey and Betty?' she asked, surprised.

'Corporal Barrett told me. He asked me to pass the news on to you.'

'Ah,' she nodded, 'he's a good man, Rupe, that's very kind of him. Very kind of you, too, Captain,' she said. 'Thank you.'

Samuel added the other necessary word of advice. 'The news is strictly for you and Betty only, you do understand?'

'Oh yes, I understand.'

'Right then . . .' He started to edge towards the door, 'I'll leave you to talk to Betty and break it to her as gently as possible. I'm sure you'll know the right way.'

Samuel beat a hasty retreat, grateful to escape, and Val was left to ponder his final words. What *right way*, she thought. There's no fucking *right way*!

Less than five minutes later she broke the news to Betty in the only way possible. At least in the only way she considered possible. Brutally.

'I had a visit from an army officer,' she said. 'Kasey's dead. They're calling it an accident.'

As the harsh truth hit home and the girl slowly crumpled, Val took her in her arms. Any further talk could come later. Christ, she thought, life can be such a bastard.

During the next two days, as they awaited the arrival of Lieutenant Colonel Carter from HQ, Samuel meticulously went over all he'd previously covered with Rupert Barrett, Amos Cole and Willie Parker while the MP lieutenant noted down for the record every single word of every single interview.

The tediousness of the days was broken up, however, by the sheer joy that awaited Samuel each night, and each morning too when he awoke to find her beside him. They slept in Amelia's quarters now. They had since the night of his return when she'd led him to her bedroom.

As if they'd been lovers for years, Samuel and Amelia had embraced their affair to the fullest. They'd made no particular declaration to one another, there seemed no need, but Samuel couldn't help recalling Rupert Barrett's simple statement regarding Kasey Davis and young Betty. *It wasn't just an affair. There was a bond between them, they truly loved each other.* That's us, he thought with a sense of wonderment, that's Amelia and me.

A private man who rarely shared his feelings, yet who now appeared to have no qualms at all about revealing himself – to Amelia anyway – Samuel wondered how he'd come to reach the ripe age of thirty-two without ever experiencing love. Certainly he'd had affairs with women, which he'd enjoyed both sexually and companionably and which he'd presumed to be love, or at least love of a sort, but he was now proven wrong. It was obvious Amelia too had blossomed and in much the same way, no longer withdrawn, shedding her inhibitions to become a different person altogether. Extraordinary, he thought. We're like two broken pieces of something that have come together to form a whole.

'I find it amazing that I don't feel even the smallest shred of guilt,' he mused as they lay in each other's arms, naked and sated, her thigh still slung wantonly over his. It was Wednesday night. Lieutenant Colonel Carter would be arriving in the morning, but he wasn't going to think about that yet.

'Why should you feel guilty?' she asked, studying him in the light of the bed lamp. Amelia liked the bed lamp left on as they made love. She liked to see him. The sexual experiences of her marriage had always been conducted in total darkness.

He stroked her hair and smiled. 'Because what I'm doing is against military regulations, that's why. I should be thoroughly ashamed of myself.'

'I'd have thought I'm the one who should feel guilty,' she said lightly, 'certainly the one who should be thoroughly ashamed. I'm still a married woman, after all. Martin hasn't been officially declared dead yet.'

Her statement, bold as it was, shocked him, yet she'd made it as casually as he'd professed his own lack of guilt. He remained silent, staring up at the ceiling, not sure what to say. Finally, '*Do* you feel guilty?' he asked.

'No,' she answered without a moment's hesitation.

Again a brief silence. Then he couldn't resist asking, 'What would you do, Amelia, if by some remote chance Martin were to return?'

'I would request a divorce,' she said, again without a moment's hesitation.

He propped himself on an elbow and gazed down at her, thinking how lovely she looked.

Amelia laughed; he seemed so very serious. 'Don't worry, Samuel,' she said, 'please don't worry. I wasn't seeking a marriage proposal, I was simply acknowledging the fact that I didn't love Martin. That I never loved Martin. Just as he never loved me. I didn't know that, you see, not until now. I must say it comes as a great relief to find out.'

It was true. In the four short days of their affair, Amelia's entire life had changed; the view she'd had of herself throughout her marriage, the guilt she'd suffered, the blame she'd shouldered, all had disappeared with the awakening of her sexuality. She wasn't frigid after all. She had never been frigid. And poor Martin, who had wasted those years trying so desperately to satisfy her . . . That hadn't been her fault.

She recalled their furtive coupling in the darkened room, aware of her parents' proximity in the bedroom across the hall, how she'd blamed herself for having forced such a situation upon Martin, a private man at the best of times. Little wonder the intimacy of their marriage had been found wanting. And as Martin had stifled any sound he might have wished to make, servicing her as best he could in the hope she would conceive the child they both wanted, her lack of passion must surely have further smothered his desire.

She recalled also the terrible night when she and her mother had been walking down The Strand. A balmy evening, dusk, there'd been a couple furtively kissing beneath a palm tree, well away from the street lights, difficult to see. She had paid them no attention herself. But her mother had.

'Good God,' her mother had quietly exclaimed, coming to a standstill. The couple had broken apart, and it was Martin who had stepped out of the shadows.

'Evening,' he said, joining them. 'A pleasant night for a stroll.'

They'd continued, the three of them, walking down The Strand as if nothing had happened. But Amelia had seen, as had her mother, that the person walking rapidly away in the opposite direction was a man.

She'd blamed herself for that, too. To what terrible lengths had her sexual inadequacy driven her husband that he should seek solace in such an unnatural way?

No-one had ever mentioned that night. But not long after, her parents had moved to Brisbane, leaving the house to her.

'You and your husband need privacy, Amelia,' her mother had said tightly, she too perhaps blaming herself, perhaps believing such deviancy in a marriage might be the result of parental intrusion.

But following the departure of her parents and the privacy the house afforded them, nothing had changed. Things had remained exactly the same. And Amelia had continued to blame herself and her frigidity.

Then, abruptly, Martin had left Townsville, quitting his job with the Post and Telegraph Department. Already a lieutenant in the militia, he had transferred to the Australian Army and was sent to Victoria Barracks in Sydney to help form the 22nd Brigade, 8th Division. When his brigade had been posted to Malaya in early 1941, he hadn't even returned to bid her farewell, although leave would certainly have been granted him. He'd telephoned her with the news instead, abruptly, self-consciously, as if aware he was running away. Running away from what? Obviously from her.

Amelia had convinced herself she was personally responsible for ruining her husband's life. And if he died on the battlefield that too would be her fault.

She knew better now. Samuel would never know for she would never reveal Martin's secret, which would remain safe, his memory intact and unsullied, but Samuel had released her from a life sentence of guilt. He had awakened her to the fact that her marriage had been simply one huge mistake, through no fault of her own and, Amelia believed, although she was aware few would agree with her, through no fault of her poor, tortured husband.

'A pity . . .'

His voice broke into the kaleidoscope of images and memories that were tumbling through her mind. He was still propped on his elbow gazing at her.

'A pity about what?'

'A pity you weren't seeking a marriage proposal.' He was smiling, but they both recognised the remark wasn't altogether flippant.

'Well, who knows,' she said, returning the smile. 'Perhaps one day I might be.'

It was their first declaration of love.

The following morning, Samuel was deeply disappointed to discover his direct link with HQ was unlikely to serve any purpose in exposing the injustice perpetrated upon the troops of the 96th Battalion.

'General MacArthur wishes it to be made abundantly clear,' Lieutenant Colonel John Carter stated, 'that we are under considerable pressure from the Australian Government to keep our Negro servicemen under control . . .'

Hank Henry's face was a study in barely concealed loathing, his expression clearly stating, *Do you think I don't know that!*

Carter, a rather colourless man with steel-rimmed spectacles, probably in his early forties and carrying a little more weight than a soldier should, was typical of many an army staff officer Hank had encountered over the years. Stuffy, self-important, pompous desk-men with no balls. At least that was Hank's considered opinion. He didn't exchange a look with Samuel, but kept his gaze resolutely trained on the prick from HQ, perhaps in the hope of intimidating him.

Hank's intimidation tactic failed miserably, however, as Carter went on unperturbed. 'The impression that we cannot successfully manage our coloureds plays into the hands of those insisting we remove all black soldiers from the continent,' he said.

Samuel's eyes kept flickering between the two, studying Hank's reaction, aware that the major must surely be simmering close to boiling point. No-one spoke down in this manner to Hank Henry.

There were only the three of them seated in the provost marshal's office. Carter had insisted upon a private meeting in order to convey MacArthur's instructions before personally interviewing the men involved in the mutiny.

'We must therefore do whatever it takes to contain this unfortunate incident.' Concluding his speech as pompously as he'd started it, Carter glanced from Hank to

Samuel and back again, his bland, bespectacled face set in the self-satisfied lines of one who had performed his duty to perfection.

'I think you'll find, Colonel,' Hank said, his measured tone as steely as his gaze, 'that this is exactly the action we have taken and will continue to take.'

'Good, good.' Carter remained unperturbed, nodding approvingly and even giving one of the tight little smiles he was known to share when things were going well. 'Personally, Major, I've no doubt I'm of the same opinion as you,' he said amiably. He'd heard that Hank Henry was a tough man, the sort who took no prisoners, and in a situation such as this Carter himself believed in the tough approach. He now decided it wouldn't do any harm to make an off-the-record comment in the interest of cementing their relationship.

'Oh?' Hank's voice was dangerous, but he maintained his self-control. 'And what particular opinion would that be?'

'Frankly, I'm all for putting a dozen of these trouble-makers before a firing squad myself,' Carter said with brazen flair. 'Teach the whole damn lot of them a lesson, focus the rest of the blacks on the job at hand.'

If he expected an answer, he was destined for disappointment, but Hank's expression clearly said, *That's not my opinion at all, you dumb prick.*

Carter, however, was not good at reading expressions. 'Unfortunately,' he went on after a pause intended to impress, 'a firing squad would require an official court martial, which would call far too much attention to the case. We can't go that way, of course.'

'Of course we can't.'

While Hank Henry's self-control was admirable in the face of the bureaucratic style of officer he abhorred, Samuel's reaction to Lieutenant Colonel Carter was becoming rapidly despondent. Not only did there appear no interest in establishing any form of reason for the mutiny, this man would be the last to condemn the appointment of an officer like Maxwell to command a Negro battalion. In fact, from this their very first meeting, Samuel already had the vaguest feeling that John Carter might well be as biased and racially prejudiced as Chuck Maxwell himself.

Over the following days, Samuel's despondency deepened as it became apparent he was right. The 'investigation', if it could be termed such, was getting nowhere. For all of their joint efforts, he and Rupert Barrett seemed unable to penetrate the desk-bound mentality of Lieutenant Colonel Carter, whose only interest lay in the fact that drunken Negro troops had turned on their white officers. Any possible motive, any driving reason for such aberrant behaviour appeared immaterial. Indeed, when Rupert Barrett attempted to voice an opinion he was barely listened to at all. Carter was not accustomed to receiving the views of a black man.

At the end of the work day on Friday, having had more than enough, Samuel decided to seek some relief over a bit of camaraderie and a few beers, and automatically he headed for his favoured drinking hole, The Brown's.

When he walked in to discover Betty at the piano, his first instinct was to walk right out again. But she seemed in fine form, playing up a storm, smiling flirtatiously at the men gathered about the piano, American soldiers for the most part, so he stayed.

Skirting around the fringes of the lounge, carefully avoiding her line of sight, he arrived at the bar where Val and Jill were serving. He headed directly for Val.

'G'day, Captain,' she said, 'what'll it be, a beer?'

'Yeah, a beer would be great, thanks.'

As Val delivered his beer, he glanced over towards the piano, where Betty was chatting brightly while she played, still all smiles and flirtation.

'How's she doing?' he quietly asked.

'Putting on a brave face,' Val answered, 'as you can see.'

He gave a brief nod, enquiring no further, and Val offered no further information, bustling off instead to serve other customers.

But as she busied herself, Val's mind was on Betty. Oh yes, she thought, Betty's putting on a brave face all right. She's a casualty of war, that girl, and she knows it, what's more. She'll get bugger all answers about Kasey's death. An accident, my arse! Christ, you've got to admire the way she's handling it though.

'I hope I'm pregnant,' Betty had announced just the previous night when she and Val had sat in the upstairs office counting the takings and doing the books. Thursday was always tallying-up night, staff pay day being on Fridays. Betty had refused any time off. To the contrary, she insisted upon working harder than ever.

'I hope I'm bloody well pregnant,' she repeated defiantly, 'that'd teach them all a thing or two, wouldn't it.'

The girl can't be serious, Val thought, although she couldn't help feeling a stab of alarm. 'But you played things safe, didn't you, lovey,' she gently queried. 'You used condoms, didn't you?'

'Yeah, but so what?' Betty was more than defiant now, she was positively belligerent. 'Hell, those things often fail, they're not foolproof, you know. Well, I hope like mad I'm pregnant! A little brown baby, that'd show 'em all, wouldn't it. That'd get 'em going all right!'

Betty was actually serious. Her period was due any day now and she was praying it wouldn't come. What she wouldn't give for a little brown baby, a piece of Kasey!

Who cared what people thought! But she wasn't going to let the hurt show, not to anyone. Anger made things easier.

'Oh yeah,' she gave a mirthless laugh, 'that'd really get 'em talking, wouldn't it, if I popped out a little brown baby.' A toss of the head. 'Well, who knows?' A careless shrug. 'You just wait and see.'

'Sure, lovey,' Val said, 'sure.' The girl's all bravado, she thought, but good for you, Betty, good for you. You're tough. You'll survive. Although I'd bet my last ten bob you'll never be in love like that again. Never.

There's always the one, isn't there, Val now thought, watching Betty rebelliously thumping away at the piano, always the one who'll stay with you forever. Funny though, she mused, I can't quite recall mine.

'G'day, fellas, what'll it be?' She put aside her thoughts and grinned at the two Americans who'd just arrived at the bar.

Samuel too couldn't help watching Betty. There was something magnetic about her animation, her flirtatiousness, something slightly unreal. He felt as if he were in a movie theatre, watching a performance.

Then all of a sudden as if sensing his gaze, she looked directly at him, and in that instant the animation and flirtatiousness dropped away altogether.

Betty had never been told which army officer had delivered the news of Kasey's death, but now as her eyes met Samuel's she knew it would have to have been him. The nice bloke, the one all the boys liked, the one who appreciated music.

She flicked back her hair, a gesture of defiance, and held his gaze boldly, all the while pounding away at the piano like an automaton. But she couldn't disguise the truth. The hardness in her eyes spoke to Samuel of nothing but pain.

He didn't even finish his beer. Giving her the slightest nod of recognition, which he hoped signalled his sympathy, he left the bar. He needed to get home to Amelia.

At the very moment Samuel left The Brown's, Pete Vickers was settling himself into another bar, the Seaview down on The Strand.

The Seaview was a raucous pub without the architectural elegance and gentrified atmosphere of the Queen's Hotel, home to the American Officers' Club further along The Strand. But the Seaview was after all home to the Australian Officers' Club, and Aussies were known to be raucous. There was never any sense of decorum and certainly no recognition of hierarchy at the Seaview. In fact, the bar was known to attract the rowdiest of customers, and the rooms upstairs, which housed the officers when in town on leave, were considered little more than a brothel.

Pete was following through with his plan. It was Friday night and he was at the pub where the Aussies hung out. If he was going to get any information from the Queensland Nasho boys of the 51st Regiment, this was the most likely place he'd find them and tonight was the most likely night they'd be here. Tonight or tomorrow, and if none of them turned up tonight he'd come back tomorrow.

He'd enquired at the bar and Alf, the old bartender whom he'd known for years, had said yeah, a number of the young blokes from the 51st regularly came in on a Friday or Saturday, and yeah, he'd be happy to point them out when they did.

Pete sat at the bar sipping away slowly at his beer. He'd arrived early. The pub wasn't yet overly noisy, but with only a few hours of opening to hand it wouldn't be long before it was; men needed to make the most of the limited drinking time at their disposal. He hoped the boys he was after would turn up before things got too rowdy.

He was in luck. About halfway through his second beer, they arrived, three of them, very young, barely twenty.

'That's a few of 'em,' Alf prompted with a none-too-subtle jerk of his head as they walked through the main doors. 'Good kids.'

Pete actually recognised one of the young men. Ron Kibbey was a Townsville boy, and he knew the Kibbey family well. Handy, he thought.

'G'day, Ron,' he said, rising from his bar stool. 'Can I buy you a drink? You and your mates of course.'

'G'day, Pete. Sure, why not.' The two shook hands and Ron made the introductions.

'Pete's a crash-hot journo with the *Bulletin*,' he announced to his mates, Pete rather wishing that he hadn't. 'This is Frank Midgely and Paddy Sullivan,' he went on, 'we're stationed at Mount Louisa with the 51st.'

'Yeah, I thought you were.' Cover now blown, Pete decided there was no point pretending his was just a passing interest, so when they were settled at a table with their beers he cut straight to the chase.

'Everyone's talking about last week's riot,' he said casually. Everyone wasn't, as a matter of fact, the general talk around town had already died down. 'So what exactly happened, do you boys know? Strictly off the record, of course,' he added hastily. 'They wouldn't allow me to write anything, and if I did they wouldn't print it anyway. I'm just interested as a local, you know, from a historical point of view.' He smiled amiably from one to the other, sharing his camaraderie particularly with Ron Kibbey, the impression being they were just a few North Queenslanders having a chat.

Ron was flattered by the 'matey' treatment he was getting from Pete Vickers. Pete was a really intelligent bloke who was held in high regard by the people of Townsville.

'We were called out to block off the Ross River Road,' he said, eager to impress and, focused upon Pete as he was, unaware of the warning look from Midge.

'You mean to halt the blokes from the 96th Battalion,' Pete chipped in encouragingly. Unlike Ron, he was only too aware of the warning signal cast by Frank Midgely and knew he was on borrowed time.

'Yeah, that's right,' Ron said, 'but we didn't see any action, they didn't come our way. They took the other route into town.'

'So what happened there —'

'We can't say, mate,' Midge cut in. 'We weren't there, we weren't in on the action.' Midge's tone was not rude, nor even unfriendly, but he was definitely calling a halt to the conversation.

Paddy added his say, too, he and Midge exchanging a glance. Ron wasn't really that bright. 'We weren't there and we don't know,' he said, directing his comment as much to Ron as to Pete. 'You've got to be aware there's such a thing as the *Official Secrets Act*, mate.'

Ron looked guilty and Pete backed off, duly chastised. 'Sure, sure, I understand,' he said. 'Didn't mean to put you on the spot, didn't mean to be pushy.' He had of course meant to be pushy and it had paid off, to a certain extent anyway. His theory about trouble with the black troops of the 96th Battalion had been confirmed, and he now knew they'd been on their way into town. He'd previously thought the trouble had been contained out at Kelso.

He smiled apologetically nonetheless. 'I'm sorry,' he said, and he really did mean it. He didn't want to get these boys into trouble.

'That's all right, mate.' Realising the man was genuine, Midge added in all honesty, 'We Nashos are shit-scared, I have to admit. You won't find the other blokes saying a word either. We can get shot for talking out, you know.'

'Yeah. Not a word. I promise.'

Pete had every intention of honouring his promise. There would be no mention, no hint, of where he might have obtained the information he now had, but everything would go into the report he was compiling. The report that would find its way overseas through whatever, as yet unknown, contact he might find.

And that contact was only days away.

'You're telling me *what*!' Hank Henry was not as successful this time in disguising his contempt. In fact, he didn't even try. He looked open-mouthed from John Carter to Samuel Robinson and back again, his expression verging on comical. As before, there was only the three of them in his office.

'FDR himself,' he went on, outraged, 'the goddamned President of the United States of America is sending a congressman to Townsville to investigate a Negro mutiny we've been ordered to *cover up*! I mean, we've been told this shit fight must never see the light of day! And he's sending a fucking *congressman*, for Chrissakes?'

'Well, the guy's actually a navy lieutenant commander,' Carter stammered a little nervously, adjusting his spectacles. This time there was no mistaking Hank's body language, which Carter was reading loud and clear. The major was mad as hell and John Carter found him most daunting. 'He's been sent out as an observer on bomber missions in the Pacific, but President Roosevelt's ordered he return with a report on the black uprising in Townsville.'

John Carter's explanation didn't help matters.

'The guy's a fucking politician who's been given a military rank simply to enhance his career after the war!' Hank exploded. If there was one thing Hank Henry despised above staff officers it was politicians who, in his opinion, should stay safely behind their desks doing the bureaucratic shit they were born to do. 'He'll be some weedy, little brown-nosing son of a bitch who knows fuck-all about anything military. What's the prick's name?'

John Carter was by now so nervous that Samuel actually felt sorry for him, while also suppressing a huge desire to cheer. They were finally going to get the attention they deserved.

'Lyndon Baines Johnson,' Carter stammered.

'Lyndon-Fucking-Baines-Johnson . . .' Hank gave a snarl of derision. 'Yeah, with a name like that, he's bound to be a weedy little prick.'

CHAPTER FIFTEEN

'**M**y time is limited, Major. I'm officially here as an observer on a combat mission, but during the several brief days of my stay in Townsville, I have direct orders from the President of the United States to get to the bottom of this downright disgraceful mutiny within our ranks. Black troops firing on their white officers! Shameful! The president is appalled, as is General Eisenhower, as indeed am I. Such disunity among our troops in a time of war simply will not and cannot be tolerated. So let's get down to business, shall we?'

Hank was taken aback. Lyndon Baines Johnson was anything but the 'weedy little prick' he'd anticipated. Resplendent in his naval dress uniform, well over six feet tall, in fact several inches taller than Hank, who at just under six feet cut an impressive figure himself, everything about Johnson was big. The air of confidence, the swagger in his walk, the voice with its Texan drawl, but above all the man's sheer arrogance. Good God, Hank thought, he can't be more than mid-thirties and yet he's placing himself alongside FDR and Eisenhower, dropping their names as if he's their equal. The gall of the guy. However, much as Hank didn't warm to Johnson, which was hardly surprising, he had to admit he'd rather have this sort of congressman than the one he'd expected. At least he's got balls, Hank thought.

Johnson dumped the file he held in his hand onto the major's desktop. 'I glanced through this here chicken-shit report of Carter's as we drove into town,' he said, casting a scathing glance at the unfortunate John Carter, who was standing nearby positively quaking and had been ever since he'd picked up this dynamo from the airfield. 'But it says fuck-all. Just dates, times, facts and figures, nothing more. I want the whys and the hows and the wherefores, you get my drift?'

'Yes, I believe I do, Commander,' Hank said in a measured tone. Well, at least that's one thing we have in common, he thought. Johnson's obviously registered Carter as the ineffectual prick he is.

'Glad to hear there were no deaths among the white officers,' Johnson went on, 'two injured, no more than that, which is good. But I know darn well FDR will be none too happy about the numbers of black casualties. And I can tell you here and now he'll want to know *why*.' He cast another withering look at John Carter. 'Being drunk and disorderly hardly constitutes a reason for attempting to murder your commanding officers,' he said with contempt, 'at least not to my mind.'

'Captain Robinson and Corporal Barrett will be eager to answer whatever questions you have,' Hank assured him. 'They're at the stockade awaiting your arrival, together with two of the men who were involved in the riot, and who I'm told have been most helpful.'

'Then we'd best get started, hadn't we,' the big Texan said, retrieving the file he'd dumped on the desk. 'Whatever we come up with will have to be better than this load of shit.'

The arrival of Congressman Lieutenant Commander Lyndon Baines Johnson in Townsville was no doubt intended to be low key, and his mission supposedly covert, but from the outset the man himself had foiled all such objectives. Johnson had every intention of being noticed, and furthermore of being recognised for exactly who he was. Far more than a mere lieutenant commander, a member of Congress, no less, and under the direct orders of the President of the United States.

Senior Sergeant Bruce Desmond rang his good mate Pete Vickers at the *Bulletin* that very morning.

'There's a bigwig in town, Pete,' he said, 'thought you might like to know. An American congressman by the name of Johnson flew in an hour or so ago, fresh from HQ. According to one of my boys out at the airfield, he was big-noting himself the moment he landed. Said he was acting directly on instructions from Roosevelt. Wouldn't say what of course, but he was driven straight to Hank Henry's office. I reckon it'd have to have something to do with the riot you were telling me about the other day, you know, the Negro troops out at Kelso.'

'Yeah, too right it would. Good on you, mate.' Pete was immeasurably excited by the news. As always, he'd confided his frustration to Bruce.

'I've pretty much pieced things together,' he'd said over a beer at the bar of the Queen's Hotel, omitting specific mention of his meeting with the Aussie boys from the 51st Regiment, as promised. 'But word won't get out, you can bet on it. The military, the government, they'll bury this whole sordid mess. And as for the numbers of deaths, the wounded . . .' he'd shrugged hopelessly, 'I reckon we'll never know, mate. Bloody criminal in my opinion. I reckon it's something no-one will ever know.'

But now, the arrival of a US congressman supposedly to investigate the mutiny put a whole different slant on things, certainly from Pete's perspective. Unlike the Australian authorities, it appeared the American government was not about to bury this terrible incident. Pete didn't anticipate for one moment he would be offered any inside information. *No, no, mate,* he could hear himself say, already conducting in his head a conversation with the congressman, *it's not what* you *can offer* me. *It's what* I *can offer* you . . . To Pete Vickers, here was the chance of a lifetime, a journalist's dream, the perfect opportunity for his exposé to reach overseas. The congressman would no doubt welcome the endless reports he'd compiled, particularly with regard to the treatment of Negro soldiers in Northern Queensland. This is a story the world needs to hear, Pete thought.

'I presume the bloke's staying at the Queen's Hotel?' he queried.

'Bound to be,' Bruce replied, 'but I'll check it out and get back to you.' Then he hung up.

Samuel registered instantly Johnson's arrogance. It was impossible not to from the very moment John Carter made the introduction.

'Don't you let this here insignia distract you from my true purpose, Captain,' Johnson said, tapping the three bars near the cuff of his dress uniform jacket that signified his rank. 'I am a member of Congress and I am here under the direct orders of the President of the United States to investigate this almighty fuck-up that should never have happened, do I make myself clear?'

'You certainly do, sir, yes.'

'I intend to get to the bottom of this whole goddamned mess your boys have put us in. I want and will have answers, you hear me?'

'Yes, sir.' Despite the man's belligerent attitude, Samuel thrilled to the words he was hearing. At last someone was interested in the truth, or at least in discovering the reason why the troops of the 96th Battalion had mutinied. 'Follow me, Commander,' he said.

He led the way through to the main interview room, where Rupert Barrett was already waiting, together with Amos Cole and Willie Parker, who'd been brought in from the cells. Standing guard by the door that led to the cells were two MPs, and as Samuel Robinson and Lyndon Johnson entered, Lieutenant Colonel John Carter abjectly trailed behind, having by now become invisible.

Samuel's respect for Johnson grew exponentially over the next two hours as he watched the congressman listen intently to the men's stories. After he and Rupert Barrett had briefly outlined the situation, explaining the deprivation of the men's liberty and the bullying factor in the form of Chuck Maxwell, Johnson demanded to hear directly from the two men involved. And as he listened, his focus was absolute and his questions, although barked out imperiously, brief and intelligent. Samuel was impressed. Lyndon Johnson might well be arrogant, overbearing, dictatorial and at times downright rude, but he was certainly accomplished.

'We was drunk, sir,' Amos said. 'No two ways 'bout that – we was drunk . . .' Even seated though they were, it was strange to see the Texan so dwarfed by big Amos Cole, not just in height, but in build and vocal power. By comparison, Johnson appeared strangely small.

'We knew we was wrong, but we was angry, see,' Amos went on, 'angry 'bout bein' barred from town, angry 'bout them closin' our club after just one night . . .'

Johnson gave a curt nod, the captain and the corporal had filled him in on these details. 'You consider that sound enough reason to fire upon your commanding officers?' he snapped.

'Oh no, sir, no,' Amos shook his huge head vehemently, 'that were never our intention. We just wanted to go into town, is all, go into town and get us a decent drink.' He looked shamefaced, like an enormous, guilty child.

'That was my idea, sir, all my idea,' he admitted. 'It was me egged the guys on, you know, just wantin' to have some fun . . .'

'So you decided to arm yourselves, just for fun?'

'Well, yes, sir, in a way.' Amos looked guiltier than ever. 'We was showin' off, that's all. The guns was just for show, sir, I swear that's the truth. No-one was goin' to fire them.'

'Kase was.' It was Willie who interjected. Willie had pondered the situation for quite some time. *Why Kase, why*, he'd wondered on that dreadful night. *Why did you have to do that?* He knew now. 'Kase was out to get Maxwell right from the start. He was prepared to go down for it, what's more.'

Johnson opened the file he held in his hand and glanced at the first page, searching for a name among the many listed there.

'Private Kasey Davis, sir,' Rupe prompted, 'the soldier considered to be the principal ringleader of the mutiny.'

'Ah yes, thank you, Corporal.' Johnson found the name among those listed dead.

'Kase wasn't out to have fun that night,' Willie went on. 'Kase wanted to kill Maxwell because of Ant.'

Johnson didn't consult his list this time, but looked directly at the corporal, seeking an answer.

'Private Anthony Hill, sir,' Rupe replied. 'You won't find him on the list, he wasn't involved in the mutiny. He died the week before it happened.' Rupe cast a glance at Samuel, who obligingly took up the baton. This was the form of hearing he and Rupe had been hoping for.

'A number of troops have cited their anger at Private Hill's death as further provocation to riot,' he said with care. 'They believe his death, although recorded as accidental, was a direct result of Captain Maxwell's bullying, which I'm led to believe was extreme.'

'And it was, sir,' Willie interjected once again, this time with fervour. 'Captain Maxwell always had a whipping boy. Started out being Kase, right from when we left home, but Kase was tough, so he switched to Ant. That's why Kase wanted to kill the captain. That's what he planned to do that night.'

'If you knew this, Private Parker, it makes you an accomplice to attempted murder,' Johnson said crisply.

'I didn't know it, sir, not then. I just figured it out since. Kase was angry, I knew that much, angry about Ant and Captain Maxwell, and he was stirring the other guys up about it, too, but . . .' A forlorn shrug of his shoulders and Willie's voice trailed away.

'So why did you go along with this mutinous action, Private?' Johnson demanded, thinking the young black soldier before him looked like anything but a mutineer.

'Because Kase was my buddy, sir. I was just following Kase like I always did.'

Johnson paused for a moment, then settled back in his chair, elbows on armrests, fingers linked, signalling a different attitude altogether, his voice even verging on amiable. 'So tell me a little about this Captain Maxwell of yours,' he said casually.

Samuel and Rupe didn't dare look at one another, but they were both thinking the same thing. A white officer asking black rank and file their personal views of a fellow white officer? Unheard of and more than they could have hoped for.

Seated apart in a corner of the room, aware his inclusion was not welcome, Lieutenant Colonel John Carter said nothing, but had anyone chosen to take note, which no-one did, his outrage was readable.

The talk remained about Maxwell for a while, Amos and Willie speaking openly, although having been warned by Samuel, avoiding any direct mention of murder, and

Johnson listened intently, interjecting with the occasional question. Then . . .

'Right, well I guess we're done here.' Reverting to his previous manner, Johnson rose abruptly to his feet, calling an instant halt to the proceedings. 'Corporal, if you'd be so good as to accompany Captain Robinson and me, I have a few further questions to put to you both.'

Within only minutes, the two prisoners had been returned to their cells, and Samuel and Rupe were back in the office with Johnson. John Carter, having followed behind them like a shadow, maintained his uncomfortable silence.

The four remained standing as Johnson briskly stated his plans. A driver had been placed at his disposal by Major Henry, and he would go directly to the camp at Kelso before checking into the Officers' Club.

'I plan to have a word with our Captain Maxwell,' he said. 'Seems he and I could do with a bit of a chat.'

'Certainly, sir, I'll radio ahead and make sure he's awaiting your arrival.' As always, Samuel's face betrayed nothing. 'Would you like me to accompany you?'

'No thank you, Captain, I think a one-on-one meeting would be more advantageous. Now,' he said without drawing breath, 'tell me about the illicit alcohol and its source of supply.'

'We know the source to be a guy by the name of Baz Taylor, sir. He provided the liquor for the Negro Servicemen's Club that we tried to . . .'

'Yes, yes, I read all about that in the report I was given,' Johnson replied with a touch of impatience, and without even deigning to glance in Carter's direction, which in itself was a deliberate comment. 'Some black-market racketeer supplied the hooch, but who was the inside man?'

'Corporal Barrett made enquiries among the troops of both Company A and Company C, sir,' Samuel said.

'Yes, Corporal, and . . . ?' Johnson was all but clicking his fingers as he turned to Rupe.

'The men admitted to handing their money over to several of their NCOs, sir,' Rupe said. 'The NCOs were corporals in rank, and when I spoke to each of them they said the money was paid directly to Baz Taylor.'

'And you believed them?'

'I had no cause not to, sir.'

'I beg to differ, Corporal Barrett. There's a poisoned apple inside every barrel, and our poisoned apple may well be the man who aided and abetted the supply of alcohol. Who's to say this insider wasn't a major influence in the mutiny? Who's to say he didn't deliberately fuel the men, inciting them to riot? Anyone think about that?' Johnson gazed around accusingly at the group, this time including John Carter. 'No, obviously not,' he said. 'I would have thought myself that an inside influence would have been one of the first areas to be thoroughly investigated.'

Lyndon Johnson did not actually hold either Robinson or Barrett responsible for such an oversight. They were not after all 'investigators' as such. His accusatory glare was now directed at John Carter, whose report had come to the simple conclusion that as a result of liquor supplied by a black-market racketeer, drunken men had mutinied and turned on their white officers. *Incompetent prick*, Johnson's eyes said. And Carter squirmed.

'I should like to talk to this Baz Taylor,' the Texan said, 'but strictly off the record. Calling him in for a formal interview would attract too much attention, and word would get around. So where might I find him?'

'At The Brown's Bar, sir,' Samuel replied. 'He works for Val Callahan, the publican there. Actually, Val herself would be a handy person to talk to,' he added as the thought occurred. 'She knew the men well. Before they were banned from town, The Brown's Bar was one of the troops' favourite haunts. What's more, Val was the force behind the club we tried to set up —'

'Yes, yes, Captain, good idea, I shall do just that,' Johnson interrupted, eager to get on with things. 'I shall most certainly speak with her this afternoon, and also with the racketeer, Taylor. Right now I'm off to Kelso.'

He strode out of the office to meet up with his driver, who was waiting outside, and the others were left in his wake. The man seemed indefatigable.

Chuck Maxwell presumed the newly arrived congressman who was conducting an investigation into the riot wished to speak to him about the fact he'd been so specifically targeted by the mutineers. He was irritated by what he saw as a sheer waste of time. He'd been interviewed by Carter, the staff officer from HQ, and every facet had been covered. He was further irritated by the fact the congressman was turning up at camp right on lunchtime. He was ravenous and had looked forward to a full hot meal in the officers' canteen. Now having been instructed to await the arrival of this Lieutenant Commander Johnson in the Company C Officers' tent, he'd had to settle for a hamburger instead.

He was halfway through his hamburger when the jeep pulled up outside and only seconds later the MP lieutenant ushered Johnson into the tent. Chuck rose to attention.

Following the introductions, the lieutenant said, 'I'll be waiting in the vehicle, sir.'

Johnson gave a curt nod, the driver disappeared, and the two men were left alone. The clerk, Percy Owen, normally present at his desk in the corner, was having a hot meal in the general mess tent.

'Don't let me interrupt your lunch, Captain,' Johnson said affably, taking a seat – he'd already decided to conduct their meeting informally. He was skipping lunch himself, as he often did when his focus was directed else-where. For a man with a normally voracious appetite, he could go a long time without food.

Chuck sat and readdressed his hamburger, waiting for the inevitable questions he'd already answered. But they didn't come. The Texan wanted to talk about Anthony Hill instead. Why? Chuck didn't feel particularly threatened. He and Strut Stowers had their story down pat and the death had been well and truly established as accidental, but he was a little mystified nonetheless. What did Anthony Hill have to do with the riot?

'I'm told the men were somewhat troubled by the way you singled out Private Hill, Captain,' Johnson said, his manner still affable.

'Singled him out, sir,' Chuck queried through a mouthful of hamburger, 'how exactly do you mean?'

'As a target for bullying,' Johnson replied patiently, 'that's what I mean.'

Chuck returned a wary look, the hamburger losing a little of its interest.

'I believe you ripped up a book that was very precious to the boy, at least that's what they tell me.'

Chuck Maxwell resisted the urge to laugh out loud. Hell, for one minute there he'd thought the congressman was going to accuse him of inflicting serious physical damage.

'That's just exactly what I did do, Commander, and I don't mind admitting it.' His grin was comradely. The congressman was a Texan, for God's sake. They were bound to speak the same language, have the same point of view. 'C'mon now, you and I both know niggers need bullying. It's what they want. They're happier knowing their place in life. You give them too much freedom, they get confused. It's called command where I come from. There's rules that have to be obeyed, sir,' he said as if making a truly profound statement, which in actual fact Chuck believed he was. 'There's black and there's white in every meaning of the term, you and I both know that, don't we.'

The Texan stood, a towering figure looking down at the man with the remnants of a hamburger in his hands. He studied Maxwell thoughtfully for a moment. This was why he'd come out to Kelso, to see what kind of a guy this Maxwell really was. Now he knew.

Lyndon Johnson had understood every implication made at the meeting in the stockade, every space between the lines, every single little thing that had been carefully left unsaid. Yes, Maxwell, you piece of dog shit, he now thought, I do believe you could well be responsible for the death of that boy. What a damn shame there's no proof. I'd so like to put you away.

'You're just a bag of scum, aren't you, Maxwell,' he said coldly, his voice a monotone. 'You're a right, low-down, son-of-a-bitch bag of scum,' and he walked out of the tent.

Chuck Maxwell watched him go with a sense of surprise. A Texan who's a nigger lover, he thought, well now that's something new.

Chuck wasn't unduly perturbed by the congressman's animosity, nor by the interest displayed in Anthony Hill, but he decided to have a word with Strut Stowers nevertheless. If by any chance Stowers were to be interviewed, best they re-rehearse their respective stories so there were no discrepancies.

After leaving Kelso, Lyndon went directly to the Officers' Club, where he booked into the hotel room reserved for him. He changed from his dress uniform into his khaki fatigues with the insignia of rank on the epaulettes. He preferred the smarter appearance of his navy jacket, white shirt and tie, but khaki was less likely to call attention. The whole town appeared to be khaki, and given the fact he was about to make contact with civilians and invite discussion 'off the record', he decided it was wiser to remain low key.

He didn't bother with lunch. And he dismissed his driver. Upon receiving directions, he decided to walk to The Brown's instead.

Walking's probably quicker anyway, he thought as he marched up the hill, passing the heavy military traffic that was all but at a standstill. Townsville sure was a busy place.

The bar was closed when he arrived. Men hadn't even started queuing up in the street, as they did each late afternoon. The Brown's wouldn't be open to drinkers for a couple of hours yet.

The main doors to the hotel were unlocked, however, and Lyndon stepped inside to the reception area, where standing behind the counter was a fair-haired young woman. Her head buried in the paperwork before her, she didn't hear his approach.

'Excuse me, Miss . . .'

'Oh.' Betty's head jerked up. She hadn't really been seeing the items of supplies and the figures listed beside them, she hadn't been seeing or hearing anything. Her mind was floating somewhere else altogether, somewhere numb and painless. She painted on the automatic smile that was always there at her beck and call.

'Hello, soldier, what can I do for you?' She noted the insignia on his shoulder, a fairly high ranking Yankee naval officer; she was quite adept at reading rank. Perhaps he wanted to book a room.

Lyndon Johnson was not accustomed to being addressed in such a familiar fashion and by one so young, but he returned her smile nonetheless. Of course, he thought, she would know nothing of rank, and besides, how could one possibly take exception to such an extraordinarily pretty girl?

'I wanted to see the publican,' he said, 'a Mrs Val Callahan by name, am I correct?'

'Yep.'

'Is she here?'

'Yep. In her office.' Betty indicated the stairs. 'Want me to take you up?'

'Why yes, if you'd be so kind.' He gave her another smile, a dazzling smile this time. She was one of the prettiest girls he'd ever seen.

'Rightio, follow me.'

As she came out from behind the counter, he noted the body matched the face. The whole package really was perfect.

'Who shall I say?' she asked as she led the way up the stairs.

'What was that, sorry?' He'd been a little distracted. 'What name?'

He very much wanted to impress. 'Congressman Lieutenant Commander Lyndon Baines Johnson,' he said.

They'd reached the top of the stairs and she turned, aware he'd been eyeing her backside on the way up. 'Wow,' she said, as if suitably awestruck, 'that's quite a mouthful.'

'Commander Johnson will do,' he said. Another dazzling smile just to let her know he'd been joking, which of course he hadn't.

Betty tapped on the door. 'Me, Val,' she called, 'you've got a visitor.'

'Come on in,' a strong female voice called back.

Betty opened the door. 'Commander Johnson to see you,' she grandly announced as if introducing royalty. What a jerk, she thought as she closed the door behind her.

Val rose from her desk, but didn't cross to him. 'After-noon, Commander,' she said, eyeing him up and down. Was this the Texan bloke Baz had told her about just this morning? Looks like it, she thought, they said he was tall. 'What can I do for you?' she asked. 'Take the weight off your feet,' she added, gesturing to one of the visitors' chairs as she sat.

'Why thank you, ma'am,' Johnson replied, and crossing to the desk, he seated himself opposite her. 'Most obliged. Just wanted to ask you a few questions is all.'

Yep, he's the Texan all right, Val thought. 'Ask away,' she said, 'I'm all yours.' Her smile was more than friendly, it was decidedly inviting. She was hoping he'd ask the questions she wanted to answer, and if he didn't, she'd tell him her thoughts anyway.

Lyndon had been wondering just how much information he should impart to the civilians with whom he intended to conduct interviews. It was imperative word should not get out to the general public about the true purpose of his investigation. That a mutiny had taken place in the US Army, that Negro soldiers had turned upon their white officers. Such truths must never be exposed to the world. He could not resist, however, revealing his identity.

'I am a member of the United States Congress, Mrs Callahan,' he began.

'Yes, so I heard,' Val replied pleasantly, 'and under the direct orders of President Roosevelt. Most impressive, I must say.'

'Ah.' His instinctive reaction was a mixture of surprise and gratification. He did like to impress. 'And how would you happen to know that?'

'Word can get around in a place like Townsville,' she said. Then, noting his brief look of concern, she added, 'I keep my ear close to the ground, Commander, and I hear things many don't.' She gave him a smile that seemed somehow intimate. 'Little gets past me, I have to admit, but let me assure you, I also know how to keep a secret.'

'I'm glad to hear that.' He found her smile most reassuring, as if they were complicit in some form of clandestine agreement. 'I'm glad indeed, for there are some questions I'm keen to put to you, Mrs Callahan.'

'This'll be about the trouble out at Kelso, won't it – the boys of the 96th Battalion. And do call me Val.'

He was momentarily stumped for an answer, which was unlike him.

'I told you, there's not much that gets past me.' Their eyes were locked, and this time her smile was more than intimate, it was positively flirtatious. 'If you don't mind my asking, Commander, what's your first name?'

'Lyndon.' For some unfathomable reason, his response was instantaneous. He didn't give it a second thought. 'Lyndon Baines Johnson.'

'Lyndon.' She seemed to savour the word, rolling it around on her tongue. 'Lyndon. I like that name. I've known a lot of men, but never a Lyndon. Would you like a drink, Lyndon?'

'Yes I would, thank you, ma'am, I'd like that very much.'

'It's Val, remember?' She rose to her feet. 'I'll bet you're a bourbon man, am I right?'

'You most certainly are.'

'Well, I'm going to give you something else, something that beats the pants off bourbon, in my opinion anyway. Ever tried Bundy?'

He watched her as she crossed to the cabinet in the corner. A fine figure of a woman despite her age, she'd have to be well into her forties, he thought. Tough and confident. He admired women like that. Full-breasted and fleshy what's more – in fact, what most men would call 'a sexy broad'. And she knew it, he could tell.

'Bundy,' he said, the word sounding quaint, 'no, I can't say I have ever tried Bundy.'

She returned with a bottle and two glasses. 'Bundaberg Rum,' she announced, placing them on the desk. 'Made right here in Queensland,' she said as she sat, 'you won't get better cane sugar anywhere else in the world.' She poured them a healthy shot each. 'I reckon this'll tickle your fancy, Lyndon,' she said. 'Bottoms up, eh?'

They clinked glasses and drank.

Val was flirting shamelessly. She'd had Lyndon Johnson pegged from the moment he'd entered her office. This big boy liked to play. She'd seen how he'd looked at Betty as the girl left the room. She'd seen too, as he'd seated himself opposite her, how his gaze had taken in her breasts. Here was a man with a wandering eye.

'Oh my Lord,' Johnson said after knocking back a good slug of the Bundy, 'this stuff's got a kick like a mule.'

'My oath it has,' Val agreed. 'Most Aussies drown it with ginger ale and ice, but to me that's a bloody crime. It's far better neat.'

'I'd have to go along with you there, Val,' he said, savouring the effect, then taking another swig. He genuinely liked both the taste and the kick.

'Yeah, I knew you would, Lyndon, I can always tell a man who appreciates good-quality, strong liquor.'

Another complicit smile was exchanged, another secret shared, then Val stopped playing the game and got down to business, determined to voice her views.

'Now, about the boys at Kelso,' she said, topping up his glass, 'I know a bit of trouble went on out there, I don't know what it was, nobody does, but whatever happened I can tell you those boys wouldn't have been to blame.'

'What makes you so sure of that?' Johnson's manner changed in an instant, and as acutely as Val's had. The flirtation now over, she had his full attention.

'Those poor young bastards were sadly done by, Lyndon. I knew a lot of them, they used to drink right here at The Brown's, never any trouble, nice kids every one of them. But they were made scapegoats right from the start, blamed for any brawl that happened between blacks and whites, and there was quite a bit of brawling going on, I can tell you. It was all pinned on those kids and they were banned from town. Bloody shameful that.'

Johnson nodded as if he'd not heard all this before, which of course he had. Throughout the morning, he'd heard all the versions, views and arguments; the political-necessity version from Hank Henry, the sheer racist view of John Carter, the humanitarian argument of Samuel Robinson . . . He wasn't hearing anything new, but this time he was hearing it from a civilian, an Australian civilian, and a smart one at that.

'I even got roped into starting up a Negro Servicemen's Club for the boys,' she said, 'well out of town so they wouldn't get into trouble.'

'Yeah, I was told about that,' Lyndon said, 'it's actually one of the reasons why I wanted to talk to you, Val.'

'I didn't set the club up just as a business venture either,' she went on with a passion. 'Although there's always that aspect, of course,' she was forced to admit. 'I mean, if you're a businesswoman you're not going to throw good money after bad just because you feel sorry for blokes, are you?'

'Of course you're not.'

'It would have solved a lot of problems, that club,' she said. 'But there you go,' a shrug of resignation, 'it got knocked on the head after just one night. And all because of a couple of stitched-up farmers' wives who didn't like blacks, or so I'm led to believe. They put in a complaint, I was told.'

'Yes, they most certainly did.' He'd heard all this from Hank Henry, but he was enjoying hearing her version as well.

'We're a strange mob, we Aussies,' Val said thoughtfully, appreciative of the Texan's avid attention. 'We like to pretend everyone's equal here, but they're not. Our blackfellas are treated like shit, always have been. We even had slave labour just like you Yanks, and not all that long ago either. "Blackbirding", they called it. Pacific Islanders were kidnapped and brought here to work the Queensland sugar plantations. We grew fat on the labour of Kanakas for a good fifty years.' She held up her glass by way of demonstration. 'That's where this comes from, Lyndon, the land of Bundy Rum.' And she took another swig as if to emphasise the point.

'So you see, we're not really all that different, are we, your mob and mine,' she went on. 'We've been pissing on black people for years, the whole lot of us. And that's exactly what's happened with the boys of the 96th. At least that's my opinion, for what it's worth. Your blokes have been treating those young men appallingly. They're good, honest boys, here to help us fight a war, and they've been treated like shit.'

Good, honest boys here to help us fight a war. Lyndon wondered whether Val knew of her own government's initial reaction to Negro soldiers. He recalled his recent meeting with Roosevelt and Eisenhower, and Ike telling him about the White Australia policy. '*When we first raised the prospect of sending Negro troops they said they didn't want them,*' Ike had said. And he recalled Roosevelt's reply when he'd voiced his own amazement and enquired of the outcome. '*We said if no black troops, then no US troops,*' Roosevelt had barked. '*Period!*'

No, Lyndon thought, Val Callahan wouldn't know that. Few civilians would. Governments don't share their secrets with the public they represent, and certainly not in times of war.

'I respect your views, Val,' he said, 'and I'm taking on board all you say, believe me.' He did, and he was. She was only confirming his own gut reaction, after all. Following this morning's interviews at the stockade, he too felt a certain sympathy towards the boys of the 96th Battalion. But the sympathy vote didn't provide answers. He needed to move on.

'I'm keen to talk to one of your employees,' he said, 'a man called Baz Taylor.'

Val gave a derisive snort. 'Employee? Well, I'm not sure if that's quite the right term. I think Baz'd see himself more as a sort of "partner". And it's true I do rely on him for a lot of things that might otherwise be difficult to come by,' she admitted in all honesty, 'given wartime shortages, you know how it is.' She left it at that, the implication obvious.

'Which would include the alcohol supplied to the club you started up for the Negro troops,' he prompted.

'Exactly,' she replied, 'and a whole heap of other stuff, too. Baz can pull a rabbit out of a hat like no-one else I know. He's a bloody magician.'

'Or a black-market racketeer,' Lyndon said.

'Same thing.'

They shared a smile.

'Any chance I could have a word with him?'

'Of course.' Val rose. 'You hungry by the way?' She gestured at his glass, which was all but empty. 'That stuff can go to your head on an empty stomach. Would you like a sandwich?'

Lyndon suddenly remembered he hadn't eaten. 'Yeah, thanks, a sandwich would be great.'

She crossed to the door, opened it, and looking out over the landing, she bellowed down the stairs. 'Hey, Betty, get Baz up here for us, will you, love? And while you're at it, pop into the kitchen and ask Jilly to make us a couple of sandwiches.' She turned back to Lyndon. 'Ham and tomato all right?'

'Fine.' He nodded.

'Ham and tomato, thanks, love,' she yelled and Betty's voice answered back with equal power.

'Rightio, Val.'

Closing the door behind her, Val crossed to the desk, sat, and poured them both another healthy measure of rum. 'What are you after Baz for?' she asked unashamedly. If he didn't want her to know he could always tell her to bugger off.

But Lyndon didn't mind. Things had progressed far enough between them that he could see no reason why she shouldn't be included in this next step. Besides, he trusted her. 'The men out at Kelso got drunk,' he said, 'which was how the trouble started. I want to know about their liquor supply.'

'Oh, it would have come from Baz,' Val said with a nod that was unequivocal, 'it would have come from Baz, that's for sure.'

'Yes, that has indeed been established,' Lyndon agreed, 'but I believe the situation is a little more complicated. I believe your Mr Taylor had an inside man, a member of the 96th Battalion who aided and abetted the supply of alcohol to the troops.'

'Yep, that'd make sense.' Of course it would, Val thought. Jeez, Baz's got 'inside men' all over the bloody place.

'I have to tell you, Lyndon,' she admitted, thinking it only fair she should be straight with him, 'most of Baz's business is conducted with the Americans here in Townsville. I mean it's hardly a surprise, is it? Your blokes are the ones with all the supplies and all the money. Barter, that's what the black market's all about.'

'Yes.' Lyndon studied her closely. You're one cluey gal, he thought, you know exactly the game you're playing and the business you're in. You're probably as much a racketeer as he is.

'You wouldn't happen to be aware of a particular contact your "Baz" might have among the men of the 96th now, would you, Val?'

Val threw back her head and laughed heartily. 'If I did, do you reckon I'd tell you?'

He gave a nod that Val read as 'fair enough' and she continued in all seriousness.

'I don't know any single one of Baz's contacts, Lyndon,' she said, 'I make it my business not to. It's safer that way.'

'I understand.' He did.

They were both silent for a moment, sipping their Bundys. Then Lyndon put his glass down and once again studied her, as if somehow sizing her up, or perhaps offering a challenge.

'Do you think your Mr Taylor will tell me who his contact is in the 96th?' he asked.

Val met his gaze, and also his challenge. 'He will if I tell him to,' she said.

Lyndon smiled. That was exactly the answer he'd been hoping for.

There was a tap at the door.

'Come in,' Val called.

Lyndon turned in his chair, expecting the arrival of the unscrupulous Mr Taylor, but instead it was the pretty fair-haired girl carrying a plate of sandwiches.

'Thanks, love,' Val said as Betty placed the plate in the centre of the desk, plonking down a couple of serviettes as well.

'Baz's on his way,' Betty said, and turning to go she flashed a smile at the commander, knowing he'd been studying her body every step of the way as she'd crossed the room.

Val was aware of the wandering eye too, and also of Betty's smile to the Texan. It was the smile Betty could turn on at any moment of any day; hard, brittle, but winning any man upon whom she turned it. That was the way the girl coped, Val thought. But she couldn't help wondering how Betty might feel if she knew that right here in this office they were talking about the 'accident' that had killed Kasey Davis. Val couldn't help wondering also, how many others had been killed in that 'accident'. It must have been something pretty catastrophic, she thought, to warrant the President of the United States sending a congressman all the way out here to investigate.

'Dig in, Lyndon,' she said as the door closed behind Betty. She pushed the sandwiches in his direction. 'They're all yours.' She wasn't hungry herself.

The big Texan was ravenous. Barely a minute later, one of the sandwiches had disappeared and he was halfway through the next when there was another tap at the door.

'Come in,' Val called, and Baz appeared.

'You wanted to see me, boss?'

'Yeah, Baz, come on in and close the door behind you. This is Lieutenant Commander Johnson,' she said, introducing Lyndon, who'd risen from his chair, sandwich forgotten. She didn't bother adding the 'congressman' title. After all, it had been Baz who had told her about the new arrival in town. 'This is Baz Taylor, Commander,' she said and the two men shook. 'Take a seat, gentlemen.'

They sat, both busily appraising each other. Baz was unimpressed. So this is the Texan who big-noted himself at the airfield. Well, he's tall, they were right about that.

Lyndon Johnson was thinking how typical of his type Baz Taylor looked. From the Ronald Colman moustache, to the snappy clothes and glossy shoes, he looked the kind of man the English would call a spiv, a very handsome and very readable spiv.

'Over to you, Commander,' Val said.

Lyndon got straight to the point. 'I'm making enquiries about the supply of liquor to the men of the 96th Battalion, Mr Taylor,' he said, 'to Companies A and C, that is, stationed out at Kelso.'

Baz smiled, his cheeky charm lighting up a face that was, to most, truly engaging. 'Oh, that was me, Commander, most certainly me, and I'm not ashamed to admit it.' No harm in admitting it either, he thought, and certainly no point in hiding the fact, everyone bloody well knows. 'Those blokes had been given a really hard time, they deserved —'

'Yes, yes, I'm aware of all this,' Lyndon interrupted tersely. 'I know you supplied the liquor itself, but I'm seeking the identity of your man inside the ranks.'

Baz's smile faded and his expression became blank, bewildered, as if he were genuinely trying to follow a link that was somehow eluding him. 'Not sure what you mean, Commander.'

'I mean, Mr Taylor,' Lyndon said, his tone measured, he wasn't about to be played for a fool by the likes of Baz Taylor, 'the particular soldier with whom you did business.'

'Oh, I see, yes, of course.' Baz smiled again, a light appearing to have suddenly dawned. 'A few of the corporals it was, can't remember their names. They collected the money from the boys and I delivered the grog, simple as that.'

'No, it wouldn't have been as simple as that at all. You would have made a deal with one man in particular, and I want that man's name.'

They were eyeballing each other now. Johnson demanding, Baz meeting his gaze defiantly.

You don't scare me, Mr Big-shot-from-Texas, Baz was thinking. I'm not part of your bloody army, mate. You don't own me.

Baz had no intention of backing down. Not through any sense of loyalty to Strut Stowers, but simply because Stowers was too valuable a contact to lose. The two of them had done a lot of business together and Baz planned they should continue to do so.

'Don't have any particular name, I'm afraid, Commander . . .' He sounded vaguely apologetic, but his eyes were clearly saying, *You can go and get fucked.* 'Just the corporals, like I said, and I never knew their names.'

Johnson held his look for a moment, then glanced at Val.

'Tell the commander what he wants to know, Baz,' Val said.

Baz turned to her. He knew an order when he heard it, and one look at Val told him this was most definitely an order. 'Sure, boss.' He grinned winningly. There was no way he was going to risk his relationship with Val. Val Callahan was worth a hundred Stowers, a thousand even. When he turned back to Johnson, the same grin remained in place, as if he were saying, *Happy to oblige.*

'A bloke by the name of Stowers,' he said, 'Sergeant Strut Stowers of Company C.' Pity to lose a contact like that, Baz thought, but what the hell, there are other fish in the sea, and I don't really give a shit anyway.

'Thank you, Mr Taylor,' Lyndon said, but he was looking at Val. Good, he thought, here was the name he was after. He'd call Stowers into the stockade for questioning first thing tomorrow morning.

CHAPTER SIXTEEN

Strut Stowers looked warily about the interview room. Was he in some sort of trouble? Hell, these were the big guys seated before him. He'd been told who they were and his eyes flickered from one to the other. The newly arrived congressman, Lieutenant Commander Johnson; the staff officer from HQ, Lieutenant Colonel what's-his-name – Carter, that's right; Provost Marshal Major Henry – well, like every other soldier in town, he knew Hank Henry; and his own commanding officer, Captain Samuel Robinson. 'Just an interview,' he'd been informed, 'that's all.' Yet seated in the corner was an MP lieutenant poised over his typewriter, ready to note down every word, and two more MPs were standing by the door that led to the cells.

Oh fuck, Strut thought, here I am lined up in front of these top-ranking white guys. What sort of deep shit am I in?

He felt the quickening of his pulse and the beads of sweat already forming on his forehead. This must be about Anthony Hill. Just yesterday afternoon, Maxwell had insisted they go over their story of that night; the ripping up of the book to teach the kid a lesson, how they'd left him in the tent to pick up the pieces and got on with their patrol; Maxwell had wanted to make sure that the times and the details all matched. He hadn't seemed worried.

The congressman had come out to camp and asked him a few questions, he'd said, nothing more than that.

'We got to get things spot on just in case the guy wants to talk to you, too, Stowers,' he'd said, 'no cause for alarm, I can assure you.'

But Chuck Maxwell hadn't had to face a line-up like this, had he? Strut was feeling distinctly spooked by now, and he cursed his commanding officer. If these guys come at me I'll make sure you go down right along with me, Maxwell, he thought. I'll see you in hell, I swear I will.

'Sergeant Stowers . . .' It was the big Texan, the congressman seated opposite him, who opened the proceedings. 'I'm here to investigate the mutiny that took place on the night of 22nd May and the events that led up to the riot.'

Strut exhaled a huge sigh of relief, although he disguised it with a heartfelt shake of his head that such a shocking and tragic event had occurred. 'Yes, sir,' he said, 'a terrible night that was.' Shit, is that all this is about, he thought. He was off the hook; he'd had nothing to do with the riot.

'The troops had been supplied with illicit liquor that night,' Johnson continued, 'which has been reported as one of the principal factors that led them to mutiny.'

Seated near the wall at the end of the line of officers, John Carter couldn't resist a mildly rebellious nod. Despite Johnson's disdain, as far as he was concerned liquor most certainly remained the overall governing factor that had led to the mutiny.

'Yes, sir, there was liquor all right,' Strut confirmed, 'the troops were certainly drunk, sir, that's for sure.'

'And where did they get this liquor, Sergeant?'

'From a man called Baz Taylor, I believe, sir. The same man who supplied the liquor for the club Captain Robinson tried to set up for the troops.'

Strut cast a glance in Samuel's direction, signalling he was only too eager to help by giving as much detail as possible and getting everything right in the process, but he didn't receive a reaction by way of return.

'Do you have any idea how this liquor was obtained and distributed, Sergeant?' Johnson asked.

'I didn't at the time, sir, of course I had no idea. That night came as a terrible shock to us all.' Another heartfelt shake of the head. 'But I've since learned several NCOs collected money from the men and paid Taylor, who then delivered the liquor. At least this is what I've been told, sir.'

Unaware he was walking into a trap, Strut felt perfectly safe. The corporals had told him they'd taken the rap, that they'd been questioned and had admitted to dealing directly with Baz Taylor. They'd cop a bit of flak, sure, Strut thought, but he'd make it worth their while. And what's more they knew that. This had been the agreement from the outset.

'You're lying, Sergeant.' Johnson dropped his simple question-and-answer technique and started to ride in hard, as had been his intention. 'The NCOs collected the money certainly, but they did not pay it to Taylor, they paid it directly to you.'

The accusation, unexpected as it was, shocked Strut from his complacency. His mind started to race. Which of those bastard corporals had ratted on him? But more importantly, how was he to play this?

'You had a business arrangement with Baz Taylor, Sergeant,' Johnson continued relentlessly, the background clack of the MP's typewriter equally relentless. 'You took money from your own men and sold them hard liquor, and I want to know why. Were you just lining your own pockets or was there a more sinister reason?'

What the hell was the man getting at, Strut wondered. He felt threatened; and threatened far beyond the act of simply aiding the supply of booze to the men. The Texan was implying something, but what the hell was it? Strut knew he was cornered, so he started to grovel.

'I did wrong, sir, I admit I did wrong, but I meant no harm, I swear. You see, when the servicemen's club that Captain Robinson tried so hard to get going was closed after just one night, the men were unhappy, they were sorely unhappy, sir. And I thought —'

'You thought it might cheer them up just a little if they could get their hands on some liquor, is that what you're saying?'

Strut registered the Texan's ominous tone, but he persevered nonetheless. 'Yes, sir, I —'

'That's a mighty altruistic motive you have there, Sergeant, but I don't believe you for one second.'

Strut hadn't really expected he would, but he wondered why the guy was coming on so strong. Was it just because he was a Texan and hated blacks, or was something else going on here? What was the term the congressman himself had come up with? Something 'more sinister'. Strut was confused, and panic was starting to set in.

His eyes darted about the gathering of officers before him, none of them saying a word, all of them appearing to await an answer, all of them complicit in the trap that was being set for him. Of course they would be, wouldn't they, he thought, fucking white dogs.

'I've been making some enquiries about you, Stowers,' Johnson said, no longer observing the courtesy of rank. 'Your men don't like you, do they?'

'I'm a sergeant, sir . . .' Seated though he was, Strut's attitude signalled he was standing to attention, at least this was his aim as he fought to retain his dignity. 'My men are not expected to like me.'

'But they're expected to respect you, surely, isn't that the duty of a sergeant?' Here was the sort of man Lyndon

Johnson despised. A man, black or white no matter, in a position of power over others who abused that position and betrayed his men as Strut Stowers had, and as he apparently had been doing on a regular basis. Johnson had listened very carefully to the views of Amos Cole and Willie Parker.

'You don't give a shit about your men, do you, Stowers?' The question was rhetorical, Johnson charging on relentlessly. 'You'd sell your own men down the river if there was a buck to be had in it.'

This guy's out to get me, Strut thought, his panic now turning to fear.

'Your motive in supplying the troops with liquor was anything but altruistic,' Johnson sneered. 'It was a downright low act. You deliberately set out to cause trouble for the men you bullied and betrayed on a regular basis, while also reaping a profit for yourself.'

Trouble? Set out to cause trouble? Strut's brow was once again beaded with sweat, his mind juggling accusations he couldn't comprehend. What sort of trouble?

Strut Stowers was not alone in his confusion. Hank Henry was wondering where Johnson was going with his argument. It had been established Stowers was the insider who had masterminded the liquor supply, surely that had been the object of the exercise. John Carter too was somewhat bewildered, although he did recall Johnson's view on the insider possibly being a major influence in the mutiny, a view he'd found rather fanciful himself.

Samuel Robinson was the only one present who had the slightest inkling of where the Texan's tirade might perhaps be leading, and even he was far from certain. This can't be Johnson's intention surely, he thought. It's not possible. It can't be. But as he watched and waited in breathless disbelief, Samuel prayed desperately that he just might be right.

'It's my belief, *Sergeant* Stowers . . .' This time Johnson observed the man's rank, but he made it sound like a further indictment of guilt, 'that you deliberately fuelled your own men, inciting them to riot.'

Jesus Christ, Strut thought, horror-struck, this fucker's going to pin the whole thing on me!

'You knew how unhappy the troops were, you said so yourself. You knew they hated you, and rightfully so given your treatment of them. You fuelled a lot of angry men, Stowers,' Johnson said accusingly, 'you drove them to a point where they determined to make a statement. In fact, I'd go so far as to say you're the major reason they mutinied.'

'That's not true!' Strut burst out; he couldn't take any more. 'They mutinied because of Captain Maxwell. I heard the men talking. They were all fired up because they believed Maxwell killed Anthony Hill. And they were right. He did. I was there.'

The room fell silent. Even the clack of the typewriter keys came to a brief halt before once again starting up with renewed purpose.

Samuel stared disbelievingly at Johnson. You did it, he thought. How clever. But then, did you? Johnson, whose eyes remained on Stowers, actually appeared surprised by the man's admission. Did you deliberately entrap him or not, Samuel wondered. He recalled Johnson's attentiveness just the previous day as he'd listened to Amos Cole and Willie Parker, and also to Rupert Barrett. Stowers' name had come up for mention several times. How Stowers had been on patrol with Maxwell that night and had witnessed the tearing up of the book, this was common knowledge; how Stowers had always turned a blind eye to Maxwell's bullying and how the men detested him for it. But never at any time had there been any mention of murder, or the suggestion that Stowers may even have been an accessory.

The men had been warned that with no proof, there must be no hint of accusation. Had Johnson come to his own conclusions and deliberately set out to entrap Stowers? Or in hounding the man so hard, had he unwittingly wrought a confession?

'Captain Maxwell will say it was an accident, sir, but it weren't no accident at all. He'll say Private Hill attacked him when he ripped up the book, but Private Hill, he did no such thing . . .' There was no stopping Stowers now, the typewriter chasing his every word in an attempt to keep up. 'That kid just tried to rescue his book, and Maxwell killed him stone-cold dead. Bashed him so hard his neck broke.'

'I see,' Johnson said thoughtfully. 'A difficult situation for you, Sergeant, I can well imagine, so what exactly did you do?'

'There was nothing I *could* do, sir.' The Texan's comment and even the tone of his voice had been so reasonable, Strut felt a sudden surge of hope. He could see his way out now; this had been a smart move on his part. 'Captain Maxwell said he'd pin the kid's death on me. Said I'd go down for it, said no white officer would listen to the word of a black soldier. Ordered me to get rid of the body, make it look like an accident.'

'So you did just that.'

'I had to, sir. I was obeying orders when all's said and done. I was obeying the orders of my commanding officer, sir.'

'Despite the fact your commanding officer had just committed murder?'

'What option did I have, sir?' Strut looked the Texan directly in the eyes, and this time his appeal seemed entirely without guile. 'It would have been the word of a white officer against that of a black NCO. I wouldn't have stood a chance.'

'I see.'

For the first time since the start of the proceedings, Johnson exchanged looks with his fellow officers, who in turn exchanged looks with each other. The general reaction appeared one of agreement: the interview had undoubtedly proved a success, although Lieutenant Colonel John Carter's face bore a worried frown.

A further ten minutes ensued while Johnson checked the finer details with Stowers, including the disposal of the body, the timing of events, and then apparently all was over.

'I guess that just about rounds things up,' Johnson said, leaning back in his chair with an air of self-satisfaction. His attention, however, remained on Stowers. 'You're a lifer, aren't you, Sergeant,' he continued without drawing breath, 'a career soldier. How long have you served?'

The Texan's tone once again was so reasonable that Strut didn't feel threatened. 'Coming up for twenty-two years now, sir,' he said with pride, 'joined the army when I was nineteen.'

'And you worked your way up to First Sergeant over those many years of service.' Johnson nodded his head as if in congratulatory fashion.

'Yes, sir, I did.' Strut accepted the congratulations as his due.

'Well now, I'm here to tell you things are about to change.' Johnson's tone was no longer reasonable. He'd played his game, he'd had his fun, and his voice was now icy cold. 'There'll be no more perks for you, Stowers. I'll see to it that you're demoted to private as of this very day.' Johnson had the courtesy to direct a look to John Carter, although he really didn't deem it necessary, and John Carter returned a nod, grateful to have been recognised.

'You'll just be *one of the boys* from now on, soldier,' Johnson said, lending sarcastic emphasis to the term, 'one of the good old rank and file. Interesting to see how being one of the rank and file will suit you,' he went on, 'but even more interesting to see how it'll suit the rank and file to have you among them.'

The prospect sent an immediate chill through Strut. They'll fucking kill me, he thought.

'Yes,' Johnson agreed, Stowers' expression clearly readable, 'I doubt you'll win many hearts.' He stood, the other officers also rising to their feet, and turned to Hank Henry. 'I suggest we put this man in the cell with the other two witnesses for now, Major,' he said, 'until all three are transferred back to camp.'

'Yes, of course.' Hank Henry gave a brisk nod to the two MP guards, who collected a now decidedly fearful Stowers.

As he was escorted from the room, once again in a cold sweat, Strut's mind was desperately planning the only defence tack he had. Maxwell. He had to spread the news about Maxwell. He had to let the men know all the facts . . . how Maxwell had blackmailed him . . . how he'd played no part whatsoever in the kid's death . . .

'I'll arrange the transfer right away, Commander,' Hank Henry said when the guards had disappeared. He and Johnson had previously agreed that Amos Cole, Willie Parker, and now Strut Stowers, should be returned to camp. The official investigation over, there was only the outcome to be discussed now, which was principally how to keep the whole ugly episode a secret from the rest of the world.

'Thank you, Major.'

As Hank Henry left the interview room, Samuel shared a quiet aside with Johnson. 'Well done, sir,' he said, 'my congratulations.'

'On what, Captain? A lucky break, that's all.' The slightest smile appeared for just one instant, then was gone. 'An unexpected bonus, shall we say.'

Samuel still didn't know whether Johnson's ploy had been deliberate. He supposed he would never know.

Lieutenant Colonel John Carter may possibly have heard the brief exchange, but it was immaterial anyway. He had far more important things on his mind as he waited impatiently for the clerk to gather his papers together.

'I'll get these notes properly typed up for you, sir,' the young MP said. 'I'll attach them to yesterday's report and have the whole file delivered to the Officers' Club by early afternoon.'

'Much obliged, Lieutenant,' Johnson replied.

'The man was *lying*!'

The door had barely closed behind the lieutenant before Carter burst forth, unable to contain himself any longer. And his frustration was targeted directly at Lyndon Johnson, who, to his mind anyway, had appeared to believe every word of Stowers' admission.

'The death of that boy *has* to have been an accident,' he vehemently declared. 'And even if it *wasn't*, it has to be *seen* to be an accident. Maxwell didn't *intend* to kill the boy. We can't pin the murder of a black soldier on a white officer, for God's sake. Particularly not now. Good grief, man, we're an army at war! We have to be seen as a unified military force!'

'I agree.' Johnson appeared if anything slightly amused by Carter's passionate outburst. And he was. Ah, he thought, the worm has turned. 'I agree with you entirely, Colonel.'

Carter, his tirade brought to an abrupt halt, seemed confused. Which particular part did the commander agree with?

Johnson decided to spell it out in detail, aware that for a bureaucrat like Carter, such a process was necessary. 'I agree that under the circumstances we can't try the man for murder. I even agree that Maxwell didn't set out to kill young Anthony Hill,' he said patiently, 'but the fact is he *did* kill the boy. Accidentally perhaps, but with vicious intent to do physical harm. Maxwell caused the death of an innocent man, Colonel. Such a wantonly heartless act should not go unpunished, surely. Wouldn't you agree, Captain?' he asked, turning to Samuel.

John Carter's lips pursed disapprovingly. Why was the congressman referring to Captain Robinson of all people? The captain was not an official investigator, he was present merely as a commanding officer of the 96th Battalion's Company C.

'Yes, sir,' Samuel replied with care, 'I certainly believe such an act should not go unpunished.' Samuel himself was surprised Johnson should seek his opinion. What was he supposed to say? After all, they both knew the US Army would allow no official court action to be taken. But Johnson was full of surprises today.

'What would you do with Maxwell, Captain?' Lyndon Johnson's unwavering gaze remained trained upon Samuel Robinson. He was definitely seeking an answer. 'You know the man,' he said. 'Tell me about him. What would you do with him?'

Samuel deliberated for a number of seconds, which seemed a long time as his eyes locked with Johnson's.

'Maxwell is a coward, sir,' he said, prepared to give his opinion with absolute honesty. 'He's a coward who uses his position and rank to bully in order to justify to himself a sense of his own manliness. At least this is what I've come to believe.'

'Yeah,' Johnson nodded, recalling the man he'd met briefly out at Kelso, the man to whom he'd taken an intense dislike. 'That makes sense to me. So what would you do with him?'

'I'd take away his rank and assign him to the toughest combat unit in the US armed forces.'

'And that is . . . ?'

'The US Marines Combat Division, sir. They'll be in the firing line before too long, they're usually first in every time, and it's my guess that time is only weeks away.'

Lyndon Johnson let out a short bark of laughter; the answer pleased him. 'That'd scare the shit out of a prick like Maxwell, wouldn't it?'

'Yes, it would.'

'Thank you, Captain Robinson.'

'My pleasure, Commander.'

Samuel hoped like hell Johnson would follow up on his suggestion. You deserve everything they can throw at you, Chuck, he thought. And I can promise you, your daddy won't be able to save you from the marines. If you don't cop it in combat, you'll cop it from the men. Those guys can smell a coward a mile away.

From the glowering look John Carter was giving him, however, Samuel gathered the colonel considered he'd overstepped the mark, so he decided it was time to take his leave. The two senior-ranking officers assigned to investigate the riot and its aftermath would need to confer anyway.

'Now if you'll excuse me, sir, I'll return to camp. I'd like to be there before the men arrive, they've had a tough time of things lately.' He was referring to Amos Cole and Willie Parker, he didn't give a damn about Strut Stowers. In fact, he was gladdened by the knowledge that Stowers was now destined to get the kind of treatment he'd been doling out to others for years.

'Of course, Captain. Thank you for your help.'

Johnson's thanks were obviously genuine, and the silent exchange between the two men might have been something approaching a form of congratulations.

With the departure of Captain Robinson, John Carter fought to regain the dignity of which he considered he'd been sorely deprived. He was very much offended by the way Commander Johnson had sought the captain's opinion in preference to his own. Such behaviour in not showing recognition of his rank was unfitting, unseemly and highly irregular.

'Well, Commander,' he said stiffly, 'I suppose the time has come for we two as senior commanding officers in this investigation to consider what action should be taken with regard to the mutinous troops of the 96th Battalion.'

'I'll tell you exactly what we'll do, Colonel . . .'

Johnson strode the several paces that separated them and stood staring down at Carter virtually nose to nose, the shorter man having to look up a good six inches to meet the eyes that bored into his.

'*I* shall report to *my* superior,' Johnson went on, meaning as they both knew President Franklin D. Roosevelt, 'and *you* shall report to *yours*,' meaning as they both knew General Douglas MacArthur. 'And I suggest you recommend to your superior he transfer Companies A and C of the 96th Battalion to service duty outside this country, which I am quite sure will be exactly what the good general will wish to do.'

Carter cleared his throat, again intimidated by the big, brash Texan, but determined not to let it show. 'Yes perhaps,' he began, about to embark on further discussion, 'that does seem a workable suggestion —'

But Johnson didn't want to listen to any more. 'And as for Maxwell,' he said, 'well, you heard Captain Robinson. The Marines Combat Division sounds spot on to me.' He strode off to the door. 'I guess that's about it, Colonel,' he called over his shoulder as he went. Although having opened the door, he did have the courtesy to turn and even offer a brief smile. 'You have a good trip back to HQ now mind.'

And he was gone.

*

By the time he arrived back at the Queen's Hotel, it was one o'clock in the afternoon and Lyndon had decided upon his plans for the rest of the day. First of all, he would go for a pleasant walk along the seafront; having been cooped up indoors with interrogations the previous day and now all morning, he hadn't yet acquainted himself with the prettier aspects of Townsville. He would walk up The Strand, he'd decided, perhaps all the way to Kissing Point Fort, which he'd been told was at the northern end. Then he'd return to the hotel for a late lunch, after which the clerk's notes of interview would no doubt be delivered, and he would settle down to the arduous task of writing up his full report to be presented to Roosevelt upon his return to America.

But no sooner had he walked into the foyer of the hotel than he found himself accosted.

'Lieutenant Commander Johnson, I believe.' A man rose from an armchair nearby, an armchair that was within clear sight of the main doors. He'd obviously been lying in wait.

'Pete Vickers,' the man said on approach, a sizeable folder tucked firmly under his left arm, right hand extended, smile friendly. 'I left a business card yesterday afternoon. A note, too, actually,' he admitted, 'I called in twice.'

'Ah yes.' Lyndon had no option but to shake the hand on offer. The pleasant-looking young man, who appeared in his mid-twenties, was obviously a cripple, and being rude to a cripple didn't seem at all right. 'I received both your card and your note, Mr Vickers,' he said, 'but I have no wish to talk to the press.'

'Oh, I'm not after an interview, Commander,' Pete said, 'far from it, I assure you. As I said in my note, I'm of the firm belief *I* can be of assistance to *you* rather than *you* to *me*.'

Of course that's exactly what a reporter would say, isn't it, Lyndon thought with a flash of irritation. 'I have no desire whatsoever to talk with the *Bulletin*, Mr Vickers,' he said rather sharply.

'Nor do I,' Pete replied. 'That is, not about you and the purpose you're here anyway, there wouldn't be any point. They wouldn't print a word I wrote.'

The young man's manner, while remaining polite, was so assertive Lyndon couldn't help being intrigued. 'Oh?' he asked in a way that invited explanation.

It was exactly the reaction Pete had been aiming for, so he dived straight in. 'You're here to investigate the riot of the 96th Battalion on the night of the 22nd of May,' he said, 'the confrontation between black soldiers and white.'

The intentionally blunt statement had its effect: he'd garnered Johnson's attention, the commander's expression clearly saying, *How the hell did you know about that?*

'I'm sure you have all the relevant information regarding the actual mutiny itself,' Pete continued. He knew he was taking a punt using the term – he hadn't heard the word 'mutiny' applied – but surely that's what it must have been if road blocks had been set up to prevent the Negro troops entering the city. He could see from the steely look in Johnson's eyes he'd hit the right chord. 'I mean all the *military* information of course, material that's hardly available to me.' He gave a disarmingly humble smile that might have worked had the time and the recipient been right. Neither were. Johnson remained unmoved. So Pete decided to lay off the charm.

'There's been trouble here in Townsville among black and white troops for some time, Commander,' he said. 'Things have been covered up naturally, but there have been so many precedents leading up to this latest disastrous event, that quite frankly the military should have seen it coming.'

He had Johnson's full attention now and he knew it.

'Trouble's been brewing with regard to black soldiers throughout the whole of North Queensland,' he went on. 'Of course, the Australian Government's demand that Negro troops be kept away from major urban centres hasn't helped,' he added cynically, 'but the US military's failure to provide their black soldiers with adequate recreational outlets has openly courted disaster. I believe the mutiny to be a direct result of all this.'

'You seem to have made quite a study of the situation, Mr Vickers,' Johnson said.

'Yes, sir, I have.' The very opening he was after. 'I've written reports about every incident that's occurred in Townsville over the past several months.' He held out the folder. 'It's all in there, Commander.'

Lyndon accepted the folder. 'What do you expect me to do with this?' he asked.

Pete wasn't going to push his luck by voicing his hopes out loud. Not yet anyway, not until the man had read the contents of the folder. 'Whatever you see fit, Commander,' he said. 'I believe my report will speak for itself.'

'Very well.' Lyndon was most certainly intrigued, but he was not about to have his day spoiled. 'I'm going for a walk, I need some fresh air,' he said abruptly, 'I shall read this sitting on a park bench.'

'An excellent idea, sir.'

'I'll get back to you in due course, Mr Vickers.' And with that, Lyndon Johnson turned on his heel and marched out of the hotel.

Once outside, he crossed the road and started to walk briskly up The Strand, admiring the view; to his right the glistening sea and far in the distance the mystery of Magnetic Island, and to his left, towering above the township the rust-red edifice of Castle Hill.

He slowed his walk in order to more fully appreciate

the beauty. It was a day in late autumn, but a Northern Queensland late autumn, crisp and clear, and if one could ignore the military traffic grinding its way up and down The Strand . . . Well, in a tropical kind of way, Townsville's mighty pretty, he thought, admiring the broad coastal boulevard lined with lush trees and the palms that were dotted along the foreshore. Birds too . . . Big, black, crested birds, some sort of parrot, he supposed, quite a number of them feeding on the ground and in the trees. As two took flight from the branch they were perched upon, he caught the vivid flash of red tail feathers. How exotic, he thought. Lyndon had never before encountered black cockatoos.

Some distance ahead, he could see coiled barbed wire and sandbags lining the beachfront. He decided not to walk up to the fort at the northern end of The Strand, where the view would be distinctly militarised, but to stay here where the aspect was more attractive.

He found a park bench looking out over the ocean, sat, and opened the folder. Inside was page upon page, fifty, possibly more, of neatly typed, single-spaced notes. Each report of each incident, varying in the number of its pages, was individually titled and dated. A detailed study indeed, he thought as he settled down to flick through the file for any key notes that might be of interest.

From that moment on, the view was forgotten. Lyndon found himself caught up from the very start by both the style and the content of every single report, and not once did he flick through the pages. In fact, he took his time perusing each. This guy sure can write, he thought.

But the material itself . . . The comment it made . . . Without labouring the point, the reporter had clearly and concisely allowed each episode to speak for itself before following it up with an intelligent, analytical view of cause and effect. And much of the reportage was shocking. Dead

Negroes in coffins secretly shipped from Mount Isa? Was this really true? There was every reason why such incidents should remain highly confidential, Lyndon thought as he read on further of other black deaths also kept secret, but these incidents should never have occurred in the first place.

An hour and a half later, he closed the folder and looked out at the ocean, but he wasn't seeing the view. His mind was still dwelling upon what he'd just read.

Vickers is right about the plight of our Negro troops, he thought. And he's sure as hell right when he says we've been courting disaster. Right here in this folder is every reason why black labour forces would seek to rebel.

He stood, stretching his back. The bench had been hard, and he felt chilled in his light khaki now, the mid-afternoon air seeming to have developed a bit of a bite. Perhaps it was just because he'd been sitting around too long in the breeze that whipped off the water.

He strode briskly back to the hotel, his intended lunch long overdue and forgotten, food immaterial now. He would ring Pete Vickers and arrange a meeting.

But the moment he stepped into the foyer, there was Pete, still waiting, still in the same armchair, where, by now, he'd spent most of the day.

At the sight of the big Texan, Pete jumped to his feet and crossed eagerly to meet him.

'Well, Commander,' he said, 'what do you think?'

'I think we need to talk. Is the bar open yet?'

'Not quite. I checked. Four o'clock, another half-hour to go.'

'Right. Coffee, then.'

Lyndon set off for the lounge, checking his stride so the reporter wouldn't have trouble keeping up. But the reporter had no trouble keeping up at all. Pete Vickers, in his enthusiasm, seemed to be checking his own ungainly stride so he wouldn't get ahead.

It's as if the guy doesn't even know he's a cripple, Lyndon thought, kind of impressive that.

As they waited for their coffees, which seemed a long time coming, the Texan remained silent, apparently thoughtful, and Pete curbed his impatience. Things were going so well he didn't dare risk irritating the bloke.

Then finally, once seated, coffees before them, he couldn't resist asking again, 'So, Commander, my report, what do you think?'

'Fucking remarkable,' Lyndon said. Then, his eyes keenly trained on Pete's reaction, he added, 'That is if it's true.'

'Every bloody word of it's true,' Pete's response was unwavering, 'I can swear to that. No embellishment, no exaggeration, just the facts as I discovered them through my investigations. Followed by my comments and analysis, of course,' he added, 'I'm a journalist, after all.'

Yes, Lyndon thought, you certainly are, and a good one at that.

'Mind you,' Pete went on, 'I'm sure you'll have noted there's no specific data regarding numbers of deaths. I have no idea how many Negroes have been killed during black and white riots in town, or how many died drinking cyanide-laced hooch at Mount Isa. Or of course,' he added meaningfully, 'the numbers of dead resulting from the recent mutiny. The US military guards its secrets very closely.'

'Of course,' Lyndon said, 'as it must.' He took a long swig of his coffee, and looking down at the folder that sat on the table before him, asked the very same question he'd asked earlier. 'What do you expect me to do with this?'

And this time, Pete was more than prepared to answer. 'I want you to take it back to America,' he said, fighting hard to contain his excitement at the possibility of a long-awaited dream about to be realised. 'No-one in Australia will publish it, you see. Wartime censorship's far stricter here than in any other Allied country. But it might well find a release in the United States . . .' He halted, aware that his passion was beginning to show and that Johnson was looking at him quizzically. 'This is a story that must be told, Commander,' he said.

No, no, no, Lyndon thought, this is a story that must *never* be told. A story the world must never hear about. How naïve can the man be, he wondered, does he honestly believe I could allow this to be published?

'You do realise, don't you, Mr Vickers, that I am a member of the US Congress and that I am investigating the Kelso uprising on the direct orders of the president himself.'

Pete recognised how absurdly naïve he must have sounded, to the point even of stupidity. As was so often the case he'd got carried away, and he now frantically attempted to correct himself.

'Of course,' he said hastily, 'yes, of course I know the mutiny itself can't be mentioned, and the specific details of other incidents also, but as a human-interest story . . .' Oh Christ, he thought, I just used the same tired old term Jim bandies about whenever he wants me to dumb things down. 'I mean, the predicament that Negro troops face working in the remote regions of this country . . . a comment about racism on both sides . . .' He started trailing off, feeling his argument was sounding somehow inadequate. 'Surely that's worthy of note.'

'It is,' Lyndon nodded encouragingly, 'it most certainly is.'

The entire report was worthy of note as far as Lyndon Johnson was concerned. Here within this folder was everything he needed to present to FDR. Here was the most detailed analysis of events and conditions that could well invoke a rebellious action by black troops against their white officers, as had occurred at Kelso. He would make this report his own. Along with the clerk's interrogation notes and the facts and figures contained in John Carter's abysmally scant account of the event, he needed nothing more. The perfect opportunity had landed in his lap.

He picked up the folder. 'I will not lie to you, Mr Vickers,' he said, 'there is no way this will be published in the United States, not even as a human-interest story, and certainly not while there's a war going on. But I can tell you this much. It will go to the White House and be read by the highest authority in the land. This report will be seen by the eyes of none other than President Roosevelt himself, I can assure you of that.'

Pete was speechless. The President of the United States of America. His report would be presented to Roosevelt, after which it would remain in the White House for posterity. Perhaps one day when the war was over, it might even be published. Well, you couldn't ask for much more than that, could you?

'Thank you, Commander,' he said with a smile that was heartfelt. 'Thank you so much, I'm truly grateful.'

Lyndon glanced at his watch. 'Four o'clock, the bar's open,' he said, 'shall we adjourn?'

CHAPTER SEVENTEEN

The following day was to be Johnson's last in Townsville. He was due to fly out to Port Moresby with the 22nd Bomb Group that afternoon, the aerial raid upon Lae to which he'd been assigned as an observer, due to take place the next morning.

With a couple of hours to spare, he decided to call in at The Brown's and say goodbye to Val Callahan. He'd walk up Wickham and Flinders streets into the city centre, allowing time also to walk back to the Officers' Club, collect his gear, and meet up with his driver. He felt somehow drawn to see Val, he wasn't quite sure why, presumably to thank her for her help, but he chose to wear his dress uniform nonetheless; he was keen to impress.

He did.

'My, my, Lyndon,' she muttered, eyeing him up and down in such a lascivious manner he wasn't sure whether she was genuine or joking. 'Very smart. And very, *very* sexy.'

He'd arrived presuming the bar would be closed. It was only ten in the morning, and the doors leading from the street were certainly closed, but as he'd stepped inside the hotel it was immediately obvious the bar was seeing some action. The door to the left that led directly from the reception area was wide open and the sound of men's voices rang out loud and clear.

He stepped inside. At least a dozen men, all in uniform, all officers, were lounging around drinking beer, several of them gathered about a glass enclosure in the centre of the room.

Val and the devastatingly pretty young girl were behind the counter, Val at the till having just accepted some money from a soldier, the girl at the far end cleaning glasses.

He smiled at the girl, noting how attractive her breasts were in the silken Jean Harlow–style blouse she was wearing, wondering whether perhaps she was bra-less beneath, and crossed to Val.

Betty acknowledged the commander's smile, proffering a bright one of her own in return. It's the jerk again, she thought, and all dolled up this time.

'My, my, Lyndon,' the surreptitious mutter from Val as he joined her, 'very smart. And very, *very* sexy.' He gave a careless shrug as if he knew she was joking, but he *felt* smart, and yes, sexy too in his navy jacket, white shirt and tie. He certainly stood out among the drab khaki that surrounded him.

'What's going on here,' he asked, 'how come the bar's open?'

'A private party,' she said, 'just for a few officers, maybe a bloke's birthday, I don't know. Not strictly legal,' she admitted with a smile, 'but what the hell, when boys are fighting a war you can't really say no, can you?'

'I guess not.' You can't really say no to the extra bucks you're making either, can you, Lyndon thought, wondering how many private parties Val hosted here at The Brown's.

'Can I get you a beer, Commander?' she asked. 'On the house of course,' she added, 'or something stronger if you prefer.'

He wondered if the offer was intended as a form of bribery, although he noted she didn't appear in the least concerned by his presence.

'No, no,' he said, 'good God, too early in the day for me.'

He looked about at the drinkers, his expression readably critical, but was relieved to note there were no Americans present. Well, of course, he thought, American officers would never behave so blatantly; they had more respect for their uniform. The officers present were all Aussies and Aussies were known to flout the rules.

'What's happening over there, is that a goddamned snake?' he asked, indicating the glass enclosure on a plinth in the centre of the bar where three men were focused upon the action about to take place.

'Yep,' she said, 'one of the blokes has just laid a house bet. Snake versus man,' she explained, 'three to one in the punter's favour if he can keep his hand on the glass.'

Lyndon watched fascinated as the snake, agitated by the drumming of the stick on the plinth and the tapping on the glass, lifted the front part of its body from the ground and started swaying from side to side, black tongue flickering. He watched the punter raise his hand and place it flat upon the glass at chest height.

'Rule number one,' Val said, 'the bloke has to maintain eye contact with the snake at all times. If he closes his eyes or looks away he's lost the bet. That's what the other bloke's doing on the opposite side of the pen, he's the referee.'

Lyndon watched the referee watching the punter. Then he watched the punter watching the snake. The focus of both was intense. But his eyes kept getting drawn back to the snake, whose focus was now more intense than either man's. The snake was preparing to attack. It reared up vertically, displaying its pale underbelly, tongue still flickering, neck coiling threateningly.

Although he wasn't meeting the animal's gaze himself, Lyndon was becoming as mesmerised as the man whose hand rested upon the glass and whose eyes were locked with those of the snake.

Then the black tongue stopped flickering, the mouth in the broad, bulbous head opened frighteningly wide, and in that split second the snake struck. In that same split second, the man's hand was instinctively whipped from the glass, a self-preservation instinct beyond his control, or so it seemed to Lyndon.

'Wow,' he said, enthralled by the spectacle. He turned to Val. 'Has anyone ever managed to win the bet?' he asked.

'Oh yes,' she replied airily. A blatant lie, but sensing his interest, she longed to throw out a challenge. 'There's always a bloke who can stand the test. Course, they're mainly blackfellas,' she was forced to admit. 'Why, Commander? Do you want to have a go?'

They eyeballed each other. He knew she was daring him. 'I never have a go at anything I can't win,' he said.

She laughed, breaking the moment. 'Wise man.'

'G'day, Commander,' a cocky voice called from the far end of the bar.

The door to the storage room had opened and Baz had appeared. He'd been unloading a fresh delivery of spirits that had just 'fallen off the back of a truck', to quote his favourite catchphrase.

He sauntered along to join them, standing beside Val, elbows lounging on the bar in a nonchalantly proprietorial manner designed to irritate. At least that was Lyndon's interpretation.

'Good morning, Mr Taylor,' he replied stiffly.

'How'd everything turn out with Stowers?' Baz asked, flashing his friendliest grin, which was intended to further infuriate. 'Hope I was able to be of some help.'

The insolence of the man, Lyndon thought, did he expect to be thanked? 'I doubt you'll be doing any further business with your former associate, Mr Taylor,' he said icily, 'Sergeant Stowers has been demoted.'

'Oh dear me,' Baz's face bore an expression of the deepest concern, 'dear me, dear me, he won't like that.'

'Bugger off, Baz,' Val intervened. 'You're being fucking annoying, stop taking the piss. Excuse me, Commander,' she said, moving off down the bar to serve two Aussie officers with empty glasses, 'back in a tick.'

Baz stopped lounging and stood up straight, as if obeying the boss, but his manner remained insolent. 'Oh dear me no, poor old Stowers,' he said, shaking his head sympathetically, 'he won't like it at all.' And still shaking his head, audibly and annoyingly tut-tutting as he did, Baz sauntered off out of the bar altogether.

No, Lyndon thought, you're damned right he won't like it. *Private* Stowers won't like it one little bit. I wonder if the men have beaten the shit out of him yet. I wouldn't blame them. He might well be half-dead by now.

Stowers was not half-dead, and as yet he'd not been beaten, but this was only due to his own cunning. Throughout the previous afternoon and evening, and this morning, too, as he laboured beside the very men who hated him, he continued to spread the story about Maxwell. How Maxwell had brutally killed young Anthony Hill . . . 'In cold blood, I swear, no provocation at all . . .' How Maxwell had blackmailed him . . . 'Said he'd pin the whole thing on me if I didn't help make it appear accidental. Said who'd believe me, white officer's word against nigger NCO? He's one evil fucker, that Maxwell . . .'

Stowers was not winning the men's sympathy. He knew it, and they knew it. But they were listening to him. And as he frantically sought his own avenue of escape, he was doing exactly that of which Johnson had accused him. He was fuelling the troops, inciting their desire for revenge, and the distraction ploy was proving successful. The men's attention was diverted from him and turning towards Maxwell as talk circulated throughout the battalion, burning surely and steadily to bushfire proportions. It was only a matter of time.

'Sorry about Baz,' Val said, rejoining Lyndon, 'he's a pain in the arse at times.'

'Yeah,' he agreed, 'Baz sure is that.'

'Valuable though.' She looked around the bar. 'Bit noisy in here. Want to come upstairs? I'll get us a cup of coffee.'

Val didn't drink coffee herself, preferring tea – 'strictly a "cuppa" girl', as she was wont to say – but with the Americans in town, she'd learned to 'stomach the muck', as she was also wont to say. Furthermore, she'd taught Jill how to brew coffee just the way the Yanks liked it, so she was rather proud to have the stuff readily on offer.

'Why thank you, Val,' Lyndon said appreciatively, 'coffee would be just fine.'

She circled the bar, signalling to Betty, a forefinger pointing upstairs, and Betty gave a nod.

As they stepped into the reception area they all but bumped into Aunty Edie coming down the stairs. She'd been sorting out the washing, which Baz would then deliver to the laundry at Rose Bay.

Edie often called in to 'sort out the washing', although she could easily have left the task in her daughter's capable hands. But she thoroughly enjoyed the walk into town and she liked to sit in the kitchen chatting with Jilly over 'a cuppa and a biccie'. Her Palm Island girls back at the laundry could easily manage things without her; she had a good set of girls these days.

'G'day, Edie,' Val said as she and Lyndon started up the stairs.

'G'day, Val.' Edie halted immediately, awaiting an introduction.

Val obliged. 'This is Commander Johnson,' she said, 'Commander, this is Aunty Edie.'

'How do, ma'am,' Lyndon said politely to the Aboriginal woman who was eyeing him up and down as astutely as Val had.

'American navy . . .' Edie was studying the buttons and the cut of the jacket. 'No two ways about it, you Yanks got style. Just look at that, will you,' she went on with a quick glance to Val and an admiring wave of her hand that took in the overall uniform, 'better fabric, better finish than anything the Aussies got, zips in the pants, too, not buttons like our boys.'

'Aunty Edie's an expert,' Val explained to Lyndon.

'Yep,' Edie grinned proudly, 'best laundry in Townsville.' Her eyes momentarily leaving the uniform, she gazed up at the Yankee officer's face. Jeez he's tall, she thought, somebody important, too, she could tell just by looking at him, and she liked the way he talked, with that drawl some of them had. 'You bring your clobber to me and you'll get it back like brand new every time.'

'Thank you, Aunty Edie, I swear I'll remember that.' Lyndon had gathered from Val's tone that the 'Aunty' was some form of title, so he was appropriately respectful in his use of it.

Val initiated their move. If she didn't Edie'd stand here and chat all day. 'Ask Jill to bring us up a coffee, will you, Edie,' she said as she started up the stairs.

'Sure, Val,' and flashing another smile at the Yank, Edie set off for the kitchen.

The two of them alone in her office, Val didn't settle herself behind the desk, thereby creating a barrier, but chose one of the armchairs instead.

Lyndon chose another, seating himself opposite her with just the small coffee table between them, the air of informality and friendliness pleasing him.

'So, Lyndon . . .' she said, displaying a neat pair of ankles and knees as she crossed her legs. For a full-bodied woman, Val had shapely legs and she liked to display them. 'To what do I owe the honour of this visit? Can I be of further assistance in your enquiries?'

'No, no,' Lyndon said hastily, drawing his eyes away from the distraction of her legs. 'My investigation is over, I leave this afternoon. I just called in to thank you for your help. Which was most substantial, I can assure you. More substantial than you could possibly know,' he added meaningfully, hinting that he wished he could tell her, but that the matter was top secret.

'Oh I am glad,' she smiled warmly, 'I do so like to be of "substantial assistance". So where to from here, back home, or . . . ?' She left the query hanging as if she was intensely interested. Val was having fun flirting. It was nice to be found attractive at her age, particularly by someone twenty years younger.

'Oh no, most certainly not home,' he said with a deadly serious shake of his head. Her smile was so seductive, so suggestive, he was determined to impress. She was obviously drawn to him, as many women were. 'I'm to fly out on a bombing mission, although of course I can tell you no more than that.' He offered a smile of apology.

'Of course you can't.' Her reply said, *Apology accepted*, and she continued, the voice of concern, 'Well, you make sure you get home safely, Lyndon.'

'Oh I intend to do just that, Val, I surely do.' He could see she was impressed so far, but this was only the beginning, he had a great deal more to offer. 'Actually, I can tell you this much,' he said, leaning forward conspiratorially, 'the investigation I've been conducting right here in Townsville was of even greater importance than the mission I'm about to fly on.'

'Oh really, is that so?' Good grief, Val thought, how funny, he's taken me seriously. He thinks I fancy him.

'Yes, really, that is a God-given fact. I can't tell you the details of course, but I am here on the direct orders of Franklin Roosevelt himself, the President of the United States of America.'

'Heavens above,' she said, stifling a laugh. I know all this, lovey, she thought, half the town knows it.

'To tell you the truth, Val, and just between you and me, mind, FDR and I are kinda close,' Lyndon admitted with all due humility. 'So close, indeed, that I doubt he would have trusted anyone but me with this assignment.'

Val uncrossed her legs, signalling a halt to the flirtation. You're coming on too strong, mate, she thought, time to back off with this kind of shit. 'In which case, Lyndon,' she said, 'I have to admit it's been an absolute honour to meet you.'

Lyndon was aware of her body language and that perhaps it meant their brief flirtation was over, but he misread Val's signal altogether. 'Perhaps then you might like a little keepsake of my visit,' he suggested, slipping a hand inside his jacket and taking out one of the cards he kept in his breast pocket. 'With my sincerest compliments,' he said, passing it to her.

Val took the card, and looking down at it was utterly dumbstruck. Is he serious, she wondered, he can't be, surely, this has to be some kind of joke. In her hand was a postcard-sized picture of Lyndon himself, posing in his naval dress uniform and gazing down the barrel of the camera with a self-satisfied smile that could only be described as a smirk.

'My, my,' she said finally, no other words coming to mind.

'Yes,' he agreed, 'very effective, isn't it?' Lyndon was proud of his personal portrait cards. All the major film stars had cards like this, or so he'd been told. 'I had them made up in Hollywood just before I came over.'

'Why?' she asked, still dumbfounded.

'I guess to sort of hand out as souvenirs,' he said, 'you know, mementoes of my visit. I'd be happy to sign it for you if you so wish, make it nice and personal.' He thrust his hand once again into his breast pocket and produced a fountain pen.

'I'm supposed to be impressed by this, am I?' she asked.

He stopped unscrewing the top of his fountain pen and stared at her, more than a little surprised. 'Ah . . . yes,' he said, 'I had assumed you might be, yes.'

Time to take the bloke down a peg, Val thought, but she would do so in good humour. Despite his insane conceit, she rather liked Lyndon. 'Now you listen to me, lovey,' she said, dumping the card on the coffee table. 'I don't give a shit about you and your best mate, FDR. In fact, I don't give a shit if you're lining yourself up to be the next fucking President of the United fucking States. To me, you're just plain old Lyndon Johnson and you always will be.'

'Oh.' Lyndon was completely deflated. 'So you don't want me to sign it, then,' he said lamely.

The door, which had been ajar, suddenly opened wide and Edie appeared, backside first, carrying a tray. She'd decided to bring the coffee up herself in order to score another chat with the tall Yank, and she'd brought Jill along with her, keen for her daughter to meet an American officer of such obvious importance.

Jill lingered politely at the door while her mother breezed into the room.

'Yeah, of course I want you to sign it,' Val said. 'Sign it for Aunty Edie. Hey, Edie,' she said, picking up the card and making room for the tray that Edie dumped on the coffee table, 'want a picture of the commander? He'll be happy to sign it for you.'

'Oh . . .' Edie breathed an ecstatic sigh as she took the card from Val. 'Oh, above and to Betsy, just look at that, will you.' She breathed another sigh, clasped the card briefly to her heart, then thrust it at Lyndon. 'Yeh, will you sign it for me, Commander?'

Val lifted up the tray and rested it on her knee, giving access to the coffee table as Lyndon signed the card.

'That's Aunty with a "y",' she said, 'and Edie with an "ie".'

To Aunty Edie from Lyndon Johnson, he signed. He handed the card back to Edie, who examined it admiringly.

'Yeh, that looks real good,' she said. Then, suddenly remembering her daughter, she added, 'Should have got you to sign it for my Jilly too.'

Val looked up, for the first time noticing Jill, who was still waiting patiently by the door.

'Come on in, Jill,' she said with a wave of her hand, 'come on in and meet the commander.' Just like bloody Edie, she thought, to bring the girl upstairs then forget all about her.

Jill shyly approached the table.

'This is Aunty Edie's daughter, Jill,' Val said, 'Jill Yiramba.' And to her great delight Lyndon stood.

'How do you do, Jill.'

Dear me, Lyndon, what a pleasant surprise, Val thought.

'Do you reckon you could put Jilly's name on this too,' Edie said, thrusting the card at him.

'I can do better than that.' Seating himself, Lyndon took another card from his pocket and signed it. *To Jill, with best wishes, Lyndon Johnson.*

Looking over her daughter's shoulder as Jill accepted the card, Edie was impressed. By golly, she thought, that's something to be proud of. Jilly's scored 'best wishes' on hers. That's really something, that is.

'Thank you very much, Commander,' Jill said, her face lighting up with a smile, which Lyndon found unbelievably pretty.

'It's my pleasure, Miss Yiramba.' He'd even remembered her name. But of course Lyndon always remembered the names of the pretty ones.

Edie grinned happily. 'Can't wait to show the girls.' Then a thought occurred. 'Eh, you wouldn't have a couple more pictures for my girls at the laundry, would you, Commander?' she asked hopefully.

Lyndon was about to produce another several cards from his pocket, he always carried a good half-dozen or more, but Val intervened.

'The commander doesn't have any spares, Edie,' she said. 'Those two pictures are very special, and they're just for you and Jill. You understand me, don't you?'

'Too right we do, Val.' Edie nodded vigorously on behalf of both of them, and hugged the card to her chest. 'No-one's gettin' this from me, I can tell you that. Over my dead body they will. Thanks, Commander, I'll treasure this picture, I will.'

'Me too,' Jill added, and in many ways her words held more meaning than her mother's. Jill's picture would not merely be something to boast of in the future, but a memory of treasured times.

Jill still attended the dances. She loved to jive and jitter-bug with the Americans. She didn't go to the dances with Betty, because Betty didn't want to dance anymore. Jill wasn't sure why, but presumed it was because Betty missed Kasey since the boys of the 96th had been banned from town and their club had shut down after just one night. Instead she went with one of the brown Palm Island laundry girls, a half-caste just like herself, and they had the best of times dancing with whites and blacks alike. They were very popular. This picture the commander had given her would remind Jill of these precious days, which surely couldn't last forever.

Edie and Jill left, hugging the cards as they went, and Val answered the query in Lyndon's eyes. 'Edie's laundry girls moonlight,' she said, 'at least quite a number of them do. Your image would have ended up in every brothel in Townsville.'

'I see,' he replied. 'Thank you, I'm obliged for the rescue.' He was most certainly grateful. His picture circulating throughout brothels would have been injurious to both his career and his marriage.

But Lyndon was bewildered nonetheless. Val's lack of respect had left him feeling confused rather than foolish, as might have been expected. His portrait cards had made quite an impact upon the number of people to whom he had given them. The recipients had been most appreciative, at least they'd appeared so. Val, however . . . ? But then Val Callahan was Val Callahan, wasn't she, a woman quite different from any he'd previously met.

Aware of Lyndon's confusion, Val decided to make amends. The bloke can't help being the arrogant, self-opinionated bastard he is, she thought.

'Let's make this coffee more drinkable, shall we,' she suggested, and rising from her armchair, she crossed to the cabinet in the corner and returned with two bottles of Bundaberg Rum, one half-finished, and one unopened.

She sat, plonking the unopened bottle on the floor beside her, and after pouring them both a coffee from the jug on the table, she topped up their cups with a healthy jig from the half-finished bottle. Then she raised her cup.

'Here's to your career, Lyndon.' She meant it; she could read the hunger and ambition in him. Good luck to you, she thought. Even an arrogant shit like Lyndon might get somewhere; hell, that's what happens in America, isn't it? 'Here's to your career, and here's to friends in faraway places, and here's to Bundy Rum,' she said.

He raised his cup and clinked it with hers. 'I'll drink to all of that,' he responded with utter sincerity.

They chatted comfortably for another twenty minutes or so, downing a second rum-laced coffee, then as he was about to leave, she picked up the unopened bottle of Bundy and placed it on the table.

'A little something to remember us by,' she said, 'call it a *souvenir* if you like, a *memento* of your visit to North Queensland,' she added with a smile that had just a touch of mockery, albeit good-natured.

'I'll sure as hell remember *you*, Val,' he replied, 'I know that much.'

'Course you will, Lyndon, I'm not easy to forget.' She stood. 'C'mon, I'll see you downstairs to the front door just in case Edie's lying in wait.'

They'd escaped Edie, who was already well on her way back to Rose Bay, but as they crossed the reception area, Val had an idea.

'Hang on a tick,' she said, 'why don't you sign the visitor's book? That'd mean more to me than just a signed picture. It'd show people you really were here, right here in my hotel.'

'Happy to oblige, Val, more than happy.' Lyndon was delighted she wanted a record of his visit; it proved she did respect him after all.

Val watched as he produced the fountain pen once again from his breast pocket, and with a well-practised flourish, signed the open book that sat on the reception desk.

It's only the visitor's book, she thought, hardly the hotel register, but what if one day he actually *does* become President of the United States, which is obviously his ambition. Hell, I can say he stayed here at The Brown's. Now that'd be something to boast of, wouldn't it?

They shook hands at the open front door of the hotel.

'Goodbye, Val,' he said, 'I won't forget you, I promise.'

'I know you won't, Lyndon. And who can tell? We might well meet again.' She stood and watched him walk off down Stokes Street towards Flinders, the bottle of Bundy tucked under his arm.

A week later, Companies A and C were posted to New Guinea, where they joined the others of their regiment who'd been transferred to Port Moresby not long after their arrival in Townsville. All the Companies of the 96th Battalion were now serving in New Guinea. The trouble that had arisen in Northern Queensland, the unfortunate uprising which had taken place just outside the city limits of Townsville at a place known locally as Kelso Field, could be relegated to the past. It had never happened.

Despite the fact that the troops of Companies A and C had been employed as a labour force and had not seen combat duty, among those now posted to Port Moresby there was a substantial number missing from the names originally listed. One such name was that of white commanding officer Captain Charles Leroy Maxwell of Company C. The records showed Maxwell had been stripped of his rank and was to have been transferred to the US Marines. But he hadn't been. Nor had he been posted to New Guinea with the troops he had formerly commanded. His destiny had taken a different course altogether.

Three days after the closure of the investigation into the Kelso uprising, Chuck Maxwell's body had been discovered by the riverbank about a mile from camp. Strangely enough, not far from where the body of young Anthony Hill had been discovered, and in a further strange coincidence the cause of death had been a broken neck.

Despite the coincidental nature of both deaths, an investigation had been unable to provide any evidence of foul play. There were no witnesses. The wintry banks of the Ross River at this particular juncture were steep and slippery, and the tangled undergrowth could easily cause a man to trip, as was evidenced by the path of damaged vegetation indicating the fall of the body. There was no option but to declare the death accidental, particularly with the troops shortly to depart for overseas. And although the military would never admit to it, the finding of 'accidental death' in the case of Charles Leroy Maxwell was really most convenient.

In the days that followed, as they awaited their departure, Samuel Robinson pondered Chuck Maxwell's death. Everyone knew he'd been murdered, of course, but no-one spoke of it, not even shared whispers among themselves. The men had closed ranks; justice had been served. No point in wondering who might have been the particular culprit, Samuel thought, this death had without doubt been a group effort. Maxwell had been found guilty by judge and jury and summarily executed.

He couldn't help wondering, though, about the circumstances. They wouldn't have killed him in camp and transported his body to the riverbank, they wouldn't have dared risk it. No, no, they would have kidnapped him and taken him well away from any possible witnesses.

Samuel tried to imagine how Chuck must have felt, all on his own surrounded by black men. The balance wouldn't have seemed at all right, would it? Memories of his daddy and the Ku Klux Klan must have flooded through his brain – hooded white men surrounding a defenceless Negro. And knowing what those white men did to that Negro, Chuck must have been absolutely petrified.

Had they taunted him, Samuel wondered. Possibly. But they hadn't tortured him. There had been no marks on his body to suggest any injury other than a cleanly broken neck. Perhaps you should consider yourself lucky, Chuck, he thought, your death might possibly have been more merciful than the future you would have suffered serving with the marines.

Samuel decided it was pointless pondering the subject any further. He couldn't bring himself to feel any sympathy for Chuck Maxwell, and the true circumstances of the man's death would never be known. You're just another mystery, Chuck, he thought, another mystery among so many.

Two days before their departure for Port Moresby, Samuel spent the night at his billet in the city. The following day, the troops would be breaking camp and he would stay the night at Kelso.

Determined the prospect of their parting should not be maudlin, he and Amelia eked out every moment they could of their last night together. They barely slept at all. They made love, certainly, but they talked too, not about anything particularly consequential, but about their favourite books and music, his passion for jazz, hers for orchestral, and they discovered a mutual love of poetry. They talked and laughed and loved, and then at midnight, they ate sardines on toast in bed.

'King Oscar tinned sardines,' she said, relishing the taste, 'a childhood favourite.'

'Yeah, for me, too, as a kid,' he said, 'although I can't remember the brand. I don't think ours were King Oscar.'

The same thought occurred to them simultaneously, although she was the one to voice it. 'We haven't spoken at all of our previous lives, have we,' she said, 'of our childhoods or our families, isn't that strange?'

'Perhaps.' He was thinking there was a lifetime ahead to do all of that, or rather he was hoping so. If the war didn't claim him anyway. He waited until they'd finished the last of the sardines. Then putting the plate on the bedside table, he casually asked, 'Does that marriage proposal still stand, by the way?'

'Oh most definitely. I'm all prepared. Look.' She held out her left hand, splaying her fingers.

'No wedding ring,' he said.

'I took it off last night before you arrived. You didn't notice, did you?'

'I didn't have time. There's been so much happening.'

They kissed, aware of the taste of sardines.

Around three in the morning they finally dozed off, awaking at dawn among the tangled sheets and toast crumbs to make love a final time. Then there was barely half an hour left.

'I'll make you a *huge* breakfast before you go,' she said, 'you must be absolutely starving.'

'No, don't.' He pulled her back to him as she started to rise. 'I'd rather stay hungry and stay here.'

'Me too.' She snuggled in close, and they both lay gazing at the ceiling.

'I'll be back, Amelia,' he said, 'you do know that, don't you?'

'Yes,' she said, 'I do know that.'

They would ignore the threat of war.

Propping on an elbow, he looked down at her in a puzzling way that may or may not have been serious. She couldn't be sure.

'I have a secret I feel I should share with you,' he said.

'Oh? What's that?'

'My name's not Robinson. It's Rabinowitz. I'm Jewish.'

'Yes,' she said, studying the aquiline face that she found so attractive. 'Yes,' she said thoughtfully, 'you look Jewish.'

EPILOGUE

1964

Lyndon knocked back the rum that remained in his glass; a third of the bottle was gone by now and Bobby had had only three shots, but Lyndon Johnson could hold his liquor well; he showed no ill-effects.

'So there you go, Robert,' he said, 'that's the story of the 96th Battalion and Townsville in forty-two. Another Bundy?' He picked up the bottle, nodding encouragingly for Bobby to polish off what was left in his glass.

Bobby obediently did as he was told. 'Jesus, Lyndon, that's one hell of a story,' he said, watching distractedly as his glass was filled with another healthy shot of rum. He was definitely feeling the effects himself.

'Yeah, it sure as hell is, isn't it,' Lyndon agreed, pouring his own shot. 'You can see why FDR wanted the whole mess kept under wraps, can't you. Few know about it to this very day, and those who do "ain't sayin' nuthin",' I swear.'

'But what about the families of the men who died,' Bobby asked, 'what were they told?'

'I believe they were told their boys died of Ross River Fever,' Lyndon said, 'a tropical disease spread by mosquitoes in that part of the world. At least that's what I heard they were told, I can't be sure. I wasn't kept in the know all those years back, you understand,' he added with a self-deprecating smile that didn't work, 'being the young, naïve congressman I was.'

I doubt you were ever naïve, Lyndon, Bobby thought as he watched Johnson down another swig. In fact, I find it difficult to believe you were ever young. I think you were born into this world a hard-nosed, power-hungry, self-opinionated shit.

'My, oh my,' Lyndon set his glass of Bundy back on the desk, 'doesn't quite have the finesse of a good Scotch blend, but it carries a sting that satisfies, you've got to admit. Goes well with coffee, too, I might add.'

Bobby resisted the urge to ask for some coffee, the raw rum on an empty stomach inviting trouble, but he didn't want to cause a distraction. He was far too intrigued.

'How did Roosevelt react to your report? Did he accept your analysis of the situation?'

'He most certainly did. FDR embraced my analysis wholeheartedly,' Lyndon replied with the utmost admiration, although whether his admiration was directed towards Roosevelt or himself was impossible to tell. 'Said my report had the damnedest effect on him, that he hadn't realised things had gotten so out of hand with our black troops.'

There were certain elements of his investigation that Lyndon had chosen not to share with Bobby Kennedy, particularly any mention of Pete Vickers and the report he'd presented to FDR as his own. He considered the fact incidental in any event. His analysis of the situation had been the same as Vickers' and any detailed report he might have written would have come to the same conclusion. Where was the harm in using the Australian's material when it would never see the light of day anyway? His had been simply a labour-saving decision, practical and efficient.

'FDR agreed we'd created the problem for ourselves by posting all those men out there in the tropics with no form of socialising, no women, no way of letting off steam,' Lyndon went on. 'He concurred totally with my personal view that we'd been just asking for trouble placing our black troops in such a position. Damnedest thing is, would you believe, he actually went right on ahead and built them a brothel. Slap bang in the middle of town what's more.'

'He did what?' Bobby was amazed. 'A brothel?'

'Not a brothel exactly, they called it a servicemen's club and it was set up with the support of the Red Cross. But it was for black troops only, and I'll bet my last buck there would have been women available. They opened the place later that very same year. Shit, FDR even sent Eleanor up there to visit the club during her trip to Australia in forty-three. Giving it the royal seal of approval so to speak.'

Bobby raised a querying eyebrow. 'I wonder what she thought of *that*.'

'Oh I'm sure she would have approved,' Lyndon said knowingly. 'Eleanor was a woman who understood sexual desires and needs, believe me. I don't think there's much could've shocked *that* first lady.'

Another swig of rum and he continued. 'Of course there were some locals not keen on the establishment of a club for Negroes, some who still wanted to keep our black troops out of town. But that's human nature, I guess, isn't it? Like I said earlier, Robert, the Australians and us, we're not all that different really. We don't do the right thing by black folk.'

Lyndon grinned. A genuine grin this time, humorous, the grin that illuminated his face and could be quite winning when he was sharing a joke as he often did over a few drinks, the joke more often than not a bawdy one.

'Hell, the Aussies really give themselves away, don't they? I mean, "the White Australia policy"! What sort of dumb shit-for-brains title is that? If they'd just stuck to the *Immigration Restriction Act* they wouldn't have shown themselves up as the racist fuckers they are.'

A short bark of laughter and he was serious again. 'That policy still stands today and it still means what it says: those Aussies don't want a shade of anything that's not white in their country. But we're one up on them, Robert, as is only right, we being the leaders of the civilised world. We have that.'

He stabbed a finger at the file that sat in the middle of the desk. 'We have the *Civil Rights Act of 1964*, and as of tomorrow, it will become law throughout the land. That's something to be proud of, wouldn't you agree?'

'I would, Lyndon. Yes, indeed I would.'

Bobby was forced to admit to himself, in that moment anyway and perhaps with reluctance, that he actually respected Johnson. Lyndon remained everything he'd always been in Bobby's opinion – loud, brash, vulgar, and so much more. But he was basically a good man. His values were right. He'd worked hard to push the bill through after Jack's assassination, and he was, as Jack himself had always maintained, one hell of a clever politician.

'We'd never have achieved the presidency without him, Bobby,' Jack had said, 'we'd have been nowhere without Texas.'

Having very much enjoyed recounting his adventures to Bobby Kennedy, Lyndon could now sense the younger man's renewed respect, which, although he would always maintain meant nothing, somehow pleased him. He'd formed a good working relationship with John during the time he'd served as Kennedy's Vice-President, but he'd always known both brothers looked down on him a little. As those of the Kennedy clan tended to do. Nice to feel a mellowing change, he now thought. Or is it just the Bundy?

'You're getting behind there, Bobby,' he said, topping up his rum. Bobby's had remained untouched. 'I'd like to propose a final toast,' he raised his glass, 'to Jack, and America, and equal rights for all.'

'I'll drink to that, Mr President.'

They clinked and drained their glasses.

AUTHOR'S NOTE

FACT OR FICTION

*K*haki Town is a work of fiction, inspired by factual events about which very little is known. This makes for an interesting combination for the reader (at least I hope so) and something of a test for the author (I know so).

Here are a few examples of such 'combinations'.

All the characters in the book are fictional, with the obvious exception of the four American historical figures, FDR, Eisenhower, LBJ and Robert Kennedy, together with the less obvious exception of Tom Aikens, deputy mayor of Townsville from 1939–44.

The Brown's Bar is fictional as is the nameless hotel in which it is situated. However, for narrative purposes, 'The Brown's', as it becomes known in the novel, stands on the site of the old Herbert Hotel. Formerly the Court House Hotel, built in the latter part of the nineteenth century, the name was changed to Herbert in 1910, and the original building replaced by the current brick structure in the 1920s.

Pete Vickers, local journalist for the *Townsville Bulletin*, is a fictional character, but the part he plays in the novel is not. The report Pete gives to Lyndon Johnson is inspired by that of American war correspondent Robert Sherrod, who was based in Townsville at the time. Sherrod gave Johnson a report of the 96th Battalion's mutiny, rather naïvely hoping to bypass the wartime censors, despite Johnson warning him the subject matter was 'too hot'. Upon his return to America, Johnson apparently presented the report to FDR passing it off as his own. A copy of it remains today in the LBJ Presidential Library.

The North American Service Club, created exclusively for African-American soldiers, opened at 380 Flinders Street, Townsville in 1942. Eleanor Roosevelt did indeed visit the club during her trip to North Queensland the following year.

The shocking events of the mutiny in Townsville and the deaths of African-American troops in Mount Isa are true, but despite various rumours no numbers have been substantiated, and I doubt the full truth will ever be known.

Lyndon Johnson made an official trip to Australia as President of the United States in 1966. He was the first US president to visit Australia while in office, and for personal reasons unknown to most he chose to have Townsville added to his itinerary.

A brief note in order to avoid confusion: Rose Bay, where Aunty Edie has her laundry, is in fact Rowes Bay, named after Charles Seville Rowe, one of the first settlers at Cleveland Bay. However, this name only came into use after World War II, prior to which time the area was variously known as Rose Bay and Ross Bay.

ACKNOWLEDGEMENTS

First and foremost my love and thanks to my husband, Bruce Venables, who remains a source of inspiration and encouragement while at times a distraction, which is to my mind a very healthy mix.

My thanks also to those dear friends who offer both encouragement and assistance of the most practical kind in their various areas of expertise: James Laurie, Sue Greaves, Michael Roberts, Colin Julin and Susan Mackie-Hookway.

Many thanks to my publisher, Beverley Cousins; my editors, Catherine Hill and Alexandra Nahlous; my publicists, Jessica Malpass and Karen Reid, and the entire hard-working team at Penguin Random House Australia.

For assistance with research, my warmest thanks to Anne Jackson, who shared with me her childhood memories of wartime Townsville and was most generous in lending me wonderfully insightful material, including a copy of her personal memoir *Bits and Pieces of My Life*.

I'd like also to thank the many helpful people of Townsville. In particular those at the Townsville City Library who provided such a wealth of historical data: Debra Close, Simone Rostenne and Robyn Maconachie.

The staff at the Army Museum of North Queensland: Coby, Allen, and others.

Kim and Rod of the Museum for the Performing Arts in Townsville.

Local historian, Ray Holyoak.

And on a more personal level, my old friend Danny Meares, whose restaurant Watermark became the headquarters for my research trip. Oh, that such an office with food and views like yours could always be at the ready – sincerest thanks, Danny.

Among my research sources I would like to recognise:

'It Was a Different Town': Being Some Memories of Townsville and District 1942–1945, compiled by Gai Copeman and Diane Vance, Thuringowa City Council, 1992

A Majority of One: Tom Aikens and Independent Politics in Townsville, Ian Moles, University of Queensland, 1979

'Australia 1942: The Most Dangerous Year', Heather Brown, The Australian Magazine, Nationwide News Pty Ltd, 1992

The North Queensland Line – the defence of Townsville in 1942, Ray Holyoak, Honours thesis

Wings Around Us, Rodney G. Cardell, Amphion Press, 1991

North Queensland WW11 1942–1945, P.D. Wilson, Department of Geographic Information, 1988

Townsville at War, 1942: Life in a Garrison City, Darryl McIntyre, Townsville City Council, 1992

While the Music Lasts: Life Stories, compiled and edited by Helen Menzies, and including the short story 'World Wars One and Two', Anne Jackson, Hilliard Hudson, 2016

Sanctuary
Judy Nunn

In this compelling novel, compassion meets bigotry, hatred meets love, and ultimately despair meets hope on the windswept shores of Australia.

On a barren island off the coast of Western Australia, a rickety wooden dinghy runs aground. Aboard are nine people who have no idea where they are. Strangers before the violent storm that tore their vessel apart, the instinct to survive has seen them bond during their days adrift on a vast and merciless ocean.

Fate has cast them ashore with only one thing in common . . . fear. Rassen the doctor, Massoud the student, the child Hamid and the others all fear for their lives. But in their midst is Jalila, who appears to fear nothing. The beautiful young Yazidi woman is a mystery to them all.

While they remain undiscovered on the deserted island, they dare to dream of a new life. But forty kilometres away on the mainland lies the tiny fishing port of Shoalhaven. Here everyone knows everyone, and everyone has their place. In Shoalhaven things never change.

Until now . . .

Spirits of the Ghan
Judy Nunn

In this spellbinding No.1 bestseller Judy Nunn takes us on a breathtaking journey deep into the red heart of Australia.

It is 2001 and as the world charges into the new millennium, a century-old dream is about to be realised in the Red Centre of Australia: the completion of the mighty Ghan railway, a long-lived vision to create the 'backbone of the continent', a line that will finally link Adelaide with the Top End.

But construction of the final leg between Alice Springs and Darwin will not be without its complications, for much of the desert it will cross is Aboriginal land. Hired as a negotiator, Jessica Manning must walk a delicate line to reassure the Elders their sacred sites will be protected. Will her innate understanding of the spiritual landscape, rooted in her own Arunta heritage, win their trust? It's not easy to keep the peace when Matthew Witherton and his survey team are quite literally blasting a rail corridor through the timeless land of the Never-Never.

When the paths of Jessica and Matthew finally cross, their respective cultures collide to reveal a mystery that demands attention. As they struggle against time to solve the puzzle, an ancient wrong is awakened and calls hauntingly across the vastness of the outback . . .

Elianne
Judy Nunn

Elianne, another No.1 bestseller from Judy Nunn, is a sweeping story of wealth, power, privilege and betrayal, set on a grand sugar cane plantation in Queensland.

In 1881 'Big Jim' Durham ruthlessly creates for Elianne Desmarais, his young French wife, the finest of the great sugar mills of the Southern Queensland cane fields, and names it in her honour.

The massive estate becomes a self-sufficient fortress and home to hundreds of workers, but 'Elianne', and the Durham Family, have dark and distant secrets; secrets that surface in the wildest of times, the 1960s.

For Kate Durham and her brothers, Neil and Alan, freedom is the catchword of the decade. Rock 'n' roll, the Pill, the Vietnam War, the rise of feminism, Asian immigration and the Freedom Ride join forces to rattle the chains of traditional values.

The workers leave the great sugar estates as mechanisation lessens the need for labour – and the Durham family, its secrets exposed, begins its fall from grace.

This is a story of honour – family honour among hard men in a hard environment. But when honour is lost, so too is love, and without love, what becomes of the family?

Tiger Men
Judy Nunn

Set in Tasmania, this is another brilliant work of historical fiction from master storyteller Judy Nunn.

Van Diemen's Land was an island of stark contrasts: a harsh penal colony, an English idyll for its gentry, and an island so rich in natural resources it was a profiteer's paradise.

Its capital, Hobart Town, had its contrasts too: the wealthy elite in their sandstone mansions, the exploited poor in the notorious Wapping slum, and the criminals who haunted the dockside taverns. Hobart Town was no place for the meek.

Tiger Men is the story of Silas Stanford, a wealthy Englishman; Mick O'Callaghan, an Irishman on the run; and Jefferson Powell, an idealistic American political prisoner. It is also the story of the strong, proud women who loved them, and of the children they bore who rose to power in the cutthroat world of international trade.

This sweeping saga tells of three families who lived through Tasmania's golden era and the birth of Federation and then watched with pride as their sons marched off to fight for King and Country.